Kings and

MW01520703

First Kindle Edition, January 2014

Copyright © 2013 by Ted Durbin

All rights reserved. This book may not be reproduced in any form, in whole or in part, without written permission from the author.

For my family, who encouraged me to always live out my fantasies.

And a special thanks to Brittney, without whom I would still be correcting all my mistakes.

Table of Contents

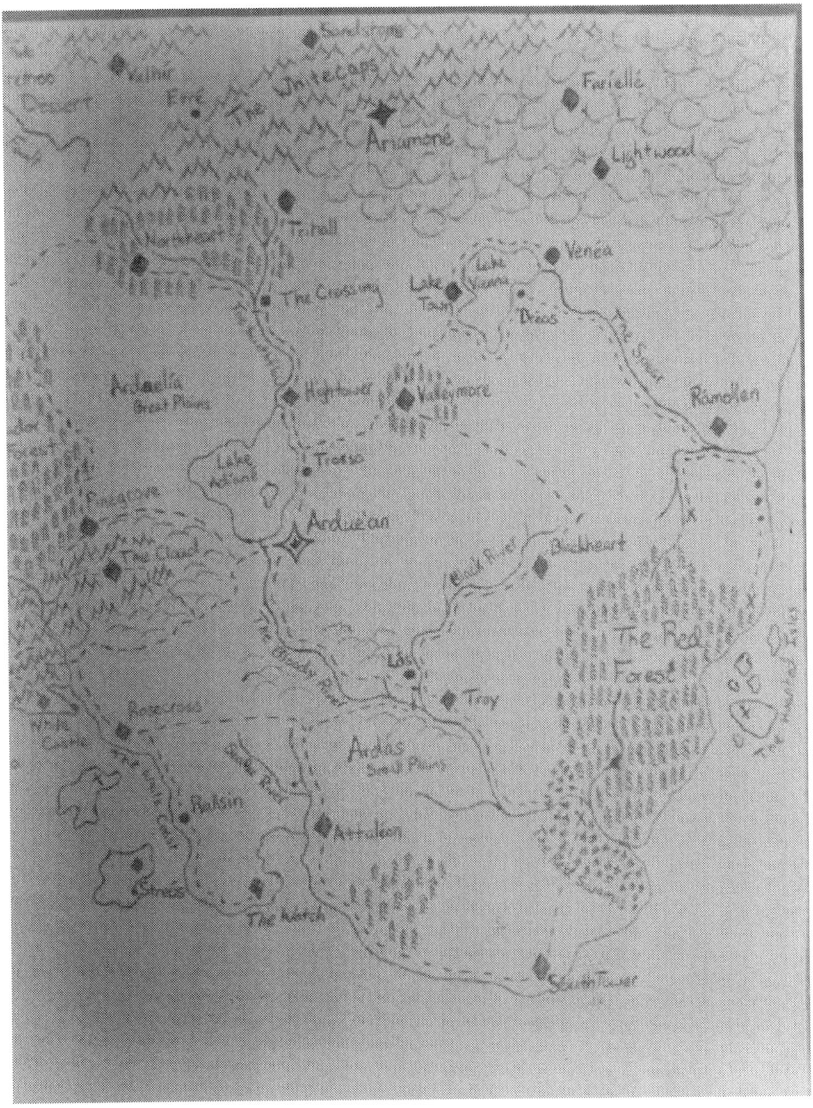
Sandstone
Valnir
Desert
The Whitecaps
Ariamoné
Fariellé
Lightwood
Trihall
Northheart
The Crossing
Venéa
Lake Town
Lake Vienna
Dráos
Rámollen
Ardaelia
Great Plains
Hightower
Valleymore
Lake Adiund
Troeso
Arduè'an
Pinegrove
The Cloud
Black River
Blackheart
The Red Forest
The Bloody River
Lás
Troy
Rosecross
White Castle
Ardás
Small Plains
Ralsin
Attuléon
Streös
The Watch
South Tower

Chapter 1: Darkness Returns

It was dark. The kind of night that makes it difficult to believe that there was ever light in this world. It was a dark that enveloped and consumed everything. Like a veil had been used to cover the stars. There was no moon. Land blended with sky and not even the crests of the distant mountains could be distinguished. The sand of the desert floor was still. There were no movements, no noises, not even a fleeting howl of the wind; it was unnaturally quiet. It was like the Gods had forgotten to finish this place when they created this world; had forgotten to fill it with anything but silence and darkness.

But then the Gods didn't favor this place. It was his kingdom, not theirs. It would take time to rebuild; to rebuild what was lost all those ages ago. It didn't matter now though, there were other things that needed to be finish.

A gaping hole formed in the black abyss that was the sky, and out of it he fell, like a hawk plummeting after its prey. He landed softly, and with an unusual amount of grace, for he was not by any means the type of figure that one would assume to move in such a way. He was enormous, far greater in size than any normal man, and yet he did not leave any mark in the sand. As he landed the wind came to life, howling in rage and protest at this new, unwanted arrival.

They knew he was there, and they wanted him gone. It did not matter much. It had been a long time since he had any fear of these Gods. They could not touch him, could not intervene, and could not stop him. Not him. Not this time. Now they would be the ones to know fear, now that he was back.

The wind continued to howl and thrash. It was bitterly cold, and the once peaceful sand flew like fragments of glass, biting and stinging, but he was unfazed by it. It swarmed around him like millions of angry bees, but it could not touch him. He adjusted his cloak and took a step forward when he noticed something. He didn't see it, but knew it, could feel its presence. Slowly he turned his head to the right and glanced at the rebelling sands beneath him, catching sight of the source of the bothersome presence. Even through the suffocating darkness he could see it as clearly as if it were in a spot light. There, on the floor of this haunted domain, was a single rose, growing out of the sand; perfect in every way, and undisturbed by the storm that raged around it. It was laughing at him.

This could not be, not here, not in his kingdom. He took two steps and crushed the flower under his massive boot, crushed the abomination before it could laugh at him again. It was weak, powerless, unwanted, and could be killed. It was not worthy to reside in his domain. Nothing like this would ever be welcome in his kingdom, he would see to it. He lifted his boot and prepared to continue on his way, but the rose was still there. As the seconds ticked by it began to straighten, rebelling against him, as it returned to its original position. He stared at it as his anger began to grow.

There was no warning, only a movement and a flash of silver. The blade moved so fast it cracked the air like a whip, silencing the howls of the wind. The sand fell back to the ground and resumed its unnatural stillness, and on the ground near his feet lay the severed rose, which slowly turned to ash in front of him. He stared down at the small pile of dust, watching as it gradually became one with the sand.

Finally he sheathed his sword and began to walk away. The wind no longer stood to defy him. No footprints were left in the sand as he moved. He did not make a sound, did not seem to even breathe; just walked. He cut through the dark like a knife, unable to see, but knowing where he was going. He would not fear the dangers of this desert; he knew them all to well. He knew his way around death; knew how to use his knowledge and sense, even when his sight was lost to him. It would be a long journey, but he would not get tired, nor get hungry.

He walked for hours, day's maybe, but light never came; it was not welcome here anymore. Finally, he reached the edge of a cliff that stretched as far as he could see in either direction. Its face shot downward at a near perfect ninety degree angle and continued to fall for close to a mile. Finally, he knew he had arrived. He looked down into the deep dark canyon below, and with his penetrating eyes was able to make out the faint outline of an oversize military style fortress. Its gray walls a mere shadow in the night. A wicked smile began to creep onto his face as he slowly stroked his blood red goatee. He took two steps forward and jumped over the edge... He was finally back.

Chapter 2: Terrick Looks Like an Idiot

He was in a forest, a forest that he knew very well. He couldn't tell you why he was there, but for some reason it didn't seem odd to him. He looked around, and saw his old, worn, wooden bow on the ground. A quiver full of arrows was beside it.

"Maybe I've been hunting." The boy said to himself.

He picked up the bow and the quiver and slung them both over his shoulder. A bird could be heard singing near by. He could tell by the cheery, high-pitched sound that it was a cardinal. The song seemed to fill his body and mind with energy. He knew all of the animals in the forest by heart. Knew their sounds and behaviors, where they made their homes and where they went to feed and drink. He knew how to track and locate them. Knew what areas to avoid, what areas were dangerous, and where to find certain plants and animals that could be of use to him if he was hungry, or in danger. After all, he had lived, explored and hunted in these woods for as long as he could remember.

The forest was dense, much more so than a normal forest, but it was also much denser in beauty. It contained hundreds of varieties of trees that grew many times taller and thicker than normal due to the unusually rich soil of the Jericho Province. The canopy was easily a hundred feet in the air and in the autumn, as it was now, was alive with dozens of magnificent colors, from different shades of sunset red and orange to the clearest gold and most brilliant yellow. The trees were always full of animals, and were so laden with their sounds that it was easy to believe the trees were actually speaking to one another.

The forest floor was always full and healthy, covered in lush green grass and turquoise mosses. Insects could be seen scuttling in every direction, carrying home food for their colonies. Streams fragmented the forest floor every so often, filled with fresh water, the clearest blue one could ever hope to find. There were no fish in the streams, but multicolored frogs and salamanders could frequently be seen darting in and out of the waters flow. Many considered this particular forest in Northern Jericho to be the most naturally beautiful place in all the land. The leaves never fell, just changed from their amazing shades of green in the spring and summer to their barrage of brilliant colors in the fall and winter, and then back again.

The boy looked up through the treetops and smiled at the flurry of activity. He could spend hours sitting alone here; lost in its vastness, talking to the animals he knew would never respond. The sun was beginning to set over the western tips of the trees. He took a deep breathe and sighed. A squirrel ran slowly past him and up a tree to his right. It climbed high in the tree and disappeared into a hole in its wide trunk.

"It's getting late." He said to himself, "I should be heading home too."

He had just turned to start his journey out of the forest when he heard a noise behind him. There was something odd about it. It wasn't a familiar sound, but was a noise that should not have been in the forest. It certainly didn't come from any of the animals he knew and loved. It sounded suppressed, as though whatever made it did not wish to be heard, and yet it sounded strangely like a whispered cry for help. The boy pulled his bow from his back and strung an arrow. He started to move slowly in the direction of the sound when something caught his eye. There was a faint silvery glow emanating from between two trees to the left of where he heard the noise. He had never seen anything like it before. Whatever it was, it kept moving slowly east. The boy crouched down and began to follow it. He crept slowly behind it for a few minutes in complete silence, hardly daring to breathe, before realizing that the glow was becoming stronger. Whatever was causing the light had stopped moving, and he was gaining on it. It was only twenty yards or so away….. ten yards….. five….. right behind the next tree….. something was tapping him on the face.

"Aaron, wake up." A distant voice said.

I jerked awake and sat bolt upright in my bed.

"Whoozare?"

"It's me silly, Lisa. You've overslept again. You're supposed to be out helping Terrick and Jarron."

I rubbed my eyes and the small room that was the upper level of my home began to come into focus. It was a small circular room with windows that pointed north and south. The room was lit solely by the light streaming in from the two windows and reflecting off the wooden floor. There was a set of circular stairs that could be seen behind an old wooden door that was left open in the eastern part of the room, opposite the bed. It led to the lower floor of the home. The entire room was the same light brown color, with the exception of the green curtains that framed the outer edges of the windows. The room was relatively large for the fact that it was located inside a tree. All of the locals lived in the largest and oldest trees that grew in the northeast corner of the Northern Jericho Woods. Everything the village had and used was derived from their natural surroundings. I lived in one of the smaller houses in the village, but as I'm the only one who lives in it, it didn't need to be very large.

Finally getting the sleep out of my eyes, I turned my attention to the little girl kneeling at my bedside. She was young, only ten years old, and small, even for her age, with shoulder length blond hair that was always pulled back into pigtails. Her face, when not entirely concealed by a book, was bright and circular and slightly overlarge in proportion to the rest of her body. She has round checks that would blush uncontrollably whenever she spoke to anyone of importance in the village; although this trend was beginning to fade and be replaced by a smart mouth. Because of my skill as a hunter, I qualify as one of these important people, even though I'm pretty young myself.

"What time is it?" I yawned while stretching.

"It's late. You were supposed to be in the field by midmorning; they wanted to start early today." Lisa replied, her cheeks already turning cherry red.

"Where are they?" I asked, already on my way to the door.

"They said they'd be on the eastern edge of the field tending to the crops there."

"Thanks a lot Lisa." I called over my shoulder as I sprinted out of the room leaving Lisa blushing, and beaming with joy from delivering her message properly.

I flew out of the house, slamming my door a little too hard in the process and cracking the old bark frame. Beside the front door stood my girl, I didn't really have any time to talk, but I couldn't just leave her standing there without saying a word. I loved everything about her, she was strong, daring and brave, as well as being unnaturally intelligent. We worked perfectly together; it was almost like she was able to read my mind. She was absolutely beautiful, with big brown eyes that could make you melt on the spot, and long flowing white hair that fell gracefully over her silky brown coat, and matched her tail perfectly... Wait, I guess I need to clarify this a bit, her name is Elma, and she's a four year old mare. You need to know I get a little mushy when I talk about my horse.

"I'll see you tonight Elma, I promise." I whispered as I stroked her mane. Sighing, I turned around and began making the long jog to the eastern edge of the crop field just outside the boarders of the forest. It was a beautiful autumn morning, with clear blue skies and the sun already out in full force. Birds were singing as the morning dew was slowly baked away in the rising heat. The Blue Rock Mountains were nothing more than a distant outline to the north, their white, snowcapped peaks blending in with the distant haze of the sky.

Weaving in and out of the trees, and jumping over the many streams that crossed my path, I tried to rack my brain and remember what I'd been dreaming about before Lisa had woken me. It was a useless attempt though, like trying to keep water cupped in the palms of your hands. Already the details were slipping away from me and mixing with other dreams I'd had in the past. I remembered a light that I had never seen before, but the rest was vague. I could no longer remember if I had been hunting, or fighting a goat with fangs... My dreams are always weird.

As I ran, the birthmark on the back of my right shoulder, the one that looked like a flaming sun, or maybe an old guy's wrinkled face, stung a little, like skin that's been stretched too tight. But I was used to it. It had always bothered me; not badly, but just enough to be an annoyance, to make me remember it was there. I tried to think harder about the dream, but the cold morning breeze was beginning to sting in my lungs from the large distance I'd already covered at such a high speed and it was beginning to break my concentration.

As I ran I jumped the fence to old man Parton's yard, snagging a pair of apples from one of the smaller trees he kept and immediately had to dodge the rake that was thrown at me from the doorway of his home.

"You'll pay for those you will ya lit'l rascal!" he shouted at my back as I sprinted away with a smile on my face. Sure, it may not have been a nice thing to do, but a guy's gotta eat right? And it's not like he wasn't use to it by now; borrowing a few of his apples every morning had become my routine. That's what I called it at least, borrowing without the intent of return. It shouldn't have been a big deal. I'd wind up paying for it one way or another.

It took most people a long time to make their way to the crop field from the village, but I'd always been unusually athletic. I'd been able to outrun everyone in the village by the time I was eight. I'm seventeen now, a full month into manhood – awesome, I know right? – I'm average height, but I'd like to think that I'm pretty well built and toned from all the years of plowing fields and digging up crops, and I'm really even stronger than my size lets on… seriously, I'm not just egotistical. Along with being pretty athletic, I've always seemed to have better control of my senses than the rest of the villagers. I can see things at far distances and I can pick up on small details that no one else seems to be able to notice. I can hear sounds that no one else can hear, distinguish their differences, and tell what is making them, without even opening my eyes. These are the talents that have led to me being named the best tracker in the village.

I've got long blond hair that covers my ears and nearly comes to my shoulders. It always falls unkempt all over my head and it's never neat while managing to never really look all that messy. The older people think it's sloppy… I kinda like it. I've got hollow cheeks, and a square jaw, but people always tell me my best feature is my eyes. I've got really blue eyes… like piercing blue, like melt really clean snow in a glass blue. When I was younger I always thought people might think they were creepy, but it turns out most girls dig um, so I don't really feel that way anymore. In my ears, I always wear a set of bright blue ear rings made of polished stone, which I was told had belonged to my father. I'm always darkly tanned from all the hours I spend in the fields, but I've been told I still keep a rather graceful and angelic look about me. Believe me, I would rather go for tough and rugged, but I guess it's better than odd and frumpy, so I'll take it. Anyways, you can't really change how you look, and even if I could, I wouldn't. I think how I look fits me pretty well.

As a stitch began to form in my side, I rounded the southern eastern edge of the crop field and could see my cousin and uncle come into view a couple hundred yards away, planting oats by hand. Terrick was digging with a spade while Jarron was on his knees laying the seeds in their freshly dug homes. As I approached them I slowed to a jog, my face flush from the half league I'd just sprinted.

"Sorry I'm late; I forgot we were working early today."

"It's alright Aaron, everyone knows that a pretty guy like yourself needs all the beauty sleep he can get while the real men do work." Terrick, my ogre of a cousin, retorted sarcastically. "I'm just glad Lisa was able to rouse you from your dreams of pretty flowers and fluffy bunny clouds."

"Actually, I was dreaming about how nice it would be if I had a cousin who was smart enough to spell his own name." I shot back with a laugh.

Terrick gave a small smirk, and muttered something to the effect of "one time three years ago," under his breathe as I tossed him the second apple. "I hope you got raked." He said harshly.

"Nope, but the old man's getting more accurate. Actually made me jump today."

My uncle Jarron just shook his head at me. "You know you'll be weeding his garden again this week for that. Now grab a spade and give Terrick a hand, we need to get these planted before the rains come this week."

Terrick was eighteen, but as he was closing in on nineteen, nearly two years older than me. He was my best friend as well as my cousin, but you wouldn't be able to tell we were related by looking at us. He was five or six inches taller than me and was easily the tallest person in the village. He was also a lot thicker than me, mentally as well as physically. He had very muscular arms, a broad neck and chest, and very powerfully built legs. He was the guy the villagers would call if they needed something abnormally heavy moved, and there wasn't a horse around to drag it away. However, for what he excelled at in brawn, he lacked in brains. Like most of the village, including myself, he was completely illiterate, with the exception of being able to scroll out, rather sloppily, his name, and with even that he struggled. He was the kind of guy that would rather solve a dispute by cracking a man in the jaw than by reason, even though he was actually quite kind in nature. Terrick claimed that it was just easier that way. I knew verbal disputes just made his brain hurt.

Terrick had dark brown hair that was very close to being black, and had been cut so short it almost looked shaved. The fuzz on his head that could be seen came down to a neat widow's peak in the middle of his forehead. Unlike myself, he had bright green eyes that were the same as his fathers and seemed to compliment the rest of his facial features quite well. Compared to me, he had a much rounder face and an undefined chin, which was often covered in stubble. He was slightly darker in complexion than me and much more rugged looking, partially due to the rather angry looking bull he had tattooed on his shoulder. Believe me, no one was going to confuse Terrick with angelic and graceful any time soon.

Jarron was Terrick's father (my uncle) and while he was a few inches shorter, he was built in the same mold. It was easy to see that they were father and son. Jarron was looked at by the villagers as an unofficial mayor of the town, and was overall, much more intelligent than his son. He, along with Terrick and I, tended to all of the crops in the northern field of the village. We grew oats, corn, beans, wheat, and rye, along with hay for the livestock. All of the fruits and vegetables of the village were grown in a clearing to the east of the village, and were tended to by one of Jarron's friends, Bray, and his family. Jarron was a hardworking man and relished the manual labor of seeding and maintaining the field. He, Terrick and Lisa, his daughter, lived right next to the field, on the opposite side of the village from me. I'd moved out a year prior, into the only available house at the time. You see, both of my parents were dead, as was Jarron's wife, Sarah, who had died giving birth to Lisa ten years earlier. I can't really remember either of my parents. My mom,

Brianna, had died in a storm that flooded the village almost fifteen years ago, and all I knew of my father was that he was foreign and for one reason or another didn't come to Jericho Province with my mom. But I figured if he wasn't good enough to come here with my mom, he really wasn't good enough to be in my life, so I was a little relieved I didn't know him. I had lived with Jarron, who was my mom's brother, ever sense she died. I'd grown up treating him like a father, and Terrick and Lisa like a brother and sister, ever since. I tried questioning Jarron about my parents a few times, once I was old enough to understand that I wasn't really his kid, but I might as well have been talking to a tree for all the good it did me. Jarron claimed to have not known my father, and refused to talk much about his sister after she had shown up on his doorstep pregnant with yours truly.

A particularly rough patch of dirt ended my mind's aimless wanderings, forcing me to concentrate on the work at hand. I broke up the clot and went back to digging next to Terrick It was tedious work that took us until around midday, working mostly in silence. Nothing but the steady sound of shovels cutting through the earth like a bizarre muffled heartbeat to keep us on pace.

"We've been working for o'er five hours pa, if we don't break soon we're gonna miss out on lunch." Terrick finally said. His brow was drenched in sweat, and some small blisters were beginning to form on his hands.

Jarron sat back on his knees and sighed. "This is going to take longer than I thought." He looked around at the remaining field that had not been seeded, and then down at himself, covered from head to toe in the rich Jericho soil. "But I guess you're right. It'll do no good to starve you two. I suppose we'll work better on a full stomach anyways. You can go back in to town and get something to eat. Make sure you're back here in an hour though. I'm going keep on working."

"Come back into town with us pa. It won't do you any good to starve yourself either." Terrick responded

"Nah, I have to stay here. You know, try and catch us up a bit. I'm not very hungry anyway. Besides, if I'm not there, I can't embarrass you in front of that nice Sienna girl." Jarron said smiling. I had to look down at the ground to conceal the wide smirk that was now pushing at the edges of my mouth. I loved it when Terrick got teased about girls. He couldn't handle it. In fact, it was a good thing he was so covered in sweat and dirt, because at his father's words, it was nice that his deeply reddening checks were well hidden.

"Would you like us bring you something back Jarron?" I offered, trying to spare my cousin by changing the subject.

Jarron turned his sly smile away from Terrick, who I knew was glad to be able to look away from his father. He thought for a moment, while his son made rude hand gestures at his back, and then began, "Well now that you mention it, a sandwich and some fire whisky from the tavern would really hit the spot."

With that we turned away from Jarron and began to walk back towards the village.

"How's he know bout Sienna?" Terrick asked under his breathe. Now not even the dirt could conceal the redness of his cheeks.

I couldn't help but laugh at him, "The whole village should know, shouldn't they? You don't exactly hide it very well. Every time you see her your jaw hangs open and your eyes go out of focus. I'm surprised you haven't started drooling yet. It's like watching a dog stare at a steak that's out of its reach. Maybe if you bark at her she'll let you have a nibble."

Terrick turned and punched me hard in the arm – which, for those of you who have never been hit by Terrick, is not fun. "Not cool." he scowled.

"Fine, then don't bark, but at least say something. All you ever manage is a grunt around her. It's like fifty brain cells die for every step she takes towards you. You need to loosen up or you'll run out of 'um entirely." At Terrick's saddening face, I added. "Hey, relax. You may be an idiot, but you're a good guy, I'm sure she gets that."

"I'm not sure whether to take that as a compliment or hit you again."

"Take it as a compliment. You hit too hard."

"Sorry bout that." Terrick laughed. "Sometimes I forget how fragile you are."

"Ha! So it's fragile that keeps out-dueling you whenever we fight."

For a moment I thought Terrick must have run out of comebacks because he fell very silent and looked down at the ground. I was all smiles, ready to savor my victory when I looked forward and realized what had caused Terrick's momentary inability to continue verbal warfare. Sienna had just walked off a path up ahead and turned into the village tavern, where she sometimes tended bar for Dane, the elderly man who owned it, and his grandson Erik. She was apparently working today.

"Let's find somewhere else to eat." Terrick said quietly.

"Don't be such a pain; we have to go in there for your father's food anyway. You need to calm down a bit, it's not going to be that bad. Just comment on her hair or something. Say she looks nice. Girls love that kind of stuff." With that I pushed open the door to the tavern and walked in, dragging Terrick's lifeless body along behind me.

The Tavern was located in the largest of the forest's trees and it was surprisingly dark for the fact that there were windows every few feet around the trunk. There were tables around half of the trunk's perimeter with the bar stretching across the other half. There were a few tables in the space in the middle of the room and small oil lamps were scattered about the ceiling. A small fireplace was ablaze by the left side of the bar. Overall it was big enough to fit about twenty or thirty people, but there were never many people in it. Some of the villagers couldn't afford to eat out while most of the others just preferred to make their own food. Jarron was one of the more important and wealthy members of the town however, and I'd inherited all my mother's money, as well as being paid by Jarron for my help, so I had quite a bit of money as well. As a result, we ate in the tavern almost every day, with the exception of when Sienna was working and Terrick made us eat elsewhere. The Tavern was owned by the overly charismatic and very old Dane, who was rarely seen outside of his back room where he brewed his own beer, ale, and mead. He was the only source of such drinks in the town.

Sienna was only two months younger than me and was exceedingly beautiful. I mean, I'm a pretty good looking guy, but next to her I looked like some dog's old chew toy. She was a good half a foot shorter than me and had dark brown almond shaped eyes, with matching hair that fell down past her shoulders and had a horribly attractive habit of falling gracefully over the left half of her face. She had shallow cheeks, skin that seemed to have been baked permanently tan by the summer sun, and was one of the only people in the village to have their ears pierced other than me, with small silver loops hanging from both. Her face ended in a small pointed chin and she had thin lips that ended in dimples whenever she smiled, which was a majority of the time. Now that I think about it, I'm not sure I've ever really seen her upset. I would have been strongly attracted to her myself if I didn't have such a horse-crush on Elma, and if I didn't know that Terrick would be destroyed by it.

When we got inside, the tavern was empty with the exception of one incredibly old looking villager named Abok, who sat in the corner drinking some kind of thick yellow liquid that must have been honey liquor. When Terrick saw that there was no one behind the bar he let out a sigh of relief.

"Doesn't look like anyone's gonna be serving us. We should probably find somewhere else to eat."

"Shut up Terrick, she's probably in the back talking to Dane." I smirked, "Look, here she comes now."

Sienna had just appeared out of the back room of the tavern, with her long hair tied back into a pony tail. I really wished she would have tied back the hair covering the left side of her face too. I knew it drove Terrick crazy. His cheeks were already beginning to exchange their embarrassed red color for the putrid green one of someone very close to being sick.

"What's up Shorty?" I called as I walked up to the bar. I figured some light conversation was in order, you know, something Terrick could ease his way into.

Sienna, rolled her eyes, "Hi to you too Aaron, Terrick. What are you boys up to?"

"We're just getting a bit to eat, we've been tending to the fields all morning." I responded, as Terrick grunted in agreement, looking like he would rather still be in the fields with his father.

"It looks like it. You guys are filthy; you should go wash up while I get your food. The usual right?"

"Yea, and a turkey and rye with a fire whiskey for Jarron."

Sienna nodded, smiling, and turned her back to get started on the food.

"Let's go Terrick." I said, turning to walk away, thinking that he clearly wasn't ready to add to any conversation.

But Terrick wasn't coming. I looked back over my shoulder about to ask what he was doing when I had to stop short. To my complete astonishment, a still slightly green Terrick was standing, staring at Sienna with a very forced look of bravery and pride on his face. You know the look, it's the one people get right before they do something incredibly stupid, usually ending in a gruesome death or some form of heinous disfigurement. For a split second I hoped that Terrick was just trying to change his order, or else say something clever like '*Hey Sienna, you have something in your eye. Oh wait, it's just a sparkle.*' but any hopes of that were dashed immediately.

"Youlookwonderfultoday!" he blurted out overly loud with his words jumbling together.

Sienna spun around and looked towards Terrick with a mixture of confusion and amusement. "I'm sorry? I couldn't really hear you." she said.

Terrick looked back at her, horrified at what he had just done. His face was waging a fierce battle to decide what color it most wanted to turn, and was now a very bizarre mix of pale red green. Meanwhile, I was having the hardest time of my life trying to force myself to suppress a fit of laughter so strong it could crack a rib. It was only my strong bond of friendship with Terrick that kept me from rolling around on the ground. There would be plenty of time for salt-in-the-wound moments later, but right now I needed to keep it together for his sake.

"I… I… go… wash hands," he stammered before turning and half running out of the tavern, with me close on his heels. Once we were halfway out the door I stole a quick glance back and saw that Sienna was now wearing a very broad smile, as well as a slightly redder set of cheeks herself.

"That's it, apparently the Gods want me to kill myself," said a very shaken Terrick, once out of earshot of the bar. "What was I thinking? I have to be out of m'mind! *I* don't even know what I just said in there!"

There was no way I could control myself any longer and I was finally forced to burst out. "What... is... wrong... with... you..." I said between breaths of laughter. "That was the funniest thing I've ever seen. Seriously, I'm cramping."

Another hard punch in the arm. "It's not funny, I can't go back in there; I have to leave."

"No no no, it's not as bad as you think... Well I mean it was bad, but it wasn't a complete disaster. I think she thinks your incredible ability to make even the easiest of sentences incomprehensible is cute. She was blushing when we left."

"What! That ain't a good thing! I embarrassed myself so bad I've started to embarrass her!" Terrick was starting to lose the color in his face.

"You need to calm down and relax." I replied.

Terrick didn't respond, but began to wash his hands in silence. I joined him by the well and began to wash up too.

"Just act like she's a normal person for once. Pretend it's old Dane behind the counter, and maybe you'll be able to say something that makes sense."

"But that's the thing, it's not Dane behind the counter, it's Sienna, incredibly beautiful Sienna. No beard, no out-of-control nose hairs, no stupid lisp; just those dimples and brown eyes, and that bit of hair that drives me insane, and every time I see her I completely lock up like some kind of overgrown farm animal!"

"Umm, guys?" said a small voice behind Terrick, and immediately what color was left in his face was gone. Terrick now uncannily resembled a ghost.

"I didn't know what you wanted to drink." Sienna said silently, her face now unmistakably blushing a dark shade of red.

"Umm, I'll take a water. Terrick, what do you... umm, he'll take a water too," I said, really wishing the previous conversation had not taking place in the same Province as Sienna, let alone right around the corner. Sienna turned and walked from me and a stone white Terrick statue that couldn't look anywhere but straight ahead, with eyes the size of watermelons. It took close to ten minutes before I could get anything out of him.

"How much of what I said did she hear?" stammered my horrified cousin.

"She might not have heard anything; she just came around the corner when you finished your rant." I forced myself to reply.

Sienna *had* only just come around the corner, but to think that she hadn't heard any of our conversation was optimistic to the point of madness, and both Terrick and I knew it.

We ate in silence, neither of us mentioning what had just happened. Terrick kept avoiding eye contact with Sienna, even though she kept trying to make small talk in desperate attempts to end the awkward silences. Just like he had said earlier, he completely locked up like a big dumb animal, hardly speaking and resorting mainly back to grunts of agreement at whatever I had to say. We left in silence, with me being the only one to say goodbye to Sienna, but we still had a little time before Jarron needed us to be back in the fields, so we sat down under an old tree to relax.

"She wanted you to say something, she kept trying to talk to you." I said in my best supportive, 'I'm there for you' tone.

"She doesn't want to talk to me. She thinks I'm an idiot. Who would wanna talk to me?"

"Hey, I think you're an idiot and I still talk to you."

"Ugh." Was all he could respond.

"You're way too hard on yourself. I mean sure you are a bit of a meat head, but like I said before, she knows you're a good guy."

Terrick let out a bit of a muffled chuckle. "Always poking fun aren't you?"

"Wouldn't be a good cousin if I didn't, would I? Anyway, in a couple minutes we'll be back in the fields digging hundreds and hundreds of little holes in the ground and if that doesn't excite you, you have to be dead inside."

Terrick chuckled again, "Ugh... well I guess digging holes has been the highlight of my day... sad as that seems."

With that, we began to make our way back to the fields.

"Cheer up man. Eventually things will get easier, and when they do you'll be able to look back at this and laugh. I mean, look at me, I can laugh at it already."

A third punch in the arm. "I hate you..."

"Oh now come on, no you don't."

"Yes... yes I do."

"You know your life would be hollow and empty without me Terrick, and you know if the roles were reversed you'd never let me hear the end of it. Besides, you can't hate me for being honest... it was really funny." I continued, beginning to chuckle again as the memory came back to me fresh.

"Ugh..." Terrick grunted again continuing to stare straight ahead.

We walked to the field exchanging small rips at each other, with me assuring Terrick that if he continued to draw blanks in front of Sienna, he could always resort to bench pressing a plow mule to impress her, and Terrick threatening the safety of my kidneys in return; an afternoon of seeding, sure to remove the disastrous memory, at least temporarily, from Terrick's mind.

Chapter 3: The Visit

The rains came even worse than expected at the end of the week. Jarron, Terrick and I had only finished seeding the field when the first drops began to fall. The storms worsened steadily until even the great canopy that stretched over the villager's heads wasn't enough to keep a steady downpour from falling on the forest floor. Most of the villagers had fled to the inner cover of their trees, and very few people could be seen venturing out into the rain. Jarron happened to be one of those people, and as such, Terrick and Lisa could be found invading the sanctity of my tree; Lisa was sprawled out on my bed with her nose stuck in a book, as it so often was, and Terrick seated on the floor, engaging me in a "high stakes" game of chess. The room was fairly dark, with only a few strategically placed lanterns yielding any visibility. Not even the brilliant flashes of lightning could give extra light, as they were completely blocked out by the high canopy. Only the roar of thunder, like that of an angry lion let us know that there was even a storm going on outside.

"Aaaaaand, now another of your pawns is dead."

"Who cares, s'only a pawn." Terrick mumbled back.

"You keep sacrificing them like that and you'll run out of men to protect your king."

"Yea yea, you worry about your own men, cause I'm'a mate you soon, and then we'll see who's talking."

"Hear that Lisa? The dumb ox you call a brother wants to mate with me."

"I hate you so much." Terrick mumbled again, barely audible over Lisa's giggles.

"Aww, it's no use lying to yourself, you know you luuuurve me."

"Shut up and let me think."

"Try not to think too hard, I don't want your brain overheating." I continued jabbing. I knew the angrier Terrick became, the more likely he was to make a mistake.

Terrick moved his knight into position to take my queen if I didn't move her, but in his haste he had completely overlooked one of my bishops. It was perfect. I moved immediately, taking the knight.

"Check."

"Piss!" Terrick cursed under his breathe. He moved a pawn forward to block the bishop's path, but it was only a temporary solution. Soon the pawn was off the board too.

"Check."

Terrick's second knight took the bishop, only to be replaced by my queen.

"Check."

We both knew it was over, but Terrick refused to give up. He slid his king over into the corner, and I pounced, moving in for the kill, in the most humiliating fashion: I slid a pawn I'd marched up the board one more space forward pinning the king between it, my second bishop, and my queen.

"That's mate, mate." I laughed, "And I believe you get to feed Elma for me for the week."

"Ugh…" Terrick grunted in disgust at his defeat, kicking the board aside.

"Why do you two care so much about that stupid game anyway?" Lisa interjected.

"Why don't you mind your own business?" her brother shot back. "What are you even reading anyway? One of your stupid fairytales? You know that garbage isn't real right? Crap like that doesn't happen in real life. There aren't no princes or princesses, and if there were any princesses, there sure as hell wouldn't be any princes risking their asses to save'um."

Uh-oh, I thought to myself. Lisa may have been a scrawny little ten year old, but if you insulted her books she wouldn't hesitate to jump down your throat and rip out your liver… I know, graphic right?

Lisa jumped up off my bed, with tears welling up in her eyes, "Shut up Terrick! Don't be mad at me just because Aaron's smarter than you. You're just jealous that *you're* not smart enough to read *my* stupid fairytales on your own!" And with that she stormed to the stars leading to the bottom floor of my tree. Right at the door she turned with daggers in her eyes and retorted, "At least *I* can talk to Sienna using complete sentences," before she slammed it shut, causing it to shake on its hinges.

Terrick looked shocked and a little ashamed, but no longer as angry.

"Well she's got us both on the reading thing mate." I chuckled a little, trying to dodge Lisa's Sienna crack, and prevent Terrick from sliding into another depressing stupor.

Most of the people in the village couldn't read. No one really understood how Lisa caught on to it so young, or who had even taught her for that matter, and she wasn't about to tell anyone. It was the one thing that she was really proud of. For all me and Terrick knew she had somehow managed to teach herself, because Jarron certainly hadn't. He never had a lot of time for things that didn't concern the fields or the general wellbeing of the village.

"You better go after her. I'll get us dinner while you try to calm her down."

"Whatever." Terrick responded in an indifferent voice as he got up and started walking to the stairs. "I'll get you back for that chess match by the way!" he yelled over his shoulder as he left to check on his sister.

The walk to the tavern wasn't a long one, but it was enough to soak me to the bone and I was glad for the warmth of the fire blazing silently at the far end of the bar. I was hungry, but the fact that I was freezing took precedence, so I sat down on the hearth and placed my hands so close to the tongues of fire that I was surprised they didn't manage catch on their own. The warmth was like a hot shower, or a soft blanket, that engulfed me completely.

"Hi Aaron." Came Sienna's friendly voice as she emerged from the back room of the bar carrying a fresh bottle of some of Old Dane's whisky. She tilted her head and gave me her usual flawless smile. "You look miserable." She said pointedly.

"Ha! It's nice to see you too Shorty."

"You need a towel or something?"

"Nah. No point is there? I'm just gonna get soaked again when I leave aren't I?"

"Touché. Something to eat then? Or did you just come here to sit by the fire?" she asked sarcastically.

"Wow, can't a guy warm up a little first?"

Sienna walked to the door leading to the back room and stood on her toes to glance through the window, before returning to the bar.

"Here. This'll warm you up." She said as she pulled a glass and an almost empty bottle from under the bar. Hopping on the counter and gracefully swinging her legs over, she walked to the fireplace and sat down by me. "Fire whisky." She winked, pouring the smooth amber liquid into the glass and handing it to me. "I told Dane we were out."

I took the glass and had a sip, almost choking as the liquid burned the back of my throat. It was like I had managed to suck the fire right out of the hearth. My eyes began to water, and I made a stupid embarrassing little gasping sound, but the effects of the fire whisky were immediate. My whole body seemed to warm up with its heat.

Sienna gave me a sad, condescending smile before downing the rest of the bottle. "Don't be such a girl Aaron." She scolded me, grinning even wider and heading back to the bar.

"Done that before have you?" I sputtered, trying to balance my shock with the disappointment that I had just been out-drank by a girl.

"Shhhhh." She responded, hopping back over the bar. "Wouldn't want to give the old man back there a heart attack." Hooking a thumb over her shoulder to indicate Dane, "Don't think he'd approve much do you?"

"Not so much."

People weren't allowed to drink in the village under the age of twenty. A dumb rule, Terrick and I thought, seeing as how we were considered men at seventeen.

"Seriously Aaron, stop being a girl and finish that before Dane sees you with it."

"Oh, right!" I snapped out of my thought and finished the drink. The second gulp wasn't nearly as bad as the first, now that I knew what to expect, but it still made me cough a bit, causing Sienna to laugh again.

"So where's your sidekick at?" she questioned, in what seemed like a forced uninterested voice.

"Ehh, he's back at my place trying to calm his sister down, she's all mad at… uh, about the storm. All the thunder you know." I lied.

"Makes sense, I didn't like storms much at her age either. Sweet of him though."

I thought it was better for Sienna to think Terrick was sweet rather than a jerk, so I just nodded back.

At that moment, the door to the bar opened and tall lanky man named Arctone walked in. He was a sandy haired man with a well-trimmed beard, around the same age as Terrick and the only person in the village who could give him a run for his money in height. He had light brown eyes and a thin, smart looking face that gave the impression of a keen intellect. He was thin, but well built, and had big powerfull hands that he said allowed him to better grip his sword. His father, Hollowsworth, was the village sword master, which made him the de facto second in command when it came to weaponry in the village.

"Hey y'all."

"Hi Arctone." Sienna smiled back, "What can I get you."

Arctone placed his order and then walked to the fireplace to warm up a bit while Sienna worked to prepare his food.

"You chose the wrong time to come." He laughed, "Rain's starting to let up."

"So I see." I scowled a bit, noticing that Arctone was almost completely dry, and while I was no longer cold – the fire whisky solved that problem – I was still thoroughly soaked.

"If the rains continue to let up tomorrow would you and Terrick want to get some sparing in? You guys haven't been able to go much with all the work you've been putting in on the fields, but I suspect there won't be much to do tomorrow with as sloppy as it'll be."

"Yea sure Arctone, I'll talk to Terrick about it."

"At-a-boy! It'll be good for you, you could use the work. I might even spar with you myself if I think you're up to it." He gave me an exuberant slap on the back.

"Yea, that'll be great Arctone."

I caught Sienna's eye and she smiled at me before looking down to hide her smirk from Arctone. I'm gonna be honest, I liked the young swordsmen enough, but sometimes he could be insufferably arrogant, not to mention condescending. In other words, he was a bit of a dolt. I didn't think it was intentional, but it could still be really annoying on occasion. At least I was more subtle about it than Terrick, who had hit Arctone on multiple occasions for calling him boy or sport or tiger like a five-year-old, even though he was older than Arctone. I smiled reminiscently at the thought of Arctone on his back after the last time he annoyed Terrick.

"Great!" Arctone exclaimed after retrieving his food from Sienna. "I'll see you tomorrow then Aaron. I sure do love it when you come around kid."

"Yea, I appreciate all ya do for me sport." I smiled back sarcastically.

Arctone didn't pick up on it though and waved back friendlily before walking out of the tavern.

"Well handled." Sienna said slyly.

"What?" I responded innocently, "Oh come on, just cause you can't stand Arctone doesn't mean I don't like him. He really… well at least he means well."

"Sure sure. Have you decided what you want yet?"

"Ehh…"

…

I returned to my tree later to find Terrick sitting on the bottom floor by himself, with a look on his face close to what could be expected if someone had insulted his mother.

"The lil punk won't even let me talk to her! As soon as I came down here she ran back past me up the stairs and locked the door to your room. I've been yelling for her for half a bleedin' hour! She never says a word the whole time! I hate having a little sister! And what the hell took you so long! I'm starving!"

"Wow, you need to cool it a bit." I laughed, "No sense yellin' at me, I was just warming up a bit, talking to Sienna. I was soaked when I got there."

Terrick scowled at the sound of Sienna's name. "I bet you were."

"Now what's that supposed to mean." When Terrick didn't respond I continued, "Oh you're impossible when you're in a bad mood. You're worse than your sister by far you know that? Here, it's ham and swiss." I said shoving the food into Terrick's hands and walking up the stairs to talk to Lisa myself.

I got to the second landing and knocked on my door (which by the way is really annoying, a guy shouldn't have to knock on his own door), "Hey Lisa, it's me. Can I come in?"

After a minute the door slowly cracked open. Lisa was grinning from ear to ear and she pressed a finger to her lips shushing me before letting me walk into my own room.

"Lock the door behind you."

"Well you smiling wasn't what I expected." I stated, a little bewildered. I was anticipating the whole teary eyed, sad little girl bit, and having to spend hours calming her down, so in all honesty, I was pretty relieved.

"Oh I'm fine," she responded, "I just like making *him* mad. And it's far too easy."

"Oh you're cruel... I like it."

Lisa giggled, and sat back down on my bed to continue reading her book. A moment passed and then there was another knock on the door.

"Lisa, can I please come in and talk to you." Terrick pleaded from behind the wooden door.

"No Terrick!" Lisa yelled, twisting her voice into an imitation of someone painfully hurt, "Y-You a-always make fun of m-me! No one makes me as s-sad as you d-do." She sniffled and I had to hand it to her, she did an incredible job of masking her giggles with fake sobs.

"Come on Lisa!"

"NO! J-Just go away!"

Terrick punched the door hard enough I thought it might give way, before his footsteps could be heard thundering back down the stairs.

"Oiy! Don't break my door!" I shouted after him before turning back to Lisa, "Well done. And here I'm thinking Terrick's the mean one. You're awful."

"Shut up Aaron." She laughed, before going back to her book, "He deserves to feel bad. He can sleep down there for the night."

I took a bite of my sandwich and looked back to the little girl on my bed, "Lisa, who taught you how to read?"

"You know I won't tell you."

"Well why not? Why's it such a big secret for you?"

"Because no one would believe me even if I told them."

"Try me. I promise I'll believe you."

"Noooo, you won't. And I'm not going to tell you anyways, so drop it or I'll make you sleep downstairs with Terrick."

I laughed, "Hey, don't you go forgetting who's house you're in and who's bed you're on there little girl."

Lisa scowled at me, "An elf taught me." She said pointedly before going back to her book.

"Come on Lisa," I rolled my eyes, "Seriously, who taught you?"

"Fine!" She said in an exasperated voice, "A yeti came down from the Blue Rock and taught me, right after he taught me archery and how to make things fly with my mind."

"Nice Lisa… really, I like the sarcasm."

"I told you you wouldn't believe me."

I rolled my eyes at her again, "I don't understand why you can't just tell me."

"Seriously Aaron, ask me again, see what happens."

…

"So she kicked you out too eh?" Terrick mumbled as I appeared at the bottom of the steps.

"Yup." I responded, dropping a pillow onto the floor.

"That's what you get for taking her side earlier."

"Yup… Oh, and she's totally playing you upstairs. She's not even upset anymore. She just wants to chafe you."

"Agh! She's a little-"

"Yuuup."

"I can't believe sh-"

"Yuuup."

"I should go an-"

"Nooo no-no-no you shouldn't."

"You know, she's getting really-"

"Yeeea she is… she learns it from the best though."

"True."

There was a moment's silence before I started back up, "I think maybe I should go back and-"

"Won't work." This time Terrick cut me off.

"Well why won't it wo-"

"Tried it already, mate."

"Fair enough... I concede." As lame as it sounds, we're actually pretty good at the whole thought finishing thing.

"Good choice buddy. You can't beat her. She fights dirty. It's really just impressive."

I chuckled before changing the subject, "I saw Arctone at the Tavern." I said with mock enthusiasm.

"Wonderful… what he call you, scooter or booster?"

"Ehh, I think it was just kid this time."

"What an ass." Was his only reply.

I laughed again, "He wants us to come and spar tomorrow. I think we should, we haven't been out there in forever."

"Why do we have to go to the field and spar? You know I can't stand that guy."

"Because, when you throw you're sword in disgust there, there won't be anyone around to be decapitated by it."

"'Cept Arctone…" Terrick mumbled, a dreamy expression on his face, "maybe I'll let it slip just once."

I laughed one more time before rolling over and falling asleep.

I jerked awake the next morning, my head swimming with images of the forest and a strange out of place glow, the exact same, image for image, as the dream I'd had nearly a week earlier. I remembered the dream had cut into another, rather more exciting dream, where I was fighting a yeti with a fairy tale book as Lisa shot arrows in the corner saying she told me so, ham and swiss sandwiches flying around her head. I rubbed sleep from my eyes and tried, once again to no avail, to retain anything from the dream. Of course, I could remember every single snowy hair on a big dumb yeti, but I couldn't remember anything of my second dream. Terrick was still out cold beside me, snore-drooling into one of my pillows so disgustingly that I would probably have to just burn it as it would never be usable again. Lisa however, was now sitting at the table at the edge of the room, nose right back in the same book it had been stuffed in the previous night. She looked up at the sound of my movement and smiled.

"How was the floor?"

"Huh?" I asked, slightly confused as her unexpected voice interrupted my musings about the dream. "Oh!" I finally realized what she was talking about, "Oh you know, a floor's a floor whether it's down here or upstairs. I'm actually surprised I slept as well as I did. How was my bed?" I countered, feigning interest to disguise the displeasure I still had about being kicked out of my own room by a ten year old.

"Oh I couldn't sleep up there… I get scared when I'm alone in the dark. You know that. I had to come down here, but you two were already out. Turns out I can't sleep at all on the floor though, I'm still exhausted."

"Ha, serves you right! Kicking me out of my own room."

"Well you deserved it!"

"Sure, sure. If you say so."

"You just missed daddy, he stopped by a few minutes ago. The fields are a mess, so he said you and Terrick could have the morning off. He's still gonna be there though. You know how he is - it'd kill him to take a day off. He says he still wants you to stop by after lunch though. He thinks that the ground might dry up enough by then."

"Hey, troll boy!" I hit Terrick across the face with my pillow, "Wake up."

Terrick snorted and sat bolt upright, making a stupid punching movement into nothingness, and taking a moment to realize that he wasn't dreaming anymore. Finally he looked over at me grinning innocently at him. "What is wrong with you? What the hell'd you hit me for?"

"You hear your sister? We have the morning off."

"Great, now let me sleep." He said, lying back down and burying his face back into his soggy pillow, "And you can tell the brat, I'm no longer talking to her."

Lisa giggled and hopped off her chair, "I'm gonna head home for a bit Aaron. You can tell *the troll boy* I'm okay with him not talking to me."

"Good, get out of here." Came Terrick's muffled voice from in his pillow.

"Bye Lisa." I called to her as she left. "Terrick, stop bein a bum and get up." I hit him again with the pillow.

"Alright, alright, I'm up. You're far too much of a morning person."

"And what's wrong with that."

"Morning people are three times more likely to die young in life. You gonna eat that?" he said, pointing to the half a sandwich I had left over from the previous night.

"Take it. And why's that?"

He shoved half of what was left in his mouth at once and began to answer "Cauzzay get on da nervfsof people ike me." He swallowed, "Wake me with that pillow one more time and you'll find out. You'll just be another statistic mate." He shook his head in mock sadness.

"Yea, you'd have to catch me first, and plow mules aren't exactly known for their speed. You coming or what?" I was already half way out the door, sword and bow in hand.

"Yea, hang on a sec." He threw the other half of the sandwich in his mouth, "I'b catch ou someow." He insisted as he swallowed.

The walk to the sparring field was not a long one. It was located much closer to my house than the field where Jarron worked. To Terrick's displeasure, Arctone was already there and waiting for us when we arrived at the field. Terrick had been hoping that in arriving as early as we did, we would manage to beat Arctone there and get our sparring done before he could show. Instead we were greeted by the usual condescending call of "Hey! Great you kids could make it out here so early. Beautiful morning isn't it?"

"Sure is Arctone." I responded halfheartedly, while Terrick grumbled, "Kid... I'm older than you asshole." under his breathe.

Once the greeting had been taken care of, I took time to scan the rest of the sparring field, happily noting that Hollowsworth had also arrived this morning. He was always much easier to work with than his son. Suddenly, there was a glimmer of hope that we wouldn't get stuck with the younger swordsman. Terrick seemed to realize this as well because his groan of displeasure was apparent when two of the younger boys from the village, Ebar and Damian, seemed to appear out of nowhere to work with him, once again relegating us to suffer through Arctone's obnoxious instruction.

"You know Arctone, I think me'n Aaron are old enough to work without you babysitting us." Terrick rumbled in an overly aggressive tone. However, Arctone either didn't pick up on it, or else he simply brushed it off because he responded as cheerfully as ever with an, "Aww you're a funny one you are. Nah I'll just watch you guys for a bit. You won't even know I'm here."

"Yea, and my sword's made of chocolate grasshoppers." Terrick responded just loud enough for me to hear, causing me snort-laugh and Arctone to give me weird what-was-that-about look.

I got myself steadied and finally turned to face Terrick, my wooden practice sword out in front of me, "Just ignore him. You ready? I don't want you crying that you weren't prepared when I take your leg off."

Instead of responding, Terrick just turned and attacked. I had figured this was coming, so I easily parried the blow before countering with an upward thrust of my own that Terrick had to bend backwards in order to avoid. My sword was batted out of the way before Terrick spun on the spot swinging at my head, which, once again, I could see coming a mile away and easily ducked.

"Strike lower there Tiger," came Arctone's voice from our right. "You lose your center when you swing that high."

Terrick ignored the instruction and sent a cutting strike at my hip which I deflected before backpedaling easily away from him. I smiled and gave Terrick a nice taunting wave for him to come closer. He moved forward and as soon as he was in range I sent a hooking chop at his head before deploying a similar three-sixty spin like Terrick had just used, only much faster, sending another blow at the opposite side of his head, only to wheel back around the correct way once both attacks were blocked, dropping to a knee and hacking hard on Terrick's unprotected shin. It was my favorite move, I was fast, and the spinning always confused Terrick while masking where I was going to strike.

"Agghh!" he screamed and hop-limped back away from me several yards.

"You have to be faster there kiddo!" Arctone shouted again as Terrick cursed out loud, "Try dropping your base a bit."

Terrick gave Arctone a venomous hiss as I goaded him further, "Yea, try dropping your base a bit kiddo. You're too slow for me."

Terrick charged forward and we reconnected with a flurry of blows. Cutting and slashing at each other, splinters flying from our weapons with each block. Unlike with most things, Terrick always managed to get better at dueling the angrier he got. I never understood how that worked. He sucked at everything else when he let his emotions come into play. But with every correction Arctone threw out at him, he got a little more miffed, and I saw my openings for a good strike become fewer and fewer. I'd only managed to hit Terrick two other times, and only one of them would have been a damaging blow. I'd even thrown my double spin at him again, but he was ready for it this time, managing to deflect the third blow for a change.

After nearly half an hour of dueling I was beginning to wear down and it was taking all my concentration to keep Terrick from landing a blow. I had to start using the flat of my blade to simply misdirect his swipes rather than blocking them entirely. Terrick took a shot at the left side of my head, and I had to twist my body in ways that it should never be twisted in order to avoid the blow. As I turned, two things happened simultaneously, one, my back groaned in agony, making me wish I'd have just let Terrick bash my skull lopsided, and two, a movement in my periphery caught my attention as something green moved in the trees on the outskirts of the sparring field. I brought my attention back to the fight just in time to see Terrick delivering another blow. I raised my sword just a hair too slow and he was able to catch the blade with enough force to knock it clear of my hand.

He held the point of his sword to my neck, "Dead," he said in a triumphant tone that would have been more pronounced if he hadn't been so angry at Arctone.

"'Bout time." I shot back, "I thought we'd be here forever. I was beginning to think I'd have to let you hit me." I decided to use this tactic rather than blame my defeat on being distracted. Terrick would think I was just making excuses.

"Whatever."

"Great work guys!" Arctone exclaimed in his typical exuberant manner, "Really, you work so well together. I just can't get over how fast your improving there sport." He directed at me, and I silently wished for some of the previous night's lightning to come back and char him into dust. "You've just come so far so fast."

"Yea our little boy is growin up so fast, isn't he?" Terrick responded, his voice heavily layered with sarcasm. "It's hard to believe he's a teenager already."

This time it seemed Arctone was able to pick up on the sarcasm just fine, because his smile faltered ever so slightly before he threw another of his bizarre compliments in our direction and walked off to talk to his father. With our sword training out of the way we decided to leave the sparring fields before Arctone could come back and give Terrick another reason to hit him.

The rest of the morning passed rather quickly. There was another game of chess ending with a tossed board after yet another match where Terrick went down in a blaze of glory, and a surprisingly pleasant lunch at the tavern, due to the fact that Sienna was not working, so Terrick didn't have a chance to embarrass himself. Instead, we were able to discuss things such as our morning training session and how the planting was going in the Northern fields with the old tavern owner Dane, before he digressed onto a hilarious rant about how Melinda, an elderly lady who knitted clothing, had the "hotts" for him because she had specially made him a sweater for the upcoming winter.

."Has a bucket'o ale stitched init and e'erything!" he exclaimed, flashing us a typically adorable senile-old-guy smile.

Terrick and I conveniently decided to leave out that Melinda would be knitting sweaters for everyone in the village. Why crush the old man's happiness?

The sun was high in the sky by the time we left the Tavern, and I had to remind Terrick that Jarron was expecting us to meet him in the fields after lunch. The walk seemed shorter than usual due to the fact that the sun was out for the first time in nearly a week and the forest was once again alive with activity. We had just rounded the southeast corner of the field, finishing an argument on who was the better swordsman when the sight that greeted us stop us in our tracks. Up ahead, seven hooded and masked men on horseback were surrounding a defiant, but somewhat scared looking, Jarron.

Chapter 4: Some Bald Guy Tries to Kill My Uncle

"Pa!" Terrick shouted out to his father.

Jarron immediately snapped his head in Terrick's direction, as did all seven of the men on horse. The only man without a hood slowly drew his sword as he stared murderously at my cousin.

"Stay there, boys!" Jarron yelled back.

All of the men turned their attention back to Jarron. The hoodless man however, allowed his eyes to linger on us for an extra second and when he turned away, did not sheath his sword. Even while he was on horseback, it was easy to see that he was far and away the tallest of the men,, and he had an aura about him that made it impossible to ignore certain inescapable facts: one, that he was not to be crossed and two, that he usually got what he wanted. It was hard to tell whether his skin was a dark shade of ebony, or just extremely tan, adding to his mysterious aura, and making it difficult to tell where his sleeveless black cloak ended and he began. The sun gleamed off his freshly shaved head, his dark black beard was recently trimmed, and he looked plain cruel. I mean this guy wore an expression on his face that screamed *I use my free time to kick puppies.*

As if his exotic features weren't unnerving enough, the large golden earring piercing one ear accented them and the tribal bands that stretched tightly up his muscular arms left no room for argument; this was not a man you wanted to cross. Along his left bicep a tattoo wound its way up his arm seeming to twist and slither with each movement of his sword, finally forming into the head of a fierce-looking serpent on the upper part of his shoulder, just beneath the sleeve of his shirt. It wasn't the tattoo that disturbed me most however; it was the rider's eyes. He had my eyes. My penetrating blue eyes. But unlike mine, his eyes didn't compliment his features, instead standing out in stark contrast. Where mine were a warm, inviting blue, his were ice cold, and unsettling.

Golden rings lined his fingers, fingers that tightly grasped the ruby laden hilt of a large curved sword, complete with a strange language scrolled down the length of the perfectly folded blade. It was beautiful in its lethality, and showed that he was obviously a very wealthy and powerful man. The beautiful stallion he rode on alone would have been worth more than some of the farms in Jericho.

As I tried to make out what I could about this stranger, the men continued to talk to Jarron while a very tense Terrick, who was already terrible at listening to orders, became increasingly restless. After several failed attempts to calm him down, he completely lost his ability to stay put.

"This ain't no good. You can do what you want, but I'm gonna go help my dad," he growled as he began to jog toward Jarron.

I knew it was no good to argue with Terrick once he had his mind made up, so I just followed along silently behind him. We were quickly at Jarron's side and the seven men fell silent at our arrival. I hadn't noticed from the distance we were at, but now that we were close to the riders I realized that something was wrong with them. They were completely covered from head to foot even in the sweltering mid-afternoon heat, with black leather gloves and boots to go along with their hooded cloaks. They all wore iron masks that resembled faces of birds of prey, with long metal beaks and sharp slits for their eyes. However, nothing but darkness could be seen through the slits and the deep, rasping breaths that came from behind the masks were haggard and reeked of rotting meat. What's more, up close the riders did not appear to be shaped like normal humans. Their arms seemed longer and thicker than normal, their legs shorter, giving them an almost apish appearance, and they all had the same unnatural hump on the back of their shoulders, like they were all wearing miniature horse saddles. It all gave them a rather eerie and formidable look.

"Well? Whatever you have to say to him you can say to me." Terrick blurted out confidently, a smug look stretching across his face.

"Son, these matters do not concern you. It would be better if you were not here." Jarron didn't say it unkindly, but there was a hint of pleading in his voice. Terrick, however, was unable to pick up on the hint, and instead just seemed put off that his father wasn't glad of his company. At that moment a beautiful peregrine falcon called out loudly as it soared overhead. The bald man eyed it intensely for a few seconds before turning his attention back to Jarron.

"Your son should learn to keep his nose and tongue out of business that is not his own," he said in an unnaturally deep voice, "before he loses them both." A small sneer crossed his lips and his grip had tightened on his sword.

"If we had weapons you wouldn't be so quick to threaten, rider. Now speak or leave." Terrick snarled back. I found it incredible how easily Terrick could insult and command things of these men and yet not be able to string a coherent sentence together in front of Sienna. If the situation would have been different I might have laughed, but the fact was we were outnumbered and unarmed, and therefore Terrick really did need to shut up.

"My cousin means no insult sir, but whatever you need to say can be said in front of us. As we do not know you, we would prefer not to leave our father alone." I interjected, trying to salvage the peacefulness of the meeting.

The rider's smile had gone at Terrick's words, but I seemed to have been able to keep his urge to remove Terrick's head from his shoulders at bay. He turned to fix his glare upon me for the first time, but as he did his expression changed. I could have sworn that there was a mixture of shock and surprise in the riders face, but it was hidden quickly. He squinted at me for several uncomfortable minutes as if trying to make his mind up about something, and then twisted in his saddle and muttered something in an odd tongue to his companions before turning his attention back to Jarron.

"You have two weeks to reach your decision. May your Gods help you if it is the wrong one."

He looked at his fellow riders again before turning and racing away into the trees, leaving before anyone could respond.

"What'd he want, pa? What'd he mean by reach your decision? Reach your decision bout what?" Terrick asked, his tone more nervous now that the riders were gone.

Jarron gave his son a sorrowful look, "Son, when will you learn that there are some matters that do not concern you. They could have killed you without thinking twice about it." Terrick looked a little stunned by his father's disapproval, as well as his unwillingness to share information. They had always told each other everything.

"Now pick up a spade, there is work to be done. The fields are dry enough."

"But fath-"

"That is enough!" Jarron cut him off in a tone that brokered no arguement, "I'm going to eat, and there will be no more discussion of this."

Jarron walked past his son, picked up a meal that he must have made for himself, and went to sit underneath an old tree, deep in thought. Terrick picked up a shovel and began to dig holes again while I started to seed the areas Jarron had dug up earlier in the morning. We were soon rejoined by Jarron, who proceeded to work for a few hours in total silence before wandering over to us and finally saying that we could go home and take the rest of the evening off. He also said that Terrick and Lisa should stay at my place for the night while he tended to other matters. After several more failed attempts to get information out of his father Terrick conceded that it was a hopeless endeavor and began the long walk back to the village with me.

"What do ya think that was about?" Terrick finally spoke, breaking the silence of our walk.

"I don't know. Can't have been anything good though, could it? I mean they didn't exactly look like they wanted to take your dad out to dinner, did they? Someone, here must have done something to offended them."

"Where do ya think they came from? I've never seen anyone that looked like them; with those armbands and whatnot."

"I think they came from the desert." I said in a flat tone.

"What, Eremoo?"

"Yea." I responded.

"How do you know that? You ain't never been anywhere near the desert. Besides, nothing's lived in Eremoo for ages. There's hardly even any animals left there anymore, let alone people. You just can't survive in a place like that. It breeds death."

"It's the tattoo, you know, the serpent that was on the bald dude's shoulder. I've seen it before, on the old nomads that use to live there, remember? Came through here a while back looking to start over. You don't remember seeing it at all? They used it as a kind of brand, to show where they came from. I heard they had all left though, and obviously none of them stayed around here long."

"They didn't look like any nomads I've ever seen. You think they've started to go back then?"

"Maybe, but I doubt it. Like you said, nothing can survive in that place for too long."

"I bet they came here looking for land to build a settlement on." Terrick said confidently. "Yea, I bet they thought that a bunch of farmers wouldn't be hard to push around."

"Whatever they wanted it can't be good. They looked like they were prepared to fight for it."

"You think that's what the two weeks' notice was, time to give up what they wanted before they used force?"

"That would be my bet. Doesn't make much sense though, they would need a lot more than seven men to bully us around here. Even with a small army they would struggle. We're too well protected; maybe they don't know that though. I'm more curious about the men than I am worried."

"What are you talking about?"

"What? Didn't you see them? They were all… bizarre looking."

"Nah, I didn't notice um, I was kinda busy sizing up the big bald one… I think I could take him." Terrick smiled at the idea.

"Don't be thick. He looked like he knew how to handle a blade. You don't get a sword that pretty unless you know how to use it."

"Ugh, I don't need a pretty sword…" Terrick mumbled, his face turning back to its original shadowy expression.

We walked in silence the rest of the way to my tree, having exhausted the topic of the hooded strangers, and by the time we arrived the sun was beginning to set over the western tree tops.

"You can go on inside, Lisa's probably here already." I said as we approached the house. "If I ignore Elma any longer she might start taking bites at me. I haven't ridden her in forever."

"You wouldn't want any company on the ride would you?"

"Ha, what are we dating? Go keep your sister company." I laughed back.

"No you idiot, I just don't think it's smart to go out exploring by yourself. Those riders are probably still out there. If you're right about them coming from the desert, they won't exactly have the time to go home and back again in two weeks will they? They could have people stationed all over."

"I'll be fine. You worry too much. Elma's the fastest horse in Jericho, and I'll take my sword and bow with me. Plus, if they really are from the desert they won't know their way around the forest. I'll lose them easily enough. I'll only be an hour or so. We'll be at the spring."

"Fair enough, but don't blame me if that big bald bloke tries to crush your head with his bare hands. He looked like he had a lot of pent up rage. '*May the Gods help you if you don't like my armbands*'." Terrick said in an uncanny impression of the rider's voice, while flexing his muscles and baring his teeth.

I couldn't help but laugh at him, he looked like an idiot, "I'll try to keep my head out of his reach then."

I grabbed my sword, bow, and quiver from inside and greeted Lisa before heading back out to where Elma was tethered.

"Hey there, my beautiful girl." I cooed to her, as she glared at me in a way that screamed *where the heck have you been!*

"Hey, don't hate me cause the weather's been awful. You wanna go for a ride or not."

She whinnied back her answer as I slid my hand through her long white mane, and over her silky brown coat. I had bought Elma off a traveling merchant three years ago when she was just a filly. He had named her Elma after some foreign God of horses. At the time, I never would have been able to guess how good of a horse I'd actually purchased, even though the merchant claimed she was the best he had ever bred. I was incredibly skeptical when I bought her – I mean, who sells the best horse they've ever bred to a fourteen year old for practically nothing – but like I said before, the eyes just made you melt into a giant puddle of 'I love this freakin horse', so I had to buy her. As it turned out, Elma really was incredibly well bred. She was the fastest horse in the village, and I found it hard to imagine a horse anywhere that could outrun her. Her intelligence was unmatched amongst horses as well. I had found that she seemed to understand everything I said, every order I gave, and if there was ever a time that I needed her, she seemed to be able to find me on her own. It didn't seem to matter how far away I was, she would always show up, ready to help out in any way she could. All I ever had to do was whistle.

I climbed up on her back and took a deep breath. It was these moments that I enjoyed the most, the times when I was riding Elma. I loved them more than anything. The freedom of it. I could go anywhere; do anything.

"Where shall our next adventure take us Elma?" I leaned down over her long neck and whispered in her ear, "Shall we go to the grove, stop by the spring?"

Once again she shook her head up and down and whinnied in a kind of agreement. She began to walk forward into the trees, along the path that we had journeyed so many times before. I didn't need to guide her at all; she knew where we were going. The grove was located deep in the heart of the forest, and was even more beautiful than the rest of Northern Jericho. It had something deeply magical about it. The trees seemed to be alive; they moved and swayed even when there was no breeze, seemingly of their own accord. The spring was located at the far southern edge of the grove and had mysterious healing power. If one was to swim in the spring, deep cuts would heal themselves completely, broken bones somehow managed to mend, and a person's energy seemed to be entirely replenished, like you had just woken up from a long nap.

The ride to the grove was usually a very peaceful one. I'd lie back on Elma and watch all of the animals in the tree tops above. But tonight was different. I decided to at least pay some heed to Terrick's warning and pay extra attention to my surroundings. I kept my eyes peeled, looking for any movement that seemed out of place, and listened to every sound the wild forest made. My attentiveness was wasted though as we had walked for close to twenty minutes without the slightest hint of anything odd or mysterious jumping out at us.

Finally, when we had closed in on the outer boarder of the grove, I noticed two things that caught my attention. First, that we were standing exactly where I had found myself this morning in my dream, and second, I heard voices. Not the same muffled sound of something trying to escape, but the sound of men arguing. Gently, I reined Elma in, and slowly climbed down from her back.

"I want you to stay here unless I whistle, alright?" I whispered in her ear.

Elma gave a small snort of consent. She seemed to understand that silence was a must at the moment.

"If you see anyone but me come through these trees, I want you to run back to the house and get Terrick." She looked down and started to eat some grass, but I decided to take that as her understanding.

I turned away and began to creep forward through the trees, never making a sound.

Was this what I was dreaming about this morning? I thought to myself. *Have I been seeing into the future?*

I moved forward a little more and the voices began to get louder. It sounded like there was a heated discussion going on just ahead. I pulled the bow from my shoulder and strung an arrow.

This couldn't have been my dream. There were no voices in my dream, only that silvery glow. I'd only now begun to recall the details of the dream. Now that I thought about it, the glow had stopped right outside of the spring, meaning I was heading in the opposite direction.

I finally managed to convince myself that the dream was unrelated to what was happening now. Although I was slightly disappointed by this fact, I now had a new sense of apprehension about what lay ahead. I took a few more steps before stopping abruptly, realizing that I had heard these voices before. The sudden realization of what was happening hit me like a kick from a horse. There was no mistaking it; the voices up ahead belonged to none other than the large black rider, and Jarron. My heart felt like it had filled with lead and went to hide somewhere in my colon, and the fact that it was beating uncontrollably didn't ease the sensation. I crept forward a little farther until I could finally see the whole scene through a small gap in the trees. Jarron was standing, unarmed in the middle of what looked to be a small army of men, all wearing sleeveless black tunics, all with a large serpent tattooed on their shoulders. Talking to Jarron in the middle of the circle was the large black rider, and not far behind him were the six other riders, still hooded and masked. They looked even more deformed and misshapen standing on the ground, hunched over with their knuckle practically dragging through the grass.

"I will talk to the villagers, but I assure you they will never summit to your rule. You would do better to turn around and go back to where you came from. For your men's sake." I couldn't believe the courage and force with which Jarron said these words.

The large rider laughed, "I assure you that it is not for my men's sake you would have us leave. You would do better to reconsider your stance on this matter, or you may no longer have a village to stand for at all. Besides," the rider continued while turning his back on Jarron, "we may not need to stay here long after all. You have certain… assets… here, which we wish to acquire. If you submit to us willingly, you will be rewarded, and once we have what we need, we will be gone."

"I have given you my opinion, and I doubt strongly that it will change in two weeks. If you plan to return to my village, you best prepare for a war."

Turning back to Jarron, the rider's confident tone suddenly turned angry, "You are bold and naive like your son. You have no idea what you are up against. I have warned you that you are challenging the wrath of a God, and yet still you take no heed. I will see to it that your forests are burnt to the ground, and that your citizens pay the price of their resistance with blood."

"Your threats hold no value here. They do not frighten us, and I assure you they will not make anyone wish to give up their land, nor bow to any king. We are free men and women here, and we wish to stay that way. The fact that you have brought an army of thugs will not change that."

At the moment Jarron called the black rider's men thugs, several of the soldiers around the clearing drew their swords. For a brief moment I could see Jarron's courage falter. He had never liked swords, and the sight of so many of them being drawn at once seemed to make him lose a bit of his nerve. He recovered quickly enough, but his moment of fear had betrayed him. The black rider had noticed and a small sneer grew across his face.

"Frightened old man?"

"It would take more than the stingers your men carry to frighten me." Jarron lied.

The rider laughed at Jarron in his unnaturally deep voice and then said, "You are a fool... a brave fool... but a fool none the less. I'll ask you one more time to reconsider. Go back to your people, *take* the two weeks, *make* them see. This is my final warning."

"My answer remains as strong and unchanging as this wilderness around you."

"I see. That is a shame." The rider turned his back on Jarron and began to walk away, but as he did so, two of the soldiers seized Jarron by the arms, causing him to cry out in shock.

"Muzahara! Zaroof! Darcon!" the rider called. Three sulking soldiers on the edge of the grove stood up. "Take our friend into the woods, beyond earshot, and execute him."

"You said this would be a peaceful meeting!" Jarron cried to the riders back. "I am not even armed!"

He stopped, and without turning around spoke, "Like I said old man, you are naive, and now your life will end because of it. As will all those who live in your village. By the end of this week the streams will run red with your family's blood." And with that the three soldiers grabbed Jarron and began to drag him, struggling, into the woods.

I was dead. I had to be. Why else wouldn't I be able to feel anything? Hear anything? No, I needed to snap out of it. I needed to go get help. No, that would take too long. They were going to execute Jarron. I was the only one that could help. It was time to grow up. The time for sparring in the fields had past. Now there was a life depending on me. My uncle's life. But there were three of them, and only one of me. No, that didn't matter, I needed to think. I was an exceptional marksman with a bow and no one knew the forest like me. This forest was my castle, I was its king. I knew how to move like a shadow. They didn't. I knew how to maneuver in the trees. They didn't. I had the element of surprise. I could use that. Use it to my advantage. A new sense of confidence began to pump through me like fire whisky. The blood in my veins was like ice on fire. All of a sudden the mission I needed to accomplish not only seemed possible, but almost a bit unfair.

I kept close to the ground, and moved like a ghost behind the soldiers; never making a sound, bow taut and ready to strike. Through streams and over downed logs I flew like the wind, fueled by anger and the will to save my uncle. Finally the three soldiers stopped in a small clearing and the largest of the three, a dim looking muscle head with an ugly uno-brow, pinned Jarron down on a small tree stump in the middle of the clearing. A small greasy haired soldier that closely resembled a rat moved into position behind him, dirty mats of black hair dangling over his twisted face. I settled in between two large trees and waited.

"Any lasst requestsss old man?" The rat-like soldier hissed, his face contorting into a sneer.

I raised my bow and drew back on the arrow. I had never taken a human life before, but I'd hunted for as long as I could remember. The thought would normally disgust me, but at the moment, the three warriors seemed more beast than men in my mind.

"I have nothing to say to you." Jarron said defiantly, although his pale face gave away his fear.

My hands were steady and my aim was true. I slowly exhale in order to keep my hands from shaking.

The soldier laughed a raspy laugh, which sounded almost as greasy as his hair looked, and raised his sword.

My heart was still beating in my colon like a haunting drum. I aimed to kill, not to wound.

The soldier gave one last look at Jarron, arms raised over his head.

The twang of a bow, the flash of a sword, but the blow never fell. The rat-like soldier dropped to the ground, an arrow between his eyes. I took off through the trees, running at full speed but still careful not to make a sound. There would be another gap between two trees ahead. I whistled as loud as I could for Elma as I ran, hoping to whatever Gods were out there she could hear me; I'd need my horse to get Jarron back to the village. I drew my bow tight again. Three... two... one... I released between the next gap while on the run. It wasn't as accurate as my first shot, but it did the trick. My arrow struck the large soldier, who had been holding down Jarron, in the shoulder and he toppled off him backwards howling in pain.

The unharmed soldier was looking all over the borders of the clearing, confusion clearly written on his face. How many people were out there? His sword was drawn but he didn't know where to go. He couldn't hear anyone. The arrows had come from in front of him, and then to the right. He was a sitting duck here. He began to take off in the direction of the second arrow but didn't make it far. My third arrow lodged itself deep between his shoulder blades and he fell to the ground in pain. The larger soldier was back on his feet, sword drawn, the arrow still sticking out from his shoulder. A forth arrow sailed by his left ear, skinning his cheek. He started spinning in circles for any sign of his enemy, taking a moment to break the shaft of the arrow still lodged in his arm.

"Where are you?" he finally screamed, "Show yourself! Fight me like a man!"

"Okay." I hissed from directly behind him.

The color drained from the soldier's face. He spun on the spot swinging his sword wildly, but never had a chance to land his blow. He fell to the ground before he had completed his turn.

"Aaron, what are you doing here!?" Jarron questioned in a whisper, like he had just seen a ghost.

I sheathed my sword. "I don't really know." I laughed, remembering Terrick's words. "I'm not supposed to be within arm's reach of anyone who can crush my head with their bare hands."

"But, how did you know I was here?"

"It's a long story. I'll tell you about it when we get you home. We have to warn the villagers." I said while helping Jarron to his feet.

We started to walk out of the clearing together, Jarron's arm around my shoulder for support, when there was a rustling in the trees to our right. I looked over as an arrow went flying past my head, missing me by inches. I dropped Jarron on the spot and had my bow back in my hands and strung in a flash. I aimed in the direction of the shot, and pulled back to fire at the shadow between two trees, the spot where I had been shooting from only moments before.

Chapter 5: Meeting in the Night

I pulled back on my bowstring preparing to loose another arrow when the man who had missed me yelled from deep within the shadows. "Don't shoot me Aaron!"

"Terrick?" I hollered back, my voice betraying my shock. I looked behind me at where the arrow had gone. On the ground not twenty feet from me was the third soldier, the one I'd struck in the back with an arrow. He had a bow of his own in his hand, and a new arrow sticking out of his chest. "How did you find us? And nice shot, by the way. I guess you're not completely worthless after all."

Terrick laughed, "Thanks, I think. Even after I save your life you keep with the insults." A smile was growing across his face.

"You, save *my* life?" I said in mock surprise. "I knew what he was doing. I just figured I'd give him at least a little hope of survival. You know, build up for a more dramatic victory."

"Is that so? Well then I apologize for stealing your moment of glory. Next time I'll just let him skewer you with an arrow."

"Yea alright." I laughed back, "How'd you find us anyway?"

"Elma. She showed up back at the tree without you, so I knew something was wrong. I grabbed my bow and she started sprinting through the woods, and we just kinda showed up here. We arrived just in time to see you finish off that big bloke. She was incredible. You're always going on about how smart Elma is, and she finally showed me what you were talking about."

"I whistled for her, she knew where I was." I had never been prouder of my horse.

"She's pretty banged up though," Terrick continued, "It looks like a couple of arrows may have clipped her backside. None of them stuck, but she's still a little cut up."

I whistled again and Elma came trotting out of the woods. I again ran my hand through her mane and over her back, before moving to examine some of the deep cuts on her hunches.

"That's a good girl." I whispered to her, "You did well today."

Elma nudged me with her nose affectionately.

"Terrick, do you think you can get your father back to the village from here? I have to get Elma to the spring, and get these wounds cleaned up."

"I was only a bit shaken up. I can get back the village myself. I don't want you wondering by yourself Aaron." Jarron interjected.

"With all due respect uncle, you're unarmed, and you'll have to walk past the rider's camp in order to get back to the village. I'm headed in the opposite direction, and I know other routes to get home once I reach the spring. I'd feel better if Terrick was with you, and I'm sure he would too."

Terrick nodded in agreement, "I'm staying with you pa. We need to get you home. You need rest."

"Rest is the last thing I need." Jarron said stubbornly. "We need to warn the villagers of the danger they're in."

"What do you mean danger? How many men do the riders have with them?" Terrick questioned. He had not seen the small army of men with the black rider like I had.

"I'll explain it to you when we get back son, I promise. But now we must hurry."

With that Jarron and Terrick walked off in the direction of the village, leaving Elma and me behind. The journey to the spring was a slow one. But when we finally made it there, all was peaceful. Elma waded out into the water until nearly half her body was submerged. I meanwhile, took off my dirty clothes and dove in for a swim. The cool, crisp, water was refreshing and revitalizing, and after a few minutes, all of my worries seemed to melt away. It seemed impossible to believe that less than an hour ago I had been fighting to save my uncle's life.

After fifteen minutes or so of relaxing in the pool, I swam back over to Elma and again examined her side. The gashes that had been bloody only a short time earlier were now only faint scars where fur had not yet grown back. I climbed out of the spring and put my clothes back on. Whistling once more, Elma reluctantly began to back out of the water as well.

"We'll come and get you some more of this spring tomorrow. How's that sound?"

She gave a small snort and nudged me with her nose again. I took that as an "okay" and climbed up onto her back.

"Let's go home." I whispered to her, and she started a brisk walk along a new path on our way back to the village.

When we got back to the village it was nearly high moon and I found Jarron knocking on doors, and rounding up the villagers for the meeting that was sure to take place shortly. When Jarron saw me, he yelled over to inform me that there was to be a gathering in the large barn outside the northern field. I rode back to my tree and put some oats in a pen for Elma before heading back out to the barn. By the time I got there I saw that most of the village was already inside. Jarron and Terrick were standing outside the entrance waiting for me. I gave the two a slight nod of my head, and they returned the silent greeting before turning and heading into the barn. When the three of us entered, the chatter began to slowly die away into total silence. The whole village seemed to be holding its breath, waiting for Jarron to speak.

"Well Jarron, ya mind explainin the pressin need to drag all us out'r bed at such a late hour." Dane, the owner of the tavern finally broke the tense silence. He was one of the oldest members of the community and it was well known that he got rather cranky when woken. I was not surprised to see that a large number of the villagers seemed to share in his agitation at being herded together like cattle.

Jarron looked down at the floor for a moment, then back up at Dane and began, "I have gathered you all here tonight to warn you that our village is in danger of being attacked."

A hushed murmur began to travel through the barn, buzzing like a swarm of bees.

A man named Johan stood up in the back of the room and spoke. "What gives you this crazy idea that we are in any danger?" He demanded. "We have no enemies, who would want to attack us?" Johan was the village blacksmith, and while he was generally a good man, I knew he could be ill tempered and overaggressive.

"They are riders from the desert. They visited me in the fields today." Jarron explained, holding his hands in front of himself in an attempt to calm simmering blacksmith.

"The Eremoo desert? You're starting to lose your touch Jarron. Nothing's lived in that wasteland for ages." The man pushed back.

"It's true Johan." Said a small but muscular man I knew as Jarron's friend, Bray. "They came to me in my field first, looking for the "lord" of the village. When I told them that we didn't recognize any one person as a ruler, they seemed to become agitated, and well, they were an imposing group to say the least, so I directed them to Jarron, he's the closest thing to a mayor this village has ever had. Sorry buddy." He added as an afterthought to Jarron.

"Fine, so there were men, but what gives you any idea that they were from Eremoo, or that they wish us any harm?" Johan persisted, the fear slowly beginning to edge into his tone.

"To answer your first question, they have the Erai-Surka tattooed on their shoulders. It's a trademark, or brand of sorts that the old nomads used to mark themselves." Jarron spoke calmly to ease some of the tension in the room, while proving my theory that the tattoo really was a brand of the desert. "To answer your second question, I know because they told me so."

Johan opened his mouth to speak again but seemed to be out of ways to insult Jarron's integrity and shut it before slumping back into his seat with a huff.

A middle aged man named Blackert stood up next. "So le me get dis strai', riders from da desert tracked you down in yer field. Told ya they were gonna 'tack us, an den went away back inter da trees."

Jarron took a deep breath and began again. "When they came to me this morning, they came to give me a choice, an ultimatum. They wished to take our land for their own, and place us under the rule of their leader, a man by the name of Ronan Hazara. We could submit, or we could die fighting. He said that we had certain assets here that they wished to acquire, but he didn't elaborate. This Ronan said he would be back in two weeks for our decision. Death or servitude."

Another intense murmur passed through the crowed. Bray's wife Illiana, spoke next. "What did you tell them Jarron?" Her voice quivering slightly.

"I didn't say anything. The boys came back from lunch and the riders didn't want to speak in front them. So they left."

"Well that's just great." Johan seemed to have regained his confidence. "So now we'll be forced to fight for our homes in two weeks?"

Jarron laughed, "I'm afraid we don't have nearly that long Johan."

"What have you done you cracked old man?" Johan hissed.

"Watch who you're talking to blacksmith!" Terrick stepped into the argument. "My father's risked his life tonight in ways you can only imagine." Terrick caught Sienna's eye for a moment and immediately began to blush, but incredibly was able to keep his composure. "You know nothing of bravery or honor. He was willing to die tonight to try and protect your families."

"That's quite enough Terrick." Jarron finally said quietly. However, the gleam in his eye that said he would have very much liked for Terrick to keep talking. "Tonight I tracked the riders down in the forest. I entered their camp and had another discussion with their leader. I told him that we would never be slaves to any master, that his threats were worthless here, and that for his men's protection, he should turn around and leave."

"I bet he didn't take that to well, did he Jarron?" Dane said in an exasperated voice, a sort of scared amusement etched onto his face.

Jarron laughed again, "No, not very much Dane. He had his men drag me into the forest to have me executed. If Aaron and Terrick wouldn't have shown up I would dead right now."

Every eye in the barn seemed to have found my cousin and me. It was like a very bright spotlight had been cast on us and I became very aware of how hot it was in the barn. I'd never been one who liked attention. The whole crowed started murmuring to each other again, except for old man Parton who had fallen asleep in the corner and begun to snore.

"So wha' now, dey plan ter 'tack us soon?" Blackert jumped back into the discussion.

"Yes," said Jarron "But I don't think they are in much of a rush. They think I'm dead, and thus think that we will be unprepared for them when they strike. There leaders didn't seem to think very highly of their men though. None of their solders looked well cared for, and there were enough of them that they might not notice three missing soldiers; but that's not to say we shouldn't begin preparing"

"But you accomplished nothing with your stunt but narrowly being killed!" Johan shouted, shooting back out of his seat. "And now they may even know that we are preparing for them."

"Johan, sit down or we'll throw you out for being ignorant." Bray responded, causing some of the crowd to chortle.

"Oh, I think I accomplished something Johan, at least something other than almost meeting the Gods a little early. I now know what numbers they have with them, and I know that they will not attack immediately because I heard one of Ronan's officers telling him that reinforcements were a few days out. When they arrive I would expect their numbers to be around two or three hundred." There was another series of murmurs throughout the barn, but it was silenced quickly as Jarron continued. "I know that they have come prepared for heavy hand-to-hand combat, but in doing so they lack the proper protection for long range weapons such as bows and spears. I know that they are planning to attack at night because of the clothes they were wearing. Their black tunics and cloaks would be too easy to spot in the day. I know which direction they will attack from due to the location of their camp. And finally I know what their officers look like, so we know who to target in order to send the rest of their forces into disarray." Jarron paused for a second. "How worthless do you think my endeavor was now Johan?"

Johan said nothing and remained seated this time.

"How is a small village like ours supposed to hold off an army of three hundred men?" said a large man named Aberin, who was known as Chisel due to his work with carpentry.

"Well, we'll need to have a good plan, one we can put into action quickly, and one where we can turn their own tactics against them. Exploit their weaknesses."

The room lapsed into silence, leaving everyone to their own thoughts and devices until Bray finally broke the silence. "So what do you recommend we do, Jarron?"

Jarron thought for a moment before responding, "I believe there will be plenty of time to formulate a plan tomorrow. As for right now, I suggest you all go back to your homes and try to get some rest. We will have much to prepare tomorrow, but it will do us no good unless we have fresh minds. Tomorrow, we secure our village." With that, Jarron turned his back on the villagers and walked towards the exit of the barn. When he reached the doorway he turned and beckoned for Terrick and me to follow him, which we both obliged immediately.

Once out of earshot, Jarron turned to the two of us. "I need both of you to do me a favor. I have ideas on how to defend the village, but the bottom line is that we just don't have enough men here to hold them at bay for long."

I didn't like where this conversation was going, but I continued to listen.

"We need help if we want to last the week."

"You want us to be messengers?" Terrick questioned incredulously.

"Yes. I need you to go to the villages in Eastern Jericho, and Alleron. I need you to tell them what's happening here."

"No deal," Terrick argued, "What if the battle starts while we're away. You ne-"

"Then at least I'll know you are safe." Jarron cut Terrick across.

Terrick bit back his rebuttal as Johan walked past, shooting daggers at the three of us with his eyes. Once he had gone, Terrick hissed at his father, "You need us here to fight. We're two of the best swordsmen in the village, and no one's as good as Aaron with a bow!"

"This is more important Terrick! Without help from those villages we are doomed."

Terrick didn't say anything in response, but I could tell he still wanted to fight his father.

"Now coming from the desert this is the first village the riders would have reached, so there's a good chance those towns have not gone under siege yet. I want the two of you to take Elma and a horse from the stables, and I want you to leave first thing in the morning. Ronan was told reinforcements were a few days out, so if we're lucky you'll be able to get there and back with help before they arrive."

"But pa-"

"Don't start with me Terrick! Just listen. I want you to take your sister with you." Jarron's request caused his son to scoff, "Terrick, listen! I want you to take her with you. If the battle comes before you get back I want to know all of you are safe."

On top of the barn a falcon screeched, taking flight into the night.

"We'll look out for her uncle." I said before Terrick could start arguing again.

"Thank you, Aaron. It's a longer ride to Alleron, so Aaron, you and Elma should take that trip. The lord of the city there is named Bo. He's a good man, and if you make it there in time he *will* send aid. Terrick, I want you and your sister to take the road to the towns in Eastern Jericho, it's not as far, but the road may be more dangerous. I want you to stay off the road and in the trees so it's harder for you to be seen. Understand?"

We both gave silent nods. All the fight seemed to have finally left Terrick

"Alright, I want you two to get some sleep. There's a long journey ahead of you and it will do no good for you to be exhausted. The fate of the village may be resting on your shoulders, carry it well."

With that Jarron turned and went back into the barn to address some of the people that had remained behind to talk to him leaving Terrick and I to trudge back to my house. Tired, and with a thousand thoughts running through our minds we didn't speak until we had reached my tree, well after the moon had begun its decent to the horizon. I went upstairs and found Lisa was already asleep in my bed, her book lying open on the floor beside her, like she had fallen asleep while reading. I smiled at her. Jarron must have thought it better not to tell her of the day's events.

How good it would feel to be naive. I thought to myself as I looked down at the little girl in my bed. I turned around and headed back downstairs to join Terrick. We took turns getting cleaned up from the day's work and then settled on the floor with a couple of pillows and blankets.

"I can't believe so many bad things can happen on such a beautiful day." Terrick finally said.

I laughed, "Yea, and to think, all we're worried about a couple days ago was how stupid you looked in front of Sienna."

"Aww, why'd you have to bring that up again? I was just starting to feel better about myself." Terrick said with a chuckle.

"It's a shame the riders didn't know you better, if they wanted you to hold your tongue, all they had to do was stick Sienna on a horse behind them and all you would have been able to do is grunt."

Another punch in the arm.

It felt good to get back to this simple bit of jawing back and forth with Terrick. It brought a sense of normalcy back into my life and made me temporarily forget about the task we were about to undertake.

"You know, she smiled at you when you were sticking up for Jarron in the barn." I said once we had stopped laughing.

A minute passed before Terrick responded, "Yea, I know, I saw her."

"I thought you did. You started to blush a bit. You managed to keep going alright though. I was afraid you would shut down again."

"I think it was only because I was so mad at Johan that I didn't."

"I don't understand you, how can you back talk those riders, and yell at Johan, and yet not be able to say anything to her."

"It's complicated. I don't really want to talk about it alright." Terrick responded, rolling over so his back was facing me, and before long, I could tell he was asleep.

Chapter 6: I Run a Guy Over with a Horse

Sleep came over me quickly, and before I knew it I had faded into darkness.

I was riding Elma through the forest, and while I couldn't see the sun through the canopy, I knew it must have been nearing sunset because the quality of light reaching the forest floor was only enough to allow some of the grass' dark green color to reflect into visibility. As I rode through the trees I kept coming across members of the village: Dane wanted to know if I had scissors so he could cut his nose hair and Johan wanted to know where Jarron was because he wanted to call him an idiot again. The minutes stretched by as I rode deeper and deeper into the forest, and finally, after telling Illinna that I had no idea how many soldiers were coming to the village I entered the grove to a bizarre sight, Jarron was by the spring's edge kneeling over a stump with all white eyes. Every few seconds his head would fall off and another would grow out of the stump of his neck to replace the one he had just lost. Standing beside my uncle was the black rider. He was exactly the same as I had seen him by the fields; same bulging muscles, same tribal arm bands, same ruby hilted sword sheathed at his side, same disturbing blue eyes. He was exactly the same, except that he now he was juggling four of my uncle's lost heads. I pulled Elma to a stop and stared at the scene, while the rider stared back at me with his dead eyes. Finally, he opened his mouth and spoke in his same bone chilling, unnaturally deep voice, *Beware of the Retreat. It will be your first taste of defeat...*

I was in a forest again, but the scene had changed. I couldn't tell you why I was there, but for some reason it didn't seem odd to me that this was where I was. I looked around, and saw my old, worn, wooden bow on the ground; a quiver full of arrows was beside it.

"Maybe I've been hunting." I said to myself out loud.

I picked up the bow and the quiver and slung them both over my back. A bird could be heard singing nearby. I could tell by the sound that it was a cardinal. All the sudden something clicked.

I'm back in the dream. I thought to myself. *But if I've realized I'm dreaming, why aren't I waking up?*

I pushed the thought from my mind. *It doesn't really matter if I know it's a dream, does it?*

I started looking around for the glow. It should be arriving soon, shining through the trees, but I couldn't see it anywhere. I kept looking for it.

What if it doesn't show up this time? I thought. *What am I supposed to do if I can't find it?*

I never had to answer that question however, because just as I finished thinking those words I heard it. The noise that didn't belong. The silvery glow shone through between two trees on my left. Just as in the previous dream the glow began to drift away through the trees, becoming fainter. But this time was different, I knew where I was, and I knew where the glow was going. I took off sprinting in the opposite direction of the light. I ran and ran; through the borders of the grove past the area where the riders should have been camping. I was going to beat it there. I wanted to see what the cause of the light was, wanted to see it as it drifted to the edge of the magical spring. I weaved in and out of the trees, and jumped over the dead logs lying over the path. I ran past a large statue of a hunter, a bow still clutched in his outstretched right hand, while his head and left arm had crumbled into several barely distinguishable small boulders at its side. Finally, I turned a corner and the spring came into view.

The spring was as beautiful and peaceful as ever. The trees here were all a wonderful shade of silver while their leaves stayed a beautiful gold all year around. The spring was full of water the purest shade of blue one could imagine, and there were four small waterfalls that silently fed it from some thirty feet up, falling down the side of a cliff, through the tree tops. There was a path to the top of them that I had used on several occasions, whenever I was in the mood for a particularly stunning view of the forest. All you had to do was climb through an ivy covered tunnel that bore right through the cliff face at the other side of the grove and the path from there was easy climbing. It was a small tunnel though, there would have been no way for Terrick to fit through it, and it was barely visible if you weren't looking for it. No one knew about it but me, and I liked it that way. It was my little secret. The place where I'd go to escape from everyday life.

I slowly crept closer to the spring, moving through the brush as quietly as I could. I knew that whatever was creating the glow would enter the spring from the western edge, so I positioned myself between a pair of trees on the opposite bank, in a perfect place to see but not be seen. There was nothing left to do but wait and after a few minutes I could begin to make out a slight silver glow making its way through the trees.

Anticipation began to mount in my chest as the glow began to get brighter and brighter. I was desperate to see what could cause such a light. It was getting closer. The glow would be coming through the trees at any second when suddenly it disappeared, like a light being switched off. I began to panic for a second, not knowing what had happened to kill the glow that I was seeking. My shock turned to amazement when a young woman walked out of the trees and over to the side of the spring. She was shockingly beautiful, like Sienna beautiful, but different. She had straight, stunningly blond hair that fell over her shoulders like a golden waterfall and a thin, pale, feline face that was sharp and wild while still presenting an aura of graceful beauty. Her eyes were slanted and foreign looking, but mesmerizing. They were like pools of the clearest spring water, full of youth, energy and power. And yet she had a sign of age and wisdom about her, like she had seen and felt things way beyond her years. Suddenly, she looked up at the spot where I stood rooted under cover just yards away, like she knew that I was there. Knew that I was watching her. She stared in my direction for a few short moments before a sad smile crossed her face.

A crack of thunder woke me, and I sat bolt upright on the floor of my home. I closed my eyes and for a third time quickly tried to recapture the final images of my dream, trying to see to woman's pale, glowing face again, but just as before the details were quickly fading from my memory. I looked over at Terrick, still asleep on the floor beside me, another perfectly good pillow ruined by a fatal attack of snore-drool.

Can't he sleep on his back just once? I thought to myself before standing and walking to the window to watch the storm that had returned during the middle of the night. Knowing that the chances of me falling back asleep were about as likely as Lisa telling me how she learned how to read, I continued to watch as the rain lashed against my window and thunder shook the tree like a stampede of angry beasts. I smiled silently to myself; the soldiers in the forest could hardly be having a good night. They would be cold, damp and tired the following morning.

I watched the storm until the early hours of the morning when it had finally started to subside. The sun had begun to climb over the tips of the trees by the time Terrick was finally roused from his slumber. Together we sat in silence contemplating all that had happened the previous day, and all that needed to be accomplished in the coming days. After fixing a small breakfast out of meat I'd accumulated over the past week while hunting during breaks in the storm, we went upstairs to wake Lisa, and then set out to the stables to find Terrick a horse that would be fast, and strong enough to journey to Eastern Jericho and back in a few days.

"I still don't understand why we have to leave." Complained Lisa as we passed into the stables and started examining horses.

"I told you already, pa wants to expand who he sells our crop to this year." Terrick began, careful not to give any hint as to the real reason we were leaving. "Aaron and I are to go to Eastern Jericho and Alleron to look for potential buyers. He wants you to come so you start to learn some of the trade routes in the area. There may be a time when you're old enough, and me and Aaron are away, that he'll have you make this trip for him."

This must have been a satisfactory answer for Lisa because she stopped pressing the subject and turned her attention to a pretty light brown mare in the stall next to where she was standing. She whispered to it and fed it a carrot. "I like this one," she said, her childish grin lighting up, "Can we take it?"

"No Lisa," her brother sighed, "that horse is too young, she won't be fast enough."

"Why does it have to be fast?" she asked curiously.

"Father wants us to be able to report back within a few days. Besides that horse is too small to carry both of us. We'll take one of the larger stallions."

After a few more minutes we settled on a stallion named Windfoot. He was an older horse but he was strong, and Urbank, the stableman, swore by his speed and intelligence. Terrick accepted Urbank's recommendation with a little trepidation due to the fact that the great white horse had gone partially blind in his left eye.

"He can hear things a mile away though, he can." Urbank reassured him, "You'd be hard pressed to sneak up on a horse as smart as Windfoot you would. And that name was given to 'im for his speed and agility ya know."

So Terrick took Windfoot's reins and walked along side me and Elma, as Lisa rode upon the tall stallion. We were about to leave the stables when Sienna stepped around the corner and cut us off.

"Hey guys." She said with her typical smile, but it faltered at the end like she was nervous about something.

"Hey Shorty." I smiled back cheerfully as Terrick managed one of his patented grunts. I waited for a moment for her to say something else, but when she remained silent I continued on instead, "Well hey, we'd love to stay and chat but we're kinda in a hurry. Jarron needs to see us in the fields."

"I know," she said back, "I heard you three would be leaving for a bit." Once again she attempted a smile, but the same uneasy look worked its way back onto her pretty features..

"Where'd you hear that?" No one else was supposed to know about our departure, but Sienna once again stayed quiet. When the silence began to stretch on I added, "What's wrong?" In my mind I told myself that she must simply still be nervous about the information that had been divulged at the previous night's meeting. It had to have been a lot for her to take in.

"I just…" She tried to glance at Terrick for a second but he was busy examining the ground at his feet like he was afraid it might open up and swallow him at any moment. When she finally realized that Terrick wasn't about to make eye contact she looked back at me and continued, "I just wanted to say good luck."

"Uh thanks." I responded uncomfortably, not really knowing how to act. A lack of confidence was so not Sienna.

Finally she glanced back at Terrick once more before adding, "And take care of yourselves." Then she did something I never thought I would see, taking a step forward, she rocked up on her toes and kissed Terrick on the cheek. My jaw dropped in disbelief, but she didn't pause long enough before leaving to see Terrick's shocked expression.

"Eeewwww!" Lisa giggled, as I burst out laughing. The look on my cousin's face was beyond priceless. He raised his left hand to the spot where her lips had just brushed, his eyes as wide as an owl's, and for a moment I was a bit afraid he may hyperventilate and pass out.

"I... but..." he looked back into the trees where Sienna had disappeared. Unable to put his emotions into words he simply gave the weirdest looking smile I have ever seen.

I could tell he was ecstatic, but we had a mission to do and time was slipping away, so I had to bring him back to reality. "Alright lover boy, we need to get a move on." I said, slowly prodding him back into moving. It took a while with Terrick off in a perpetual daydream, but the three of us finally made our way back to Jarron.

The entire time we walked however, it was easy to see that there was something odd happening in the village. Everywhere we looked the signs of fear and despair could be seen. Doors and windows were shut. No children ran around in the yards. The faces of all we passed were sullen and deep in thought. If I hadn't known this was where I had grown up I would have found it hard to believe that this was the same joyful place I'd awoken every other day of my life. The forest itself seemed somewhat diminished, as if it knew what lay ahead for the village. It lacked its usual bustle of activity, leaving the path to the other end of the village appearing altogether too quiet and borderline depressing. On our way we passed Bray, but he brushed by as if he hadn't noticed us at all. He kept his head down and was muttering to himself.

When we had finally made it to Jarron's it was nearing mid-morning, and the air was thick with the scent of wet grass from the previous night's storm. I always thought storms gave the landscape a good clean look, and I enjoyed walking beneath the trees high ceiling, letting it spray me with droplets of water whenever the wind blew. We saw Jarron sitting at the base of a tree smoking an old, twisted pipe of his, which was set in the shape of a battle ship with deep red embers smoldering in its prow. As we approached he looked up with worried eyes and then tapped his pipe out on the base of the tree before storing it away in his front pocket. Gingerly, he got to his feet with his backside soaked by the water that still saturated the morning ground and had not yet been dried up by the young sun in the sky.

"I see you've found a horse." He said looking at Terrick. "I hope he's up to the journey that lies ahead of you."

Jarron waited for his son to say something but Terrick was still busy reliving the last few moments by the stable so I spoke for him, "Urbank swore by his strength and quickness, and I don't think that he would mislead us. Especially knowing what we're off to do. I trust him."

"And that you should." Jarron said, turning to me while still eyeing his son suspiciously. "Urbank is a smart man. Terrick, do you have enough supplies to last both you and Lisa?" When his son again was unreachable he shouted, "Terrick!"

This was finally able to snap Terrick out of his trance but did nothing to dispel the goofy smile on his face. "Huh?" he grunted.

"Terrick got a kissssss." Lisa taunted from on Windfoot's back, finally clarifying Terrick's mental absence for his father.

"Shut up you little runt." He growled back at her, but Jarron had already moved on, surprising me by passing on the opportunity to raze his son.

"And you Aaron?"

"I have everything I need." I responded.

"Good. Then you need not delay any longer. Ride strong and fast and make sure you come back with good news." Jarron gave us all a weak smile, "Travel well, and stay safe and in the trees."

With that Terrick jumped up onto Windfoot, settling in front of his sister, as I leapt upon Elma. "We'll return soon." said Terrick with another dreamy smile and' wheeling his horse around, took off down the village path with me in hot pursuit. We traveled at a slow pace at first, using cloth to cover the horse's hooves and thus muffle the sound of our presence until we were well past the soldier's camp. Once we felt we were a safe distance away, we untied the cloth and quickened the pace, not speaking, and slowing down for nothing; winding our way through the trees and along the path south from the village. We cut through the trees for hours as the leagues disintegrated under our horse's hooves, only stopping once for food and something to moisten our dry throats. We moved at such a furious pace that the trees began to blend together, forming a solid sheet of brown and green at our sides. The sound of the horse's hooves on the dirt roared like thunder in the afternoon sun.

I looked over at Terrick and suddenly saw a strange smile cross over his face. A second later Terrick pulled on Windfoot's reins in a way to cut me off.

"What are you playing at Terrick? Cut that out!" I shouted.

Another moment passed and again Terrick cut across Elma's path again. Terrick looked back with a playful smile and a gleam in his eyes. At first I was perturbed by his behavior but then a realization settled over me. Still riding the high from his kiss he thought he could race me.

I knew that this wasn't the time or place for such antics, but I couldn't help myself from grinning, "Come off it Terrick, not right now."

"What, are you afraid that me and this old horse will outstrip you?"

"Ha!" I laughed, my fierce competitiveness beginning to worm its way into my consciousness. "You know you're no match for Elma and me, but if you wish to subject yourself to humiliation, I'll have to teach you this lesson one more time."

With that I dug my heels into Elma's side and took off like a bolt, shooting past Terrick, whose face had changed from a playful smile to a look of fierce determination. Terrick took a sharp right into a group of trees, bypassing the longer turn in the path which I had to take, and came out in front of me by more than a dozen yards. Lisa looked back and gave a laugh at me, clearly enjoying the ride. I knew Elma was much faster than Windfoot, especially being that

Windfoot was carrying the weight of a second passenger, so I had half expected Terrick to resort to cheating. I dug my heels into Elma's sides again coxing an extra burst of speed. She'd made up the ground between us in a heartbeat, but with Lisa telling Terrick where I was, I found it impossible to make a pass. Every move I made was quickly cut off by Terrick and I was forced to pull on Elma's reins, slow down, regroup, and attempt to make another pass. Another turn was coming up and this time, anticipating Terrick's next move, I was ready when he cut into the forest to take another short cut and turned in directly behind him. Together we weaved in and out of the trees like fish through water, cutting one direction and then another in order to find the path of least resistance through the forest and its underbrush. Elma leapt over a downed tree and I looked over to see that we were pulling ahead of Terrick and Lisa again. A smile spread over my faced and I urged my girl for another burst of energy. We flew out of the trees and back onto the path, this time with me in the lead. Now without Terrick to cut me off I began to easily pull away from an exhausted Windfoot.

I laughed and raised my hands in victory, when a falcon screeched overhead. The noise startled me so badly I almost fell off of Elma. I looked to my left in time to see several men in black cloaks hidden in the trees.

Windfoot's almost blind in his left eye. I thought in a panic. *He'll never see them coming.*

"Terrick! Look out left!" I shouted, but it was too late. A large man had jumped out from behind his cover in the trees and crashed into Windfoot who staggered wildly at the jolt, throwing Lisa from her seat on his back. Terrick who was the far superior rider had managed to just barely stay in his saddle after the blow. Lisa screamed as she hit the ground hard and tumbled along the path like a rag doll, falling unconscious immediately; as did the large warrior who had collided with Windfoot, and had clearly underestimated the force of contact a sprinting horse would deliver. Meanwhile two more warriors had jumped out of the forest and into my path. Elma however, with her two good eyes was able to see them coming and at the last moment dodged to the right, allowing her attackers to tumble harmlessly across the path.

I pulled on Elma's reins and turned her around on a dime, facing our assailants, bow already drawn and an arrow nocked. Terrick had his sword drawn but had abandoned Windfoot in order to sprint to his injured sister. As he was distracted another warrior dashed out of the woods, sword drawn, racing at Terrick who, with his concentration solely on Lisa, could not possibly see him coming. I had a split second to transfer my aim from the two men who had regrouped after their failed attempt at ramming Elma, to the most recent attacker from the forest. My aim proved true and found its target, piercing the warrior through the chest where I knew his heart to be, and knocking him to the ground a second before his sword would have found Terrick.

I soon found however that my move to save Terrick had sacrificed myself, and before I could nock another arrow I was forced to fall backwards off of Elma to avoid a swipe from one of the warrior's swords. I landed hard on my back as arrows scattered from my quiver. Quickly, I rolled to my right to avoid another blow from the second warrior. Unable to draw my sword fast enough I grabbed the first thing I came to: one of the arrows that had scattered when I fell. As I rolled past, I clutched it firmly in my hand and managed to thrust it into the foot of the first warrior, who dropped his sword, howling in pain, and fell to the ground grabbing his foot. Still on the ground, I had to somersaulted backwards to avoid yet another blow from the second warrior and upon rising to my feet, I was finally able to draw my hand and a half sword. As I eyed my opponent I could feel fear seeping into my veins like a deadly toxin, threating to freeze my wits. I trusted myself handling a blade, but was still nothing more than a hunter, and the bow was definitely my weapon of choice.

As I circled the warrior, two more men raced out of the woods, and Terrick, who realized that there was nothing he could do for his sister, turned to face them. They clearly didn't know that when Terrick is angry people get hurt, or in this case, get dead. He parried a swipe from one of the warriors and attacked with a ferocity that would have been hard for a king to defend against. All the rage he had in him for the soldiers who injured his sister coming out in every blow of his ringing sword. The first warrior fell almost immediately to his blade while the second backed off, seeming almost frightened to confront him. Once they reengaged however, the soldier seemed to gain back some of his confidence, as his blows became more focused than Terrick's erratic, yet powerful hits. I realized that up to this point both Terrick and I had gotten fairly lucky in that we were still alive, for now that we were both locked in battle, it was apparent that while we were considered fine swordsmen by the village's standards, we were no match for the warriors. After a few minutes both Terrick and I had sustained numerous small injuries and I began to wonder just how long we would be able to keep fighting before we would both be overwhelmed.

Just as I was beginning to tire and the warrior started to gain the upper-hand, Elma came bolting back out of the forest and, with a crash, ran straight into my assailant, knocking him to the ground, once again fully justifying the massive horse-crush I have on her. I didn't let my shock at her maneuver distract me for long however, and I used my new found advantage to quickly end the battle. Turning from the downed warrior I began an assault on the soldier whose foot I had wounded earlier. Up to this point he had pretty much been sitting at the edge of the forest sulking about the fact that he had an arrow in his foot rather than helping his buddies out. The soldier fought bravely, but with his injury his speed was diminished, and it was only a few minutes before he fell to my blade as well.

A scream of pain pulled me from my last victim and cause me to look in desperation over to where I knew Terrick had engaged the last soldier. He had a long cut down his right arm that was bleeding profusely. Losing energy quickly from his wound, he was barely able to knock away the soldier's advances, but as the warrior raised his sword to issue a final blow, an arrow cut through the air and struck him in the neck. The warrior staggered backwards, a look of shock on his face, and slowly crumpled to the ground.

I picked another arrow up off the bloodied ground and nocked it; not taking any chances that there might be more warriors in the trees. Slowly, and completely aware of my surroundings, I made my way over to Terrick, his right arm cradled in his left, sword embedded in the ground at his feet. I examined the wound and was relieve to see that it wasn't nearly as bad as it had first appeared.

While it looked grotesque, it was not overly deep and seem like it would be relatively easy to clean and bandage.

"Terrick, we need to move, I don't want to be anywhere near here if more soldiers come." I looked wearily at my cousin, feeling bad about having to ask him to move, "How long do you think you can ride before you'll have to stop for the night?"

"I'll survive," was his deadpanned response, the victory of Sienna's kiss all but forgotten.

"We should bound the unconscious soldier and drag him with us. We could use the information."

With that, we slowly move into the trees for cover while I first cleaned and bandaged Terrick's arm with some herbs I was able to locate in the forest, before binding the unconscious Eremoo soldier and securing him onto the back of Elma. I settled Lisa onto Windfoot in a similar manner behind Terrick before seating myself upon my horse. It took some work to coax Windfoot back onto the path. The horse was badly shaken from the attack, and I was slightly worried that he would bolt, even with Terrick and Lisa on his back. However, this proved not to be a problem, and before long we were back on our way. We moved at a much slower pace, only covering a few leagues before night began to fall, forcing us to set up camp.

We moved off of the path and slid silently into the forest until we found a small clearing in the trees. By now we'd traveled well outside of the realm of Northern Jericho, and the forests here were much different, and foreign. The trees were smaller and skeletal looking. Their leaves had begun to fall and already the forest floor was covered in a thick layer of them, still damp from the previous night's rain. After spending so much time in the captivating forests of Northern Jericho, this forest had an unhealthy and malnourished look to it. The bright crescent moon in the cloudless velvet sky threw eerie shadows on the ground, making it look like all the trees were reaching out for us; the unwelcome strangers who now sought shelter in their twisted arms.

After our camp had been set up, I fixed dinner over the small, pathetic fire that I'd been able to produce with the wet timber I'd gathered, while Terrick sat nursing his wound and cradling Lisa's head in his arms.

"How do you think they knew where we were?" Terrick finally asked, breaking the long silence that had plagued us since the battle. "That path isn't the main road to the near villages, and we're leagues away from the rider's camp. How could they have set up an ambush that far down the path without having any warning of what we were doing?"

The question unsettled me something awful. I'd been mulling over the same thing since the battle. It didn't make sense to me. In order for them to set up the attack they either had to know exactly what we were doing, which no one but Jarron and Urbank knew, and they would have needed to know in advance because they would have had to leave nearly half a day before us in order to make it to that point on foot. The other explanation was that the warriors were scouts from other villages that had already gone under siege, and that didn't seem likely because the attack seemed to have been planned, although poorly executed. Also, scouts just didn't move in those kinds of numbers. I chewed on a piece of meat as I thought about Terrick's question.

"I don't know, the attack had to have been planned and organized, and I don't like to think about what that means. Somehow they must have found out what we were doing."

"That's impossible. The only person who knew what we were doing was pa."

"Na, Urbank knew too."

Terrick contemplated the meaning of this for a moment before continuing on, "You don't think he would have sold us out do you. I mean I don't know him very well, but pa seems to think that he's trustworthy enough."

"I don't see how else they could have known."

"But even if Urbank did tell them about us, I don't understand how they could have made it this far on foot that fast. Urbank didn't know what we were doin' 'til early this morning, and we left only a few hours after that. Unless... do you think they had horses?"

"No, the only people at the rider's camp with horses were the six masked rider's and Ronan. Besides, if they had horses they would have used them. Attacking us on foot put them at a disadvantage, and they would have known that." I stared at the ground for a moment. I was sure that they would have used horses if they had been available to them. However, now that I thought about it, it seemed like a tragic mistake not to look in the woods for possible horses. I was in such a hurry to get out of that place, with Terrick wounded and Lisa unconscious that I'd over-looked this possibly important piece of information. "But then again, you are right. There was too little time to move that far on foot without more warning. We'll make sure we question the soldier about it when he wakes up."

Terrick nodded his head, essentially ending our conversation and leading to us finishing the rest of our meal in silence. We decided to take watches throughout the night in order to be better prepared for another attack, so I said goodnight to Terrick and secured our unconscious prisoner to a tree before taking up a station in a location where I could easily see all my surroundings. To my left, Terrick was already drifting into sleep, his arms wrapped around his little sister.

Chapter 7: Terrick Wants to Skewer a Bad Guy

"Aaron! Wake up and get over here!"

The shout roused me from my sleep, and I sat upright, startled. It was still dark out, probably a few hours before dawn.

"Ugh!!" I groaned as I rubbed the sleep out of my eyes and looked around while the blurry scene slowly came into focus. I looked toward where Terrick was standing over the once unconscious soldier, who was clearly beginning to stir. A little further to the left was Lisa sitting against a tree, her eyes wide as she stared at the soldier, her arm in a makeshift sling.

I stood up and walked over to the soldier. He was a large man, bald and freshly shaven, with a flat nose and a scrunched face that made him look like he was squinting even though he had his eyes closed. It almost looked like someone had hit him in the face with the flat side of a shovel. Like all of the other Eremoo warriors, he was darkly tanned and had the Erai-Surka tattooed on his broad shoulders. He was mumbling incoherently in a language that Terrick and I didn't understand; like he was having a bad dream. With every line he spoke Lisa's eyes seemed to grow. I had almost forgotten that she knew nothing of the strange men who were planning to attack the village.

"How long has Lisa been awake?" I asked.

"She woke up right before this guy started rambling. I haven't had time to explain anything to her properly. But she deserves to know everything now." Terrick responded.

I nodded my head in agreement and continued to wait silently for the man to start making sense. For almost an hour the soldier continued to mumble, during which time the sun had begun to creep into the sky. Slowly, the incoherent mumbling died away and the warrior began to open his eyes. He let out a grown of pain and stared at the ground for a couple minutes, clearly not grasping the situation. He tried to move his arms, but when he realized he was bound, a look of comprehension slowly worked its way onto his scrunched face. He lifted his head so that Terrick and I came into his field of vision, and then proceeded to blink his eyes stupidly a couple of times as if he was sure that he wasn't really bound and that this was just a continuation of whatever bad dream he had been having.

"Hi there!" Terrick shouted in a tone of mock welcome before driving his fist into the soldiers jaw. "That was for my sister."

"Terrick!" I yelled, "Knocking him out again won't help us at all."

"It'll sure make me feel better." He mumbled back before addressing the soldier once more, "What is your name?" he asked in a voice of forced calm, to which the warrior just continued to stare stupidly, first at Terrick and then to me in quick succession, his eyes lingering for a moment on my own.

"Hey! Smash-face, over here." Terrick started again, snapping his fingers to regain the man's attention. "I asked you your name. Or does the desert breed such stupidity that you do not know?"

When the warrior again did not respond and Terrick threatened to lose his cool, I stepped in. "Soldier," I questioned, "what is your purpose here?" As I spoke, the warrior changed his blank stare back over to me, but still remained quiet. To this Terrick pulled out his broad sword and stuck the point of it against the soldier's throat.

"Terrick, stop!" I ordered in an exasperated tone, as the warrior began shouting in the same foreign language that the black rider had used back in Jarron's field.

"We need answers." he said back, "If this is the way to get them than so be it."

"Not like this." I responded, and slowly I reached forward and grabbed Terrick's arm, pulling the blade away from the soldier who had gone cross-eyed trying to keep its point in view. Immediately the soldier's foreign muttering stopped, but sweat was starting to slide down his forehead. Terrick glared at me, but did not move his blade back towards his target.

"Soldier," I started again, "I know that you can speak this language, so do not play me like a fool. I saw your leader Ronan..." and at the warriors shocked expression at hearing his leaders name, I continued, "yes soldier, I have seen Ronan, and I saw him giving you soldiers orders in this language, so I know you can speak it. I would suggest you start to give us some cooperation, otherwise you'll be of no use to us, and I'll be forced to allow my cousin here to continue on his impulse to turn you into food for the crows. You should know he has a very bad temper."

The soldier gave me a very calculating look, and then adjusted himself, struggling momentarily against the ropes that held him in place, as if wanted to make sure they really were still there.

"Speak now." I said again.

The soldier chewed his tongue for a moment more before glancing once more at Terrick, his eyes traveling slowly to the sword still held in his hand. Then he looked down at the ground and spoke in a rough heavily accented voice, "My name is Ratkursk Volhuon." He paused.

"And?" I prodded.

"And vut?"

"And how did you know what we were doing? How did you get here so fast, and on such short notice?"

"Ronan knows… Ronan alvays knows?" A small smile came across his lips, "You do not know vut you are up against. He vill crush your village."

"This is useless." whispered Terrick, "He'll never tell us anything we can use."

"Hold on, give me a minute." I retorted, "That doesn't help us. How does he know? How does Ronan know about us?"

The warrior looked down at the ground, "Do you really believe he vould share that with a mere foot soldier like me? I am not important enough for him to speak to. I vos told to come here, to stop you from reaching your destination, and to bring you to him… alive."

"When were you told this?"

"Two night prior. Ve set off immediately."

I pulled back, shocked. Two nights ago Urbank didn't even know of the plan. It didn't add up, and it certainly didn't seem possible that the soldiers could have heard about our plan that quickly. It was the same night Jarron had shared it with us.

"This isn't right." I said, turning to Terrick. I signaled for him to follow me out of earshot of the warrior. Once a good distance away I said, "We should keep moving. I don't think we will be safe until we get to the next villages. That is if the next villages are actually still there."

Terrick had a look on his face that told me he was thinking painfully hard about something, but after a few minutes he finally responded, "Okay, we'll leave."

I was glad to see that Terrick wasn't arguing with me on this point.

"What should we do about him?" He asked, returning Ratkursk's look of disgust, as he stared at the dirty warrior. "Kill him? I don't suppose he'd spare us if the situation was reversed."

"He's unarmed, I won't become an executioner."

"Ha, well I've got no problem with it." Terrick responded with a smile, spinning his sword in his hand. "That dumb ox broke my sister's arm with his stupid stunt. I wouldn't mind taking one of his clean off to return the favor."

"No. We're not having this discussion. I won't kill an unarmed man."

"We could throw a knife to him... then he wouldn't be unarmed."

"Terrick!" I chastised, turning my back on him to walk away

"Well I'm just sayin..." He replied, running after me, "I mean, it's not a bad idea."

All I could do was glare back at him. I couldn't believe he wanted to kill him that badly.

Terrick's face turned to something that looked like pity. I hated him for it. It was like he thought that I was being weak, or ignorant. But to my relief, he simply shrugged and didn't press the subject any further. Only shook his head a bit as he walked back to Windfoot.

"Well we have to do something with him, and I'm not big on the idea of taking him with us." He shouted back over his shoulder.

"I know," I responded, "he can't come with us. We should let him go."

Terrick spun back around looking shocked, and somewhat angry at my response, "We can't just let him go! He'll go bring more of his dirty little friends after us."

"He doesn't know where we are. He just spent half a day unconscious, and he doesn't know which side of the path we set up camp on. He could wonder for days before he found the path again, and that's if he even finds it at all."

"You'd let him die wonderin' around the forest? Getting caught by a swampdragon or a bear? It seems less cruel to just finish him off now. And what if he did happen to find his way back to the other men?"

"I told you, I won't kill an unarmed man. At least this way he has a chance to survive. It depends on his fortitude, and if he has his wits about him. I'll play no part in his death though. And I don't think it much matters if he finds his way back to their camp. They already know what we're doing, and when the men don't report back they'll no we survived their attack. There's nothing more they can do to us here unless they already have men deployed and that's why I want to keep moving."

When Terrick didn't say anything I continued, "If they were able to find out what we were leaving to do only moments after Jarron told us, it means we were either betrayed by someone who overheard us, or they have spies of an unnatural kind. And if that's the case, than there's a chance that they've already become aware of the fact that we've defeated their pawns. More of the soldiers could be on their way as we speak. We have to keep moving."

Terrick chewed on his tongue for a second before responding "Whatever, lets hurry up and leave then." After a brief pause he continued, "I'll go fill Lisa in on what's happening. After the attack... well... she has the right to know now. She's frightened. You can do what you want with him, but get him out of here before I lose my patience."

With that Terrick turned his back on me and walked to his sister, who was still staring wide eyed at the soldier tied to the base of the tree. I slowly made my way towards the bound warrior, who had not moved his gaze from the ground. When I got close, the he looked up again.

"You vill regret your defiance. You're friend vill be killed, and worse vill be in store for you. Ronan vants to deal vith you in person." Ratkursk smiled evilly, "You should know that it is a great honor to be disposed of by Ronan himself. I don't see vy he vould vaste his time vith you. You are nothing."

"Well I am clearly something enough to have beaten you and your rat friends." I laughed back, but when Ratkursk continued to smile I eyed him suspiciously, "Why would he want me, I have done nothing to warrant being hunted."

"You are right. Vut have you done?" was his only response.

Scowling at how maddeningly unhelpful the soldier was being, I prodded some more, "Speak smartly; I will not play your games."

Ratkursk went on, "He said you looked like him. I vouldn't know, but he vould, he vas there at the end."

"Who said I looked like who? What end? What does that mean?"

Still smiling at how irritated he was making me, Ratkursk laughed, "You do not even know. You truly are ignorant young one."

I drew my sword in a flash and swiped it once through the air. The soldier flinched terribly with fear, but remained unharmed; instead the ropes that bound him fell to the ground.

"Stand." I commanded.

The soldier slowly got to his feet, his smile gone, clearly realizing that he might have gone too far with his taunts. A little of the color had gone from his face, and he looked as though he was afraid I would finish him any second now.

"Leave now, before I reconsider my choice to spare you. Next time we meet, I *will* kill you."

The soldier looked at me for a moment as if he couldn't believe his luck, and then slowly broke into a run out of the other side of the clearing, through the dense trees and out of site. I smile for a moment, realizing that he was going the wrong direction.

Chapter 8: A Big City With a Tiny Lord

With the Eramoo soldier out of the way, we turned our attention back to the task at hand, but not before Terrick and I had a heated discussion about how Ronan had found out about our plan. Terrick was quick to pin the blame on Johan, claiming that he was so upset at Jarron after he was embarrassed at the meeting that it would have been easy to see him turning us in to get back at him. He also pointed out that he had walked right by us while we were having our conversation that night. His theory made sense, but I refused to believe that anyone from the village would have sold us out. Maybe I was being naïve, but I hoped that my trust wasn't misplaced.

It took longer than we wanted it to get moving. Lisa, having been fully informed of the danger of our situation by her brother, was reluctant to depart and wanted to go back to her father, but after several minutes of pleading, she was finally coaxed back onto Windfoot and our trio was again ready to head back to the path. With the idea that there may be fresh soldiers on our trail, we took off at a neck-breaking pace; once again racing against the time we knew was running short. We tore through the trees at a furious clip and with a reckless abandon, as the trees reached out with harsh painful arms, whipping and thrashing at us as if to prevent us from reaching our destination. The branches cut at our arms and faces, leaving welts and scrapes, and yet we raced on. Riding as if whips cracked behind us. Never looking back. Never slowing down.

By mid-day we had reached the fork in the road where we would separate. With a wordless smile Terrick gave me a slight nod that said more than any words he could have ever spoken. It was an act that encompassed so many different emotions that I was glad we could both keep to ourselves. The nod spoke of love and pain, of encouragement and warning, and of the importance and intense magnitude of our journey. Without a word, he jerked Windfoot's reins and took the leftmost of the paths, which would lead him and Lisa to Eastern Jericho, while I charged forward onto another path that would lead me to Alleron. Both of us ignoring the third path which lead to Allasmíra, the third of as many provinces that were outside the rule of the bordering country Ardûe`an, east of the Blue Rock Mountains.

Elma and I flew on, now feeling very much alone. With Terrick and Lisa by our side, it had somehow felt like we were still at home. Even with the danger and urgency of our mission upon us, being together had made it all seem less real, like it was really a dream that I'd wake up from at any minute. Now that I was alone it settled on me like a heavy fog. It seemed to suppress me, make me sluggish and slower, causing the odd sensation that my stomach was always in my throat, and nearly making me gag on the very air I breathed.

If I am attacked again, I won't be able to survive on my own. I tried to put the worrisome thought out of my mind, but the idea made me ride harder, only stopping when I felt Elma may suffer from exhaustion.

As dusk began to fall on the third day of my journey, I knew I would soon be within sight Alleron's walls, and by high moon I could see the harsh jagged outline of the city in the ghostly light it reflected back onto the land. The smell of the distant sea hit me in the face like a fist. The salt rode on the cold sea breeze and masked most of the scents that I was use to when in the forest. Pine, grass and fur were replaced by the scents of salt, fish and damp, rotten wood. This was not my home and I couldn't help but get the feeling the sooner I was away from here the better.

I decided to set up camp for the night, knowing that I was within a few hours ride of the city, and also knowing that no entrance to the city would be granted this late at night, as the gates had likely been closed hours ago.

The city of Alleron, which was named after the province, was much larger than anything found in Jericho, most of whose small towns were located on the eastern boarder of the province, closer to the sea. It was a port city that was built around, as well as overtop, a choke-point of the Aríalas River, whose great mouth opened to the sea nearly a quarter of a mile downriver of the city. While the mouth of the river was not quite deep enough to harbor the large shipping vessels, whose enormous masts could be seen floating out at a secondary port closer to the sea itself, it was an important river in the province.

Nearer to the city, a large number of smaller ships and dinghies, which were used to carry people and supplies, as well as exports to and from the larger merchant ships, could be seen docked off of large piers jutting out from the cities eastern border. The entire city was surrounded by a large, stone wall, which contained walkways and tiers where guards and archers could stand and fight if the city were under siege. The wall's cold, gray stone looked unwelcoming and unfriendly. There was a time in Alleron's past where pirate attacks on the city were a near weekly occurrence, and it forced the people there to take many precautions to stay safe.

In its day, Alleron had a fleet of ships that even the great country of Ardûe`an would not wish to do battle against. However, I had heard stories of how the men of Alleron, while excellent warriors at sea, were slow and clumsy in hand to hand combat on land, a notion that worried me, seeing as how they were Jericho's primary source of reinforcements, and would be battling the far superior swordsmen from the desert. Looking at the city from afar, I wondered if there was a single man behind its great walls that would come to my home's aid.

I went to work building a small fire and cooking myself a dinner from some scraps of meat that I hadn't eaten the previous two nights. When I was done I propped myself up with my back against a tree, facing the city. The forest around me made eerie, unfamiliar noises that rendered it difficult to fall asleep. With every breaking twig and every new animal noise I imagined a dozen black-cloaked men rushing out of the trees and into my small camp. Paranoia slowly overtook me and even though it was a cold autumn night, I kicked out my small fire, just to be sure it wouldn't give away my position.

When I finally did manage to fall asleep my dreams were full of unsettling images. Men with masks like hawks, and broad swords, riding a plethora of beasts. I imagined Terrick and Lisa in shackles, and hay fields on fire. I saw a faceless man, the lord of Alleron laughing at my request for aid and sending me to the stocks.

After every new vision, I'd jerk awake with a disturbingly sick feeling in the pit of my stomach.

Morning came after what seemed like days, and I could not have been happier to be on my way again. I took off at once, riding on the wings of Elma. We moved steadily downhill as we drew nearer to the coast. I had been to the sea on a few occasions before in my life, when Jarron would have time off between planting seasons, but that had always been on the Eastern boarder of Jericho, where the small towns were few and far between. I'd never seen anything of Alleron's size before. As I approached the city, a morning fog was only beginning to lift from the outer walls, revealing their true size. They had looked much smaller from a distance, and up close I was able to tell that no less than seventy or eighty of Jarron's fields would have been able to fit in the cities vast interior. Sentinels, their numbers in the dozens, walked to and fro on the high outer wall of the city, bows and quivers slung haphazardly over drooped shoulders. The distance from the night before had also concealed the second wall sitting just inside the broad, outer wall. Tall watch towers with wood stacked for signal fires could be seen every hundred yards or so along the inner wall, and large scorpions that would take at least three people to load, aimed out at different angles. I reached the city simultaneously with the raising of the bulky iron gates, and was stopped almost immediately by two armed guards, spears crossed in front of the entrance, thin sabers hanging from their waists.

"What be yer purpose 'ere laddy?" grunted the short, plump guard to the left.

I could tell by their mannerisms as well as by the way they carried themselves that, unlike the warriors from the desert, these were no swordsmen. "I seek a counsel with the lord of your city. I bring ill tidings from Northern Jericho, and fear that time may be running short for my people. Will you let me pass?"

The two guards exchanged stunned glances under their helms, clearly not expecting to hear this answer to their question. "Um…" the taller guard spoke, "um, I guess, I guess ye can pass." He looked at the other guard, "He can pass right?"

The short guard shrugged stupidly, "I s'pose if 'es towns in danger we'll have to let'em, wont we? Duddint seem right not ta. Let'em through."

I was shocked at how simpleminded the two guards seemed, as well as by the fact that I had been able to gain entrance to the city so easily while being so heavily armed. My faith in how much the city could help my town was quickly dwindling.

"If you ride straight down this 'ere street you'll reach the Lord's Manor. It's the center of the city, all roads lead to it, they do. I wish ye luck young sir, but I'm not sure 'e'll see ya. He's a busy man ya know." The guard explained while pulling back his spear so as to unblock the way into the city.

I nodded and urged Elma forward through the gate. Upon entering the city, it seemed to me that the town, while well protected from the outside, was sloppily built from the inside. The buildings were built without any conceivable pattern and were built so close together that some of them actually touched. Periodically there would be a walkway built over the street with another small gate, where a sentinel or archer stood, but it seemed as though the city had very minimal means of protection if the outer walls were ever breeched. For one, some of the tallest buildings in the city were built on the outskirts, by the walls. I assumed that it was such so that extra archers and catapults could be placed on their roofs if the city came under attack. However, if the walls were to fall, these buildings would be among the first to be captured, and as such, the city would lose its only advantage and source of high ground. Their loss would be impossible to overcome if the city was ever breeched. Due to the closeness of the buildings it would be easy to move from rooftop to rooftop all the way to the Lord's Manor.

Now that I was inside the city walls, I realized how unimpressive it really was, and I wanted nothing more than to put it to my back and ride away. It seemed like a trap rather than a form of shelter, and the further into the city I rode, the more this feeling suffocated me. It took all my effort to put these thoughts out of my mind, but after a few moments my tension began to lift and I started to actually enjoy my slow march through the city.

No one here wants to do me any harm. I thought to myself. *For the first time since I've left Jericho, I can feel safe.*

These thoughts put my mind at ease, and I began to enjoy the scenery of the city a little more. The entire metropolis was made up of the same stale gray colored shale that was found near the sea, but still the citizens had found a way to make their homes colorful in many ways. Potted plants with flowers of the sort I had never seen before, hung from windowsills, and brightly colored flags showing the Alleron Province's hawk and moon waved in the breeze over doorways. Some buildings even had paintings and symbols marked on their facades and I found the effects rather aesthetically pleasing. Men and women walked up and down the streets, some pointing at Elma's beautiful coat and staring as she strutted past, holding her head high as if she knew she was being praised.

A hooded man in a forest green traveling cloak walked beside us for a ways examining Elma a little too closely for my liking. His sharp jaw-line was barely visible and a magnificent ivory bow hung over his shoulder with a quiver full of swan feathered arrows. A pair of golden hilted sai were tucked into his belt at each hip, and I couldn't help but think what an odd choice of weapons they were. I mean who fights with sai? I could tell that this man, like myself, was not native to the city. With my hand gripped tightly around the hilt of my sword, I was about to open my mouth to speak to him when the man suddenly gave a stiff nod and turned sharply down a barely visible side street between two buildings. I felt slightly suspicious, but let the feeling pass from my mind almost immediately. The man, whoever he was, did not feel like an enemy.

The city was large and, while moving slowly, it took an unexpectedly long time to cross though the crowded streets. However, by midday I found myself in front of a magnificent manor that belonged to the Lord of Alleron, whom Jarron had called Bo. It was the largest building in the city and extended high in to the sky with many levels and beautiful stained glass windows that sparkled in the bright sunlight and stood in stark contrast to the black obsidian rock the manor was constructed from. Two sentries stood guard by the front gate of the building while two more stood on a tier at the second level with bows at the ready. As I made my way forward, I could feel four pairs of eyes bore into me like the heat of the midday sun.

Almost immediately I could tell that these soldiers were not cut from the same cloth as the men stationed in front of the city. These were Alleron's elite. They were covered from head to foot in shining silver armor that made them look both terrifying and formidable. They had gleaming helms adorned with a variety of spikes and symbols and each of their belts had a large green emerald, the size of a small child's fist, inlaid at the buckle. The swordsmen in front of the door each carried a long war spear as well as a pair of long curved sabers sheathed in an X across their backs, silver handles that had been inset with gold were visible, protruding from each shoulder.

The two archers on the second tier had long bows almost as tall as they were, made of a shining, polished wood. Their arrows, which came to an end with the feathers of an eagle, were constantly nocked, and blood red bracers covered their forearms. All of them stared at me as I neared the manor, their eyes shadowed by their war helms but I could feel the distrust rolling off them. These were not guards who would be taken unaware. Long silver blond hair fell over the shoulders of the taller of the two archers while the other had long, matted, curly brown hair that matched his dark pointed goatee.

When it became apparent that I was indeed intending to pay a visit to the Manor, the largest of the soldiers stepped forward and spoke in a rough voice, "Be quick and speak your purpose!" He spoke with none of the ignorance the soldiers at the gate had shown.

"I am Aaron, of Northern Jericho, and I bring a plea for aid to your Lord Bo. Will you allow me to seek his counsel?"

The soldier gave a hearty laugh, "If that were all you needed to reveal in order to meet with our Lord he would not have lasted very long. What is this plea?"

"My people are to be attacked. Warriors from the desert have come seeking our lands. I fear that if aid does not come, we will be overrun."

Smiling, as though he had just heard an amusing joke, the soldier responded, "And what exactly did these men from the desert look like?"

I tried to keep a confident face, but the soldier's tone was starting to make me nervous. *What is Alleron won't help us after all? What if I fail?* But I continued on in spite of my doubts, "They are garbed entirely in black, and have the desert serpent tattooed onto their shoulders. They are camped in the forest by our village as they await reinforcements, and they are led by a man named Ronan Hazara.

At the mention of Ronan's name, the soldier's smile vanished and he turned to his fellow guard, "Uthgar, go and tell Lord Detrick that he has a visitor." Turning back to me he continued, "These are ill tidings indeed. I will permit your passage, but not so heavily armed. Your sword and bow must remain here with my men, no weapons are permitted inside the Manor."

I had expected this request and immediately jumped off Elma to begin stripping myself of my weaponry as the soldier named Uthgar returned, accompanied by a servant. I handed him my sword, bow, and quiver of arrows, as well as a small dagger I had carried in my boot ever since Terrick and I had been attacked on the path. I wasn't going to get caught on my back without a weapon again anytime soon. After I had removed all my weapons, Uthgar proceeded to roughly, and thoroughly, check me for any weapons I may have "forgotten" about.

After the search, which lasted several violating minutes, Uthgar turned back to the first guard and spoke in the deepest voice I'd ever heard. "He is clear, Captain."

"Thank you Uthgar." The guard responded. "See to it that his weaponry is placed where it can be retrieved in a timely manner."

"Sir, yes sir." And with that Uthgar turned away, the servant carrying my equipment trailing at a distance behind him.

Turning to look up at the archers on the second level, the guard shouted, "Bowhard! Host!" The two men looked down, "Keep a sharp eye while I am gone."

Both men nodded and the tall blond archer pointed his arrow directly at the path in front of the Manor while the other glanced hurriedly from rooftop to rooftop as though he expected an invisible enemy to appear at any moment.

"Follow me... Aaron is it? Have you a last name?"

"No sir, it is custom of the people of my province to use the name of their father as their second name. My mother is dead, and none know of my father."

"I see. Tis tragic to grow old and not know where you came from." A shadow grew over the guard's face then as he continued, "However, sometimes ignorance is bliss."

I didn't entirely understand where the guard was going with his comment so I merely nodded my head in response and continued walking in silence, examining my surroundings. The Manor was beautifully built, with rich mahogany walls and hard oak floors. Paintings and tapestries hung from the walls depicting scenes of love and hate, and of peace and war. I was amazed as I walked through the halls. On my left I passed a painting of three children dancing in a golden field of wheat, holding hands. Butterflies floated around their heads and distant trees could be seen in the background. There was a blazing sun in the sky, and a shabby red farmhouse near the left frame. A flock of gulls flew in a "V" over the children's heads, searching for some distant sea. The painting was so mesmerizing that it seemed to me as if it was alive, like I was looking out a window of the building. The clouds seemed to drift over the clear sapphire blue sky and the children seemed to sing from deep within the art.

While the children spoke of innocence and freedom, the neighboring tapestry was steeped in blood and pain, the companions of battle. The entire painting seemed to be in a black-red haze except for two soldiers in the forefront of the picture. The darkness of the background, when compared to the paleness of the hardened faces and the smoothly polished state of the armor, made them stand out in greater relief. I averted my eyes from the gruesome image of the soldier in a shining white helm and armor, impaling the other with an emerald studded war spear. It astonished and disturbed me that the two pieces of art could be placed so close together.

On my right, a painting the size of a small house featured a hunter running through the forest with a bow drawn and readied. The painting was broken down into three segments starting from the left where the forest floor beneath the hunter shown brilliantly in the sunlight, placing a spotlight on the humanity at the center of the wilderness. Leaves fell around the hunter and squirrels and rabbits could be seen in the trees and on the forest floor.

As the painting moved to the right, the canvas gradually darkened to twilight where the scene seemed to glow with the light of a sunset. The same hunter sat in the middle of the forest on his knees, his bow lying on the ground in front of him. The hunter's features were distorted and he was bleeding from the left wrist, a look of agony on his face. The animals that had given life to the first painting were absent, driven into their homes by the setting of the sun. Instead a new life was seen; an eerie, unnerving life created by the shadows on the forest floor, caused by the last light of the sun glinting off the fallen leaves.

In the final segment of the painting, the page was dark, as the forest would be in the middle of the night. And owl sat in a branch in one tree, while a nighthawk could be seen in mid-dive aiming at a small mouse that could barely be seen at the bottom of the page. In the center of the segment a large russet brown wolf ran in the moonlight towards the right frame, his body stretched out into a full sprint. It was a beautiful painting albeit a confusing one.

After observing a few more examples of the extreme art in silence, my curiosity turned toward the soldier I had been blindly following and after a few moments of consideration my interest in the soldier became too great for me to remain silent.

"You and the other guards, you are not typical Alleron soldiers are you?"

The guard laughed and looked over at me, his brown eyes baring into my blue ones. "And what would ever give you that impression?"

"I passed guards when I entered the city, as well as while traveling through the streets to the Manor. They are not made of the same material as you and the other men guarding the entrance. Their armor is dull and scratched, they don't speak the same way, and their hearts seem to be made of lesser metal."

"Well in that regard you would be accurate, young sir." The guard responded, still chuckling. "My men and I are members of Dû Vena Ruösa, or the Bear Pack in our language. We are professional soldiers, not hired hands like those that watch our gates. We were trained as warriors from the moment we could stand. There used to be many more of us, but our numbers have dwindled in recent years. A great force we once had. However, Alleron was not as stagnant during past wars as Jericho and Allasmíra. We here have a proud history of triumph in battle. It used to be regarded as the height of honor to die in battle at the hands of a worthy opponent." He sighed and continued on, "How times change."

"The sons and grandsons of the men that gave their lives over the years have returned our order to some of its former splendor, and now their sons and grandsons have continued to uphold their names with honor. You are correct Aaron, we are not like the others you saw at the gate. We are stronger and smarter, and worthy of the name Dû Vena Ruösa."

With that the guard turned to his left and opened a door. "In here you will find the audience you seek." he said, and then led me through the opening.

The Lord's Quarters were just as magnificent as the rest of the building. The same bizarre art could be seen all over the circular room's walls, except for where three windows and another door prevented them from being hung. Gold inlay was worked into all of the wood in the room, from the window panes and picture frames, to the furniture. There was even gold throughout the maroon and black patterned rug in the center of the floor, the colored thread seemingly setting the rug ablaze. In the center of the room, hanging from the ceiling, was the most magnificent crystal chandelier. It made the room glow as if the sun had been captured and only permitted to rise and set in this room. The diamonds sparkled with ferocity and made it look as though the chandelier danced about in the room, casting its segmented light into every corner.

Lord Detrick, the man Jarron knew as Bo, stood behind a beautiful mahogany desk with ornate carvings of wolves and bears throughout its front, his hands flat on either side of a mess of scrolls he was examining. He was extremely short compared to the people of his province, who seemed to all be about Terrick's height. By a guess, I would have assumed that Bo was much closer to five feet in height, rather than six. He had long, salt-and-pepper hair and was skinny as well as being small in stature. I wondered how it was possible a man such as he was able to rule over a province. He was small and weak looking, and when I thought of the farm animals from back in Jericho, I would have thought Bo to be the runt of the litter. Standing behind him was a man garbed in a long black cloak. His hood pull over his head, casting a dark shadow over his face, his hands were placed together as if he were in prayer. He was tall, or at least he looked tall next to the miniature Lord. Upon my entrance, the man leaned forward and whispered into Bo's ear. He looked up slowly from his work and acknowledged my presence with a slight nod of his head.

"Hello Luther." He said to the guard with a small smile. "As always, it is a pleasure to be in your company."

"Thank you, sir. As it always is with you." The soldier responded.

"Uthgar has brought me some distressing news. I hope that you can alleviate my concerns. For if what he speaks is true, it will unsettle my very being."

"I know not what to think my lord, but I will let him speak for himself."

For the first time, Lord Detrick addressed me, "Tell your tale young sir, for it may be of utmost importance. You should know that I do not tolerate subtlety in my home of homes. I believe people should speak their word with all of their heart and being, and should not hold back for the mere dismay of others." He smiled gently.

I paused for a moment, still registering the fact that the lord of Alleron had just spoken to me, but I gathered myself quickly and began, "Lord Detrick, I am Aaron, nephew of Jarron Farrowsson, I believe you know him." Lord Detrick nodded slightly but said nothing, so I continued, "I come to you with a plea for aid from my province. We face an enemy the likes of which we have never seen before and I fear that it may mean the end of my people. We are free men and women, we will not hand over our lands nor be ruled over, and because of these facts, we will not flea, nor will we surrender, no matter what force is pit against us."

Lord Detrick smiled briefly before saying, "Yes, I know Jarron. Once upon a time…" He sighed and smiled again. "I admire your bravery, it speaks volumes towards your character and make up.

I have heard a generalization of your story from Uthgar, and it has peaked my interest. However, I would like to hear your own firsthand account of the happenings in my neighboring province."

I looked at Bo, and when he did not continue I took it as being time to recount my tale. I started from where the desert riders visited Jarron in our field and left nothing out. I spoke of Jarron's meeting in the woods and of mine and Terrick's daring rescue. I told of the town's meeting and of their decision to hold their ground and fight for their homes. I talked about the number of items Jarron had discovered from the meeting he had in the woods, of how the warriors awaited reinforcements, and how they were sure to attack soon. I spoke of the ambush while riding on the road to Alleron, and of my interrogation of the warrior we had captured. I explained to Bo my unease at the speed at which the warriors were able to set their trap and of their skill in battle, as well as the luck it took for Terrick and me to escape. Finally, after recounting the events of the past for nearly an hour, I found that my tale had been told in its entirety.

Lord Detrick stood a little straighter at the conclusion of my story, his hand stroking the short graying goatee sprouting from his chin, his dark eyes considering every aspect of my appearance. "And you say that the men were led by Ronan Hazara?"

"Yes sir, they were indeed."

"Impossible."

"Of this I am most sure, Lord Detrick."

"No, I fear you must be mistaken."

"And why is this?" I continued, unable to keep a little of the frustration out of my voice.

Lord Detrick shifted his gaze from me to the guard standing a short way back, nearer the door. The guard stepped forward and spoke for the first time since entering the room, "It is impossible, because I watched him die."

"Captain VanDrôck here was the one who finally managed to bring about that horror's undoing." Lord Detrick explained with another smile. "He and his men were the ones who hunted Ronan down on the fields of Arduelía, within the borders of the empire fourteen years ago. It was he who made him pay for his atrocities. Therefore, the man you met could not possibly be Ronan Hazara."

My mouth hung open for a second before I was able to quickly conceal my astonishment at this new revelation. "I tell my story how I have witnessed the events through my own eyes and ears. If this man is not who he says he is, that is of no consequence to the dire circumstances of my town's situation. For one reason or another, my village will be attacked, and we will not be able to hold them off on our own. Who leads these desert warriors into battle does not change our predicament."

"Ah, but here I beg to differ my young sir." Lord Detrick responded. "It could make all the difference. This man may not be Ronan, but if he leads the Urröbbí into battle using a name as feared as that, he must be powerful indeed. Luther, what opinion are you of this?"

"My Lord, Ronan was the Urröbbí's greatest leader and warrior. I do not believe they would hand that title out lightly. Could it be possible that he is a sorcerer?"

I shook in shock at these words. *Sorcerer?* My first thought was *Ha! That's a funny joke.* But all I managed to say was "Huh?"

"No Luther, I do not believe that he is a sorcerer. As far as I know there are only three sorcerers still alive in these lands, and they are all under the influence of the empire. That being said, however, it could be possible that a new one has come about during the last fourteen years. We have not kept a good enough eye on the desert. I would not underestimate the skills of anyone the Urröbbí saw fit to give that name."

"What are you talking about?" I finally interjected. "There are no such things as sorcerers. They are myths, children's stories made to scare younglings. No sensible man would believe in magic."

"I'm sorry Aaron, but I'm afraid that I have forgotten Jericho's lack of magicians. It has been too long since I have been outside my boarders. But I am indeed sorry to tell you young Aaron that spell weavers do in fact exist, to varying degrees of course."

"That's not possible." I objected, my mind seemed to be stuck on that one idea and I was finding it hard to control what I was saying, regardless of how childish it sounded.

Bo smiled a gentle, pitying smile that suddenly made me feel very small and naïve before he sighed, glancing back at the hooded man at his side and saying, "Foramére."

The man stepped forward and muttered under his breath. At the cloaked man's words a quill rose up from Bo's desk and hung in the air.

"Rajía!" the man shouted, and the quill shot across the room and impacted the tough wood of the door so hard, it stuck, quivering from the force of the impact.

I let out a small involuntary yelp, and stared, dumbfounded at what I had just seen. It would have been really cool if I wasn't so horrified by it. "Not... possible..." I whispered to myself. "How... how did he do that?"

Bo smiled again, "Foramére here is the best spell caster in Alleron. He uses a crude and obscure, but none-the-less effective, branch of magic. Many practice the art, but few are able to do anything useful with it. However, strong, skilled magicians can be of paramount importance in battle however. That is why Foramére here is assigned to my personal protection. One would be mad to attack a spell weaver, at least directly that is."

"I thought you said there were only three magicians in existence?"

"Oh heavens no boy." Bo said with a chuckle, "As I said before, many people practice this branch of magic. What I said was that there are only three *sorcerers* left in existence."

"I don't understand. What is the difference?"

"Ah, they have their differences, and that's really all you need to know. Needless to say, if Foramére here were ever pit against a sorcerer, he would be torn to shreds. No offence of course my dear Foramére."

"None taken my Lord." the man spoke from under his black hood. He had a grating voice that seemed to match his mysterious persona.

"Anyway, I feel that we have drifted too far from our original topic of conversation. You come seeking aid, do you not?"

My head was spinning, and I felt as if the crystal chandelier in the center of the room was laughing at me. I knew I needed to get control of my wits so after a few deep breaths; I managed to steady my mind and after regaining the use of my vocal cords I responded, "Ye-Yes... Jarron sent me to see if you would be so kind as to supply us with the reinforcements we need to repel the force at our doors. In my entire village we have but a mere forty or so men who are fit and ready to fight. The rest have seen to many winters, or else are too young to hold a sword properly. We expect the riders force to be upwards of three hundred men, and from what I have seen, they are better fighters than us."

"Well..." Bo sighed, "What I cannot do is send all of Alleron's force to Jericho's aid. In fact it would be unreasonable for me to think that even a hundred men could be sent to your aid. It wo..."

"But how will we survive if you do not help us?" I interjected, feeling as though all the air had been knocked out of my lungs.

"I did not say I would not help you." Bo said raising his voice slightly. "And I would appreciate it if I were not interrupted in my own home." My face flushed slightly at being told off, but I held Lord Detrick's gaze. "What I was saying was that it would be unreasonable to send a force of even a hundred men to your aid. It would take far too much time for the troops of a force that size to be contacted, gathered together, and supplied. It would also take far too much time to move a group of soldiers of that size. Alleron is a naval city and as such, does not have a cavalry. Our stables do not have enough horses for a force that size. Therefore my men would have to move on foot, causing the journey back to Jericho to be painstakingly slow, and by the time they reached your town, I fear there may not be anything left of it. Do you understand Aaron?"

"Yes sir, but what *will* you do? If you cannot send even a hundred men, how will your aid help us survive?"

Bo took a deep breath, "Here is what I will do for your town Aaron. I am willing to send close to half of Dû Vena Ruösa to your aid. I will not send them all, because without them my walls are too vulnerable to an attack of their own. The force will consist of around thirty men..."

"Only thirty men!"

"Thirty of my best men!" Bo continued, raising his voice again, to project an aura of power that in no way should have been able to come from a man small enough to fit in my pocket. "And you should be happy to receive that. If you had seen these men fight you would not be so quick to judge them by their numbers. As I said before, any more than that would be unreasonable do to the time constraints. Will you accept my offer?"

"Yes sir." I responded, suppressing a tone of frustration. "I am sure my town will be honored to have your men fight beside us."

"Good. The thirty men will consist of swordsmen, archers and spearmen, in about equal numbers, and they will be led by Captain VanDrôck." Bo nodded to the guard that had let me into the Manor. "He is the finest soldier I have had the pleasure of knowing since his father. I'm sure he will perform this task admirably. Most of the members of Dû Vena Ruösa have horses of their own, they are the only ones who I feel can sufficiently aid your town, and give you a reasonable chance at withstanding these demons from the desert." Turning again to the guard behind me, Bo continued, "Luther, you shall go and alert thirty of your best men that our neighbors are in need of help. You will need provisions and a means for lodging, be sure that everyone you select is well supplied."

"Sir, yes sir." And with that the guard turned and left the room.

"Aaron, even though I have granted you my best men, it will take time for them to prepare for their departure. Men must be found and supplies must be gathered. You will not be able to leave Alleron before tomorrow morning…" upon my looking as though I wanted to argue this point Bo held up a hand for patience, causing me to still my tongue. Sighing, he continued, "I know you wish to argue Aaron but you must be reasonable. The earliest you will be able to leave is tomorrow morning, therefore, I suggest you find a place to sup and then get a good night's rest. It will do you no good to be worn out and underfed; your people will need you to have all of your energy."

"Yes sir." I said, realizing that Bo and Jarron must have spent some time together because they both spoke the same way.

"If I may make a suggestion, I suggest you sup at the Setting Sun. The barman is, rather conveniently and coincidentally, named

Barrman, if you tell him I sent you he will allow you to eat your fill as well as sleep in the upstairs inn free of charge. And may I also recommend the tuna club, it may not sound delicious, but I promise you that it is absolutely ravishing to the palate."

With a smile and a nod, I realized that I had been dismissed from the Lord's chambers. "Thank you sir, you are most generous."

"If you follow Lucious here, he will see to it that your weaponry is returned to you."

Bowing awkwardly towards Lord Detrick, I turned and followed the servant out of the Lord's quarters.

Chapter 9: A Guy with No Eyes Sings a Song

As much as I hated to admit it, Lord Detrick was right, any force that would give Jericho any advantage in regards to numbers would just take too long to organize and even longer to move. I didn't like it, but a small force was all I could have ever hoped to gain from Alleron.

If I'm going to return to Jericho with only thirty men, I might as well return with the best thirty men possible. I thought to myself. *Captain VanDrôck and the other guards in front of the Manor sure looked the part of great warriors. I hope their looks are not deceiving.*

I stood in the dimming light of the sun as it began to drift below the buildings in the west of the city, waiting on my weaponry to be returned by the servant Lucious. Captain VanDrôck and the two archers had been replaced by three new men who looked every bit as formidable, but the guard known as Uthgar stood facing me, his dark eyes boring into mine as if I was something not to be trusted. I did not shift my gaze from the guard however, but kept staring directly back into those accusing eyes as though I was trying to prove a point by not being intimidated.

After a few tense moments the servant Lucious returned and uttered a low cough trying to gain my attention. "Um… good sir. Your arms are ready. Sir?"

I shook myself from my mental battle with the guard and brought my attention back to the servant. "Thank you." I said, as I began to strap my weapons back into their proper places. As Lucious began to walk away I yelled out for him again. "I'm sorry, but could you by chance tell me how I can get to the Setting Sun?"

The Servant turned back and opened his mouth to speak but Uthgar cut him off. "You may leave Lucious," the guard ordered in his unnaturally low voice. "Your services are no longer required here. I am to accompany the boy to the inn."

The servant started for a second and then gave a small bow to Uthgar, and left.

"You're escorting me to the inn?"

"Those were the Captains commands, so yes, I will be... ah... babysitting you for the evening."

The guards comment touched a nerve with me. I didn't like being treated like a child. This guy didn't even know me and he was acting like I wasn't worth his time. "And what exactly do you mean by that?" I questioned with forced calm.

"It means that I have been set the unpleasant task of making sure you don't get lost in our big city. Someone must be there to tie the bib around your neck before you eat. Make sure you do not dribble food all over yourself."

My cheeks stung as I felt the heat rise in them. This guy made Arctone look like he could win a personality contest. I hated it, but I forced myself to ignore the soldier's words. "Well I would hate for your task to last longer than necessary. Let us be on our way."

"No! We are to wait here until a forth guard has come to replace me at this post. Then and only then can I hold your hand to the inn. You are not to leave my sight."

I hid the scowl that threatened to cross my face and climbed up onto Elma. *Who does this guy think he is?* I thought to myself, losing my cool. "Right, well seeing as how I can't recall asking you to accompanying me to the inn, I think I'll be off on my own. After all, I don't really want to attract attention to myself, and I fear having a hapless gorilla like yourself tailing me might not fall under the category of subtle." The other guard at the door quickly disguised his snicker as a rasping series of coughs, as I turned around and sped off down the street leaving Uthgar standing in a cloud of my dust.

Once I was safely out of sight I slowed Elma to a brisk walk knowing that I should not have left without my guide, but still savoring the pleasure of laying verbal abuse upon Uthgar.

He had no right to insult me like that. He doesn't know me, and I have done nothing to offend him.

Looking around at my surroundings, which did not seem familiar in the least, I knew that I'd have to find someone I could ask for directions to the Setting Sun. I had taken a quick left down a small side street in order to get out of Uthgar's field of vision, but now I found myself in what looked like a poorer area of town, and in probably the very situation that Lord Detrick and Captain VanDrôck didn't want me to be. I looked back on the road I'd been traveling down. I could have easily gone back the way I came until I returned to the main road, but that would have taken me right back past the Manor, and while insulting Uthgar was awesome at the time, I had no intensions of being found and scolded by him like a child anytime soon. I mean the guy had to have some serious rage issues to be such a complete jerk to a stranger. So instead I took a right and began to look for an alternative route that would lead back to the main road.

As I rode on, I kept sliding deeper and deeper into the rough part of the city. The people around me hurried in and out of rickety shacks of buildings, wearing tattered clothing and shrouds that covered most of their faces. Unlike the main road, there were no colorful flags or potted plants, and the few paintings that were on the sides of these buildings were darker and had a depressing feel to them. The people here were uglier than the ones I had seen in the main part of town. They had a haggard and abused look to them like they had needed to fight for everything they had. They eyed me suspiciously as I passed and mumbled things under their breath. While trying to maintain my forced look of calm, I placed my left hand firmly over the pommel of my sword as I quickened Elma's pace ever so slightly. As I realized the filth and squalor in which these people lived I became increasingly worried that I might be in danger of being robbed or mugged. While my clothes were travel worn, they were still far nicer than anything these people had. The same could have been said for my sword and bow, let alone Elma. My beautiful mare was easily better looking than any of the people in these parts.

The sun had finally passed out of sight, and the dark blood red lights that lined the tops of the buildings cast ghostly shadows into every corner of the street. With the thought that the odds on me getting shanked and left in a ditch becoming greater by the second, I spurred Elma around another corner desperate to get back to a better part of town. As soon as I did however, something caught my attention. I heard music and shouts from up ahead where a crowd had gathered outside a pavilion of sorts where a friendlier glow of orange light poured out onto the street. I pulled Elma to a halt, wondering whether riding close to the crowd was a smart idea or if I should turn around and circumnavigate them. The light and music made the scene seem harmless enough, but I knew that a large group of poor individuals could carry the kind of people who would wish to do me harm.

After a moment's indecision, I slowly edged Elma forward again, moving her closer to the scene. "No harm has ever come from taking a look." I whispered in her ear while patting her neck, even though I myself wasn't all that confident in my decision. "If we don't like what we see you'll just have to do a little running now won't you?"

She snorted as if questioning my decision and saying that I could run on my own if we were chased.

I pulled her to a halt again at the back of the group. From where I sat in my elevated position, I could see that I had arrived at a poor-man's tavern. In the center of the pavilion there was a large circular bar where four men were handing out large pints and tankards of some kind of drink. Three men sat in ragged clothing on a make-shift stage in the front of the pavilion playing an odd assortment of what I could only assume were some kind of flutes with bags attached to them. A small basket had been placed in front of the musicians where people could drop coins if they felt compelled enough to donate to the artists. The people standing inside the bar, who all looked equally as filthy as the performers, danced and drank and laughed while they listened to the wistful tones being laid around them. I smiled despite myself, and I wondered why I had ever been worried about these people. I was amazed at how these men and women could look as though they had been through hell and yet still laugh and talk as though they were having the time of their lives. Many of them looked as though they had been living off the streets like animals.

As the tune the musicians were playing came to an end the people in the pavilion applauded and cheered like they were the greatest thing in the world. The three men with their instruments stood up and bowed slightly. After the crowd had finished their cheering and had gone back to their drinks, two of the men jumped off of the platform while the third moved forward to collect the donation basket. However, before he could get a hand on it, a short man with matted shoulder length hair and a tangled mess of a beard ran past and snatched it from under his grasp. The musician roared with anger but it was unnecessary. Before the thief had taken four steps a large man by the bar swung his arm and hit him in the face with his tankard so hard that the dirty glass shattered everywhere spilling its contents on the floor, while the thief's feet flew out from under him and he lay sprawled out and unconscious, soaked in mead. The crowd cheered and clapped while the hero of the night smiled and let out a friendly roar while flexing his arms comically, and I couldn't help but cheer and laugh with them. Meanwhile more people had moved forward and while two men slowly gathered the spilt coins and handed them back to the musician, two more dragged the thief from the pavilion by his feet and threw him face down into the muck of a pig sty on the opposite side of the street. As the man landed with a crash and the squeal of pigs the crowd let out another roar of laughter.

The crowd cheered, and I cheered with them, the infectious atmosphere of the bar getting the best of me. I laughed and cheered until something caught my eye. Sitting in the corner of the room was the man in the forest green cloak that had walked beside Elma and me when we had entered the city. His hood was still pulled up over his head and his magnificent ivory bow was visible over his shoulder. His eyes were hidden by the shadow cast by the top of his hood, but he stared in my direction, never moving his head. Never yelling or cheering with the rest of the crowd. His leather gloved hand moved to his mouth and he took a draw from a long white pipe, the end glowing red from the fiery embers in its bowl. He removed the pipe from his mouth and proceeded to blow a set of perfect smoke rings into the air, before leaning back in his chair and placing one of his muddy green-brown boots across his knee, still keeping his penetrating gaze on me.

When the crowd had finally settled back down to a dull roar, an old man took the stage in the musicians place; cloaked in all black with his hood pulled up tightly over his head. I was still slightly perturbed by the stranger in the green, and I thought for a moment that I should leave the bar, but the new man stepping onto the platform brought my attention back to the stage. He was small and thin, and beneath his cloak, his back bent where it had been beaten down by the years it had walked the lands.

The man slowly pulled his hood from his head to reveal short unkempt gray hair and a rough gray beard. His lips were worn and cracked, his nose was long and hooked like the beak of an oversized bird of prey, and his skin was so wrinkled it looked like worn leather stretched thin over a lumpy rock. However, the most astonishing aspect of the man's appearance caused me to cringe. Where the man's eyes should have been, there were only two empty sockets of black, forever gazing out into the abyss without any comprehension. The skin was pulled tight around the sockets and no eyebrows resided over the gaping holes, giving the man the appearance of being nothing more than a skeleton. If he would not have been walking and moving on the stage I would have assumed he had been dead for some time.

The man held his empty stare on the audience for a few minutes, holding them captivated, and for the first time since I had arrived, silent. He studied them in a way that should not have been possible before finally opening his mouth to sing.

Cold be heart and cold be stone.
Cold be the dead all alone.
Stories told of stories lost.
Old, and forgotten, at a cost.

The Gods were young, and rich and wise.
But bored with naught to set their eyes.
And so with both great might, and care.
They brought about this world so bare.
They made the mountains and the sky.
And the desert hot and dry.
They built the oceans and the seas.
And grew the forests with their trees.

They made the humans rough and strong.
And the elves with hearts so long.
They built the Dwarves of stone and bark.
And then the beasts for places dark.
And for millennia they coexisted,
Keeping to their own.
Until the day the dark one came,
Seeking out his throne.

Many people see with eye,
But not with nose and ear.
And blur the past with images,
That I see perfectly clear.
Near a hundred eighty years ago.
He came to rule this lan'.
And united things of dark and drear,
'gainst elf and dwarf and man.

Born a son of man and elf,
He held all their greatest features.
Like strength and grace and a long life,
More cunning than all creatures.
And as the boy became a man,
He learned what others feared.
He was the greatest of all beings,
His path in life was clear.

Not one could best him, he would claim,
As strongest in body and mind.
Why should others get to rule,
When his powers, they could not find.
So he sought out the elf King Romulás,
And fought him for his crown.
But the elf King was too much to best,
And so he was beat down.

"I banish you!" the King yelled out,

For all others to hear.
"To waste your days where there are none to hurt,
And none for you to make fear."
The dark one yelled and gnashed his teeth,
And screamed into the night.
"You'll rue the day, King Romulás,
You sent me from your sight."

And so he wandered day and night,
In the wasted desert land.
Til bones were dry and muscles weak,
And soul bled through the sand.
He cried out with his dying breathe,
"Please help me, I'm alone!"
And the Gods themselves they were deceived,
By the repentance he had shown.

They sent to him the Medallion of Light,
So he could yet live on.
And grow and breathe and regain strength,
When he otherwise should be gone.
The Gods were pleased that they could help,
A lost sheep find his way.
But saw the error of their gift,
When he took away the day.

He laughed at them,
"You foolish Gods, you should have let me die.
Now because of your powerful gift,
Even you aren't as mighty as I!"
The Gods grew angry and fought hard,
To take their one gift back.
But through everything that they tried,
Their gift they could not retrac'

And so the dark one gathered to his side,
All those who had been repressed.

Creatures of the cruelest make,
The dark of heart and depressed.
For three and twenty years it raged,
The war the dark one brought.
Until at last he met the King,
And once again they fought.

But this time the King,
He was no match for the power that he held.
And so darkness overpowered him,
And his foe he finally felled.
But he withheld his final blow,
To taunt and tease and test.
"Now bow to me O King of Kings,
And tell me who is best."

But instead of bowing the king did take,
Advantage of his pause.
And stabbed the dark one in the chest,
Through the Medallion that was his cause.
The dark one screamed and raged and yelled,
His fate he could not believe.
The medallion broke and so did he,
This time there would be no reprieve.

Shattered into pieces six,
The Medallion broke, it's true.
And with the strength that he had left,
The king hid the pieces blue.
He knew that he'd be hunted still,
By evil's followers who were spurned.
So when they killed the King a century later,
The Medallion would not be returned.

For in that metal holds the key,
For bringing back the dark one.
For he is it and it is he,

And that cannot be undone.
And it is here my tale shall pause,
For its end has not been wroughten.
Of stories told of stories lost,
That should never be forgotten.

     As the old man finished his tale he pulled his hood slowly back over his skeletal head and walked back off the stage. I was shocked by the story that had just been told, and I wasn't the only one. It seemed Captain Buzz-Kill had managed to put the entire pavilion into a complete trance. It was as if the men in the bar did not realize the story had come to an end. No one made a sound, or for that matter, even moved. I half expected the eyeless man to walk back on stage and start singing again, maybe this time with an equally depressing dance. Minute after minute crept by and slowly people began to return to themselves. It was as if they had taken a stroll outside of their bodies down a path they could barely remember. The words from the man seemed to echo in my mind like the beat of a drum, and I had to shake my head to bring myself back to normalcy. I looked over to the right of the stage and saw that the man in the green cloak had now stood up; both his hands were placed on the hilts of the sai that hung at his hips.

     "I've dawdled here too long." I said aloud to myself.

     Just as I started to turn Elma around to get the heck out of there, a hand grasped my shoulder with a grip as strong as iron. With one swift move I was pulled straight off Elma's back and thrown hard to the ground with a crunch that felt every bit as painful as it sounded. The unexpected fall immediately knocked the air from my lungs and caused lights to popped in my eyes, blurring my vision as the shadow of a man moved silently over me.

Chapter 10: A Meal for Fools

Still unable to see clearly, I felt the hand close around my arm again. I tried to pull free, but the vice-like grip was about as close to letting me go as the eyeless guy was to seeing what color shoes he was wearing. Slowly I was dragged, struggling, into the sty where the thief still lay unconscious in the corner. Against my will, I was hoisted to my feet and pinned against the rear wall.

"Boy you must be some new breed of stupid!" an unnaturally deep voice yelled at me.

I blinked twice in quick succession, trying to get my eyes to focus, and slowly my surroundings came into view. Standing in front of me with a heavily armored hand on each of my shoulders, pinning me to the wall, was the burly figure of Uthgar. His helm was removed, revealing his face. He was clean shaven and his jet black hair was closely cut to his head, with short sideburns coming to points by his ears. He had a long, jagged scar that stretched from beside one angry, green eye, down his right cheek. The most shocking part of his appearance however, was how young he looked. I couldn't believe that the deep, gritty voice belonged to the man, for he looked to be only a year or so older than Terrick.

"What are you doing wandering around this part of town? You have taken a terrible risk coming here. What kind of simple mind have you to place yourself in situations that you cannot handle?"

"I was handling it fine til you mugged me." I mustered, finally getting the air back in my lungs. "I thought you were supposed to be the good guy."

"And you still have a smart tongue! Perhaps a lesson in manners is what you need."

"Those were decent people in that bar. Just because they seemed below your high standards doesn't make them all criminals. I was as close to danger there as you are to becoming a king."

Uthgar's angry stare turned incredulous before he pulled back his right hand as if to hit me. His steel fingers had closed into a fist when a voice behind him spoke up, "Uthgar! He may need a lesson, but not of the variety that you would teach."

"Captain?" Uthgar spoke with surprise, stiffening a little as he dropped me in a heap back to the floor of the sty, "What brings you here?"

"Oh, I suppose the same thing that brings you to this place. I was searching for our mutual friend. Your inability to keep tabs on him will delay our departure several hours. Instead of being able to gather supplies as we should, we have been forced to put aside preparation in order to relocate our guest."

"Sir, I could not possi –"

"You could have Uthgar. And you should have. Now stand down."

"Sir I…"

"Stand down, Uthgar! You should return home and prepare to leave the city as soon as time permits."

Uthgar looked mutinous, but submitted, "Yes *sir*." He said in a jagged voice, cold as ice, and stalked past the captain and out of sight.

"Now…" the captain turned to me. Like Uthgar, he too had removed his helm. I saw that he had the same close-cropped hair, but unlike Uthgar, he had finely trimmed hair growing down his jawbone, which ended in a neat pointed beard. He had thick black eyebrows and his face, while still looking relatively young, and kind, had the appearance of great wisdom, as though it had seen more battles than a face should ever be unfortunate enough to look upon.

"Now," he continued again, "what are we going to do about you?" His dark eyes had a shrewd, calculating look to them.

Somehow I couldn't find anything to say, but still managed to keep eye contact with the Captain.

"I have yelled at Uthgar because he was disrespectful to you. However, it is not his fault we will be late in leaving tomorrow. You should not have left your guide."

"Sir I…" Captain VanDrôck held up a finger silencing me at once. He had an aura about him that immediately commanded respect and attention.

"Because of this little… excursion of yours… you placed yourself in danger and distracted my men, and while the tavern here is not necessarily a dangerous place full of ill-minded miscreants, in this part of town a man with a fine horse and fair clothes is almost as likely to get robbed or stabbed as he is to pass through unchallenged. Now, what say you?"

I wanted to say something, to express my regret for my actions and gratitude for him stopping Uthgar from pummeling me into pig chow, but all I could manage was a pathetic, "Sorry sir."

The captain looked at me for a minute before speaking again. "Good. Let it not happen again. Now if you will follow me, I will guide you to the inn. Your horse took quite a fright when Uthgar pulled you off her. The men I was with have taken her to the stables for the night in order to try and calm her. She will be brought to you in the morning."

With my head pointed towards the ground like a child who had been caught misbehaving, I muttered a weak, "Thank you sir." and followed the Captain out of the sty and back into the street. Two new musicians had taken the stage and were now playing an odd assortment of drums that really consisted of nothing more than beating different sized trash bins with old, metal cooking spoons. The man in the green cloak was no longer anywhere to be seen. Glancing through the crowd, I could see that the people of the bar were laughing and drinking again. They must not have noticed the scene that had unfolded behind them after the old man's song. Not noticed, or not cared.

"Captain VanDrôck, I'm sorry I ran off, it was not my intention to cause your men distress."

The Captain looked over at me and gave a kind smile, "Humility is a meal for fools Aaron, but it is one that we must all be served. Everyone makes mistakes, but the wise do not make the same ones twice. You must learn from your mistakes, the lessons they teach will serve you well."

"If you don't mind me asking sir, how did you find out about me taking off? Even Uthgar seemed surprised by your appearance."

"Eric, the other guard, who was at the gate with Uthgar, informed me. He seemed to take quite a liking to your insults." The Captain gave me another smile.

I didn't smile back; instead I felt my cheeks flush with embarrassment at the fact that he had found out. "I'm sorry about that as well, I was out of line."

"Do not be sorry, it was well warranted. Do not let people insult you, it gives them power over you. Uthgar... he is still young, and he has much to learn, but he is a fine soldier, and there are very few I would rather have protecting my blind side than he. He has a good heart, but youthful prejudices are hard to break. He grew up rich and has always seen others as somewhat unequal to himself. It is a lesson I fear he may not learn until it has cost him something dear. It is not wise to underestimate people, no matter how their appearance or heritage may portray them."

We walked in silence the rest of the way to the inn. I noticed that while I was with a member of Alleron's elite guard, I didn't hear nearly as much muttering directed my way. It was incredible that a single soldier could command that kind of respect from people. We rounded a corner and a small, faded, wooden sign displaying a sun setting over a mountain range came into view. It had been a long time since I had anything decent to eat, and I hadn't noticed just how hungry I was until the smell of cooked meats and potatoes wafted into my nose. It was an incredible scent that caused me to salivate on a near uncontrollable level, somewhere close to what happens when Terrick looks at Sienna.

Turning towards me at the door to the inn the Captain spoke, "In here you will find food and a warm bed for the night. Barrman has been alerted that you will be staying here as a guest of Lord Detrick. He will give you anything you want. Make sure you eat your fill and rest easy, for tomorrow we ride hard and long. These are the last comforts you will be afforded for some time, take advantage of them."

"Thank you Captain. But I am use to the riding, and I am prepared for all that may stand in my way in the days to come. I accept you city's hospitality with many thanks, but I am ready to take whatever pace your men can handle to get back to my home." I wanted the Captain to know that I was tougher than Uthgar thought.

He nodded, "That is good to hear. I would have expected nothing less of you, from what I have seen thus far of your character."

The Captain's praise was enough to draw a smile to my face for the first time, "Thank you sir. I will see you in the morning."

"Yes, yes you will. And let us begin the cleansing of Jericho from the clutches of these desert rats. Sleep well, young Aaron."

"Sleep well, Captain."

"Ah, but a good Captain can never afford to sleep too well, young sir," and with that, he turned and strode off into the night, leaving me to enjoy one heck of a tuna club.

Chapter 11: The Honor of War

"Move now, and let us ride to our destinies!" the Captain shouted. As one, the thirty soldiers on horseback and a farmer from Jericho set out, leaving the gates of Alleron behind them. I could feel the tension around me, the mood of the men was uneasy and as I looked over the trees to the northeast and saw storm clouds in the distance. The line of dark gray was startling against the clear, bright blue morning sky that stood overhead. The sun was bright and beautiful, beating down on us, and while it was still early, it was startlingly hot for this late in the season. At the last minute, Captain VanDrôck had forced his men to pack an extra waterskin so that they would not dehydrate in the high temperatures.

The men urged their horses up the gentle slope that lead out of the river valley and into the forest. Behind us a soldier stood on the walkway above the gate playing a trumpet. The sound resonated off every tree in the forest as the sky itself seemed to be filled by the melody. As we rode further away from the city, the tune faded until it finally ceased to exist. As the sound of the trumpet died, the music of the birds took its place. The sounds of the forest were in full force on this beautiful day. The melody the wind made with the leaves of the trees seemed to defy the storm all of us knew was on the way.

I was back where I loved to be, in the forest, where the crisp, clean air and the abundance of sounds made me feel alive. It thrilled me to be back outside of the cramped confines of the city and into the place where I was most in my element. A squirrel ran off the path as the lead horseman rode by and scampered up a tree, coming to rest on a branch that drifted out over the road. I smiled up at it and closed my eyes letting my mind relax and empty. Suddenly I was hit with a strong sense of self, but not of myself. It was something different. I felt wild, but oddly afraid and worried. Winter was approaching… I hadn't gathered enough nuts yet…

I shook my head. I was back within myself. I looked back over my shoulder and stared at the squirrel in the branch, who stared right back at me.

What just happened to me? I thought, trying to convince myself that I had slipped into a momentary daydream. I let the feeling of uneasiness pass away from me and looked over at the warrior riding at my side. It was the archer with the long, silver-blond hair who I had seen when I'd first approached the Manor. His name was Bowman, or was it Everhard? His hair flew behind him in the wind like notes of music flowing from a flute. The crown of his silver helm gleamed in the sunlight, while the absence of a bottom revealed a stiff, but shockingly beautiful jaw line, and light honey-colored skin. He caught my eye and gave a swift of his head before turning his attention back to the road.

The small army of men cut through the forest like fish swimming upstream, leaving a cloud of brown dust and a beaten down trail behind us. We rode hard and never stopped to rest. When the horses threatened to give in to exhaustion, we slowed our pace, but never stopped. When we grew hungry, we ate cold pieces of meat and fruit from our packs while still in the saddle. I had never been on a horse for such a long period of time in my life. Already my legs were cramping and the insides of my thighs were chaffed from the strain it took to hold onto Elma. The constant bouncing motion made my back ache to the point where it was both painful to sit straight or slouched, and my lips were chapped from the heat and the dust the horses in front of me kicked up. It was like riding through a never-ending sandstorm.

By the time the sun was setting over the trees I wanted nothing more than to get off Elma and curl up by a fire to fall asleep, but I was determined not to complain; determined not to show any sign of weakness to the soldiers. Uthgar rode two men behind me, and I wanted to make a point of showing him that I could endure as much as any of his fellow guard. And so I rode on, lips pressed together in silent defiance to the pain in my weary limbs, my mind solely on the mission of getting home in time to save my village.

We rode well into the night and covered a stretch of land that I would have never thought possible if I had not just done it. With almost two thirds of the distance placed behind us, Captain VanDrôck finally slowed the pace until he found a good sized clearing in the trees for the men to make camp for the night. I was pleased to see that we would be able to reach Northern Jericho by mid-afternoon the next day.

"We'll rest here for the night men," the Captain barked. "Get rest while you can, we rise early tomorrow to continue our journey."

The men slowly climbed off of their steeds and began to set up the camp. As I maneuvered off Elma and hit the ground, my legs nearly gave way and I momentarily lost my balance. Having been seated for so long, standing upright and walking was a monumental task for my cramping legs. As I grabbed hold of Elma to steady myself, I heard a scoff behind me and turned, to my dismay, to see Uthgar shaking his head critically. I averted my eyes from the soldier and gritted my teeth. The last thing I wanted to do was appear weak in front of the one soldier who judged me so blindly.

I unpacked some jerky from my saddlebags, walked away to the edge of the clearing and sat down, leaning against a tree. As I chewed on the seasoned meat I stretched my legs out and massaged my raw inner thighs. The insides of my pants were damp from the seepage of small abrasions which had formed from constantly rubbing against Elma's worn down saddle. It felt wonderful to rest and I closed my eyes willing myself to fall asleep when I heard someone call my name. I glanced up to see that Captain VanDrôck stood a little way away from me.

"How are you Captain?"

The Captain smiled, and passed his hand over his short hair which was once again allowed free of its war helm. "Why I am fine thank you. How are you? That was quite a ride we just had. From the way you were massaging your legs I take it that you are not quite used to riding like that."

I hid a grimace as my hand passed a little too hard over one of the wounds under my trousers. "I am fine, Captain, I only wish for some rest."

In my haste to appear tough in front of the captain, the words came out a little harsher than I had intended.

"I see," he said with a knowing look in his eyes. "Well if you are alright then I guess I will allow you to slumber. I apologize for disturbing you," and he turned to walk away.

"Captain," I called after him, realizing that I had sounded far to abrasive. "Thank you for your concern. I did not mean to be so blunt."

The captain turned back around, "Well, you are welcome. And please, call me Luther. I am not so old, nor so arrogant, that you need to address me with such formality."

"But don't most of your men call you Captain? That is how Uthgar addressed you."

Luther laughed, "Only the pups acknowledge me as such. As I said earlier, Uthgar is still young. It is a habit I will try to break him of. Most of my men call me Luther. Captain VanDrôck was my father, and I am not him, my first name will suffice."

The captain began to turn around again when I stopped him once more, "Umm Capt... I mean Luther?"

"Yes Aaron?" he responded with a smile.

"Well I was just curious, I mean, I understand that you and your men are brilliant warriors, but... well it's just... the men from the desert, they will still far outnumber us, and well, I guess what I am trying to say is..."

"You want to know how we can be expected to save your home, as well as your family and friends with so few men."

I looked down at the ground, slightly embarrassed at asking such a question. "Well... yes."

Luther gave another small smile and he too examined the ground. Then he walked over to the tree where I lay resting and sat on the dirt beside me, his back unusually well postured.

"Have you ever seen a wolf attack a bear, Aaron?" Luther said after letting out a deep sigh.

I started, not sure I had heard Luther's question correctly, "Pardon me sir?"

"A wolf Aaron, have you ever seen one attack a bear?"

"Well no." I responded, wondering whether the long ride from Alleron in the hot sun had caused the Captain's brain to melt.

"And why is that Aaron?"

I thought for a moment, wanting to make sure that I wasn't being asked a trick question, and not wanting to look like an idiot. After a moment, I responded, "Well, it's because of their size and strength difference isn't it? A wolf is no match for a bear because of the bear's sheer size. It would get mauled."

"Good reasoning, Aaron. Now how many wolves do you think it would take to bring down a bear?"

I thought again, "I'm not sure. I've never seen it done. I suppose four or so could probably do the trick, but even then if the bear was able to kill one or two of them quick enough, they still wouldn't be able to defeat it."

"Very good again."

"I'm sorry sir, but what does this have to do with us?"

"Ah, but don't you see Aaron? Perhaps not. While there may be many more of the Urröbbí than there are of us, we are smarter, and fiercer, and better fighters. We are like the bear Aaron. Unless they manage to separate us from each other they will crash against our shields like waves on rocks, and once the wave recedes, the rocks will still remain. Four wolves might be able to take down a bear, but could eight kill two? Could fifteen kill three? Only if the bears were simpleminded enough to allow themselves to be separated from each other. To be surrounded, or taken down individually. If all the wolves could attack was the bear's front, I doubt that any number of them could overwhelm it. Do you understand, Aaron? Numbers do not necessarily matter when the smaller force contains superior fighters."

"I understand the analogy sir, but how do you know it will be as you say? What makes you better fighters than them?"

The Captain stroked his beard and thought for a moment, "Because that is how we were made my young friend."

"Not to be rude, but that's maddeningly unhelpful sir."

Luther chuckled before continuing, "The men you saw before the Manor… Uthgar, and Host, and I, as well as others you see here now before you, the men of Dû Vena Ruösa, we were born and bred for war. To be the best at what we do. To be the tools of death. From the time we were old enough to hold swords we were taught to fight, but unlike most people who are taught only enough to defend themselves, we were taught the finer points of our crafts, the many eccentricities of battle tactics and techniques. We do not have occupations. There are no farmers or blacksmiths amongst our numbers, only warriors. We are artists of death and we paint our canvases with the sword and the bow and the spear and the hammer. We train endlessly and without restraint for the one day we may paint our masterpiece with the marrow of our enemy's bones.

"We have been taught how to slice a single blade of grass with one pass of the sword; how to loose an arrow with such accuracy that we could pin a fly to a wall; how to skewer a boar with a spear at fifty yards, and we have been taught how to protect one another. No man will run when his brother is in peril and that dedication makes us dangerous. We have seen the despairs of a battle. Felt the fear before and the glory after. We know the thrill of fighting a worthy opponent, and the electricity born of felling him. Every man amongst you here has looked into Deaths eyes and defied him, and every man amongst you looks forward to doing the same again.

"Can you say the same of your people? Can you look at your blacksmith or your barkeep and feel confident with him by your side in battle? These men have known nothing but war since they were born. They live, they breathe, they survive for it. They feed off it and they grow stronger through it. It is their sun, their moon, and all of their stars, and they will never give up, never surrender, and never be denied. And if we fall, Aaron… well if we fall, we will receive the beautiful death that men of our make deserve. Falling to the hands of an opponent who was willing to stand before us, and die before us.

"And when we leave this Earth we will not go quietly, but we will be remembered. For if a battle is to be our end, then we will force it to be such a glorious end that our enemies will shriek in fear at the very mention of our names. They will know that we may be few in number, but we are many in heart, and any wise man knows that is more than enough to even the score, even if the odds are tenfold against us.

"We have made many mistakes over the years, but now, I feel that our time for redemption is near. I feel it at the very core of my heart and in the depths of my soul. The mention of my old enemy's name only strengthens this resolve. This is the beginning of our chapter; the second beginning of our history. A history that we will write, and none will stand between us and that which we deserve. This is our destiny, to live and die by our armor and the steel that runs through our veins.

"Some say that there is no honor anymore in what we do, they say that we are mercenaries. But they have never had to stand on the fields that run red, never have they had to see their fate thrust upon them. To see, react, and overcome, and know that you put yourself in danger for a cause that is greater than yourself. A cause that is worth fighting for, and a cause that will continue to endure long after all of us are gone. That is why we do what we do, that is the honor of war, and that is how I know we are the bear, young Aaron. And that is how I know we will save your village."

I was speechless. I looked into Luther's dark eyes and wanted to say something, but no words came to my lips. The Captain gave me another calculating smile that told me he knew exactly what I was thinking, and then stood up and walked away, back to the other end of the camp, kneeling down and speaking with other soldiers as he went.

I thought for a long time after Luther had left. I thought about my home and my family, and the battle that I knew would soon be thrust upon us. The world had always seemed so small to me. There were the fields, old Dane's funny stories, Arctone's annoying comments, and the chess board that Terrick always threw against a wall. It had always been in order, always been simple. Now it was in disarray. As sleep slowly began to overtake me, I thought about everything that Luther had said, and I smiled to myself. For the first time since the arrival of the desert men I felt as if there was more than just a small glimmer of hope.

"We are the bears." I said to myself, and fell asleep.

Chapter 12: Damn

Terrick looked out over a small town in Eastern Jericho, from where he sat hidden behind a fallen tree on the hillside he and Lisa had made their camp for the previous two nights. They had arrived at Rehorr village, a small establishment near the coast, only to find it overrun with men in the same black cloaks they had seen on the soldiers threatening their own village.

"Damn." Terrick muttered under his breathe.

"What is it Terrick?" Lisa whispered.

"What are you... get back to the camp Lisa, I told you not to follow me."

If Lisa caught the annoyance in her brother's voice she couldn't have cared less. "No Terrick, I wanna help."

"No Lisa you can't help with this."

"Of course I can help. I managed to sneak up on you." She retorted with every ounce of attitude she could summon.

"That's not the point you little she-devil. I need you to go back to the camp and wait with Windfoot. I don't want you being seen."

"What are you gonna do?"

Terrick sighed, "Something incredibly stupid."

"But what if they catch you? I wanna come."

"Don't be a pest Lisa, for once do as you're told!" Terrick hissed. "I'm in charge here alright. You have to do as I say."

"You never let me do anything!"

"Lisa be quiet, someone'll hear you."

"Don't treat me like a kid!"

"You *are* a kid, now go back to the camp. If I'm not back by sunrise tomorrow I want you to take Windfoot and ride home."

Lisa gave him a look of pure loathing, but for once listened, turning back towards the camp and stomping away through the woods.

"Why couldn't I have been an only child?" Terrick sighed looking up into the sky. "I'm being punished for something, aren't I? That has to be it. The Gods just hate me."

Terrick turned his attention back to the men in the valley below him. Back to the armed men in black cloaks that patrolled through the streets of the small town. It had been the same everywhere. There were three villages clustered along the coast, within a two day trip from Northern Jericho, and at each one he had seen the same thing. Together the villages would have made a formidable opponent, but separated, Terrick could see how they were either directly overpowered by the desert men, or had just surrendered, falling like dominoes. Each time he came upon a new town he hoped to see something different, but at every one there was the same sight. Dark skinned men… black cloaks… serpent tattoos.

Finally, here at Rahorr, the largest of the three towns, Terrick was planning to do what, at least at first glance, seemed to him as being impossible. His plan was to infiltrate the village, and smuggle as many willing men as he could out, with the promise that once they helped fight in Northern Jericho, they would then return here in order to free Rahorr. Yup, that was it… that was the plan, and the madness of it settled in as he recalled there were at least three dozen men patrolling the village, as well as several dozen more who simply disappeared off into the forest every day for some unknown reason. Not to mention that there were countless others hidden in buildings scattered around the village.

Terrick had spent the last two days in intense recon of the village, spying from afar. By now he knew when the warriors would change guard, and that the largest building in the southeast corner of town, as well as two smaller ones on the western edge, were being used to house spare soldiers who were not busy patrolling the town or bullying its citizens. Just that night he witnessed an altercation between one of the citizens and a drunken warrior who thought he could take liberties with a woman, whom Terrick assumed, was the man's wife. The warrior dragged the shackled, unconscious woman out of one house and towards another when the man attacked him. When the guy knocked the warrior to the ground with a pair of quick punches he was slain from behind by another warrior who was nearby. After the altercation Terrick had been forced to watch in horror as the woman was dragged away from her dead husband and into one of the soldier's barracks. The episode made Terrick furious and he vowed to himself that if he had a chance to maim the drunken warrior in any way when he entered the town, he would.

His plan, as weak as it seemed, was to move when the warriors on the south side of the village switched out, as they did every morning after the others disappeared into the forest. Once the guards left, he knew he would have about five minutes to enter the village and get into one of the citizen's homes. From there, he could use the windows inside the homes to further spy on the warriors and see when the coast was clear to move to another house. He had not yet formulated a plan on how exactly he was going to get the villagers out of the town undetected, but he figured that if by some miracle he had not been caught or killed by that point... well, he would just have to wing it.

"That's hands down, the dumbest idea I've ever heard." Lisa stated bluntly when he had told her his plan the previous night.

Terrick didn't really appreciate having his plans criticized by a ten-year-old girl. After all, he didn't exactly have a lot to work with. He had come to recruit men to help him fight for his home, and he point blank refused to let his friends and family down by going back to his village without any reinforcements. However, he had to admit, she was right. It was, hands down, the dumbest idea he had ever come up with, and that was including the time when he was seven and tried to fly off the village barn. Key point, the barn stunt ended in two broken arms and a concussion... this was likely to get him killed. For one, he didn't know the paths the warriors on guard would take. They were sporadic and there was no specific routine that they followed. And two, he wasn't overly confident that he could dispatch even one of the warriors in hand-to-hand combat, if that's what it came to. He felt that he had been lucky to survive his last encounter with the warriors and his arm still stung where he had been cut four days earlier.

"Damn." he muttered to himself again, and then sighed, "Here we go."

The soldiers on the southern edge of the village were starting to turn their backs on the border of the town and head to their quarters for some rest. As they left, Terrick strung his bow and started to make his way out of the forest. The dark storm clouds overhead would work to shadow him in the early morning hours. His hands were sweaty and his senses seemed overly perceptive. As he neared the village his stomach curled with nerves and he had to fight the urge to vomit and run away. Eventually, he was able to master himself and overcome the voice in the back of his mind that was screaming at him to flee. Jarron had always said that a coward was not worthy of the title of being a man of Jericho, and he was not about to let his father down. He would fight with every fiber of his being and when his limbs yelled for rest, his mind would carry them on. To strike one more time, or run one more step than his enemies could. Surrender would never be an option for him.

He approached a house on the outskirts of the village and peered into one of its windows. The small home was empty, but a roaring fire was going in the fireplace. Terrick pulled his gaze from the home; an empty house was no use to him. He started forward again but was forced to freeze as a warrior sauntered around the corner. It was lucky for Terrick that the warrior was just as startled by his appearance as he was of the warrior's, because it gave him just enough time to skewer the guard with an arrow before he could shout. The warrior fell to the ground with a thud at Terrick's feet.

"Damn." He hissed. "What's he still doin' here?"

He began looking around for a place to hide the body when he was struck by a sudden bolt of inspiration, which for Terrick is more like an idea that kills brain cells. Slowly he dragged the soldier into the empty house, and pulled the arrow out of his throat. It made a strange gurgling sound as it came out, like an empty stomach.

"Shut up." Terrick responded looking down at the dead man. Then he poured a small amount of lantern oil onto the tip of the arrow and ignited it in the fire. Threading his bow once more he loosed an arrow into the thatched roof above. Terrick smiled as the arrow struck the roof, but as he turned to leave the house, it fell back to the ground, putting out the flame.

"Damn."

He picked up the arrow, reignited it, and sent it back into the roof one more time, this time waiting for a second before he turned. Slowly, flames started to spread along the thatched roof and Terrick sprinted out of the house, turning back the way he had come, running out of the village, and back into the forest. Once safely out of sight, he sprinted along the outer border of the village, making his way to the opposite end of the town as smoke slowly started billowing from the house he had set ablaze, and the frenzied orders of officers could be heard above the sounds of the forest.

By the time he had stationed himself at the other end of the village the house was a raging inferno, and had spread to the only other house downwind of it. Terrick smiled to himself, his plan was working, and most of the villagers were now standing outside of their homes in order to investigate the commotion the guards were making as they ran to see what had caused the fire. Even the barracks had completely emptied, which was far more than Terrick could have hoped for. Creeping forward, back into the village, he snuck up on a guard that had his back turned and, covering his mouth, plunged an arrow into his spine. The soldier dropped and he continued moving forward. He reached a group of people standing by a house and, getting their attention, quickly explained the plight of his home. He was able to convince two men around his age to grab horses and wait for him in the woods on the southern side of the village.

Slowly Terrick made his way from house to house, twice more sneaking up on guards but having less luck at finding recruits. Not everyone wanted to help, and many had families that they refused to leave alone in the hands of the desert warriors. Some wanted to help but lacked the horses to carry them to the battle. After all his efforts he was only able to find three more men who quickly grabbed horses and fled to where he told them to wait. After finally exhausting his options he turned his attention to the warriors' barracks.

He ran to the western edge of the town, once more coming upon an unsuspecting warrior before reaching the two small buildings. He ran through the door of the first house, bow raised, only to find that it was completely empty. He looked around the room finding all the weapons he could. The better crafted ones he stole while the others he tried his best to destroy, breaking a plethora of arrows and spears and throwing swords into the fireplace to weaken their structure.

He left the first building and ran quickly to the second; not knowing how much more time his distraction would bestow him. He looked around the room spending his time in much the same manner as he had in the first barrack, damaging weapons and pillaging supplies. Finally, he moved to a small closet in the corner of the room and pulled back the door. Terrick gasped as he found a woman, unconscious and shackled to a crossbeam that bridged the length of the closet. It was the same woman he had seen the drunken soldier drag out of sight the previous day. Her beautiful, golden hair fell over her face, and there were bruises all up and down her sleeveless arms.

"My Gods." Terrick said to himself. He started to try and hack away at the cross beam holding her shackles in place when someone shouted behind him.

"Get back to your posts you worthless pieces of filth or Ronan will have your flesh."

"Damn." Terrick hissed again looking over his shoulder. "I will return for you." he promised to the woman brushing her hair back to reveal a pointed ear. A pointed ear that made him jump back from the woman and gasp. "An elf? Not possible…"

"Ah, but it is possible boy."

Terrick jumped again and turned around, quickly drawing his sword. In front of him stood the same drunken soldier he had seen dragging the woman about.

"Now wha-da-ya think yer doin here boy?" The warrior spoke as he glanced around the room at all the broken and damaged weaponry. "Dangerous game you're playin', it is." The warrior smiled and drew his sword, "How'd ya like ter play another."

Rage boiled up in Terrick as he looked at the warrior, his left eye swollen from where he had been hit the other day. He was shorter than Terrick, but thicker, with biceps that bulged from under his sleeveless black cloak. He was sweating profusely which made the matted jet-black hair that fell every which way over his ugly, pig-like face look oily and disgusting. Even standing at a distance across the barrack, Terrick could smell the alcohol on the man's breath.

"I've always like games." Terrick said as he started forward. He pulled his arms back and swung his two-handed broadsword sword with all his might, allowing all of his anger to flow through a blow that the warrior was barely able to react to in time to parry. Moving as fast as he possibly could, Terrick threw every combination of blows he could muster at the warrior, who somehow was able to block every thrust and swipe. He must have been an excellent swordsman, however Terrick could tell that the warrior was tiring, not to mention drunk, and he was finally able to flip the soldier's sword away, before dropping to a knee and cutting loose the man's left leg with another quick slice. The warrior howled in pain and collapsed in a heap on the floor.

"The whiskey on your breath smells expensive. I'll be sure to thank the man you stole it from." Terrick sneered before finally silencing the soldier.

Tearing his eyes away from the disposed warrior, he looked out the nearest window. To his dismay he saw a group of five soldiers returning through the buildings.

"Damn." He cursed again, as he searched his mind for a way to escape. When none came, he took a deep breath and prepared to face the inevitable. "I guess we're officially winging it." He said with a smile as he threaded another arrow.

Running out of the door he loosed a poorly aimed shot at the returning soldiers and missed them entirely, causing them to shout in dismay and chase after him. Terrick weaved in and out of the buildings trying to lose the men that followed him but every time he looked back they seemed to be gaining ground. He wasn't Aaron, and had never really been known for his foot speed, but he knew that if he made it back into the woods he could outmaneuver his assailants. Finally, the last house came into view in the distance. Arrows began sailing past his head and shoulders, so perilously close to him that he could hear the whistling of their tail feathers as they flew by. He only needed to make it around one last corner and he would be able to escape to the safety of the forest.

Glancing back one last time he rounded the final building and ran square into a wooden out house, crashing straight through the door and hitting the opposite wall with a sickening thud. Dazed, he fell backwards out of the hole he had created, head pounding and lights popping in his eyes. Somewhere in the distance he heard people laughing and insulting him in heavily accented voices. Gradually, his eyes focused and he saw a group of six, darkly cloaked men standing over him. The largest one stepped forward and raised his foot to stomp on Terrick's face.

"Damn…" he managed to mutter, before everything went black.

Chapter 13: I Get Knocked Off My Horse... Again

Morning came as if night had never passed, and I couldn't believe that I had been asleep at all, let alone for several hours, when the soldier with the long-silver blond hair roused me.

"It is time to go, my young sir." The man stated while shaking my shoulder.

It was still dark out, so my eyes adjusted quickly as I looked up. The man was back in full armor and his helm was tucked under his arm. I was shocked by his facial features. He had slanted blue eyes and thin, wire-like, silver-blond eyebrows that matched his long, flowing hair. His face was an odd combination of fierce determination and fine grace. It looked wild and foreign, but also strangely angelic. His face was soft and kind but at the same time had a hardened look to it that made it appear as though his facial features were carved out of granite. But the most bizarre part of his appearance was the pointed ears that jutted out beneath his hair. They were long and slender and added to the already feline-like appearance of the man.

"You're an elf!" I gasped, the realization jolting me completely awake.

The elf laughed a shrill laugh that filled the air with the music of a hundred flutes and then exclaimed, "Nothing can be kept secret from your shrewd observations, can it?"

"I'm sorry, it's just, I've never seen one of your kind before, I wasn't even entirely sure that you existed."

The elf chuckled again, "Ah but here I am, and as such I can assure you that I very much do exist indeed." He smiled and his white teeth sparkled even though there was hardly any light to be reflected off of them. "Now come, there will be time for questions later. For now we must ride." A moment later he held out a hand to help me up from the ground.

Still in shock with the knowledge that I was standing in the presence of an elf, I couldn't contain myself from asking the childish and obvious question. "Are there more of you?"

The elf's smile vanished and he shook his head sorrowfully, "No, tragically I am the last of my kind."

My smile faded immediately, "No! That can't be!"

"I must say, you really look smarter than you are." laughed the elf, his features returning to their previous state of blissful happiness. "Of course I am not the only elf left. It is not so simple to pull the wool over the eyes of a sheep!"

My checks flushed at my own stupidity, "So… so there are more of you?"

"Well I can assure you that I am the only one of *me*, however, as for elves, yes. I can promise you that there are entire cities just crawling with us. In fact there are four more elves here in camp with you right now."

"Really?" I looked around the camp as if expecting them to hop out of a tree towards me screaming 'Here we are!' before breaking into song and dance.

"Yes, young Aaron, there are." The elf laughed his same musical laugh.

"What is your name, good elf? And why are you with the forces from Alleron? I saw none of your kind within the city walls."

"Funny thing, I swear I remember saying that there would be time for questions later." The seemingly permanent smile never leaving his lips.

"Oh, right." I remembered. "Sorry sir."

The elf paused a moment before beginning to speak, "My name is Tryson, Tryson Bowhard, and certainly not sir." He winked, "But as for my life history, it will have to wait for later. Right now, we must ride. You will find Elma grazing on the far side of the clearing."

"How do you know my horse's name?"

Tryson looked at me a little odd, as if I had asked a stupid question, before he responded simply, "She told me," and then walked away, leaving me feeling as if I were five years old again, and completely dumbfounded.

I walked to the far side of the field, passing all of the men clad in their gleaming silver or green armor. Some of them looked up at me and nodded while others ignored me entirely. I found Elma exactly where Tryson said I would, and I casually began stroking her long mane.

"Are you well rested my beautiful girl?" I said to her, and she raised her head from the sweet green grass at her feet to give me her answer of yes through one giant blinking brown eye.

"Well good, because we get to look forward to a whole 'nother day filled with the fun and excitement of pounding hooves and clouds of dust."

Elma simply snorted and went back to grazing.

"Don't worry girl, we'll be home soon enough and then you can rest as much as you want. That is as long as we don't have to fight for our lives first." I smiled and patted her on the neck.

I strapped on Elma's saddle and harness and then settled myself upon her back, wincing slightly at the pain that still pulsed through my legs. At my prodding, Elma reluctantly turned away from her grazing and together we trotted back to the center of our small regiment of soldiers. I spotted Captain VanDrôck and gave him a nod, which he returned in kind.

"Prepare to ride out men!" he shouted, and all attention was turned to him.

"We are ready to ride now Luther." Tryson responded, his magnificent white smile showing under his helm. "We are not all so slow to rise in the morning as you old man."

Some of the men, including the Captain, chuckled at his comment. "Ready now you say? Well then let us not tarry here any longer, before Bowhard sees fit to leave without us. Can't say I'd be too upset to be rid of the elf though. I've always said a pretty man makes a miserable soldier." More of the men laughed at this.

"Ah, but how happy will you be to have mine arrows covering your back in battle?"

"True point, Tryson. I guess we will just have to put up with each other a little longer eh?"

"I would have it no other way."

Luther turned his back on the men and looked out toward the path that lay a short way beyond the outer trees of the clearing. A breeze from the approaching storm gusted strongly through the clearing, and a groundhog quickly scurried back into its underground layer.

"We ride!" he shouted, and spurred his stallion forward, guiding the thundering hooves of the thirty-one horses back to the path and onward toward my home.

Elma seemed to have recovered faster during her short break than many of the other horses, and she easily began to outstrip most of them. After a few short minutes I found myself riding close to the front of the pack, just a short way from the Captain and Tryson. The pounding from riding again so soon hit me quickly however, and my sore legs groaned in protest every time Elma's hooves drove into the earth. I could already feel the scabs on my legs cracking open, allowing fresh, warm blood to seep down my thighs. I longed to get off and lay down again, but like the previous day, I was determined not to show the soldiers any sign of weakness. I wanted them to know that a farmer from a small village could endure everything they could.

By midday the storm clouds had moved directly overhead, shadowing us entirely. It was as if the sun had not risen at all, and slowly the soft drum of raindrops on armor could be heard amongst the pounding of hooves. Light filled the sky as thunder cracked, and the trees tossed every which way in the steady gusts of wind. I had to lean forward into the gales, low onto Elma's back, so as to reduce the drag of air against my body and ease her strain as she ran forward harder than ever. Her muscles rippled through her body and made my thighs pulse with agony, but still we moved on. No one spoke and we never thought to slow our pace. The rain pounded on us for several hours and the wind blew like a stampede of demons, trying to prevent us from reaching our destination. We rode until Luther felt it would be detrimental to our horses' health if we continued, and finally we broke for a short period of time, seeking shelter in the trees and trying desperately to dry our soaked limbs while the horses recovered.

As we settled into the trees, the Captain walked once again to where I lay resting my throbbing legs under a tree. "Do you know where we are, young Aaron? I mean, do you recognize the area? Can you tell how far we have left to ride?"

I hadn't been able to pay much attention to my surroundings while trying to keep my head down and my eyes out of the rain, but now that I looked around I noticed that the trees had their old, familiar, larger-than-life size, and colorful leaves. They even smelt like home.

"We are close." I responded, "I've been here many times before, if we ride up over these next hilltops we should be able to see Jericho in the distance."

Luther smiled. "Good. I had hoped for such news. It has been many years since I have been this direction, and I was not entirely sure of the distance anymore. I will send a rider to scout ahead and verify what you have said." He turned to his left and spoke to a man who sat a few feet away from me, "Râven, how is your horse?"

"She is as fine as ever, Luther. She has always been blessed with a fast recovery."

"Good, would you consent to riding a bit further to the tops of these coming hills, and reporting what you see?"

"For you Luther, of course."

The man jumped up from the ground and whistled to a gray mare that was a few yards away. The horse immediately trotted over to the man and whinnied as he stroked her mane and positioned himself on her back. After giving a little kick to her side, they took off together back into the rain.

After he had vanished through the trees, Luther once again turned to me, "How are you feeling? I know you wish to be respected amongst my men, but it is easy to see that you are in discomfort."

I hesitated, on the verge of denying that I was in any sort of pain, but then thought better of it, "Sir, it's only that I have never ridden so long before. My legs aren't use to it. I can handle the pain, it's just bothersome."

"Tryson is most skilled at Elven remedies. I hope that when we return to your village you will allow him to look at your wounds. You won't be able to do your village much good in battle if you cannot stand. He can make you right again in a night's time."

"Thank you Captain, I would like that." I thought it would be best to accept the Captain's offer rather than trying to explain that my village had a bizarre, wound-healing spring. I mean who's going to believe that? It's weird enough that we live in trees.

The Captain smiled, "I see I have another pup to break of bad habits… I told you to call me Luther."

I laughed and was surprised to see I was sore enough that the action caused my ribs to ache. "I am sorry Luther. It seems you will indeed have to break me of that habit."

"Tis no matter. I am sure you will remember soon enough."

I smiled again, and looked up into the dark sky. "It's stopped raining." I stated with a puzzled look on my face. "Why has the sun not rejoined us?"

Luther looked up into the sky as well before responding, "Yes…" as a worried expression started to cross his face.

"Something is wrong. These are not rain clouds…" I said more to myself than to the Captain.

Luther spun around on the spot and looked back towards the direction of Jericho, "There is some evil at play here."

At that moment, the rider Râven came galloping back around the bend and into view, spurring on his mare as if an entire army was pursuing him. I was up in a flash. Something was wrong.

Râven came to a halt directly in front of Luther, "The forest…" he spoke in a harried tone, "it burns."

I took off like a bolt, already whistling for Elma and completely forgetting the fact that the sores on my legs made it feel like my pants were made of splintered wood. Thoughts raced through my mind at a hundred miles an hour. Thoughts of Jarron, Terrick, and Lisa. Thoughts of the harvest, the village tavern, and Sienna. Thoughts of my home, my stable, and my friends. I had ridden all the way to Alleron and after all the pain, and the effort, I was still too late to save my home.

As I ran I was transported back in time in my own thoughts. I was five and Terrick was doing a swan dive off of the village barn. I was six and Jarron was showing me how to plant crops for the summer season. How to use a spade, and how deep to dig the small seed's homes. I remembered wrestling with Terrick after a long day's work and the exhaustion I felt after, as we both lay bruised on the ground. I was seven and Lisa was being born. I remembered how scared I was when my aunt Sarah had fallen ill during labor, and when I wasn't sure that Lisa would survive the night. I could remember Sarah's funeral afterwards and standing in the shadows while Terrick cried, holding his baby sister.

I was fourteen and spending half my savings on Elma as I purchased her from a traveling merchant named La`fíndel, a strange, shrouded man with a white pipe. I remembered getting a far better price than I deserved, the rainbow colored smoke rings the merchant blew as some kind of magic trick, and the feeling I had when I first rode the magnificent mare. It was two week ago and I was harassing Terrick about how stupid he looked around Sienna. I could remember the odd shade of pale green and red he had turned as he mumbled incoherently to her. Now all of that seemed irrelevant.

Elma came running through the crowd of soldiers at top speed, and I knew she could sense my urgency. The men in her way heard the pounding of hooves and let out cries of surprise as she bolted past. Men behind me were yelling my name, but I couldn't care less. I could not hear, could not see, could not breathe, I could only run. There was nothing in the world, just the adrenalin pumping in my veins like acid, the feeling in the pit of my stomach, and the thought that kept gnawing at the back of my mind: the thought that everyone I knew and loved was gone. That I was too late.

Elma ran abreast of me, and without missing a step I had vaulted onto her back. Together we flew like lightning towards our burning homes. The homes that we knew could already be in the hands of our enemies. As I rode, heads turned towards me and muffled shouts could be heard, but nothing could slow me down now, I needed to see it with my own eyes. We turned the bend, leaving the sight of the soldiers, and continuing along the path towards the village. Within a few minutes I had reached the crest of the hill and beheld the horror of the scene below.

The whole of Bray's eastern fields were set ablaze, and as the wind had shifted and begun to blow towards the west, several trees and homes on the eastern side of the village had caught fire as well. Smoke billowed from the field and the trees like giant black snakes slithering into the sky. The smoke from the green living wood was so thick that it completely covered the sky, entirely blotting out the sun, if there indeed was one to be seen through the equally dark storm clouds. Together they merged to form premature night over the tortured landscape that was my home.

Anger welled up inside me at the sight of my own tree, one of the few that were engulfed in flames. All I could think of was the punishment I wished to give to the people who were responsible for this disgusting sight, the punishment I would give to Ronan if he was still down below in the valley. The image of the black rider was permanently scarred onto my consciousness now, and I could see him as clearly as if he were standing right in front of me. His bald head and dark skin. His gold rings and his ruby hilted sword. A twisted smile graced his lips at the destruction I knew he was enjoying. I wanted nothing more than to cross blades with the man right now, and with all of my desire and anger fueling me, I began to edge down the valley towards the village.

Suddenly there was a flash of green to my right and in an instant I had been unseated from Elma, once again feeling my teeth rattle as I landed hard on the ground with a thud. I groaned in pain and looked up at my assailant, only to realize that it was the hooded man in the dark green cloak that I had seen in the city of Alleron. His face was still hidden by his hood, but the bottom of the man's square jaw could be seen protruding from the hood into the dim and almost nonexistent light.

I wanted to get up and fight the guy, or at least yell something really insulting at him, but all I managed to do was lie on my back like an idiot and choke out "Dude?" while desperately trying to regain my breath.

"You must not go to the village!" the man shouted. "There are too many of them! You must not go!"

"Who the heck are you?" I gasped back, trying to move before realizing that the man had me pinned firmly to the ground.

"That does not matter, but he will know that..."

He never got to finish saying what he would know because at that moment Elma, who had clearly had quite enough of her rider being unseated, had come sprinting back to crash violently into the man's side, sending him sprawling across the ground. The man quickly turned his tumble into a summersault and bounced, or almost flew, back to his feet with inhuman grace and speed, turning just fast enough to evade a second charge from Elma. I stumbled clumsily to my feet and drew my sword.

The man, who had somehow managed to stay hooded, looked at me and spoke, "I do not wish to fight you, Aaron."

What I should have said was "Screw you buddy" and then cut off his head, but I was too shocked that the guy knew my name, so instead all I grunted out was "Huh?"

"All you need to know is that you are in danger, this place is not safe."

"How do you know my name and why are you following me?" I shouted, finally managing to string together a sentence.

"You must listen to me. You cannot go back to your home. You are too important. It cannot be risked."

A trickle of worry was beginning to worm its way into my intense feelings of anger for the hooded stranger, and it was causing me lose my cool. "My home burns and you want me to listen to you? I don't even know who you are! Answer my questions!" I shouted.

The man began to speak but was cut short again. Behind him a stick snapped, almost inaudibly, and the man turned his head just in time to see that he was in peril. Once again he moved with inhuman speed, barely getting out of the way as an arrow grazed him, cutting a hole in the hood of his cloak. Behind him appeared four men on horseback, Râven, Uthgar, Luther, and an archer whom I didn't know. The man in the hood raised a leather gloved hand to his hidden face and pulled it away to reveal a small amount of blood on his fingertips. He quickly drew the two golden hilted sai at his sides, spinning them wildly in his hands.

"Fancy." Uthgar taunted. "Odd weapon choice though. I don't think anyone's used sais in near a hundred years."

"I do not wish to fight you." The man yelled back as he was forced to evade Elma once more.

I could see why the man had said this. He had no chance of overcoming four elite soldiers with only a pair of sai.

Uthgar sneered at the man, "As no overmatched man should. You shouldn't be here, and now you'll wish you weren't."

"Uthgar, hold!" Luther shouted, but he was too late.

Uthgar had already drawn the two curved swords splayed in an X across his back and urged his horse forward. As he rode, the unknown bowman nocked and loosed another arrow. The hooded man twirled a sai in his hand and cut the arrow out of the sky, splitting it clean in two. I could see the Captain's eyes widen at the sight of this and he nodded to Râven, who also drew his weapons and began to ride forward into the fray.

Uthgar reached the man in seconds and took a swing with one of his swords that, if it would have connected, would have sent the hooded man's head flying half way to the burning village below, but the powerful blow only managed to cut air. At the last minute, the man had leapt sideways to the opposite side of Uthgar's horse and somersaulted to safety. As he rolled, he stuck both sai into the ground and picked up a long, thick stick that must have fallen from a tree during the storm. He spun the wood in his hands and dodged Râven's charge in a similar manner, except this time, when he had rolled clear of danger, he twirled the stick and jammed it between the racing front legs of Râven's gray mare. The stick cracked under the force of the impact and the horse fell to the ground with her front legs collapsing in a twisted mess, throwing her rider some fifteen feet to land in a crumpled heap, unconscious.

I stood frozen in place as the man once again maneuvered to avoid yet another arrow launched in his direction. Twisting to the ground, he pulled the two sai back from the soil and turned to face Uthgar's second charge. This time instead of leaping to the opposite side of the horse, the man bent backwards, nearly touching his head to the ground, to avoid Uthgar's blade. As he bent, the hooded man twisted a sai and cut loose Uthgar's saddle, causing it to slide slowly off the right side of his steed and sending Uthgar tumbling comically to the ground. The soldier scrambled to his feet quickly and faced his opponent, now only wielding one sword, having lost the other in his fall.

The hooded man was paying him no attention however as the bowman had given up on trying to slay the man at a distance and now attacked him with the broad sword that was once sheathed at his hip. Both he and Luther had dismounted their horses, realizing that the man had somehow managed to turn the disadvantage of being on lower ground against his last two opponents.

I began to step forward with my sword wanting to help out, but Luther ordered from where he stood, "Aaron no! Stay where you are!" and I once again subsided, left to do nothing more than watch the hooded man in awe.

He fought with a defined elegance and for a short time was tangled in battle with both Uthgar and the bowman, yet he was managing to hold his own. He moved with such speed that he was able to easily deflect all of the two soldiers' blows even though they attacked from opposite directions. He ducked under the slower, less maneuverable broad sword and turned to catch Uthgar's blade between his sai, thrusting it to the side. He rolled left, avoiding another swipe with the broadsword, and returned to his feet in time to parry another of Uthgar's blows.

He spun around the bowman and quickly swiped at his backside cutting the soldier where the plates of his armor did not quite meet under his arms. The soldier let out an almost mute gasp and swung the broadsword clumsily around him. The hooded man ducked it easily and cut upward, slicing at the bowman's arm, causing him to lose his grip on his weapon. Twisting back into a standing position he then hit the now unarmed soldier in the side of the head with the hilt of one of his weapons, knocking him unconscious.

As the bowman fell, Uthgar continued his savage attack with a ferocious set of blows, each time finding nothing but air and steel in his path, and each time becoming increasingly frustrated. The hooded man ducked one blow only to coil his body and flip backwards over the next. He fought like he was made out of mist;

Uthgar would swing his sword at a place where the man had once stood, only to have him momentarily disappear and materialize on the other side of his blade. At last, in desperation, Uthgar threw his whole weight into a swing of his sword and lost his balance. The man took his advantage, and with a quick spin, dipped low to the ground and swept Uthgar's feet out from under him with one of his own. The soldier slammed into the ground and the air went out of him.

Before the hooded man could do anything more to Uthgar however, Luther finally stepped into the fray. A single blade drawn in one hand and a small shield in the other, the Captain swung at the man who narrowly avoided the blow, which still managed to claim some cloth from the man's cloak.

Together the two men danced, their blades flashing almost too fast to be seen. Luther stabbed and sliced with his blade while the man dodged with increasing difficulty. Luther's sword flew past the man, who in turn spun and swiped at the unprotected areas of Luther's armor. The Captain reacted quickly and blocked with his shield, only to again swing with his weapon, which the man caught with the prongs of his sai, attempting to twist the weapon from Luther's grasp. As both the man's hands were occupied with Luther's sword, the Captain was able to thrust forward with his shield, knocking his enemy off balance, and freeing his weapon, thus allowing him to launch a fresh assault. However, the man had recovered quickly and dodged the blows, swiping at Luther's hand as it past and cutting it, causing the Captain to curse.

He thrust his shield forward again to create space before feinting at the man's head only to angle the blow down towards his knees. The cloaked man wasn't fooled by the maneuver and back flipped, easily clearing the sword. Luther's next blow was again captured by the prongs of the man's weapons, only this time he was able to get a good enough grip to wrench the sword from the Captain's hand. Unarmed, Luther let one blow glance off his shield and then another. On the third swipe, Luther grabbed the man's arm with his free hand as it passed, and spun, bashing the man's head with his shield and sending him rolling across the floor.

While the man got to his feet, Luther had the opportunity to draw his other sword and regroup. The man, however, did not attack again but sheathed his sai and held his arms away from his body.

"I said I did not wish to fight you." He announced again, sounding as if he wasn't the least bit out of breath. Slowly, he let his hand travel to the small stream of blood that continued to trickle down from under his hood. "Your men attacked first."

Luther opened his mouth to speak, but something caught his eye before he could get a word out, "Uthgar, no!"

The soldier did not hear though. He ran forward and took two quick swings at the man, who had seen his assailant just soon enough to dodge both of them. After the second thrust of Uthgar's sword the man ducked and spun while simultaneously drawing a single sai from his belt. Upon rising once more to Uthgar's level he caught the soldiers arm and twisted it violently, pinning it to the soldier's back while his weapon hand found its way to Uthgar's throat. Above him a falcon screeched in a tree. The man turned his head sharply and looked at it before turning back.

"You are in danger. They know you are here. I hope the next time we meet I am more favorably received."

With that he shoved Uthgar forward onto the ground, and with his free hand pulled something from a pouch in his cloak. Throwing the mystery object to the ground it exploded, causing a cloud of thick black smoke, which upon clearing, showed that the man had disappeared.

Chapter 14: Marcus Carves a Bear

I looked at Luther in shock at what had just happened. However, the old soldier simply gazed unblinkingly at the spot where the man had just vanished. Slowly, he sheathed his one remaining sword and walked to Uthgar, who was kneeling on the ground, one hand covering a small cut in his neck where the hooded man's sai had cut him; a small trickle of blood ran between his fingers. Holding out his hand, Luther helped Uthgar to his feet.

"Next time we fight I hope you use more sense." Luther scolded while Uthgar continued to stare at the ground. "And I hope this is the last time you disregard my orders. Your failure to listen caused us to rush into a fight we were not prepared for, and it caused us to lose order in our attack. If the situation allowed for it I would have you whipped, but for now, the loss of your weaponry will suffice."

Uthgar looked sharply at Luther, as if a good whipping would have been much preferred to the loss of his swords. "Sir?"

"Your weapons Uthgar, I see no reason that you should have them seeing as how you cannot make responsible decisions with them."

"Sir you must be joking. My weapons are all that I am, you cannot take them."

Luther's eyebrows rose, "I cannot? Are you prepared to disobey me again?"

Uthgar's face whitened and his eyes bore into Luther's with a mixture of shock, anger, and hatred, but he eventually conceded, "No, sir."

He continued to look at the Captain, his entire body practically shaking with rage, and then he turned towards his horse and began to walk the stallion back to the soldiers resting place.

Luther watched Uthgar walk out of sight and sighed. It was the sigh of a man who had seen and done too much in too short a time. He ran his hand over the short hair that grew on his scalp, and allowed his gaze to wander for a short while. Slowly he walked to the spot where the hooded man had vanished and picked up one of Uthgar's swords. He bounced it up and down in his hand for a few moments with the look of someone undergoing an intense internal struggle, and then moved on to pick up his own sword, which he sheathed in its place on his back beside its brother.

"Luther... I must go home. I have to know what's happened." I interrupted Luther's silent stream of thought.

"No." Luther said bluntly. "It could be a trap. We must scout the area before we make any moves. It would not be intelligent for us to race into the village and straight into an ambush." Upon seeing the worried look on my face, Luther's expression softened. "Aaron, you must trust me. If there was any way to speed our arrival, I would see to it that it was done."

I said nothing but nodded and turned slightly to continue gazing down into the valley towards my burning home. As I looked on, Luther walked to the crumpled form of Râven, who lay on the ground a short distance from his injured horse, and bent over, examining him.

"That man," I started, turning back towards Luther, "he fought like no one I've ever seen. His speed didn't seem human. How could he fight like that with naught but knives and sticks?"

Luther didn't look up from Râven but responded, "He could fight like that because he wasn't human. He was an elf, and a highly trained one at that. I haven't seen anyone fight that way since the king passed."

"He was an elf? Can all elves fight like that?"

"No. All elves are faster and quicker than humans. They also have stronger senses. They can see, hear, and smell things that most people would never be able to pick up on. However, they have their limitations and weaknesses, and they *definitely* cannot all fight like that. Elves have their natural advantages, but they must be trained in battle the same as men. Many elves would be no more skilled with a blade than the worst swordsman in your village. But if trained correctly, they can be lethal, as you have just seen."

"If all elves are that fast and have such good senses, what weakness could they possibly have?"

"Walk with me Aaron." Luther said after he had hoisted Râven and the unconscious bowmen onto his horse's back and turned in the direction of the rest of the soldiers, leaving Râven's poor, injured mare behind. I grabbed Elma's reins and followed without question.

"Elves have limits to their strength. They are built differently than men. A man and an elf's muscle structures are dissimilar. Elves have more muscle groups than men, and they are more finely formed and gently developed. The extra muscles allow for an elf's incredible speed and flexibility, however, the muscle groups of an elf do not develop as far as those of a man. They have a different purpose. Elves are built gracefully, if their muscles become too large it slows them down and it becomes hazardous to their health. Elves bones are thin and extremely light, once again to aid in their speed. They don't break easily because they are too completely protected by their different muscle groups. However, if an elf's muscles overdevelop, they could begin to pull apart and fracture the bones to which they are connected. Essentially, the elf's muscles would become too strong for its body to stand. Overdevelopment is actually a disease to elves, and a very painful one at that.

"In order to protect themselves, an elf's muscle growth shuts down completely at around the age of eighteen, the elven age of manhood. Once their muscle growth stops, so does their aging process. At eighteen an elf is full grown, and while their physical features may change, it takes many more lifetimes to accomplish that change than it does for a human.

"Now, back to your question about their weaknesses. An elf's strengths are also, in many ways, their weaknesses. They are developed for speed, flexibility and quickness, and because they are built this way, they lack the strength that men can develop. Essentially, a man's strength is limitless until age catches up with him. Clearly, not all men take advantage of this ability, but it is there all the same. If you wished to do so, you could work your muscles in different ways and they would continue to grow and strengthen for many years, until your strength far surpasses that of an elf. For example, you are not near full grown, and yet I would not doubt that you are already stronger than the elf which we just fought. An elf counts on its superior speed to add force to his blows, and to thus twist a man like Uthgar. It is a simple matter of momentum and inertia.

"This strength differential helps men in battle. I am much stronger than the elf I fought, and thus every one of my blows that he blocked took a much greater toll on him than it did me. Eventually, if the elf's speed did not finish me quickly enough, I would have been able to simply overpower him. Elves always look for quick kills, and their speed typically allows for them to accomplish that. However, if they cannot, they must rely on simply deflecting blows rather than absorbing them entirely, as that takes too much of a toll on their energy. However, not all elves are skilled enough in the art to accomplish that. They must be well trained in being able to avoid blows entirely.

"Also, the elves makeup in general decides what weapons they can use. You will never see an elf carry a large sword, axe, mace or lance. A heavy blade wears on them too fast and it slows them down. It would be clumsy and counterproductive for them to use one, as it would work against their greatest advantage. This is why most of the elves in my company are archers. It is also why the elf we just fought used sai, although that is still an unusual choice. Most elves fight with daggers, the weapons are light and perfectly adapted to elfin styles of fighting, the weight and shape of the weapon works to almost enhance their speed.

"That all being said, you are not nearly skilled enough to exploit an elf's weaknesses, therefore, if you ever meet one in combat, I suggest you turn and run, not that an elf couldn't easily run down most humans. But your knowledge of the area gives you an advantage in escaping, and by the way you took off today, you seem to be quite the sprinter yourself."

My head was spinning from all the new information but at the compliment I smiled, "I am the fasted in my village." Then I began to think of all Luther had said. "Do you think there will be elves with the desert men?"

Luther took a deep breath and sighed. "It's not likely. The elves, for the most part, develop terrible prejudices. That's what happens when you have a memory that's as long as their unnatural lives. But no harm has ever come from preparing yourself for the unexpected."

At this point Luther and I had made it back to the camp of soldiers. The elf, Tryson, must have not seen Uthgar return, but when he saw the two unconscious bodies on Luther's horse he sprinted to meet us. I had never seen an elf run before, so it shocked me when the fifty meters between us was covered in no more than three or four seconds. I couldn't believe that anyone could move that fast and yet make it look so effortless. The elf's stride was so deceptively long that it looked as though he was merely walking towards us. Finally, I understood what Luther had meant when he said that an elf could easily run down most humans.

"Luther, what happened?" He said in a worried voice. "Where is Uthgar?"

"All is well Tryson, no one is hurt, at least not seriously. I believe Râven's mare has broken its leg; it'll need to be put down. He'll hate it… he loved that horse more than anything. Uthgar's here somewhere, he came back ahead of us. Probably did not wish to be seen."

"Luther?" when the Captain didn't respond he asked again. "Luther, what happened?"

Luther sighed, "There was an elf who prevented Aaron from getting to the village. When we saw him, Uthgar… well you know Uthgar. He jumped to conclusions, and rushed into battle. The elf was hooded so he had no way of knowing he was overmatched. But needless to say, without any organization the elf picked us apart. He was an extraordinary fighter. He only withdrew when I began to wear him down."

"There are elves with them?" Tryson's beautiful features were distorted into a mixture of shock and disgust.

"No, I don't believe he was with them. He didn't wear their clothes, and he made a point of saying that he did not wish to fight us. But again… Uthgar… you know. He didn't exactly let him finish pleading his case"

"Of course." Tryson's repulsed look diminished significantly after Luther's assurances.

"But like I said, he didn't do any serious damage, except maybe to Uthgar's ego, and he said that the Urröbbí know we're coming."

"What is our move, Luther? If the village is burning, we may not have much time to act."

"Well it is only the field to the east that is on fire, that and a few of the trees on its outer edge. It could have been an accident, or even a scare tactic. We cannot afford to rush this as it may only make matters worse. I didn't see any homes on fire… in fact, I didn't see any homes at all."

"We live in the trees." I spoke up for the first time. Both sets of eye shifted in my direction.

"The trees?" Luther responded, cocking one of his eyebrows in my direction.

"Of course." Tryson looked like this fact was obvious. "Northern Jericho use to be an Elven village. It was many centuries ago of course, before they moved into the protection of Aríamoné. Back then we made our homes in the tree bases rather than the tree tops, as we do now. When his ancestors discovered the village, they probably found it just as the elves had left it."

"Wait, Jericho used to be an Elven village?" I responded, shocked. I had always thought Jericho's founders were my ancestors, and I was a little put off to learn that they were more free loaders of the elves leftovers.

"Not all of it, just this Northern section. That is why the trees grow in this particular way; it is the magic that elves carry with them. Some of us have the ability to shape the nature we live in as we wish. Most of us are deeply connected to their environment." He turned his attention back to the Captain. "How many of the trees were on fire?"

Once again it was me who spoke. "Most of them were just trees. Three of them were homes though… Mine included." I said after a short pause.

Tryson smiled again. "That is good." After seeing my reaction however he continued. "I mean, I'm sorry for the loss of your home Aaron, but it is good news. I do not believe that the Urröbbí would have set fire to the fields on purpose. Once they take the village they will need it as their food supply, they have no idea how to grow crops in this climate. Plus, the wind normally blows from west to east in this area, and they would have known that. It is only a rare occurrence, like the storm we just had, where the wind shifts in a different direction. If they wanted to damage the village they would have started the fire in the west."

"How do you know the wind blows to the east here? I've lived here my entire life and I wouldn't be able to tell you that."

"I can tell because of the way the branches of the trees bend. It is subtle, but it is enough for me to pick up on, and it would be enough for them to see as well. The one thing the Urröbbí are well known for is tracking. Not many of them are good at it, but their leaders have always been among the best."

I paused for a second before turning to Luther. "I see why you keep him around."

Both Luther and Tryson laughed at this. It was an odd noise, laughing, I felt it had been far too long since I had last heard it.

"Indeed," Luther responded. "Tryson, I want you to take Athéal, Gladía, Lacríel, and Ranier, and scout the area. Make sure we do not ride into a trap, and find out as much as you can without being seen. Report back as soon as you can."

The elf gave a curt nod and looked to turn away from the captain, but Luther held his finger up to still him a moment longer.

"Aaron, where did you see the riders camped?"

I thought for a moment before responding, "They were camped on the eastern outskirts of the forest, well into the trees beyond the fields that are on fire. But that was a week ago, they could have relocated by now, especially after the fire, if what Tryson suspects is true."

"Yes, you are probably right. I don't think they would have stayed near the fire. In fact, they could have used the fire as a diversion to move their entire camp. Their reinforcements would be coming from the desert, it would make sense for them to move to the northwestern edge of the village to meet up with them and coordinate their attack." Turning back to Tryson, he continued, "Meet us on the eastern border of the village. We will move right to the area I'm assuming they have vacated. We need to position ourselves closer to the town. Hopefully from there, we will be able to make contact with one of the villagers so we can begin to formulate a plan. If nothing else it will give us a place to launch a surprise attack from, no one will suspect a force to move from the direction of the fire."

Tryson took a deep breath, "Yes sir" he exhaled, and sprinted away from the Captain.

Turning back to me, Luther continued, "Get your horse, we will need to be on the move again soon." Then he too walked away.

…

We arrived at the eastern outskirts of the village at dusk, moving in the cover of the fading light that blended perfectly with the dying glow of the fire. We moved slow, not wanting to risk being seen or heard, and we found the Urröbbí's old camp abandoned, just as Luther had expected it to be. By the time we arrived by the village the fires in Bray's fields were beginning to die out, the smoke billowed into the toxic atmosphere like a dying snake struggling to reach some unseen destination on the sky's darkening horizon. No birds sang. No animals cried out into the fading sun. It was eerily quiet. The soldiers sat in the silence that surrounded them, hardly making any noise themselves. Conversations were held in hushed whispers, but all held an undertone of worry, had they arrived too late?.

It was close to high moon when the five men returned from scouting. Tryson presented his information to the Captain while another elf, named Gladía I found out later, stood beside him in silence. The two elves could have been twins if it were not for the dark, chocolate brown hair of Gladía. He had the same slanted blue eyes and honey colored skin. The same elegant fierceness about him. They talked in whispers, like everyone else, too far away for me to overhear. At one point in time Tryson came to my side to tend to my legs, but he left quickly afterwards to rejoin his conversation with Luther. They continued to talk well into the night, and I quickly began to lose track of time. I wasn't sure when it happened but I slowly drifted into sleep.

…

I was in a forest, a forest that I knew very well. I couldn't tell you why I was there, but for some reason it didn't seem odd to me that this was where I was. I looked around and saw my old, worn, wooden bow on the ground, a quiver full of arrows lying beside it.

"Maybe I've been hunting." I said to myself.

I picked up the bow and the quiver, slinging them both over my back. A bird could be heard singing nearby. I could tell by the sound that it was a cardinal. I took a deep breath and exhaled slowly. I knew I was dreaming again, but I allowed the peace and tranquility of the dream to wash over me for a moment. I had been through so much the last few days. It was nice to relax for a moment, nice that my legs didn't hurt. It didn't matter that none of it was real. It didn't bother me this time that I wasn't waking up, even though I knew this was a dream. I was happy again for the first time in a week.

Just then the sound that didn't belong brought me back to myself. I had almost forgotten about the purpose of the dream. About the strange glow. About the beautiful woman. I took off again along the same path I had run the previous time I had the dream, again beating the glow to the spring by a couple minutes. Finally, the woman moved out of the trees, the same saddened look on her face; her beautiful face. Her blond hair flowed over her shoulders like a pale river of shimmering gold, almost blinding in the sun. She had brilliant blue eyes from what I could see. They were the same blue as mine, but maybe a little more subtle. One was covered by hair that fell elegantly over the left side of her face; identical to the way Sienna's hair was always draped over hers.

I immediately thought of Terrick, *It's a good thing he's not here. He'd probably collapse.* I smiled at the thought, and then a stab of pain went through my heart. I didn't know what had happened to my clumsy cousin on his journey to the east. I prayed for a moment that he was safe.

The woman looked up at me with the same sad smile I had seen before. The one blue eye I could see, gazing deep into mine. She moved the small bit of hair out of her face and tucked it behind an ear. An ear that came to a perfect point. It was a movement that I had missed in my previous dream. I knew I shouldn't be surprised, the women was, after all, far too beautiful to be human. But I couldn't help the shock that coursed through me. I still wasn't quite used to the whole 'elves being a part of my life' idea.

"Hello, Aaron," she said, her voice ringing like a choir of a thousand bells. Then her smile faded and all that was left was the sadness. "You will fail to keep it safe…"

I sat bolt upright, gasping for breath. I stared blankly at my surroundings, knowing, and yet not knowing where I was. There were soldiers spread out over the clearing, some sleeping, some in full armor with weapons at the ready, prepared to do battle at a moment's notice. I allowed myself a minute to catch my breath. No one seemed to have noticed me jerking awake so unnaturally. Calming my shaking hands, I noticed a sitting with his back to a tree across the clearing. He looked young, too young to be with the elite warriors that surrounded me. He looked up from something he was doing with his hands and smiled at me before putting his head back down to continue working on whatever it was he had found to occupy his time. It was a few minutes before I realized that I had tears in my eyes.

"Ugh!" I groaned, wiping my eyes dry and laying back down to look up at the early morning sky. The sun had to just begun to rise over the horizon. It still couldn't be seen over the trees in the eastern edge of the clearing, but it was casting an unnatural, blood-red light into the morning sky. It was as if the heavens had been ripped open and were allowed to bleed into the atmosphere. I shut my eyes and tried to fall back to sleep. Tried to go back to the dream. All I wanted was to see its conclusion. I remembered the woman's face perfectly. How could you forget a face like that? It wasn't possible. But the rest of the dream was once again evading me. I knew that she had spoken for the first time, but I couldn't remember what she had said. It was driving me insane.

Slowly I began to realize that sleep was not coming back to me, forcing me to once again give up on my dream and wake. The boy-soldier on the other end of the clearing was still busy with whatever was in his hands. As usual, my curiosity was too much for me to contain, and I stood up, slowly making my way across the treeless area to him. As I drew closer, he looked up again and smiled once more. He had dark black hair that was long but neat. It covered his ears and came down to nearly his shoulders. His brown eyes and square jaw made him look familiar, but I shrugged it off thinking that

I must have seen him somewhere while I was near the Lord's Manor in Alleron.

"Hello." He said in a youthful voice that matched his young face perfectly.

"Hey." I responded in kind, "Whatcha doin' there?"

The soldier smiled again and waved me closer. I stepped closer to the man to get a better look at what was in his hands. At first I didn't know what I was looking at. It was so small. But after a minute I saw it. There, in the man's left, hand was an incredibly sculpted figurine of a bear, its front paws stretched out in front of it, as if it was mauling an imaginary foe, and its mouth was open in a fierce growl. His lower half was still attached to a larger chunk of un-carved wood. In the man's other hand, was a small knife that he must have been using to carve the intricate designs into the wood.

"That's incredible." I finally murmured, silently wishing that I was as good at anything as this guy was at carving. "You're very talented."

"Thank you." The soldier responded.

The man went back to work on his sculpture and I couldn't take my eyes away from it. Every detail was perfect. It was as if the bear was alive. Every fur seemed to stand out and every tooth in the bear's tilted mouth was whittled to a perfectly curved point. The bear's eyes even seemed to follow wherever you moved.

"What is your name?" I asked, not taking my eyes off the small bear.

"Marcus." The soldier responded, not stopping his delicate work.

"That's a good name. It's strong." I paused for a moment before continuing, "I'm sorry, I don't want to offend you, but how old are you?"

At the question, the soldier stopped his work and began to laugh. "None taken Aaron. Everyone asks me that. I can't be that much older than you, if at all. I'm nineteen."

I was shocked by his answer. I knew the boy looked young, but so did Uthgar, and I had heard from Luther that he was twenty-six. I never expected the answer that I had received.

"Nineteen?"

"Yes. I'm the youngest man to ever join Dû Vena Ruösa's ranks. They normally don't grant soldiers this title before the age of twenty-one. This is my first assignment with the pack."

"That's incredible. You must be as talented with the blade as you are with that knife."

Marcus smiled and let out a small chuckle, "I guess you can say I'm somewhat of a prodigy. It doesn't hurt to have a respected father as well."

I sat down beside Marcus, my back pressed against the same tree. "Was your father a good fighter as well?"

Marcus laughed again, "The men say he was the best they had ever seen when he was in his prime." He started to work on the bear again, his smile gone. "I wouldn't know… I've never seen him fight. Not really anyways. Everyone here knows him better than I do."

I felt that I had reached an uncomfortable moment with Marcus, so I quickly changed the subject.

"Why don't they let men into Dû Vena Ruösa before twenty-one?"

Marcus shrugged, "Who knows? Father says it's because we aren't *seasoned* enough… like we're some kind of unprepared meat. He says that warriors age like wine… I think they age like concrete. They grow hard and cold, and then eventually they crack." He gave me a small wink. "I'll never be a better fighter than I am right now. It's an old and out-dated rule that they've had for centuries. We don't need to be sheltered like that anymore. We train better now than they use to, so we're ready earlier.

"For the most part it doesn't matter to them though, they still abide by it. They give everyone who attempts to join early impossible tasks, just so they can deny them entry. My older brother for instance, he was sent into the mountains and told to kill a falcon with naught but his bare hands. Needless to say he failed. Next year when he turns twenty-one he'll be set an easier task and granted entry. It has to be killing him that I'm here and he's not. He hates being outdone… especially by his *baby brother*."

"What is your brother's name?"

"Darius, his name is Darius."

I nodded my head, thinking about the name while other questions swirled through my mind. "So how did you manage to get in?"

A wide smile crossed Marcus' face, "I got a bit lucky," he admitted. "I was in the hills when I stumbled upon a pair of falcons fighting. It must have been territorial, I suppose one of them must have had a nest in the area and didn't want the other around. Anyways, the smaller of the two was able to outmaneuver the other and injure one of its wings. Without being able to fly it was easy to catch. When I brought it back, there was no way you could tell that it had been wounded before I had captured it. Even that wasn't enough for them though. They had me fight Tryson upon my return. When I stalemated him, they decided to admit me even though most of them still didn't like the idea." His smile disappeared again, "Most of the men here still don't see me as truly being a member. It's really only Tryson and Athéal, who have accepted me. The others, well…" he let his thought trail off.

I thought back to my time in Alleron, and my mind immediately reflected back to the way Uthgar always treated me.

"Yea, I understand. Some of them seem like they can be a bit of a tough crowd. They all seem good at heart though. I haven't met Athéal, but Tryson seems like a very nice man, errr elf. He's one of the few who talks to me. He and Luther. Your Captain is as good a man as I've met."

Marcus didn't look up from his work, "Mmmm, yes, that's what I've heard."

"And he must respect you; otherwise he wouldn't have let you into the pack, right?"

Marcus laughed again, "He wanted me to join least of all. He just couldn't think of any more reasons to deny me entrance."

Once again there was a silence that led me to feel I had drifted back into an awkward subject area. I began to search for a new topic when my eyes settled back on the bear that Marcus had returned to.

"Do you carve often?"

"Not often no. I used to carve a lot when I was younger. Darius and I would have challenges to see who could create the most elaborate work." He smiled a playful smile again, as if the memory was still fresh in his mind. Like it had only happened days ago. It reminded me of Terrick. "I rarely won. Darius is very talented. Now I only carve when I have a purpose to."

"And what is your purpose for carving this?"

"This is going to be a gift," he stated simply.

"It'll be a fine gift. Is it for someone back in Alleron?"

"Yes. It'll be done by the time he arrives." he flashed me another small smile before settling back into his work.

I was about to ask what Marcus meant by "when he arrives" when I heard my name yelled from across the clearing. I looked up to see Luther standing with Tryson and two other men.

"Aaron, come here would you?" Luther yelled over again.

I stood up and stretched. I was still stiff from riding, even if my legs felt as though Tryson had performed a small miracle on them. "It was nice meeting you, Marcus." I said before making my way over to the Captain. Marcus nodded in response, not lifting his eyes from his work.

Chapter 15: A Dumb Idea

There was a flurry of sounds humming around him, or maybe it was just the ringing in his ears. Everything was fuzzy and his head throbbed unnaturally. Terrick couldn't remember ever feeling this horrible before. The pounding in his head made it feel like lightning kept striking his skull with the regularity of a drum beat. His face was hot, sweaty, and incredibly tender. He couldn't breathe through his nose, which hurt so badly from being boot-stomped that it could have been inverted into his face and poking his brain. Dried blood covered his face and clothes. He could feel it in the stiffness of his face; could feel the little bits of it that flaked off whenever he grimaced. He tried to move but quickly realized that his hands were shackled. The light made it painful for him to open his eyes so he couldn't tell what he was restrained to; instead he allowed his other senses to slowly come back to him.

The rope that bound his hands had rubbed his wrists raw while he was unconscious and every movement dug the coarse rope just a little farther into his already abused skin. Once more he attempted to take in a breath through his shattered nose, and once again he failed miserably, instead moving to a shallow gasping of air through his mouth. He coughed once and his whole body ached.

Ugh, I clearly have worse injuries than my nose. He thought.

"Ey…" someone in the distance grunted, "Ey Surrok, I think the rat's vakin up."

"Who cares? It's not like e's goin' anywhere. We can't question 'em til e's coherent." Was the answering growl.

Terrick sat still, keeping his eyes shut; he needed to figure out what was going on before being thrown back into the thick of the situation. He tried to control his breathing but his broken ribs screamed at him every time he filled his lungs. He tried to remember where he was, and what had happened to him, but the lightning strikes in his mind were relentless and kept disrupting his concentration.

Where am I? - pound, pound - *Why am I tied up?* - pound, pound - *Men from the desert...* - pound - *Windfoot... burning buldings... mission... a black boot...*- pound - *dumb idea... dumbest idea...really, really, really dumb idea.* - pound - *Lisa... I have to get back to Lisa.*

He started to silently struggle against his bonds, the rope chaffing even more against his wounded wrists, desperately trying to free himself without attracting attention. He shifted his weight to the left and bumped into something soft. He slowly opened his eyes for the first time and saw that he was restrained in the small closet-like area of the second bunker, right next to the beautiful elf women, the abuse she suffered still obvious in the slowly fading bruises on her arms. Her thin, pale lips were pressed together and her head tilted forward so that her small pointed chin rested on her collarbone, above a chest that moved slowly up and down with her shallow, uneven breathing. Her golden blond hair obscured most of the rest of her face.

Terrick heard the two soldiers speak once more and quickly shut his eyes again, he did not want them knowing that he was awake, at least not yet. Silently, he struggled against his bonds a little longer. Fresh blood seeped from his chaffed wrists and ran down his arms. It was warm and pungent smelling, and it almost made Terrick nauseous. It was odd, for someone who enjoyed fighting as much as him; he had never much liked the smell of blood. Finally the pain, and the fact that he was getting nowhere, forced him to give up. He sat in silence trying to come up with a new plan of escape, but no ideas would form in his muddled brain.

Come on Terrick, think. There has to be a way out of this. Any idea will do, it doesn't even have to be a good one, just an idea.

He started running scenarios through in his mind; unfortunately everything he came up with was either impossible or ended in a horrible death. His mind waged a fierce battle, and somewhere between the two extremes of desperation and reason he figured he would find a solution. The problem was, those two sides were yelling at each other instead of coming up with a solution.

No... not possible... too long... ehh, that doesn't account for the second guard... that won't work either. Well maybe... oh there's no way that's gonna work. It's better than anything else you've come up with. But it won't work. Ooorrr it could work. No, no, they're gonna kill you if you do that... you're gonna die. No, they want to question me; they won't kill me... at least not yet. What's the worst that'll happen? They'll kick your ass, that's what. Well than come up with something better... yea... damn.

Terrick started taking deep breaths as he moved his hands together. He needed to calm himself. If he yelled he would give himself away, and he needed to take his time. He cracked his eyes open ever so slightly and located the two guards in the corner of the room. One was thick and muscular; he looked like an ape and had thick jet-black hair that fell over his shoulders. The man was so large it didn't look like he would have been able to cross his arms over his chest. The other man was medium of build and also had black hair. He was an ugly man with a thin, hooked nose and eyebrows that connected in the center of his forehead, but his eyes gave him a shrewd and calculating look that at least radiated a slight level of intelligence. As if their appearance wasn't enough, both men had wicked looking sabers attached at their hips, that Terrick knew from experience that they would know how to use. As they continued their conversation, Terrick could finally begin to make out that there were talking about the fire that he had started the previous day.

Terrick inhaled few more times, steadying himself. Finally, he took one last deep breath and held it as he grabbed his right thumb and pulled with all his strength, dislocating it. He clenched his eyes shut as every muscle in his body tensed, causing him to bite down on his lip so hard it started to bleed. The pain was like nothing he could have prepared for and he couldn't help the involuntary whimper that escaped his throat. Both soldiers looked over in his direction, but apparently thought nothing of it, because after a few seconds of staring they returned to their conversation.

A few more deep breaths and Terrick was able to get himself back under control. He slid his hand partially out of its restraint and biting down on his lip again, popped his thumb back into place. Putting the thumb back hurt almost as much as popping it out, but once it was back in place a wave of dizzying relief came over him. Even with the dulling pain it still took nearly ten minutes for him to completely master his emotions. Finally, having calmed himself enough to continue, he turned his attention back to the soldiers' conversation.

They're gonna kill you Terrick. No they're not, you're gonna be fine. No no, you're a dead man. He fought with himself, wrestling with the shear madness of his plan. He needed to get close to one of the soldiers and there was only one way he knew to accomplish that goal.

"But the fire damaged more'an just the two houses that burnt down." The smaller of the two soldiers complained. "It spread ta three other buildin's fore Rayon and the others'd put it out."

"Who gives a rat's ass?" The larger soldier responded. "Let'em fix deir own damn 'ouses."

"That's what I said. But Rayon doesn't want the villagers ta do anythin' stupid. At least not while we're short on men. Havin' ta fight off them villagers would cause us to break our search. Dey submitted willingly, but dat don't mean their willing to be pushed around. The search is the most important thing. Once reinforcements show up we can start treatin' 'em like the dirt they are." The large soldier chuckled, probably at the thought of kicking an old man or punching a child. "But anyways, yer missin' the point. We needs to patch dem roofs, but those idiots cut down timber dat was too large, and I couldn't get em up to da roof. And Rayon starts screamin' at me like it's my fault. And I'm like, it ain't my fault. I can't get it up."

"That sounds like a personal problem." Terrick spoke from across the room. *Here we go,* he thought.

Both soldiers stopped dead, and turned to Terrick. "What did you say?" The smaller guard sneered, glaring at his captive.

"I was just pointing out that I really don't care to hear about your personal problems. Sounds like something you should be talking to your woman about... or boy, I don't know what you like. But anyways, me and the ape don't need to hear it." He gave a quick look toward 'the ape' and shrugged his shoulder, looking for agreement.

The soldier gripped the hilt of his saber, his face white with rage. "What?" he hissed again.

"Oh come on. Is there something wrong with your ears too?"

That did the trick. The soldier was on his feet an over to the closet in a flash, pulling back his fist and letting loose his anger as he crushed Terrick in the face. Terrick's check split where the fist had hit, and immediately blood started pumping out of the fresh wound.

As sick as he felt, Terrick forced himself to laugh. "Aww, if I wanted a kiss I'd have asked your boyfriend over there."

The soldier struck him again, causing the wound to split open wider and his left eye to swell shut.

"Seriously," He gasped, "look at his lips... I bet he could suck the cork of a whisky bottle!"

The soldier struck him again. Terrick's eyes were watering terribly as blood rushed to his bruised and mutilated face, but he was able to keep up his charade and continue laughing.

"What's so funny?" The infuriated soldier screamed.

"Nothin', it's just you hit a bit like a woman."

The soldier hit Terrick brutally hard again, this time square on his already broken nose. Terrick couldn't help it, his laughter broke and he let out a small moan.

The soldier smiled, "Not so funny anymore, are you?" he said as he turned to walk back to his post.

But before he was halfway across the room Terrick was able to regain control, forcing another weak laugh through his tears. "Aww, come back sweetheart. I wanna make you my pretty girlfriend."

The soldier practically sprinted back to Terrick and this time move right past punches and slaps. He knelt over Terrick and with both hands started to choke the life out of him. Terrick struggled and gasped, trying to maintain his laughter even though he couldn't breathe. Just as a smile started to cross the soldier's face, Terrick finished freeing his hand, quickly moved it to the soldier's side, drew his saber, and ran him through with it before he could react, leaving Terrick gasping as air flooded back into his lungs.

"Surrock!" The apish man screamed, toppling over in his chair in his attempt to quickly get to his feet.

Terrick rolled the dead soldier off his lap and quickly used the saber to cut free his other arm. He got to his feet just in time for the large soldier to crash into him. Terrick went flying into the wall to his right, and the air immediately went out of him. The broken ribs in his side screamed in agony as he lost his grip on his sword. The soldier picked him off the ground like he was a child and threw him with all his strength across the room into another wall. He was still trying to regain his breath when the soldier lifted him off the ground again, this time pinning him to the wall.

"I'm gonna kill you vith me bare hands." He snarled, a wicked grin spreading across his apish face. "And I'm gonna enjoys it."

Keeping Terrick pinned to the wall with one arm he pulled his other back into a tight fist. Terrick's eyes widened as large as the swelling would allow and he did the only thing he could think of. He used all his strength and kicked the soldier in the groin. The man howled and dropped Terrick immediately, causing them both to fall the ground in agony. It took Terrick a second to regain his train of thought and scrambled to the saber that the warrior had dropped, but he picked it up as the soldier got back to his feet.

As Terrick stood, he turned, swinging the saber wildly, and barely managed to catch the soldier under his right arm, as the surprisingly agile ape-man mostly dodged his blow. He didn't seem to avoid it entirely however, as the wound managed to be deep enough for the soldier's right arm to go limp. Trying to take advantage of the situation Terrick swung the sword again, but the soldier caught his arm in his good hand and kicked him hard in the side with a swing of one of his tree trunk legs. Terrick gasped and dropped the saber again as another one of his ribs broke, causing him to crumple to the ground in pain.

The soldier, apparently having had enough of hand-to-hand combat, finally drew his own saber, "Here is vere you die." But as he took a step forward he stumbled slightly and his face whitened. He shook his head as if trying to rid himself of dizziness and once again took a step forward. This time his leg gave out and he fell to a knee. He blinked stupidly a few times as he rocked back and forth. Dropping his sword, he used his left hand to lift his right arm, revealing a huge bloodstain that seemed to be growing at an incredible rate.

'A look of shock and horror crossed his paling face as he turned back to Terrick and muttered, "Vut did you do to me?" before falling forward onto the ground.

"What the..." Terrick whispered, gasping for air. "How the... no way that just happened."

He looked around the room and then back at the large soldier as if expecting him to pop back up and yell "Just kiddin!" before finishing the job.

"I must have clipped an artery." He guessed, still gasping, as a smile cracked through the dried blood on his face.

"I am a *God*!" He shouted as he began to laugh. "Terrick the Invincible!" he rolled onto his back and threw a fist into the air. The motion sent another stab of pain through his body. "Sweet mother of the Gods I hurt everywhere." He grimaced.

Wiping some of the blood off his face and, clutching his ribs, he slowly got to his feet. After a quick peak out a window to make sure no other soldiers were near, he turned his attention to the beautiful elf that was still bound in the closet. He stepped over the ape warrior and the pool of blood that had now formed on the ground, a crimson mirror on the dirt floor of the barrack, making his way to his fellow prisoner. To his dismay, he found that the bonds that held her were metal, rather than the makeshift rope shackles that had held him. Her bonds were obviously prepared over time rather than thrown together at the last moment like his.

Making sure the woman's hands were out of the way he took a swing at the chains with the saber, only to find that his broken ribs prevented him from putting enough force into the swing to even make a mark on the shackles. Upon further investigation of his body he realized that the wrist of his left hand was significantly more swollen than his right. With all of the pain from his ribs and face he hadn't even noticed how much his wrist hurt.

I must have a broken wrist to go along with my ribs. He thought. *Perfect.* He sighed and turned his attention back to the elf. *How am I gonna get you free... KEYS! There have to be keys around here somewhere. One of the guards must have them.* He realized, as his headache receded to a dull roar in the back of his mind.

Terrick moved as fast as his damaged ribs would allow and began to search the large soldier. Then, upon finding nothing, he moved on to the smaller of the two.

Damn! He thought as he began to tear the rest of the room apart looking for the item that would set free the second hostage, but the more he looked the more frustrated he became. *Aargh! Another one of the soldiers must have them.*

Terrick looked back at the elf and took a second to get his thoughts in order. *I can't break her free and I can't waste time looking for the man carrying the keys for her bonds. Even if I could break her free, I'm not exactly in the best shape to drag an unconscious elf the entire length of Jericho. I wouldn't make it half way in my condition. You have to leave her...* His face curled in disgust at the thought. *I can't leave her... she'll die. It doesn't look like she can take much more of whatever they're doing to her. No, there's nothing you can do for her right now, and if you wait around much longer another guard will show up and when they see two more dead soldiers they're gonna kill you... no more wanting to question you... they'll just kill you. I can't believe I have to leave her. Staying will only get us both killed.*

With that Terrick pulled his gaze from the woman, walked slowly to the smaller of the two guards, undid his belt and slipped it snugly around himself before sheathing the saber that he had dropped to the floor. He then re-examined the larger guard, and upon finding a small knife, tucked it into his belt as well.

Always smart to have an extra weapon. He thought to himself.

Once the weapons were secured, he turned and made his way to a window on the backside of the building. As stealthily as he could he scanned the area. There was a single guard wandering away, his back to the bunker. When the soldier turned around the edge of a building, wandering out of sight, Terrick silently, and painfully, slid himself out the window and worked his way to the forest.

Once under the cover of the trees he began to navigate his way back to the place where he had set up camp with Lisa two nights prior. It was slow going, with his injuries preventing him from moving with any speed. He had only covered half the distance to his camp when he started hearing shouts from the village below.

They know I'm gone. He thought as he continued on his way. When he made it to an area where he could clearly observe the village, he stopped and watched the scene that unfolded before him.

There was a large gathering of warriors on the western edge of the village; by the bunker from which he had just escaped. A dark skinned, muscular, bald man in the middle of the group was screaming incoherently in the odd desert language at the men around him. Terrick cringed as the man drew his sword and ran a fat warrior through with it. He then turned to the others and shouted some more. When he finished, the group of warriors turned and headed at top speed into the forest like a group of frightened rabbits. A cluster of four men moved to the northwest, towards Northern Jericho, while a separate party of three warriors took off Northeast, towards the other villages on the coast.

For the first time, Terrick realized how smart it had been to circle the village and make his camp on its southern edge, where there were no other villages. The warriors would never expect him to flee south; there was nothing to flee to in the south. Just more coastline, leading to Alleron, after an un-walkable distance. Even with this thought comforting him, he didn't want to stick around very long to test his theory. Looking away from the village once more, he continued his slow march through the forest to his old camp.

It took Terrick an excruciatingly long time to reach his former camp, and when he did, he found it abandoned. In the middle of the camp he found the remnants of a cooking fire that had probably been lit this morning. He smiled; the fire was not built in a way Lisa could have put together.

The men from the village must have found her, and when I didn't come back, they listened to me and left for Northern Jericho. At least Lisa is safe. The thought comforted Terrick a great deal. He felt bad about yelling at his sister before he left for the village. It was nice to know that she was okay, at least for the time being.

He gave the camp a quick scan and found a small package of meat by a tree at the edge of the clearing. It had to have fallen from someone's saddle pack while they were departing earlier in the day.

He quickly unwrapped the package and devoured the cold meat. It tasted terrible cold, but it didn't seem like a smart idea to light a fire with people out searching the forest for him, so it would have to do. Even with the poor taste of the meat, Terrick forced down every bite he could find. He hadn't realized just how hungry he was until he had food in front of him. The thought of a meal had been pushed to the back of his mind in the midst of everything that had happened.

The sun was starting to set over the treetops and an incredible wave of exhaustion surged over Terrick. He was miserably tired and every inch of his body, even the parts that weren't injured, ached. He took a deep breath, causing his ribs to grown in protest, and laid down in the soft grass of the clearing. As he looked up into the fading light, his good hand massaged his swollen wrist and the long scab that had formed on his forearm from where he had been cut during his first battle with the warriors.

Someone up there must still like me. He thought to himself, looking up into the stars as sleep slowly overtook him.

Chapter 16: Fight or Flight

"Aaron," I hurried over as soon as I heard the Captain call my name, hoping desperately to hear good news in regards to my village, "we've run into a bit of an odd situation." Luther began. "I had Tryson and Athéal," he nodded to a dark skinned man of medium build with gleaming dark green armor and long, jet-black hair streaming out from under his helm, "and some of the other men scout the area last night. They found nothing."

"What do you mean they found nothing?" I questioned, trying my best to stay calm.

Luther took a deep breath, "I mean exactly that. They found absolutely nothing. There are no members of the Urröbbí to be found anywhere near this area. Not only that, but beyond the fire, there seems to be no trace of anyone being anywhere near your village. Tryson and Athéal are two of the best trackers I have ever met and they were able to find nothing. Not a broken twig, or a crushed leaf, or a discarded cook fire. Simply nothing."

"But how could that be? There were so many of them and they don't know the land. They would be damaging everything if they moved a force that large, and that's not to mention the reinforcements they spoke of."

"Well..." he looked at Tryson for a moment and continued, "it means that they must have a magician covering their tracks. And not only that, but if their force is as large as you say it is, than he must be a very talented one as well. Even a good magician wouldn't be able to cover all of the tracks of a force that large and there wasn't a single sign of them ever being here." Luther paused for a second to allow the idea to sink into my head.

"Now on the positive side, a spell of this magnitude has to be draining their magician terribly. The longer he holds the spell the less useful he will become in battle. They take a big risk in order to gain a small strategic advantage. Most likely, it is as the hooded elf said – they knew we were coming and had their tracks hastily covered so as to conceal their movements from us. On another note, they were able to find signs of activity in the village. It seems as though most people are staying out of sight, but the men could be seen moving from the center of the village and somewhat fortifying the outskirts. Nearly the entire village has been walled off with the large trees that grow in the area. They must have cut them down earlier in the week. That will benefit us because it will most likely force the Urröbbí to focus their attack on one of several locations making their numbers less effective. We were also able to deduce that someone in the village must have seen them move northwest, for that was the area that was fortified the heaviest.

"These are both bits of knowledge that we can use to our advantage, however, due to the sheer size of the trees, securing the village will be a slow process. I fear that there is no way we will be able to finish before the battle. If we think optimistically, there will still be a several areas that will remain relatively unprotected, and the sooner they strike, the less prepared your village will be. Also, if the Urröbbí's numbers are as strong as you say they are, the trees will only slow them down, not stop them indefinitely. Therefore an attack is still plausible from nearly any direction.

"Now, what we need to do is make contact with someone in the village so we can coordinate and formulate some kind of defense. What we can't risk is moving our entire force into the village and startling them into attacking us by accident. Not that I think they could easily mistake us for the Urröbbí, I would simply rather avoid the risk. This is why I've called you over. I would like you, Tryson, and Athéal, to go into the village and make contact. I trust the three of you can be stealthy enough to get into the village unseen by anyone, and back out again once you have an idea of the situation. Stealth is of the utmost importance in this matter, we do not want a Urröbbían scout to see you and realize where we're stationed. If they do not know where we're located, they could underestimate the resistance they'll face, which is exactly what we want. Do you think you can do that, Aaron?"

"Yea. Yea I can do that." Like I was going to give any other answer.

"Good, I need you to leave as soon as you can. Athéal is rather talented at magic himself. He'll change your clothes and

Tryson's armor into something more… inconspicuous. I'll need you to report back to me as soon as you can. The sooner we can formulate a strategy for our incorporation into the village, the better."

With that, Luther gave Tryson and Athéal another small nod and walked away.

…

It turned out that Luther wasn't lying when he said Athéal was rather good at magic. Once I had thrown my bow and quiver over my shoulder, it only took a few minutes of work for a faint outline of our bodies to be the only thing that could be seen. I was still not use to the whole concept of something as abstract as magic, so it made me queasy to look down at myself and not see my body where I knew it should be. The sensation almost made me feel as though I was falling. It also made it harder to navigate in the forest. I kept forgetting where my feet were now that I could no longer see them and I found myself stumbling in places where there was nothing to trip over at all. My sense of balance seemed to have disappeared with the rest of my body, and I had to keep placing an invisible hand on nearby trees in order to keep myself from tumbling onto the ground that was still moist from yesterday's rain.

It was near midday, and despite the difficulties I had staying upright, the three of us managed to make it into the village undetected by anyone, friend or foe. Tryson, Athéal, and I stood in the trees facing Dane's tavern in the center of the village. I had been hoping to run into Jarron, but so far I'd had no luck in locating my uncle. He was the only person who knew what Terrick and I were doing so it made the most sense to take Tryson and Athéal to him, but as he could not be found, I needed someone who I could trust. I still didn't know if someone had overheard Terrick and my conversation with Jarron and I was slightly suspicious that someone had betrayed us to the Urröbbí. Therefore I wanted to be extremely careful about whom I met.

As we watched the bar, I saw Anglehurst, Sienna's father, walk out of the tavern, talking to a blond haired mouse-faced boy named Erik, who was nearly a year younger than me. They spoke in whispers and moved off towards the southwestern edge of the village where they were continuing their tree wall. A few minutes passed and Sienna walked out of the bar, her apron on, and moved to the trough to wash her hands. I thought about it for a moment and decided that if there was anyone in the village I could trust as much as Jarron, it was probably Sienna. I had Athéal remove the magic that made me nearly invisible and began to make my way to her.

"Sienna." I whispered once I was close enough for her to hear.

"Holy crows!" Sienna yelped, jerking so violently she almost fell over. She turned and her face changed to shock. "Aaron? Next time why don't you just throw a brick at me, you ass! You scared me half to death!" She yelled while punching me in the chest. "Where have you been? Where's Terrick and Lisa?" she lowered her voice to a hiss as I put my finger to my lips to try and silence her.

"They aren't back yet?" I responded, worry lacing my words.

"NO! I've been worried sick about you three. No one will tell me anything! How could you guys just leave like that? I assumed you'd only be gone for a day or two. Everyone's furious at Jarron for sending off his family while we all have to stay here in danger."

I waited to make sure she was finished before I started, "Are you done yet?" When she just glowered at me I shook my head laughing slightly, "Come here." I said, pulling her behind a small group of trees. "I don't want anyone else to see me and I don't want to be overheard."

"Aaron what are you talking about?"

"I'm sorry, but I have to be careful." I paused and looked at her for a moment.

"Well speak up!" she shouted, punching me in the chest again.

"What is it with everyone hitting me?"

"Shut up and tell me what's going on." She hissed.

I couldn't help but laugh at her, "Alright, alright, calm down. Jarron sent me to Alleron, and Terrick and Lisa to the villages on the coast. He wanted me and Terrick to try and bring back men to help us fight. He sent Lisa just so she'd be out of the village. But we were ambushed about a day's ride out, so..."

"You were ambushed!"

I was caught off guard at being interrupted, but regained my train of thought quickly enough, "Yea, but it's alright. We're all fine. Don't worry. But we did realize someone had to have tipped the Urröbbí off about…"

"Wait, tipped off who?"

"The Urröbbí… err, the guys from the desert… that's what they call themselves."

"How do you know that?"

"Oh my Gods, do you want your first question answered or not?" I laughed at her some more. Women always say men can't listen; well that's crap, women are way worse. They always have a hundred questions and they never give you enough time to answer more than two of them before pelting you with more. She scowled at me but said nothing, so I continued, "Anyways, someone told them what we were doing, that's why I have to be careful about who sees me until I can speak to Jarron. If whoever told them sees that I've brought men back, than the Urrö… err, the desert guys'll be able to prepare for them. They need to talk to Jarron first to work out a plan, and then they can start to integrate themselves into the village. Do you have any idea where he is?"

"Umm," she thought for a minute, "uh, yea, he should be in the same barn we had the town meeting. He was talking to some of the other adults about ways to defend this place."

"Thanks Sienna." I paused for a second, and then looked back at her and couldn't help but laugh again, "Holy crow?"

"Shut up!" She responded, hitting me again. But she couldn't help the smile that crossed her face and I couldn't help but smile back.

"Just promise me you'll tell me before you vanish again, okay?" she said, concern once again working its way back into her tone.

"I'm about to here in a second." I responded, giving her one last smile before slipping back to where I knew Athéal was waiting.

As I adjusted more and more to being invisible, it became easier to make it through the village without stumbling, allowing us to move with greater speed. With the increased pace, the three of us were at the barn in a matter of minutes. Again, I had Tryson and Athéal stay behind, and was surprised when they listened a second time. I couldn't help wondering if that was why Luther had sent the two of them with me. I thought of what Marcus had said, and if they were really the only two who were accepting, maybe they were the only two who would listen to what a youth told them. I was sure Uthgar wouldn't have been receptive to my giving commands to stay or follow. Maybe the others were like that as well.

This time I had Athéal leave me invisible as I made my way to the barn's entrance and peered inside. It wasn't hard to locate Jarron, but Athéal had warned me that if I got further than a dozen yards or so from him his magic wouldn't be able to hold. I couldn't see him but I could tell that the spell was already taking a toll on him as his breathing sounded ragged and heavy. Apparently, I had to be near him for the spell to stick and I kept worrying that I would wander out of his range and simply appear all of the sudden in the barn and cause everyone to freak out.

As I approached I could hear Jarron's thick voice coming from inside the barn. He was standing with Bray in the corner looking at several sheets of paper. There were only two other men present, both of whom kept shooting dirty looks in Jarron's direction. I suspected that the majority of the villagers were at work either cutting down trees or moving them into position around the perimeter of the village. I made my way into the barn and stood behind Jarron and Bray, trying to decide how to best get Jarron's attention.

When I couldn't come up with anything creative I simply tapped Bray on the shoulder and when he turned away I whispered in Jarron's ear, "Uncle, it's Aaron, I need you to come outside."

Jarron jumped at hearing my voice, not quite as bad as Sienna, but enough that if Bray hadn't been looking the other direction, he definitely would have noticed. He looked behind him and when he saw nothing, shook his head in a way that clearly said he thought he was going crazy.

"Uncle," I repeated, once again in a voice so low only Jarron could hear, "outside, now."

This time Jarron didn't turn around, but whether or not he thought he was crazy he looked to Bray and spoke, "I think I need some fresh air. You won't mind if I step out for a minute would you?"

"Of course not, Jarron. Anything you need. I'm telling you you're overworking yourself."

Jarron gave him a weak smile and turned to leave the barn, passing in silence the two other men who again shot him dirty looks. When I was out of the barn and out of earshot, I turned to Jarron and spoke again.

"Uncle, you're not crazy, just follow my voice."

Jarron jumped again, but didn't argue. I led him away from the barn and to the place where I had told Tryson and Athéal I would meet them. When we were out of sight, Athéal released his magic on me, causing Jarron to jump out of surprise once again.

"Aaron!" he sighed, pulling me into an embrace, "By the Gods it's good to see you again. How did you do that?"

"Don't worry about it," I began in a hurried whisper, "I've brought men back, that's all that matters right now. They need you and only you to come meet them and form a plan for the village." I paused for a second and then continued, "We think there may be a traitor in the village."

"No!" Jarron gasped.

"Terrick and I ran into an ambush on our way out of the village. They knew we were leaving and where we were going." At Jarron's look of horror, I continued on, "Everyone's fine. It's okay, really. But did anyone other than us know what we were doing the night before we left?"

"Only Bray, but he would never..." he let his voice trail off.

"Terrick thought maybe Johan." I said, beginning to give in to Terrick's line of thinking.

"Maybe..." was all Jarron said in response.

"It doesn't matter. At least not for the time being."

I proceeded to recount the events of the previous few days, explaining about the men I was able to bring back from Alleron, and leaving out the parts about getting lost in the city and of the hooded elf. When I had finished, Tryson and a shivering Athéal made themselves visible (to which Jarron jumped horribly once more) and introduced themselves. I could tell that the influx of information was slightly overwhelming to my uncle, but he needed to know everything.

As Tryson explained the situation in more detail, I was finally able to take in the fact that I was back home. It had only been six days since I had left, but it seemed like the trip had taken weeks. The whole getting attacked multiple times and having my life threatened seemed to make every detail of my surroundings more prominent in my mind. Near death experiences tend to do that to a guy. All of the fine points of the forest that I took for granted were thrust into focus at a much more intense level. The beauty of the trees, with all their incredible colors. The golds and oranges and yellows. The scene was breathtaking.

I had always loved nature, had always loved animals, but yet even I had been able to overlook the smaller details that made my home perfect. The way the moss hung off the trees with their stunning plethora of colors. The way a swarm of carpenter ants moved in and out of cracks in the tree's base. The way the air here had a small hint of honey and molasses to it. It was almost intoxicating.

I would have stayed in this state of peace for hours had a great horn blast not shaken me and everyone else back to the present. I looked from Jarron to Tryson, trying to interpret the worry on their faces. The horn blew out again, ringing through the village.

"Mahalíne... the horn of Alleron." Tryson gasped, "The men are under attack!"

Athéal removed a short, light-weight sword from his back. He had left his spear and shield at the camp. "Follow us." He said in a light voice, before sprinting through the village. It didn't matter who saw us now, there was no more point to secrecy. As we dashed by worried looking villagers, who were clearly bewildered by the unfamiliar horn blasts, I could hear further gasps of astonishment at my sudden reappearance in the village as well as the sight of the two men in full Alleronian battle gear.

We made it to the western edge of the village in time to see a fierce battle raging on the far end of Bray's smoldering fields. The men of Dû Vena Ruösa had been pushed back into the clearing by an almost incomprehensible number of Urröbbían warriors. I looked out onto the scene with horror, realizing we had not been the only ones to hear the horn's call, as a large group of men from the village had also assembled at the border of the field. I tried to quickly take a head count of Dû Vena Ruösa, and was shocked to see that there couldn't be many more than half of the men left, most of which were without helms and shields. They had clearly been caught off guard by their attackers.

Tryson had nocked and released three arrows before I had even finished taking in the scene and Athéal had already covered half of the distance to the men. As I watched, the last of Tryson's arrows skewered a warrior about to engage in battle with a helmed soldier. He turned and shouted to the bewildered villagers who looked out on the battle in awe. "We have come here for you! Will you not fight?"

The men were shocked and frightened, so it fell to Jarron to finally break the silence, "We have very few swordsmen here. We're near worthless to you on the ground. Get your men to fall back to the village. We can use the trees to our advantage here. They'll give us the elevation we need for good bow shots. But right now you're out of our range, not many of us can shoot like an elf."

The horn of Alleron blasted through the air again as Tryson nodded and took off after Athéal, loosing arrows like a man possessed.

Jarron looked around at the motionless villagers and screamed, "What are you waiting for? Get somewhere you can make yourselves useful!"

I looked around and saw the startled villagers finally jump into action. As I sprinted to a tree I could easily climb, I saw Sienna's father, Anglehurst, climb into a tree beside me, a bow over his shoulder. To his right Urbank, and Aberin climbed another. Once I was in a good position I readied my bow and waited for the retreat to reach a point where I could finally join the battle.

Tryson had already reached the men, who now began to fall back at an even faster pace. As they withdrew, three villagers who were better with the sword, Hollowsworth, Arctone, and the blacksmith Johan, ran out to join the fray. While more men from the village gathered I noted that Bray was nowhere to be found.

Men from the desert continued to pour into the clearing at an alarming rate, threatening to surround and engulf Luther and his men. As I watched the inexhaustible numbers I couldn't help but think it was fortunate that the Urröbbí did not have bows with them; for Luther's men would have likely been destroyed in seconds if that were the case.

Although Dû Vena Ruösa had sustained a large number of casualties in what could only have been an ambush, they regained their poise and confidence as they regrouped and were finally able to fight as a single unit. They fell back to the village in a wedge-shaped formation, in order to prevent themselves from being outflanked. Luther was leading at the head while his archers were stationed at the ends, aiming to take down any warriors who threatened to overrun them. Now that I was able to take time and watch Luther and his men in action I could understand the confidence the captain had shown in their ability to defend the village with so few numbers. Their skill was beyond anything I had ever seen, with the exception of the cloaked elf.

Even though the men were retreating they were slowly taking control of the flow of the battle. Their movements were completely synchronized. They dodged blows and delivered their own with incredible speed and accuracy, slaying two or three men at a time before turning and sprinting four or five yards closer to the village only to turn back around to face the next line of warriors who were being offered up like lambs to a slaughter. It was like watching a morbid ballet, with their movements so perfect and refined. Kill and run, kill and run, kill and run. The dance continued.

To my right, Aberin loosed an arrow that fell short of the Urröbbí, but almost clipped one of Dû Vena Ruösa's archers.

"Hold!" Jarron shouted to the villagers in the trees, whose numbers now stood around a couple dozen. Some of the men glared at him, but they listened all the same. I assumed Sienna was right, Jarron sending his family away and allowing the rest of the village to simply assume that he was sending them to safety must not have gone over well at all.

"Hold!" He shouted a second time.

A tall, blond swordsman fell as the number of warriors overwhelmed him, but his hole in the line was closed off immediately as the retreat continued.

"A little closer!" He shouted again.

Dû Vena Ruösa's "V" kept getting shorter. There were only fourteen or fifteen of the men left.

"A little closer!"

At the head of the formation Luther cut down two more men while barely deflecting a blow from a third with his shield, which he flung over his back every time he retreated further, allowing enemy swords and spears to glance harmlessly off his backside.

"Almost there!"

I could see the long flowing silver-blond hair of Tryson swirling around his head as he launched the last of his arrows and drew the double daggers at his hips. He moved like lightning slashing and cutting with the speed and ferocity a bird of prey would use to dive after a field mouse. To his left, Hollowsworth fell to a large warrior who was subsequently killed by another of Tryson's blows. His son, on the other side of the "V" fought on, unaware of the loss of his father.

"Fire!" Jarron shouted releasing the first of the villager's volley of arrows. I followed my own missile through the air, and watched as it lodged itself in the unprotected thigh of a large black warrior close to Luther. Not exactly a perfect shot, but it would do. Shortly after, a dozen or so other men fell to the ground around him, only to be replaced by the endless stream of warriors. More arrows filled the sky and the warriors of the Urröbbí continued to fall at an increased rate. While Dû Vena Ruösa was still incredibly outnumbered, they now seemed to be in complete control of the battle. They continued to retreat towards the village, but thanks to the reinforcement they now received from the villagers' arrows, the Urröbbí began to come to them at a slower rate. One that was easier for the soldiers to defend against.

Arrows continued to rain down and I could see that the numbers the Urröbbí had started the battle with, once close to three or four hundred, had easily been cut in half, and I could tell the battle would be over soon. I was confused by the warrior's tactics. While I understood the need to ambush Dû Vena Ruösa, it was near suicide to continue their pursuit once they had entered the clearing. By allowing themselves to be drawn into the open they had turned themselves into easy targets for the villager's hungry arrows, and I found myself baffled as to why they had so willingly left the cover of the trees. As time passed it became increasingly obvious that if the warriors continued their advance their entire force would be massacred. While there were not many swordsmen in the village, we were almost all respectable marksmen with a bow – we had to be in order to hunt our food – and as the battle continued, only more men had shown up to aid in the battle.

I saw a small group of five or six more villagers run out to help Dû Vena Ruösa, led by a tall, lanky man named David, who was known best for his work as the village butcher, meat cleavers in both hands. As more and more of the warriors fell and more of the villagers showed up to the battle, the Urröbbí offensive began to slow, until finally a horn blast that sounded like the screech of a falcon magnified ten times over rang out from farther in the east, causing the warriors to abandon the attack and begin a retreat of their own.

A storm of arrows followed the Urröbbí's uncoordinated retreat until they were finally beyond our range, while members of Dû Vena Ruösa give chase to cut down stragglers. As the last of the warriors disappeared into the trees, a triumphant cheer rose from the village end of the scorched field. Despite the losses that Dû Vena Ruösa had sustained, I couldn't help but yell with the rest of the villagers. Even after the full scope of the carnage on the field was examined, my enthusiasm couldn't be reined in. We were still alive. We had won the battle. Here was proof that the men in the trees around me were stronger than the Urröbbí had thought.

I jumped down from my tree looking for Luther, a broad smile covering my face. As I began to move across the field however, the mood change was tangible. It was like walking out of the sea and onto land; two completely different worlds. No one on the ground was cheering like maniacs. A quick count told me that only thirteen of the Alleronian soldiers remained. It was a number I knew Dû Vena Ruösa did not expect to shrink to, especially not in a single battle. On the left side of the field, surrounded by bodies, Arctone was knelt over his father. I could tell by the shaking movement of his shoulders that he was weeping.

I changed course and began to walk to Arctone, wanting to comfort my friend, but wound up stopping myself short, realizing that he probably wanted to be left alone with his father. He was only eighteen, a year older than me. He would be the village's new sword master now. I instead continued my search for Luther.

On the ground the fields reeked of scorched earth and fresh corpses. The smell of the blood made me queasy, and lightheaded, but I fought off the urge to vomit as I continued to the area where the small contingent of soldiers stood. I spotted Athéal talking quietly with another soldier whom I knew as the elf Gladía. Beyond them Tryson could be seen walking the field, pulling his eagle feathered arrows out of the dead and placing them back into his gleaming silver quiver. Eventually, on the other side of the field, I found Luther in deep conversation with the young soldier Marcus. I was glad to see that the young man had lasted the battle. As I moved closer, I could see that Luther looked horribly worried about something while Marcus simply looked put off. When Luther noticed my approach he abruptly ended his conversation and sent Marcus running toward the village.

As the captain turned, he said nothing, but simply examined me with his piercing gaze, waiting for me to speak. He did not seem nearly as pleased with the victory as the villagers, whose cheers of jubilation could still be heard from the border of the field.

I forced a smile back onto my face as I reached the captain, "I can't believe we did it! Your men were incredible. You'd have never known you were outnumbered. When I saw all the men come out of the forest I thought we were done for. That was truly amazing."

The captain put on a token smile that was more like a grimace as he replied, "A victory is only a victory after all the angles have been examined Aaron. And we have paid for what we accomplished with many lives."

He took a strip of cloth from a pouch at his side and began wrapping up his right hand, which was bleeding rather profusely for the size of the cut on the back of it.

My smile faltered, I could tell that Luther was troubled by something. Suddenly my words seemed rather childish.

"What happened? How did the battle begin? And what's wrong now?"

Luther chewed his tongue for a moment before responding, "They we able to catch us off guard and unprepared. The magician they have with them, whoever he is, he must be a tracker. He was able to conceal their approach completely. We never saw them coming. A few of the men didn't even have their weapons on them." He gazed back at the edge of the clearing where the battle had begun, "Foolish." He said to himself.

I noticed that Luther had dodged the second part of my question, but when he didn't look back at me, I decided not to force the subject. Instead, I turned away to walk back to Jarron and the rest of the villagers. As I trekked back to the edge of the fields I crossed paths with Tryson. Unlike Luther, the elf threw on a smile that stretched from ear to ear when he saw me.

"Beautiful weather we're having today." The elf exclaimed as he pulled another arrow from a dead warrior and examined it. "Damn shaft is cracked." He sighed, discarding the arrow. "It would be perfect conditions for some Allaío!"

"What's Ally-o?" I laughed. I liked the elf very much, it seemed impossible that he could ever be in a bad mood. Even after the fierce battle and the loss of his fellow soldiers, he seemed entirely unfazed.

"Ah! It is an elfish game." He said, grinning even wider. "Very popular in my homeland. I have not played it in many years." His eyes glazed over into a dreamlike state for a solid three minutes before he moved to retrieve his next arrow. "I always hate killing in the morning. It just seems cruel that a man should die before lunch." Looking down at a warrior who had one of his eagle feathered arrows sticking out from between his eyes, he continued, "Poor chap looks underfed as it is. I hope hell feeds him more often than his commanders."

A bit morbid, I thought, but still the comment made me chuckle. "How is Ally-o played?"

"Al-a-oo." The elf corrected, breaking the word down. "You humans never can seem to pronounce it right, and it is a most wondrous game of speed and concentration. We elves hold tournaments every year and the whole city gathers to watch. It is a magical spectacle. Alas, I have not played it sense I left Aríamoné."

"And how long ago was that?"

"Over sixteen years ago." He said while dislodging another arrow. "I fear I must be dreadfully rusty at it by now. Once upon a time I use to be quite respectable. I even captured the title of tournament champion the year before I departed for Ardue'an. As far as I am concerned I am still the champion, seeing as how I have yet to be dethroned." A sarcastically smug look crossed his youthful face. "Although the other elves will tell otherwise. Gladía's still bitter about me beating him that year. He claims I cheated but he is really just a sore loser. Never misses a chance to say that he would beat me in a rematch though, he doesn't."

I couldn't keep from smiling in the elf's presence even with the carnage around us, his mood was infectious.

"And why did you leave your home?"

"Ah, for this and that." He sighed, "I never was a very good elf. My people are too political and slow in their thinking. Too much talk and not enough action… I like action. Dû Vena Ruösa offered that for me. Avenging the king seemed a better use of my talents than Allaío. Luther always says I would have made a better human. I have to agree with him, everything seems more beautiful when your life is counted in years instead of decades. Most elves hate war and adventure, they all think I'm crazy." At this he rolled his eyes and broke into yet another smile that, given the current situation, could have easily been construed as crazy.

"Do you miss it? Your home."

"Very much. But what I do here is more important than anything I would accomplish back there. I get to visit occasionally, once every few years or so, but the stays are never very long. They are just so I may visit my wife. I miss her worst of all, but I keep her with me." And he waved the end of one his arrows at me. "Every one of my arrows are fitted with feathers from eagles that she is friends with."

"Friends with?"

Tryson laughed, "You wouldn't understand. Humans never seem to be able to grasp some concepts."

"And you've been away from her for fifteen years?" I asked, a little shocked.

"Sixteen." Tryson said as he did the quick calculation in his head, "But trust me, she doesn't mind. It gives he time to follow her passions. She is living with a family of eagles right now. They are her favorite. She can never get enough of watching them. Studying them. I believe she wishes she could be one. And you forget Aaron, sixteen years is not so long a time to an elf. There will be plenty of time for us to be together once we are done chasing the whims of our hearts."

Just at that moment, Aberin came running out from the tree line to me, a broad smile stretching across his rough face. Both Tryson and I looked up at him expectantly as he began to talk. At first I was worried that something was wrong, but my fears were quickly dispelled. "Aaron, all of the men are heading to the tavern tonight for drinks. I know you're not old enough yet but as you seem to know these men I thought you could invite them for us." Looking over to Tryson he continued, "Wow, a real elf, here in Jericho. I never thought I'd live to see the day."

Tryson laughed apparently finding Aberin funny, "Everyone is always surprised. My name is Tryson. And you are?"

Aberin seemed at a loss for words at being addressed by the elf.

"Yea Chisel, he talks and everything," I jabbed at the stunned man, "Isn't it great!"

Regaining focus after my comment he managed to recovered, "Um, well I guess ya can call me Chisel, ever'one round here does."

"Well thank you for the invite, Chisel. There is nothing more that I would like than to have a drink with your fellow villagers, but I'm afraid after the events that have just transpired, it may not be wise to open ourselves up for another ambush. The men and I will need to set up a perimeter around the unprotected areas of the village. We want to be as ready as possible for another attack."

"I do not think you need to fear that Tryson." A voice spoke behind us.

Everyone turned around to see Luther staring solemnly towards the village.

"I'm sorry Luther?" Tryson asked.

"I said I don't believe you have to worry about another attack."

"And why is that?" he inquired again, a questioning look defining his elegant face. I followed Luther's gaze back to the tree line where I could see Marcus running back out of the village toward us, a look on his face as if his worst fears were confirmed.

Luther looked at the ground for a moment before quietly responding, "Because I fear they may have found a way to swing the tide in their favor."

Chapter 17: A Demon Runs Away With My Cousin

All of a sudden something clicked in my head. It was something that had happened nearly a week earlier, something that I hadn't ever given a second thought. Immediately, the image of Ronan Hazara juggling four of my uncle's heads forced its way into my mind. Four deeply spoken words echoing back to me from my memory... *Beware of the retreat.*

I turned to Luther, the color draining from my face. I believe we had both come to the same conclusion. "We're in the wrong place." I gasped, "They attacked inside the village."

We didn't wait for Marcus to reach us. "Vena Ruösa! To the village!" Luther yelled to his men while Tryson, Chisel, and I sprinted back into the trees.

Villagers who were celebrating at the field's edge gave us bizarre looks as we flew by, not fully understanding our worry. It didn't take long for us to realize something had gone terribly wrong. We were only a short way into the village when we came across a sight that made my heart jump into my throat. The young boy, Damian, was sprawled out by a tree; the back of his head cracked wide open, a short sword lay at his feet. He was only thirteen, not old enough to even really put up a fight. Chisel knelt down to examine the small boy, but I didn't wait for him to tell me the news that I already knew. Damian was dead. Instead Tryson and I kept moving deeper into the heart of the village. As we ran, we passed a pair of women sprawled out between two trees, the bark door to one of the homes broken down. One was Urbank's wife, Mara, the other an older woman named Fiona. Tryson and I stopped only long enough to check for the pulse we would never find.

Looking up from the dead women, tears starting to form in my eyes, we could see the broad tree that was the tavern, and against its base we could make out the forms of two more people. As we neared, I could tell that the two bodies belonged to the old tavern owner, Dane, and a sweet, freckled, red-headed girl named Abitha.

Dane sat with his eyes wide open, clutching his left arm. The look on his face of a haunted and terrified man.

"T-terrible," he stammered, "they were s-so t-terrible."

Tryson bent over the old man before turning to me, "Is there any Apperborn near the village?"

"What?" I stammered, my mind having trouble processing the words.

"Apperborn! Does it grow near here?"

"I don't even know what that means!" I yelled back, racking my brain for anything that could help us. No one knew the plants of Northern Jericho like me but at that moment I froze. My mind was completely blank.

"It's a flower with green petals. It has a white stem."

"You mean Rootvein?" I questioned, thinking of the only green flower I knew.

"I don't care what you call it, just get me some!"

You always like to think that when you're thrown into a situation that is life or death, you'll react to it well and manage to save yourself or someone else. You imagine yourself having all the answers and your plans working out flawlessly. That's the way it had worked for me since the Urröbbí had arrived in Jericho. When Jarron was in danger and when Terrick and I were ambushed, everything had gone so perfectly or at least the end results were near perfect… essentially meaning that we were all still breathing. But this wasn't like releasing an arrow or swinging a sword. It wasn't simply a matter of action and reaction. I needed to pull from my memory and use my head, which should have been a positive situation seeing as how I'm a smart guy. But the bottom line was, my brain picked a horrible day to sleep in.

I ran around the forest by the village for far too long; going to wrong location after wrong location before finally returning to the tavern with a handful of flowers. The good news was that Dane was still alive. The bad news…

"I said a white stem Aaron." Tryson almost whispered. There was worry and defeat lacing his voice. I looked down at the flowers I had gathered, only now realizing my mistake. I dropped the plants like they were poisonous snakes. I could feel my whole body shaking. By this time most of the other villagers and soldiers had arrived at the tavern. Jarron looked up from Abitha, and tried to give me a look of comfort that said "it's okay." Most of the other villagers were giving me looks that said, "You're a failure."

"W-where is Melinda?" The old man questioned, his eyes beginning to glaze over.

I turned to run back into the forest, but Tryson grabbed my wrist. "It's too late, Aaron."

Like hell it is, was all I could think. I shook him off without a word and ran back to check any locations that I hadn't already. But it was futile. I returned minutes later with the right flower, only to see Tryson shutting the old barkeep's eyes for the final time.

I didn't think the situation could get any worse – Dane was dead, Damian was dead, I didn't yet know what was wrong with Abitha – but I was wrong. A moment later, Anglehurst stumbled through the trees, tears streaming down colorless checks. My stomach filled with lead, a sensation that I was beginning to become all too familiar with.

"She's g-gone!" He wailed, causing everyone to look away from Dane and instead in his direction. "M-My Sienna's g-gone!"

I should have realized it as soon as I saw Dane and Abitha outside of the tavern. Sienna was working today; I had just seen her a few hours earlier. She would have been at the Tavern when whatever attacked Dane and Abitha arrived. If she was okay she would have gone to get help.

My mind numb, I stepped away from the scene, away from the pile of worthless flowers that had been lying at my feet None of it seemed real. We had managed to go from stunning victory to tragic defeat in a heartbeat, and I couldn't help but think that everything was entirely my fault. *I* was the one who had the weird dream-warning, and I hadn't given it a second thought. I was too wrapped up in my other dream. Too wrapped up in glowing lights and pretty elves to see what other dreams may have been telling me, and it had cost Damian, Mara, Dane and who knew how many others their lives.

It would have been bad enough if only one villager had died, but I had an opportunity to at least somewhat redeem myself. *I* could have pulled back some small shred of victory from the horrible scene unraveling before my eyes. *I* could have found the Apperball, or whatever the heck it was called. *I* could have saved Dane. Instead, *I* had failed, and now there were at least four dead. I hanged my head, feeling my shoulders slump forward as I let the extent of the failure... *my failure*... hit me.

I'm not sure what happened next, for all I know my brain decide to shut down the rest of the way. Why not right? I must have been in shock, because the next thing I knew, it was night. It had to be, because the Tavern was the dark, flickering reddish glow that only happened when the sole source of light was the fire. I wonder if that happens a lot to people; some kind of awful, post-disaster, stress avoidance thing. A situation gets too hard to handle and you simply black out for a couple hours to dream about ladybugs and sunshine or something until your brain resets and you're shot back into dark reality.

Anyway, I didn't know how I got there, or what had happened in the time following my failed attempt to get the right flowers and Sienna turning up missing, but someone was shoving a glass of fire whisky into my hand and I downed it without hesitation. It didn't burn going down this time. I was numb to it. It was a long time before I began to pay attention to anything other than the glasses of whisky that kept mysteriously appearing in front of me. I looked up and realized it was my friend Erik behind the bar. He must have known how miserable I was feeling because he kept pouring me drinks, even though I really wasn't allowed. Then again he may have just been drunk. I noticed that for every drink he poured me, he took two. His eyes were bloodshot, like someone who had just finished doing a year's worth of crying in a single night, and his blond hair was disheveled and fell every which way across his face. I couldn't blame him, his grandfather had just died. Erik and I had always been pretty good friends, but at that moment I didn't understand why he was being nice to me. After all, it was my stupidity that caused Dane's death, even if I wasn't the one that attacked him.

I finished the drink he poured me and immediately felt my stomach clench, as it started to rebel against the alcohol I kept forcing it to handle.

Maybe I've had too much to drink. I thought, shoving my empty glass away. I leaned back in my chair and fell off the back, onto the dirty Tavern floor. *Yup, you've definitely had too much.*

I slowly climbed back to my seat, making a mental note to never drink and lean in a chair at the same time ever again, when someone put a steadying hand on my shoulder. I looked up into the sad face of my uncle. I hadn't even realized he was there until that moment.

"You need to let it go, Aaron." He said solemnly to me.

"Yea, no kidding." I mumbled back, "Whooo knew I was sssuch a light weight."

Jarron shook his head. "That's not what I'm talking about."

I knew exactly what he was talking about, but I didn't want to hear it. "Hey whhisky, maybe another Erik."

"He's had enough Erik, and so have you. Maybe you should go home for a bit, be with your brother. I'm sure this has been just as hard for him."

"Ebar's" -hic- "fine." Erik hiccupped back.

Jarron gave Erik the same sad look he had just given me and opened his mouth to speak again when the door snapped open sharply, causing everyone to look away from what they were doing and focus on the new arrival. Uthgar strode into the tavern with a stern look on his boyish face and one of his strong arms forcefully guiding Ebar toward the center of the bar. I had no idea where Uthgar had come from. Last I had seen him he had his weapons taken from him, and I couldn't remember seeing him in the fields during the battle. I had assumed – half hopefully – that he was dead, but not only was he standing here in the entrance to the tavern, he had both his swords back in their proper positions, splayed in an 'X' across his back.

"Ey!" Erik shouted at the sight. "Leave my bra" -hic- "ther alone!"

He tried to make his way out from behind the bar but tripped and fell, shattering the almost empty bottle of whisky on the floor.

"This boy has information about the attack that he's refusing to share." Uthgar spat in his deep voice.

Ebar looked horrible. His eyes were bloodshot and swollen from crying. The poor kid was terrified, but I couldn't tell if it was because his grandfather and best friend had both just been killed or because of the mammoth soldier who was shoving him around. At that moment my dislike of the young warrior reached a whole new level. Half of me wanted to jump off my stool and choke Uthgar, but the other half was smart enough to realize that I probably would have pulled an Erik and eaten a chunk of dirty tavern floor.

Erik scrambled back to his feet but Jarron kept him from jumping at Uthgar, which, given Erik's present state, was probably a good thing. Uthgar was a big enough jerk that he'd have probably kicked the poor guy.

"Why do you" -hic- "ave to pushhem aroun'? Can't you see he's" -hic- "been through enough?" He continued to scream; his strained voice cracking several times as his voice rose.

Uthgar responded by simply giving Erik the loathsome look that someone would give a slug. A second later the door opened again and Luther walked in, followed closely by Tryson and Gladía. The "elf twins" as I liked to think of them.

Luther quickly scanned the area before turning to Uthgar, "Leave us."

Uthgar glared darkly at the Captain but must have remembered what happened the last time he disobeyed orders and decided not to argue. He took his hand of Ebar and stalked back outside.

When Luther spotted Ebar his expression immediately softened. He crouched down so he could be on the same level as the young boy and gave him a small half smile.

"I'm sorry for what happened today." He spoke softly, "But I need to ask you a few questions. Is that alright?"

Ebar still looked like he would break into tears at any moment, and once again his brother stepped in, "Can't it wait til tomorra'?" he slurred exhaustedly.

Luther looked up, "If there was any way I thought reliving today's nightmare at a later date would ease the pain of the experience, believe me, I would wait. But we both know that no amount of time will make this any easier." He waited a moment for

Erik to say something, but when he didn't, the Captain continued, "The information your brother has may be very helpful. I must talk to him now if he will permit it."

Erik looked like he wanted to start arguing again but Ebar spoke for him. "S'okay E-Erik, I'll b-be okay."

Immediately all the tension left Erik's body, he walked back behind the bar and poured himself another drink before setting the bottle down beside me and stumbling through the door to the back room. Ebar may have needed to relive the last few hours, but it was obvious that Erik didn't want to.

Luther placed a hand on the young boy's shoulder and led him to a table near the wall of the tavern. He wasn't rough with him like Utghar. It was a gentle, comforting action, like a father guiding his own son. He pulled a chair out for Ebar so he could sit before moving to take a chair across the table from him, allowing them to face each other like friends, or equals. He had Tryson and Gladía take seats at a table within earshot, but not at the same one. It was as if he knew that Ebar would be intimidated if people crowded him waiting to hear his news. The last thing he wanted to do was continue to frighten the boy. It was the subtle actions like these that made me respect the Captain all the more.

Luther looked around the tavern to see that every eye in the building was focused on their table, causing the young boy to visibly shake with nerves.

Luther frowned, "Would it be at all possible for us to speak alone? I'm sure this young boy has been through an incredibly trying ordeal, and I don't feel that recounting today's events will be an easy task, especially with everyone here watching."

A palpable disappointment ran through the crowd, who obviously wanted a good story to help all of the day's despair make sense, but no one was cruel enough to want to make the situation any worse for Ebar.

Jarron was the first to respond, "Of course, Captain." He said quickly before turning to face the rest of the bar, "You heard the man, clear out." He said it firmly, but in a controlled voice. I knew he didn't want to be giving orders, but he wanted the others in the tavern to make no mistake that he was serious.

"Let's go, Aaron." He said turning to me. He put a steadying arm on my shoulder and started to slowly guide me out of the tavern when Luther stopped him.

"I'm sorry…" Luther paused, searching for Jarron's name.

"Jarron." My uncle quickly filled in.

"Jarron… I would like it very much if Aaron would stay for this. He is familiar with some of my men; I feel that he could serve as a good intermediary between them and the village."

Jarron gave me a look the plainly said "I wish you would have had three or four *dozen* less drinks before being asked to be town ambassador" but he must have not wanted to say "Sorry Captain but my nephew's incapacitated" so he simply gave me a small nod and took his hand off my shoulder to leave.

I wish there was a way that he could have left but kept his hand on my shoulder because no sooner did he remove it then I lost my balance and fell backwards into a table. That's right… the Great Liaison of the village can't make it ten seconds without looking like an idiot. At least Uthgar wasn't there to see me… It's not a lot, but I really needed a silver lining at the moment.

Immediately, Jarron helped me back to my feet and over to the table where they were sitting. He never looked at me. I think he was ashamed. I don't really blame him. I was ashamed as well. I would have blushed if my face wasn't already flush from the alcohol.

"Perhaps, Aaron should get some sleep." He finally spoke up, "I'm not sure he's in a condition to be of any use to you tonight." The heavy disappointment in his tone made me so sick I nearly vomited. It's a good thing I didn't; on the list of things that could have made my uncle think any less of me at the moment, I'm pretty sure throwing up on Luther would have been near the top.

Luther looked up at me as if judging whether or not he thought I could handle the situation. Instead he asked me, "What do you think, Aaron?"

It was my chance to at least gain some respect back. I needed to make the right decision, and the truth was I was drunk. There was no way I could serve in any useful capacity in my condition.

"I'm ssorry Captain, but I sshould go home." I finally stammered, looking at the floor.

Luther gave me a small smile, like he was at least happy that I was able to be honest.

"Fair enough. In that case, would you be willing to stay Jarron?"

Jarron thought for a moment, "I will if someone would be willing to help Aaron back to his home."

Luther smiled "I'll have Uthgar make sure he gets there alright."

"No!" I practically shouted, "I-I mean don't bother, I'm not that bad. I can make it home on my own.

Luther gave me a skeptical and knowing eye.

"Really, I don't live that far away."

"Alright." Luther responded quietly. He gave me a slight nod and turned back to face the still scared-looking Ebar. Recognizing that I was dismissed, I turned and left the table, using various pieces of bar furniture to help me keep my balance. I made it back to where I had been sitting earlier; the chair I had knocked over was still on its side. Slowly, in order to keep my balance, I lifted it back up into its proper position, before picking up my bow and quiver and making my way out of the Tavern.

I walked through the old wooden doors and into the cool night air. Uthgar was standing by the side of the Tavern, talking to another soldier, and when he saw me he stopped abruptly. I passed by slow enough to give him the most loathsome look I could muster, but took my eyes off the path too long and almost tripped. I could hear his deep antagonizing chuckle still going as I passed beyond the nearest line of trees.

I *hated* him. I hated the mess my village was in. I hated that Sienna was missing, and that my friends were dead. That Abitha was hurt, and that Ebar was being interrogated. I hated that I was drunk and that I couldn't help Luther, and I hated that I didn't know where Terrick and Lisa were. I hated that they could be in trouble and that I couldn't help them. And then it hit me: I was walking to a house that no longer existed. I had watched it burn down two days earlier. And that's when I lost it...

"Why is this happening?" I screamed to the darkness, tears beginning to pour down my cheeks. I yanked the sword from its sheath and started hacking at a nearby tree like everything was its fault. I hacked and swung like a man possessed, wood chips splintered and flew past my head.

I started screaming again, a sword chop punctuating every word. "There… is… no… way… my… life… could… suck… any… worse!"

And then my sword got stuck…

I tugged on it a couple of times but it didn't come loose… so I kicked the tree. Yea, great idea right? When has anyone ever won a kicking match with a tree thick enough for someone to live in? Now not only was I drunk, angry, and depressed, but my foot was killing me. I grabbed it, like that would stop the pain, and started to hop on my other foot, but I was still too inebriated and wound up just falling on my backside in the dew soaked grass.

I didn't move. I was too angry, and hurt, and embarrassed, and frustrated, and seven or eight hundred other different emotions to move. So I just laid there getting wetter and wetter as the cloth of my shirt soaked up the moisture from the wet grass, wondering what my next great move would be. There was a moment where I thought I might simply never move again. Where I thought I might just stay there, stay freezing and wet all night. Fall asleep under the clear patch of night sky that broke through the tree's canopy directly above me; stars sparkling through the leaves like dozens of fireflies, dancing above me. Slowly the tears stopped coming. I hated crying. Terrick would have ripped on me something terrible if he knew I was crying. I didn't really care though; I needed the good cry; it made me feel a little better, but at that moment I missed my cousins worse than ever.

Then a girl's scream cracked through the night air like a whip, causing a horrible chill to run down my soaked spine. It was horrifying because I knew that scream. I had been hearing it ever sense I was little, except usually it was directed at Terrick or me, and it never sounded that frightened.

"Lisa!" I screamed back.

I got up too fast and almost fell over again, still feeling woozy from all the fire whisky, but at least I was alert. Alert enough to know that Lisa was in danger. I grabbed my bow and quiver and began sprinting through the trees as fast as my intoxicated legs would carry me without nose-diving.

"Lisa!!!"

She screamed back again, closer this time.

I rounded a corner and saw Lisa sprint out of the trees not more than fifty yards from me. It was pitch black under the canopy and the forest was still spinning in my eyes, but I could tell that something was wrong. Her clothes were torn and she was carrying her already broken arm at an odd angle, like it had been hurt again. But I couldn't see anything chasing her, so I began to calm down and slowed to a more stable walk.

"Lisa!" I shouted for a third time.

Finally she spotted me, horror lining her face. "Aaron! Run!"

"Why? What's wrong?"

She never got a chance to answer. A beast shot out from the trees between us and flew towards her. I had never seen anything like it and I failed to react in time. The beast was the size of a man, but black as a moonless night, and distorted in appearance. It had short' thick legs, muscular arms that were too large for its body, and a grotesquely hunched back. If it had been standing straight it's arms would have hung well below its knees, but it wasn't standing straight, it was sprinting on all fours at an incredible speed. Lisa screamed again as the beast reached her and was immediately thrown from her feet like she was weightless, landing roughly at the base of a tree, and tumbling to a stop. I could hear a terrible, raspy growling, like something you would here coming from an angry wolf with a sore throat.

I wanted to run to my cousin, to help her, but to be completely honest, I was scared stiff. All I could do was thread an arrow into my bow and continue my stunned stare at the bizarre creature. Part of me thought that I might have fallen asleep in the grass and was now having some kind of horrible drunken nightmare, but it all seemed too real to just be in my mind. Slowly I allowed myself to unfreeze and I began moving towards the creature, as its raspy growling grew louder. As I approached it, I was hit with the smell of sewage and fetid meat, and it kicked my alcohol ravaged stomach into instant puke mode. I could feel the bile rising in my throat, but was able to keep it down and keep moving towards the beast that was shuffling around with its face close to the ground as if sniffing for something. It moved about five feet towards the spot were Lisa was lying, and stopped moving. I took another step forward, but in my need to keep my eyes on the beast I didn't see the stick that I was about to step on.

Crack… it was barely audible, but it was enough. The beast's head immediately snapped off the ground and in my direction. Now that I was closer I could see exactly what the creature looked like. Its face was that of a wolf, but with a shorter snout and no fur. Instead it had a reptilian look. It was covered in obsidian scales that glistened as if they were moist. It was like the animal was secreting mucus from under each diamond shaped plate of armored skin. Its triangular ears stuck straight up in the air and twitched with agitation, picking up sounds that I could only dream of hearing. The pitch black pits it had for eyes stared hungrily in my direction as it bared two rows of razor sharp fangs and allowed its growl to escalate. I pulled back on my arrow preparing to loose when I was nearly knocked off my feet by an awful, ear-splitting roar. It was so loud that I almost had to drop my bow to cover my ears. When the roar stopped, the beast snapped its head back to the left and began hurtling towards Lisa, whom I could see was once again beginning to stir.

"No!" I shouted as I let my arrow fly.

I'm not sure what I was trying to accomplish. Like I could see straight enough to strike anywhere near the sprinting creature, but I tried anyway. The arrow harmlessly struck the ground where the creature had been an entire two seconds earlier. The beast reached Lisa and used one massive hand to hoist her into the air over its massive shoulder, causing her to scream again. Unlike the last time however, she wasn't thrown anywhere. Instead the creature looked like it was simply content trying to carry her off.

"Aaron, run!" She yelled once more, sobs punctuating her desperate plea.

Over my dead body was this thing going to carry off a member of my family. I strung another arrow and fired again praying to the Gods that I'd manage to hit the beast I was seeing two of.

Somehow, the arrow flew true and its point completely disappeared in the beasts opposite shoulder. Immediately, another unrecognizable roar rent the air. The good news was that I now knew the creature could be hurt. The bad news was that all I seemed to accomplish was making it angry. The roaring stopped as I nocked another arrow and the beast started flying towards me on three legs, using its fourth to hold Lisa in place. The raspy growling and retching grew louder with every step it took.

Horrified at my impending doom, I rushed my third arrow and missed completely, quickly realizing that the previous shot had been nothing more than a lucky hit. Three, two, one… I felt like I had been hit with a sledgehammer. I flew through the air like a broken arrow and blacked out before I even hit the ground… once again unable to save someone I loved.

Chapter 18: Terrick Finds an Elf

"Breathing is the key… As long as you keep breathing you can't die."

Terrick kept trying to convince himself that the pain he was feeling in his… well everywhere… was going to go away any moment, just to be disappointed when it didn't. It was excruciating. He still couldn't breathe through his broken nose, his left eye was swollen completely shut, his ribs screamed in agony with every step, and his left wrist was now so swollen it looked more like an over-ripe squash rather than anything that should actually be attached to a human. All of this was compounded by the fact that he had gotten dirt in the cut under his eye, which he was pretty sure was now infected, because it had started oozing puss that smelled something like cabbage that had been left in the sun for too long.

He had been walking for over a day and knew that at the pace he was moving, he'd be lucky to make it home in less than two weeks. He kept hoping that someone might be coming back for him and that they'd give him a ride home. But they were fruitless dreams. He knew that if Lisa had done what he told her to do, no one would be coming until after the village was done handling its own problems. And even if they were coming back for him, they would come on the path to the east, which he was staying clear of because he knew the desert men were looking for him. And even if someone did somehow manage to find him, riding a horse would be anything but fun in his condition, so he'd be stuck walking at any rate. It was all very pointless.

All things considered, his morale was pretty low, and it was dropping by the minute. I mean seriously, he had resorted to telling himself to keep breathing… that's gotta be near rock bottom. He had a sword, but he couldn't really hunt, traps weren't much use because he was constantly on the move, and he wasn't very good at the whole botany thing. He knew enough to stay away from most of the berries that grew in this area, but beyond that, he didn't really know which plants were good for him and which plants provided him with really zero nutritional value whatsoever. That was all Aaron's deal. If someone ever needed some kind of plant, Aaron would be the one who could find it. Instead, Terrick had pretty much resorted to eating whatever disgusting bugs he could find and swearing a lot… the swearing help.

Over the last day and a half of walking he had become exponentially more frustrated and angry about his situation, and had to resort to talking to himself in order to pass the time. Part of him was seriously starting to wonder whether he was going crazy.

"Just think about diving into the spring when you finally get home."

"Yea, when you get home in about a year."

"Don't think that way. It'll only be a couple of days. It'll just seem like forever."

"That's if you even make it home at all; dying is definitely a possibility with you wondering around in the forest. You'll probably fall down a hole, or get caught by the desert idiots… or get eaten alive by wolves."

"Whatever, I'm gonna make it."

"Yea, I bet the animals can smell you from a mile away."

"Think positive. It's not raining. That's a good thing."

"Every time you cough it's like a dinner bell for bears."

"Nothing bad is going to happen to me."

"That's right, bears…"

"Hey, I've got a sword."

"That you can't swing without crying… wuss."

"But I do still have it. What do bears have?"

"Razor sharp claws and about a thousand pounds of rip-your-head-off strength. But yea, keep thinking the whole sword thing is cool. That'll keep ya from getting eaten."

"You know what, it doesn't matter, cause I'm not gonna come across any bears."

"Yea keep tellin yerself th-"

Terrick stopped his argument mid-sentence. A stick had just snapped in the distance, sending him into a state of ultra alert; the two sides of his mind already resuming a silent battle inside his head.

What was that?

A BEAR! A freakin bear!

There's no way that was a bear. It was too quiet.

It was a stealth bear... He cracked a smile at the thought of some kind of stealth warrior bear stalking him quietly in the woods, wondering what kind of crazy animal talked to itself.

Another stick cracked, and then another. The noise was getting closer, and whatever was making it wasn't trying all that hard to keep quiet. Terrick slid behind a tree. If it really was a bear he didn't want to be out in plain sight. That saber of his wasn't going to be useful at all, no matter how he tried to convince himself otherwise. A few tense seconds passed before, out of a group of berry bushes a dozen yards from where he hid, a brawny looking man in a black sleeveless cloak staggered into view. He was about four or five inches shorter than Terrick, but was similar in build. He had what looked to be about a week's worth of growth on what was sure to have once been a cleanly shaved head and face... a face that looked as if it was scrunched together into a permanently squinting face.

No way... Terrick thought to himself, almost laughing at his luck. *There is no way this is happening right now.*

Terrick took two steps out from behind his tree and shouted, "Hey! Smash-face! Is that you?"

The warrior froze like he had been shot and turned towards the shout. He looked awful, even more so than he naturally looked. It was obvious the time since they had last seen each other had not been good to the man. Instead of the powerful build he had sported before, the warrior looked pale, weak, and frail, even though he still had maintained a lot of his size. It was the obvious look of someone who had recently spent a lot of time being violently ill.

"By the Gods it is you. You look terrible."

Finally, a hint of comprehension grew on the sick warriors face. In his defense, Terrick couldn't have looked a whole lot better.

"Who mangled your pretty smile, boy?" The warrior grunted evilly.

"Oh, it was one of your mates." Terrick quipped back, "Don't worry though, I'm better off than he is. You see being alive has the awesome benefit of being able to heal."

"So I see…"

For a second, Terrick had to wonder why the once almost scary looking warrior had become so sickly, but a quick glance at the red berry juice that was still fresh on the warrior's face told him all he needed to know.

"Those bushes you just came stumbling out of, tell me you haven't been eating those berries. You know them things are poisonous, right?"

A quick glance at the growing expression of shock on the sick man's face told Terrick that he didn't have a clue.

"Aww, you didn't, did you? It's a pretty easy mistake to make, isn't it? They almost look like strawberries. A dumb foreign guy like yourself probably ain't ever even seen these before. Don't worry though, they aren't fatal."

The warrior seemed to relax for a second, causing Terrick to smile. "Now the vomit induced dehydration on the other hand… that'll kill ya. By the look of ya, I'd say you've probably been sick for about a week. Wha-did-ja do, start stuffing your face with these things the second we let you go? You've probably been getting sicker every day since then, but you just kept pumping them into your system didn't you? It shouldn't be too long now. There aren't many streams that run near here, and I'd say if you don't get to some water in the next few hours or so… well let's just say that on the bright side the vomiting'll stop."

Terrick was having fun with this, the guy looked like he could fall over dead at any moment, and he really needed someone to take his frustration out on. A day of limping half-broken through the woods in complete solitude tends to create a bit of pent up anger.

"You know," Terrick started again, "it was my stupid cousin's decision to let you go. I wanted to just finish you off on the spot… Although, like I said, it looks like you're doin' a pretty good job of it yourself. I suppose that's what you get for attacking us though."

"You know," the man finally jeered back, "if I vould not have been unconscious, I vould have killed you myself. And it vould have been slow." He looked angry enough to attack Terrick, even without a weapon.

·"Yea, I bet. Means a lot comin' from the guy who thought he could run through a horse... momentum's a rough ride mate."

Suddenly the warrior smiled, "Ah, speaking of that, vut of the young one... I 'ope her face is prettier than yours... Or per'aps, you do not know..."

The smile dropped from Terrick's face almost immediately at the mention of his sister. The jab cut deep, and suddenly this was no longer fun. He drew his saber and took a half step in the warrior's direction, before forcing himself to stop. In the back of his mind, Aaron's voice kept yelling at him, *"He's unarmed. He's defenseless."* But on the other hand, he *really* hated this guy.

"Not if I give him a weapon he's not." He growled, finally putting a voice to his internal battle.

The warrior gave Terrick a puzzled look. After all, he was talking to apparently no one. But then Terrick drew out the extra knife he had taken from the warrior's bunker and drove it into the ground between them.

"Pick it up." He ordered. When the warrior didn't move he continued, "I'm *going* to kill you. Whether you die unarmed or not is your choice."

The warrior contemplated Terrick for a moment, staring deep into his eyes, before responding, "You are making a very unvise decision. There are no horses here to save you now."

"Yea, and this is me not caring." Terrick shot back. He wasn't in the mood for anymore taunting. "Are you gonna pick up the damn knife or not?"

The warrior stared pensively at the knife for another few seconds, but must have decided that Terrick looked beat up enough that he still had a fighting chance, and slowly bent over to retrive the knife. He straightened back up and cleaned the blade off on his dark cloak, smiling down at the weapon.

"I am very good fighter back home. I like knives the best. You get to be close to your kill. Much closer than vith a bow, or even a spear. It makes the rush of it all, very much exciting."

He flipped the blade upside down in his hand and moved into a defensive position. The warrior didn't look nearly as weak and feeble with a weapon in his hand, but Terrick couldn't have cared less. All of his focus was on killing this one person on whom he blamed all of his recent misfortunes. He took as deep a breath as his broken ribs would allow and charged toward his nemesis. He was able to cover about five feet before he tripped over a large root sticking out of the ground and hit the forest floor hard, right on one of his sore ribs. Immediately, the air was forced from his lungs as a wave of pain washed over him with such intensity it forced him to lose his grip on his saber, sending it flying towards his foe. It turned out that with his only good eye focused entirely on the sick warrior, he couldn't get a good look at the terrain in front of him.

The warrior was so shocked at this bizarre turn of events that he didn't react nearly fast enough, and by the time he started to make a move, Terrick was able to regain a bit of his focus. The warrior lunged at Terrick, and while the attack was slow enough to allow Terrick to roll to safety, it was plenty fast enough to kick the warrior's stomach into digestive pyrotechnics mode. The knife sunk hilt deep in the ground as the warrior hit all fours, immediately losing it, and spewing sick all over everything within a three-foot radius.

Terrick was back on his feet, but having no idea where his sword had went, resorted to simply taking a step forward and kicking the sick man hard in the side. As the warrior rolled away in agony, Terrick paused for a second, thinking about reaching down for the knife that was still stuck in the ground, but as it was covered in regurgitated poisonous berry juice, decided that it wasn't worth it and instead dove forward, landing on top of his victim.

"I don't need a weapon." He sneered, "I'll just kill you with my bare hands!"

Holding the warrior down with his right hand, he pulled back his left and punched the man as hard as he could, square in the jaw. A split second later he realized that he should have used his other hand.

"Aaaaagggghhh!!!" Terrick howled as he rolled off the warrior's chest holding his broken wrist.

The moment Terrick took to nurse his throbbing wrist, gave the warrior the opening he needed to take control of the fight. He punched at Terrick twice, but was so weak he could barely put enough effort into the attack to make Terrick wince. Instead the two tumbled over each other, flailing almost helplessly against the other's attacks. The battle moved back and forth for several agonizing minutes, with each person managing to do more harm to themselves than their foe. Finally, the skirmish was forced to come to an abrupt end when the warrior had another unfortunate vomiting episode and managed to pass out from the exertion of the fight.

Terrick lay on his back, desperately trying to get air into his lungs, which he couldn't fully expand due to the pain coming from his ribs. He didn't even realize the fight was over until he looked to his left and saw the warrior face down in his own sick. As quickly as he could, he got to his feet and moved back to where his knife was stuck in the ground. He no longer cared what it was covered in, he wanted that man dead. Yanking the knife free of the bile and earth, he walked slowly to the unconscious warrior, rolled him over, pressed the blade to his throat and… couldn't bring himself to strike. In the back of his mind, his cousin's voice said three words – *Not like this.*

He wanted to kill the man more that he had ever wanted to do anything in his entire life, and yet, something kept him from doing it. He pressed down so hard that blood actually began seeping from the knife's point. But he couldn't follow through. It was too easy. Too violent. If he followed through with his instinct, would it make him an animal? Would it make him as barbaric as the people who were invading his home? In the end Terrick slid off the unconscious man and slouched back against a tree. It wasn't as easy to take a life as he thought it would be. It was different when he was saving his own life, or trying to save another's. But Aaron was right. This was wrong. It was cold.

He leaned back against the tree and closed his eyes. All he wanted was to be home. To see his family again. To know that everyone he loved was all right.

Just another couple days and I'll be home. He thought to himself. Then he felt the cold edge of a steel blade pressed against his throat. He didn't even open his eyes. He knew it was over. He'd been tricked.

"Touché Smash-face, I guess you wi-"

He was cut off as he was smacked hard across the face. Too hard to have been hit by the weak and injured warrior he'd been fighting. The stars that were popping in his eyes made it hard for him to bring anything into focus but as his vision cleared he saw that he was no longer alone in the forest. There were close to thirty men in dark cloaks spaced periodically throughout the trees. Directly in front of him was a large, long haired man with bulging muscles and a long scar down the right side of his face. The tip of the long saber he held came to an end pressed against Terrick's throat, right below his chin. The rest of the men kept their distance, barely visible through the trees. Finally, close to the back of the group he saw one familiar face.

He didn't need to go back for the elf woman after all.

Chapter 19: The Status Quo

"Stand up." The long haired warrior ordered.

Terrick shut his eyes again and didn't move. Never before in his entire life had he ever felt defeated. Never. Not when Aaron beat him at one of their childhood games. Not when he was in shackles in at Rehorr. Not even when he made a fool of himself in front of Sienna. But now, for the first time, he was seriously contemplating giving up. All he had gone through the last few days was for nothing. He had still been captured, was still unable to help his home, and the way things were looking, he was still going to die. Why should he give them the pleasure of giving in to their commands? Why should they be allowed the satisfaction of having their questions answered? If living meant suffering through torture and misery at the hands of the Urröbbí for what short time he had left, then what was the point of living?

"Stand up!" The warrior ordered again, raising his voice.

For another second Terrick did nothing. He just sat there with his eyes shut, hoping that the man would get frustrated and run him through with his saber. Slowly, he cracked open his eyes, ready to accept the end. But instead of finding it, his eyes focused on the elf woman. She was slumped against a tree, still unconscious, with her arms were painfully outstretched in front of her due to the chain that was attached to her shackled, bleeding wrists. One of the warriors had apparently been dragging her through the forest, for the dress that was once white as snow was now covered in dirt, grime, and blood.

As Terrick's eyes locked on her, he took in the pale skin covered in bruises, the filth incrusted hair that had surely at one point in time been beautiful, and the elegant face with its eyes that may never open again. He had a moment of clarity then. There was no way he could give up. Not now. Not when someone needed him. Needed him to be strong. Needed him to play the role of hero. He was overwhelmed by the feeling that even if he never made it out of this situation, she simply had to. She couldn't die. He didn't know what it was, but he could tell that this one elf was meant for something more. She had a future that she needed to survive to see fulfilled.

SMACK! A gloved hand caught him hard in the cheek, causing him to wince.

"I order you to stand!" The warrior commanded again, his annoyed tone giving way to a seething anger.

There would be a time for defiance later but for the moment he knew he must submit. Terrick shut his eyes for a third time and took in a deep breath before finally getting to his feet.

"What do you want of me?" He finally spoke, in a voice that was no more than a whisper. "I am unarmed. I pose no threat to you or your men."

The warrior eyed Terrick for a moment before pulling back his gloved hand again and punching him hard in the gut. Terrick doubled over wheezing before his knees gave out and he hit the ground painfully.

"I claim these men prisoners of war!" The warrior shouted.

Terrick looked up through watering eyes to see the rest of the men cheering. "These men? I am alone." He was able to question between gasps.

"Silence!" The man glared down at him. "Or I will kill you *and* the deserter."

It took Terrick a second to realize that he was talking about the unconscious warrior Terrick had just been trying to kill.

"Him?" he questioned in disbelief, almost laughing. "Go ahead and kill him. That guy's not with me."

Once again, a gloved hand crashed into his cheek.

"I told you to be silent." The warrior sneered before turning to the rest of the men. "Chain the prisoners."

Before Terrick could get his thoughts in order he was dragged roughly to his feet and had a new set of shackles clamped down over his wrists. They fit uncomfortably tight over his swollen arm, placing him in unnecessary pain. He glanced down and saw a similar set being placed over the wrists of his unconscious nemesis.

"Where are you taking us?" Terrick mumbled to the long haired warrior, but he got no response. The man just sneered at him and walked away. Terrick felt the point of a saber dig into his back and was forced to stumble after him. Looking to his right, he was able to see two other warriors begin to once more drag the elf woman along behind them. As he watched, the elf's head lolled to the side and bumped off of a tree root. The site of her being treated so disrespectfully made him feel sick to his stomach.

"Do you have to be so rough with her?" He growled. The two soldiers stopped and gave him a lost look, clearly stunned by the fact that their prisoner had the nerve to speak to them. "She deserves better than that."

He was immediately kicked in the back by the warrior who was behind him and stumbled forward. Without the use of his hands he fell right on his face, the deep malicious laughter of the desert men echoing in his head as he lay on the ground.

Gritting his teeth through the pain he slowly worked his way back up on to his knees. "If you unshackle my hands I will carry her." He pleaded. "I'll carry her. Just stop hurting her."

The warriors who were dragging the elf stopped laughing almost immediately. They looked from Terrick to the long haired warrior who was clearly in charge, and back to Terrick again. Their faces gave away just how badly they longed to walk without the burden of the elf, but the fear of their master made it so they weren't about to beg to be relieved of their duty. The lead warrior turned and contemplated the situation. Probably weighing how little he wanted to unshackle Terrick's hands against how much he'd like to place his already wounded prisoner in extra pain. After a moment where he simply sneered at Terrick, he turned and nodded to his men. Once again Terrick found himself being roughly hoisted to his feet, this time having his bonds removed, immediately alleviating the pain in his wrist. Another powerful shove from behind found him stumbling toward his fellow prisoner.

Kneeling down by the elf, he lifted her fettered hands over his shoulder. Her skin, while scraped and bruised, was soft and smooth to the touch, like the skin of a ripe peach. He took a deep breath, bracing himself for the pain, and stood, his ribs moaning in agony over the extra weight that they now had to carry. The warriors laughed as he took a step and winced again in a state of obvious discomfort, but he didn't give in to them. He had to be strong. *For the both of us.* He thought.

A horse will carry its rider until it dies of exhaustion, and it will never complain, and neither would Terrick. They walked for what seemed like hours. Walked until his mind went numb. Until trees and streams and grass and moss blurred into a dreamlike haze, and the forest became a solid green prison that he couldn't escape, not even into the deepest recesses of his consciousness. The only thought that passed through his mind was that of putting one foot in front of the other. The elf's river of golden hair would whip his face every time the wind blew. Its silky touch kept the pain at bay, kept it from overcoming him.

Their slow march continued on until the sun began to set behind the dark clouds that ruled the sky, daggers of red light the only thing that could cut their way through, creating ghostly shadows in the dusk. Terrick had spent the small moments of lucidity wondering where they were heading, and to what purpose, until it was made clear by the appearance of more warriors coming through the trees to the east, some of whom were men that he recognized from his stops at the other villages on the eastern coast of Jericho. For some reason, the warriors had picked up and evacuated the towns. Terrick held out a small amount of hope that they had found whatever it was that they were looking for and had left the people and their homes alone. He even allowed himself the hope that if the warriors were abandoning the villages on the coast, perhaps his own town would soon be safe as well.

As the two small forces connected, the long haired warrior that hit Terrick earlier signaled for the men to take a break. Slowly, Terrick eased the unconscious elf off his shoulders and leaned her against a tree. Sliding down next to her he wrapped his arm around her cold shoulders and allowed her head to drop against his chest. For some reason he could think of nothing else but protecting her. She seemed so fragile, like any breath could be her last.

He closed his eyes and allowed his mind to wander away from his cramping legs, aching back, and protesting ribs. Allowed his mind to wander to what the elf would have been like had they met under different circumstances. If they were free of their bonds as well as their other worries. In all his life he had always dreamed of meeting an elf. He imagined them stumbling upon each other by chance. Her white dress no longer stained with the grime of the forest, but as clear and beautiful as polished ivory. Her pale, porcelain skin no longer bruised and cut, but gleaming in the sunlight, a sapphire lily placed in her long golden blond hair, tucked neatly behind one pointed ear. She would smile at him, causing two crescent dimples to form at the corners of her cherry red lips. She would have an intoxicating personality, soft and sweet as honey, and when she laughed it would be like a thousand songbirds singing in chorus. She would be the embodiment of all the stories he had been told as a child, that elves were intelligent and compassionate, gentle and flawless. The thoughts eased his mind and allowed him to momentarily forget about the predicament they were both in.

The thoughts died however as he heard two voices talking deeper into the trees.

"Vhy haf ve been called here Malickí? Ve should be continuing our search. If you vaste our time Ronan vill haf your head."

Slowly, Terrick crawled out around the edge of his tree so the scene that was unraveling came into view. A short way through the trees the long haired warrior with the scar was talking to a tall black warrior with dark hair that was braided and woven tightly to his scalp. His arms bulged out from his sleeveless cloak with his sinewy muscles rippling as he tensed in agitation.

"Word has come to me directly from Ronan. He has seen an opportunity to gain influence in the east. We are to meet up with the main body and wait for his command."

"But vut has changed?" The black warrior questioned.

"The counsel has moved twice in the last year, they are trapped now. They have no more resources to use. All we must do now is find them. We will crush them."

"But how are ve to meet the main body? They are north of Farador. Ve vould haf to skirt ze entire range. It vould take veeks."

There was a loud crack as a stick broke in the distance behind Terrick. He flinched and quickly ducked out of site. As quietly as he could, he crawled back around the tree to the unconscious elf, not wanting to be caught eavesdropping. For some reason he didn't see that going over too well. As he made it back to the elf and resumed his protective position around her, he once again closed his eyes and allowed sleep to overtake him.

Throughout the night he drifted in and out of dreams. They were restless and dark and he kept waking up in sweats, only to repeat the process after he succumbed to his exhaustion. Finally, after a particularly horrible dream where he relived his flight and capture in Rehorr village, he was roughly woken by a hand grabbing his shoulder and dragging him onto his back and through the forest. Using the one part of his body that didn't hurt, he swatted the hand away with his left arm. "I can walk on my own." He growled.

Terrick looked up into the face of the long haired warrior, who sneered at him, but didn't resume dragging him through the forest. Slowly he made his way to his feet and was finally able to come face to face with his captor. The warrior was nearly half a foot smaller than Terrick but thick as a tree trunk. His muscles tensed like he was holding himself back from striking Terrick again and the scar on the right side of his face twitched with agitation.

"Follow me." Was all he could snarl before turning and walking through the trees.

Terrick did as he was told and followed the warrior as he was guided to a clearing, about twenty meters in diameter, which was surrounded by several old and sickly looking trees. A musty rotting stench emanated from the damp wood, filling Terrick's nostrils with every breath. In the middle of the clearing there stood two other warriors, one was short and tan with matted black hair and dark, beady eyes, while the other was the tall black warrior he had seen earlier. As he approached, the black warrior's eyes bored into him with malice, like he would like nothing better than to crush Terrick under the heel of his boot.

"Sit." The long haired warrior ordered without a glance at his prisoner.

Terrick took a moment to give the man his most loathsome look before responding, "I think I'll stand thank you." He liked the fact that he was taller than all three of the warriors, and he could tell that his size made them all a little uncomfortable. He could sense it in their body language as well as in the movements of their eyes, as each soldier kept flicking his eyes to his comrades' as if attempting to figure out what they were to do. Terrick enjoyed it. It made him feel as though the situation wasn't entirely out of his control.

The warrior sneered at his response, but didn't object. "Which village in Jericho are you from boy?"

"Tell me why I should answer your questions?"

"Because, your answers will tell us how useful you can be to us. You do not want to run out of uses."

It was quickly becoming apparent to Terrick that the only reason he was still alive was for information's sake. They weren't lying, the moment he ceased to be useful would be the moment that preceded his death. In order for him to survive he would have to keep the status quo.

He chewed his tongue for a moment before responding, "I'm a farmer in Northern Jericho."

"And what is a farmer from the north doing so far away from his home?"

"It's the growing season. I was looking for buyers for this year's harvest."

The long hair warrior took two steps up to Terrick and smacked him hard in the face with the backside of one gloved hand. "We are not so simple to believe that this is true."

Terrick spit in the dirt at his feet and glared at the warrior, wondering how truthful he should be with the men. "My town was attacked, so I fled to the east seeking refuge. It worked out just swimmingly."

"You are a coward?" The black warrior interjected.

"Must be." Terrick growled back in response.

"And haf you been to ze eastern boarders before?" He continued.

"Yes. Why?"

"Many times?"

"Yea, many times. Why?"

"If you haf been here many times than you vould be familiar vith ze terrain."

Terrick glanced at his surroundings for a moment before responding, "You could say that."

"Then you vill lead us east through ze Mountains of Blue Rock and into ze forest of Farador. You vill do this in ze fastest vay possible."

"And what if I refuse?"

The black warrior's eyes narrowed until they were nothing more than black slits concealing beady pupils. The shorter warrior turned to the side of the clearing and nodded. Terrick's eyes followed the man's line of site to where a sound of movement could be heard in the trees. Out of the forest walked two more soldiers dragging a long chain behind them, and attached to the chain was a pair of pale bruised arms.

Terrick's heart rate increased tenfold, and his eyes bulged with rage as they shot back and forth from the three warriors in the middle of the clearing to the elf that was being used as leverage against him.

"I told you to stop dragging her around," he growled.

"If you refuse," the black warrior continued, ignoring his comment, "ve'll kill the elf you seem so fond of."

Beads of perspiration started to form on Terrick's forehead, and the muscles in his jaw clenched so tightly they started to cramp. He began straining his mind, searching for the best course of action as he weighed his options. On one hand, if he refused to lead the warriors, both he and the elf would most likely be killed. On the other, if he did guide the men, he would be aiding them in a way that would probably endanger more lives. If these men were hunting this counsel, he wasn't really in any hurry to help them achieve that goal. There had to be a reason the warriors wanted them found so badly, and Terrick was starting to think that this counsel might be important enough to help him get home.

"I'll need I splint for my wrist." He started to barter.

"What?" the long haired warrior sneered back.

"It's a three day trip to the mountains, and then we'll have to hike over them. The Gods only know how long that'll take, and if you want your *guide* to make it far enough to see you safely through you'll have to get me a splint for my wrist and a pad for my ribs.

And you're gonna have to start giving me something to eat. If I starve to death, you'll have a hard time navigating the swamplands."

All three men looked mutinous, and once again the long haired warrior stepped close enough to smack Terrick, a bulbous vein throbbing viciously on his forehead.

"You ask for much." He snarled

Terrick rolled the one eye he could still see out of, "If you don't need me then kill me and you can take the long way around the mountains. But that trip will take you well over a month instead of two or three weeks." It was a bold bluff considering that Terrick had never been as far as the mountains before in his life, but he needed to buy time, and making the warriors think he knew what he was doing was one way to accomplish that task. If he was being honest with himself though he had only navigated the swamplands twice before in his life, both on hunting trips with Aaron, and he wasn't all that confident in his ability to get them through those haunted lands successfully. The best he could hope for was to stall until a better plan came into view.

Terrick held his breath as the large black warrior put his hand on the pommel of his sword and eyed him angrily, causing him to wonder whether he had pushed his bluff too far. He waited and waited for the sword to escape the sheath. For the cold steel to sink into his soft flesh. But the blow never came. The long haired warrior gave him one last quick look of distain before pushing past the others and walking out of the clearing. One by one the others followed.

At the last minute, the black warrior turned back and spoke in a threatening growl, "Do not try anything brave and foolish young one, or your friend vill be ze one who pays for it," before he too disappeared into the early morning darkness.

Finally, Terrick allowed himself to breathe again. It was a small victory, a step in the right direction, but most of all, it meant that he was going to live to fight another day. And it meant that he had once again regained a little control in his life.

Chapter 20: Back From the Dead

When I finally came to the next day, I wished I hadn't. I had such a severe headache that I could feel my heartbeat in my brain. Every time blood pumped through my veins it would pang like a hammer striking an anvil. Eventually, I gained the courage to open my eyes, only to have a bright, hazy, white light blind me. My head began to spin, and with it so did my stomach. Barely making it to my side, I vomited, the bile immediately placing the taste of stale whisky back into my mouth.

"Aaron, are you alright? He's coming to." I heard someone say in the distance. The voice sounded fuzzy and miles away though, like the person was either speaking through a cloth, or I had a major buildup of earwax.

"Bright," Was all I was able to moan back. "Why so bright?"

"You took a nasty bump on the head." The voice said again, sounding slightly closer this time, "Sensitivity to light is common with concussions. You need to rest."

Slowly I took my hand and ran my fingers through my hair. On the back right side of my head, the skin raised up into a massive welt that was so sensitive to touch I had to keep myself from unintentionally jerking away from it. The hair around the wound was matted in places and sticky in others like it had either just been bleeding, or some kind of ointment had recently been applied to it.

Suddenly, small snippets of the night after the bottle came back to me. Though all I could remember was a creature from a nightmare and Lisa, no wait, the nightmare creature had Lisa. "Did you get it?" I mumbled as it tried to shield my eyes from the light, but it was no use. The light seemed to diffract around my hand and through the cracks between my fingers only to be magnified ten times. "Did you get it? It had Lisa."

At the lack of a response I could feel the burn of tears building in my eyes. Lisa was gone and it was entirely my fault. I had managed to take the disaster that was last night and make it worse.

"Can someone please turn that light off?" The voice finally spoke. After a moment the light in my eyes dimmed from excruciatingly blinding to simply bright. It was enough to finally give a face to the voice as Luther's face to come into view. "We were hoping you would be able to help us with that. We heard screams, but by the time we arrived, all we found was you. Tryson searched the area and found footprints, very odd footprints. He tracked them as far as he could, but once they disappeared there wasn't much he could do. My guess is the same magician that concealed the Urröbbí's attack concealed these prints. They were nothing more than a dead end."

Far off in the distance I heard a door open. "Aaron! Is he awake?" I heard the desperation and anxiety in my uncle's voice.

"Jarron!" I called back, finally succumbing to the tears. "I'm s-sorry, I'm s-so sorry." Was all I managed through weak sobs.

"Thank the Gods you're alright!" He cried back, falling to his knees over my bed and embracing me in a hug I didn't deserve.

"They took Lisa J-Jarron. I couldn't stop it. I'm s-sorry."

Jarron's face turned so pale it seemed almost transparent in the white light. Luther moved forward and placed a comforting hand on my uncle's shoulder, but didn't interrupt.

"What of Terrick?" Jarron was shaking as though he feared the answer.

I shook my head trying to hold back more tears. "I didn't see him. J-Just Lisa."

"While tracing the footprints Tryson found three horses on the southern edge of the village." Luther paused for a moment before continuing. "He found the bodies of five men there, as well as three other horses. There looked to be a skirmish. There were arrows and swords lying around the clearing where they were found. But none were alive. A villager came by but…" the soldier cleared his throat, knowing the rest of his news would be difficult to hear, "there wasn't enough left of the men to identify. I am sorry."

As he spoke the words they seemed to trail off into a whisper. They sank in slowly, like a fog covering a valley, except this wasn't a normal fog. It had weight and it compressed my lungs until I could hardly breathe. I looked up into Jarron's eyes and read defeat. My cousin, my best friend, was dead. I was overwhelmed with a despair so powerful it was beyond the tears that streamed from my eyes. Beyond sobs. I simply stared, unseeing, and unthinking, into the light, and silently wished that it had been me instead of him. I'm not sure when or how it happened, but I drifted back in to a deep, dark sleep.

…

"You will fail to keep it safe…"

I awoke with the words ringing in my head. Images of a beautiful elf woman and a strange glow swimming in my mind. I would fail to keep what safe? I didn't know what the dream was trying to tell me. I had failed plenty already in the last day and a half. I wasn't sure I could stand anymore failure, but after I took my last dream warning for granted I was determined to try to understand this new one.

It was night outside. I could tell because when I opened my eyes I wasn't blinded by painful white light. Instead, I could make out the dimly lit dullness that was the basement of my uncle's tree. It took me a moment to realize that I wasn't alone. Sitting in the corner of the room, his dark, thoughtful eyes locked on me, was Luther. He didn't speak when he saw me look at him, instead waiting for me to be ready to talk. The minutes slipped by, but still he waited.

Finally, after what seemed like hours he spoke, "I'm sorry about your cousin." When I said nothing in response he continued, "They held a funeral today for those who have been lost. It was a worthy ceremony. He will be welcomed into the Lord's court with grace and honor."

After another long pause, I wiped a tear from my eye and confessed, "I don't know what to do." Choking down the emotions I was desperately trying to keep in check I continued, "My whole life has been simple. There was my family, my work, my relationships. They all made sense. They all fit. Now it's all changed. Everything I have ever known is being torn down before my eyes, and I haven't been able to do anything to stop it. I have completely lost control of my life. What do I do now? Where do I go from here?"

Luther took a minute before responding, weighing his words carefully. "What you do now is up to you Aaron. No one can choose your path for you. But whatever it is, whichever path you do choose, it will define you. Successes are wonderful things. They build confidence and pride, and boost morale. But true men, true warriors… kings… they are not defined by never falling, but by whether or not they rise again *after* they have fallen. They are defined by how they react when they have been defeated. How they respond when all hope seems to be lost. And it is in these times Aaron, when they make the most important decision of their lives; to keep fighting. Because in the end, all of the great men through history have realized that there is something greater than themselves in this world, something that is worth fighting for."

"And what do I have that's worth fighting for?" I questioned, tears starting to well up in my eyes again as I thought of all that I had lost.

Luther gave me a sad smile and thought for a moment more before responding. "That is the one question I cannot answer for you Aaron. No one can. But if you think about it, I'm sure the answer will come to you."

It was at that moment that I stopped thinking about all I had lost and started thinking about everything I still had to lose. I still had a village to fight for. Friends that were still here, that were just as scared as I was. I still had my beautiful horse Elma, and an Uncle that would need me to be strong. And I still had people to save. Lisa, and Sienna, and countless others. They were still alive, and as long as I had breath in my lungs, I could never give up, never let them down. As I thought about everything I still had in my life I made a decision to harden my mind. Things may end up getting worse before they would get better and I couldn't afford to have another breakdown, and more importantly, those who were counting on me could not afford it.

"Thank you Luther." I finally responded. The Captain gave me a nod before I continued, "I know you wanted to talk to me about what happened last night. I think I'm ready now." I took a deep breath and began to relive the nightmare that was the previous night. I talked about everything that had occurred, from my stumbling through the forest, to my breakdown, to hearing Lisa's initial scream. The memory of it sent a fresh wave of horror down my spine, making my hair stand on end almost like I was standing too close to a lightning strike. I talked about finding Lisa and my encounter with the foreign beast. I tried to put as much detail as I possibly could into the description, but the combination of the dark, the alcohol, and the concussion had made everything so hazy. Certain things stuck with me however; the moist scaly hide, the dark pitted eyes, the razor sharp fangs. Thinking about the fact that poor Lisa was in the clutches of such a beast made me hate myself, as the guilt at being unable to save her settled over me once again.

As I recalled my experience, Luther listened intently and by the time I finished his face wore an expression of deep thought.

"Your story, along with the footprints Tryson found, and the little I was able to garner from the young Ebar, verifies my suspicions and the outlook is not a bright one. If things are as they appear, then it would seem our predicament is worse than I originally expected."

"What do you mean?" I questioned as the anxiety began to rise in my voice.

"The creature you described is known as a Mazenkyrie, It is a bird demon of the olden world. Until this event they were believed to be extinct. The last of their race were thought to have been killed during the Great War. They have not been seen for over a century and the fact that our enemies have found them is a sinister twist in events . It means the Urröbbí are much more powerful than we anticipated."

"A bird demon? That thing looked nothing like a bird." I shivered as the beast's image was once again cast into the forefront of my memory.

"That's because the one you saw was still relatively young. When the Mazenkyrie are born their wings have not begun developing. The bulge you noticed on its back is a placental unit used for growing them. When it reaches adulthood, its back will split and its wings will emerge. Until that time they are relatively harmless."

"Relatively harmless?" I shouted back in disbelief. "The back of my head begs to differ! The thing swatted me like a fly. It could have killed me."

Luther gave me a sad look. "Yes Aaron, I have no doubt that it very well could have killed you. In fact, you're lucky to still be alive, but you must understand, I say 'relatively' because when it reaches adulthood it will only be that much worse. When talking to Ebar, he said the creature that attacked him and Damian was fully clothed. He said that it had a saber, but didn't use it. This goes along with my assumption. The Mazenkyrie are sensitive to light until their scales are fully developed. If exposed to ultra violate radiation it will receive crippling burns. With effort, a youngling can be taught to use a sword, but my guess is that the weapon it carries is more ceremonial. Until it is fully grown it must rely on its teeth and brute strength to attack."

"That seems like more than enough to me." I interjected.

Luther gave me a wary smile and shook his head. "It is a lot, but it is beatable. They are sloppy, wild, and unintelligent, but all this changes when they reach adulthood. They lose many of their weaknesses. They can hunt by day or night with effectiveness and within a week they will grow talons the size of daggers. Arial assaults are harder to defend against and defeat than those executed on the ground. Their clumsiness will be replaced with agility and their speed will increase tenfold. Strength will go from being their primary weapon to one that is seldom used."

"What can we do against a creature like that?" I asked in exasperation as a stone dropped into my stomach, our chances of defeating the enemy looking bleaker every second Luther continued to speak.

"Once they reach that form there is not much we can do. We must hunt and kill them while they are still young. Ebar said that four of the creatures attacked so we have to be prepared for the Urröbbí to have at least that many. Now th-"

"Six." I interrupted, as Luther gave me an odd look, as if he didn't understand what I was saying. "There are six of them. They all visited Jarron in our fields the first day they arrived. They were with Ronan."

Luther nodded solemnly. "This makes sense. He would not want his most important weapons out of his sight for long. He will keep them close. But as I was going to say, this gives rise to an even larger problem. If the Urröbbí have six younglings, they must also have the parents."

He paused for a moment to let those words sink in. It seemed obvious to me after he said it, but it was a concept I hadn't given a second thought. Of course the beasts had to have come from somewhere. They weren't exactly sprouting out of the ground.

"So there are eight of these things we have to kill?" I questioned.

"It would seem so." Luther responded. "The younglings reach adulthood sometime during the fourth year of their existence, but it is random, there could be anywhere between two days and twelve months between when the first and last change. However, I fear that Ronan would not be using them if they were not close to adulthood, and if this is the case, the clock may already be against us."

Luther's words were only just spoken, and they were already starting to weigh heavily on my mind. "What do you think they want?" I asked, fearing that our fight here in Jericho was quickly becoming more about holding back a terrible storm and less about saving my village.

"I am not sure, Aaron." He answered honestly. "But throughout my life I have been taught that our world tends to run in patterns and things are returning that have not been seen or heard in many, many years. Whatever it is they want, the return of the name of Ronan Hazara coupled with the resurfacing of the Mazenkyrie can only mean that a dark road lies before us."

No sooner were the words out of his mouth, than the blast of a horn sounded from somewhere in the forest. I shot out of my bed so fast that the blood rushed from my injured head and I was overcome with dizziness. Luther grabbed hold of my arm, until I was steady enough to stand on my own before alleviating my concerns.

"Easy, Aaron. That was no war horn."

"Then what was it?" I asked, silently praying that he was right.

"Something else." He responded cryptically, like that should have cleared the matter up entirely. Luther stood, a look of deep concentration on his withered face, before continuing, "Come with me," and walking out of the room without looking over his shoulder to see if I would follow.

As we left the house, the cold night air blew softly over my skin and gave me goose bumps. Luther stayed silent as we moved through the trees and I had to walk fast to keep up with him. Other villagers had started coming out of their homes as well, clearly just as nervous about the horn blast as I was. Even the animals seemed skittish because of the noise. It was as if the whole forest was holding its collective breath in anticipation of what might happen next. A moment later the horn sounded again. It was coming from the eastern side of the village near where the battle had taken place in Bray's fields. The second horn blast caused Luther to quicken his pace and I had to jog to catch up. As we weaved our way through the center of the town I could see Tryson running toward us from the opposite direction. His war helm was back in its place on his head and his long hair streamed behind him as he ran.

As he skidded to a stop in front of us, I was amazed to see that he was not the least bit out of breath from his sprint. "A black rider has entered the eastern field flying a white flag. He has one of the children with him. The men felt it would be best if you approached him first."

Luther stood pondering Tryson's words for a moment before nodding back in the direction of the village, "I want you to take the other archers and station yourselves in the trees at the southern edge. I don't want to let our guard down only to walk into another trap. If he is expecting our eyes to be in the east, he may be preparing to mobilize elsewhere. It is likely the rider wishes to barter with us but we must prepare ourselves against alternative actions."

"Yes, Luther." Tryson responded before sprinting off again, presumably to gather his fellow archers.

We reached the eastern edge of the village quickly and quietly after Tryson left us. As we moved through the outer ring of trees bordering the charred field, my stomach leapt into my throat, a sensation that I was becoming all too familiar with. In the center of the dead field, seated on a stallion that was so black it was nearly invisible against the backdrop of scorched earth, was the black rider who called himself Ronan. They stood like a demonic apparition in the quickly darkening night. A beast from the underworld set to destroy all that was green and good in the world. The rider sat facing the village, with a white flag clutched in one enormous hand. His ruby hilted sword was not sheathed, as it had been the last time I had seen him, instead the wicked looking blade was grasped in his other hand. The hand of an arm that was draped around the neck of my terrified cousin. He was grasping her so tightly I feared that if he flexed his bulging bicep any more he may pop the head right off Lisa's shoulders.

As we passed into the clearing, we met a group of villagers and warriors of Dû Vena Ruösa, who had apparently been waiting for Luther to arrive to approach the rider. I was happy that Jarron was nowhere to be seen. I didn't know how much more his old heart could take. Seeing Lisa with a sword to her throat may have done him in.

Luther stopped for a moment and nodded at the warrior I knew as Athéal, before continuing forward. As our crowd slowly advanced on the rider, his bone chilling blue eyes locked on mine, and an evil sneer worked its way across his face. He was taunting me. Daring me to make a move. Daring me to do something irrational. To think only about the hatred that bubbled up inside me every time I saw him, like a storm charged with electricity, just waiting to unleash a fury of lightning. Waiting to strike something down. To turn him to ash. It took all my strength but I was finally able to master my urge to charge the rider and fell in behind Luther.

Ronan seemed to sense my internal struggle, because he gave me one last antagonistic look before turning to the Captain.

"Captain VanDrôck," he spoke in the same deep voice I had heard twice before. The cold smile he had given me grew even wider as he eyed Luther. "It has been many years old friend. I did not expect to see you in this place. The boy was not to make it to Alleron of course, but it seems if you want something done correctly you must do it yourself." His voice was smooth, and if it had not been for the antagonistic word choice and cold tone, it would have almost been pleasant.

Luther gave Ronan a calculating look before responding, "I know not who you are rider. You should introduce yourself before you assume such things."

Ronan gave a deep chuckle, "Don't remember me? I'm offended Luther. I thought killing your father would warrant me a permanent place in your memory."

At the taunt, I could see Athéal's hands twitch around his spear, as if he was fighting the urge not to throw it. Luther simply lifted a calm hand to stop the warrior, his face remaining emotionless. I had no idea that the original Captain VanDrôck had died at the hands of this man. Luther had never mentioned what happened to his father and certainly had made no illusions of a connection between his father and the man known as Ronan.

"You are not Ronan Hazara." He responded steadfastly, never taking his eyes off the rider, "I watched him die."

Ronan smiled again, "And I can assure you that it was very painful. I should like to return the favor someday." When Luther didn't respond his smile faded and he continued, "But today will not be that day. Today we have business to discuss."

"What business do you have with me, rider?" Luther calmly questioned.

"I have traveled a long way to get here, Luther. Through shadow and dust and I will not return to that world. Not ever. But I have a debt to pay and pay it I shall." As he spoke his icy eyes bore into Luther's. "As we speak there is a force of incalculable numbers moving towards this village. Those of you who have survived our last little skirmish will soon be destroyed. All that is left of you will be wiped clean of this world and history will never remember those who lived, fought and died here. All of your heroic efforts will fade into obscurity and your honor will be lost to the decay of time. But I am offering you hope, Luther. For the last week this village has been little more than a thorn in the paw of a wolf and its defiance has begun to perturb me.

"Yet I am not entirely unforgiving and I have come here today to offer you a fleeting chance. You see, this wolf is starting to draw weary of the stench radiating from this forest. I wish for a new task to conquer, but I cannot move on until I have extracted what I need from this place… this… zoo. You see, I could continue to hide my men and wait until my force is joined by thousands. I could wait until the moment is perfect and bleed this forest dry. Purge the world of your existence. But if all of you die, I may not receive the information I need, and that Luther, that could prove to be an inconvenience. It could keep me in this wooden prison for much longer than I would prefer, and so I offer you an alternative to annihilation."

"You should get to the point rider. My patience is not unlimited." Luther interjected.

Ronan made a tisking sound as if reprimanding the Captain and tightened his grasp on Lisa, who squeaked like a frightened mouse. "Luther, Luther, Luther, we both know that I have the upper hand. I could speak all night if I wished and you would simply stand there and listen to me. You don't want this poor child's blood on your hands, do you?"

At his words, my hand instinctively moved to my sword. It was a small movement, but it was enough to catch Ronan's attention and he turned to give me another wicked smile. As if he knew that by threatening Lisa he was hurting me.

"My proposition Luther," he began again while shifting his vision back to the Captain, "I will leave this place. I will take my men and I will leave this forest and these… people, without any further scars. But you must do something for me first. Or perhaps I should say you must trade me something first."

"What is it that I have that you could possibly want?"

Ronan's face lost its toying expression and replaced it with a seriousness that radiated anger. His voice grew into a deep rattle as he spoke, "I want the elf."

Luther paused for a moment and I couldn't tell whether or not the request had confused him. I couldn't blame him. If he knew what Ronan was talking about he would have been the only one. Everyone else who was close enough to hear the conversation looked completely bewildered, soldier and villager alike, and there was an outbreak of hushed whispers amongst the crowd.

"Whom is it that you seek?" Luther finally responded. "There are still three elves under my command."

"You know who it is that I seek!" Ronan spat.

"Why?"

"The reasons are no concern of yours."

"On the contrary, we are at war. Everything you do is a concern to me, and if you will not elaborate I may be hard pressed to grant your wish."

Ronan practically shook with rage and Lisa had started to cry. Whoever it was he was after, he wanted him badly. "There is a broken statue southwest of the village. He will come to me tomorrow night or you will pick up the body of this girl. And every night you delay will mean the death of another captive. So you can either do nothing and watch as this village and your men are crushed by the storm that approaches, or you can sacrifice one to save many. That is my offer." Ronan took one more moment to scowl at Luther before letting a cold smile creep back onto his face, "You should take the offer Luther. It is not as though this would be the first time you have helped me."

For the first time during the entire conversation, Luther's façade slipped and he seemed to lose his edge. His eyes grew wide in surprise at Ronan's words, almost an unperceivable amount, and he simply watched as the black horse disappear into the trees at the far end of the smoldering field, Lisa's terrified sobs echoing back to us long after they were gone from view.

Slowly, Luther turned and began to walk back to the village, ignoring the questions of the bewildered villagers and signaling for his fellow soldiers to follow him. As he walked, I began to drift into the background, not sure if I was supposed to follow. But my concerns were alleviated when he nodded in my direction.

As I fell in behind some of the soldiers, I saw Uthgar and Athéal in the front in deep conversation with Luther. My mind immediately went to the idea of Uthgar spewing protests at my being brought along, and I once again prayed for a falling tree limb or an angry squirrel or anything else to drop from the sky and knock him out. My life was broken up enough as it was without having to put up with his insults.

I was interrupted from my attempt to kill Uthgar with my mind as an armored hand was placed on my shoulder. As I turned I realized that it belonged to Marcus, the young soldier that I liked so much. He gave me a small smile as if to say '*welcome to the pack*'.

"Why is Luther keeping me with all of you?" I finally got to ask what my heart was wondering. "I may try to convince myself otherwise, but I am no soldier."

"I have no idea." He shrugged. "He must have taken a liking to you." When I didn't say anything he continued, "Hey I'm not going to complain. It'll be nice having someone else around who will talk to me. I mean Tryson is nice, but that elf is crazy."

I had to suppress a chuckle and it made my injured head throb. We walked until we reached the tavern. The fire cast ghostly shadows on the walls and I kept expecting old Dane to come flying out of the back room with drinks. So much had changed in such a short time.

Luther marched up to the bar and turned back to his men, his face a mask of concentration, like he was trying to piece together a puzzle that he couldn't see from anything more than his memory. Calculating chess moves without ever seeing the board. As he thought, the door opened and Tryson walked in, closely followed by Gladía and a third elf I didn't know.

"So what did the rider want, Luther?" he asked cheekily as he turned a chair around and sat down in it backwards, taking a moment to fold his arms over its back. "Giving us the typical friendly chance to surrender so we can be killed without a struggle?"

"It's Ronan, Tryson."

Tryson's face turned from joking to confusion in a heartbeat. "The rider claimed to be Ronan?"

"The rider *is* Ronan. I'm not sure how, but it's him."

The poor elf looked just as lost as I felt, and the rest of the men did not seem to understand any more than us. "I've always liked your sense of humor Luther, but I must admit I'm not quite getting this one." When Luther took too long to respond he leaned forward over the back of his chair and continued, "The last I checked Ronan Hazara was a pale, dead elf who has spent the last decade rotting in some unmarked grave in Arduelía, and not a dark skinned man with a pulse."

"Whoa!" I pulled myself away from the shock of what I just heard. "Ronan Hazara was an elf?"

Uthgar shook his head like I was an embarrassment and Luther responded to Tryson like I hadn't spoken.

"I told you Tryson, I'm not sure how, but it *is* Ronan. He knows things that only he could know."

"It cannot be him, Luther. I will not believe it."

"Believe what you want Tryson, I'm not trying to convince you."

"What did he want?"

"I believe he wants you."

There was a palpable silence in the room as all eyes turned towards Tryson, waiting for his response.

"Well you can tell him I already have a wife, so he's a bit out of luck." He finally spoke causing Gladía to chuckle under his breath. Luther's somber expression did not waiver however.

"This is serious, Tryson. If the rider really is Ronan, if he has indeed found some way to return, he's looking for something and on his way to that goal he wants revenge."

"Why would he want revenge on Tryson?" I interrupted again, this time a little louder.

Hearing my voice for a second time must have been too much for Uthgar to stand, because this time shaking his head wasn't enough. "Luther, why is this child here? We still have more than enough men to carry out any action you would have of us." The anger was evident in the frustration of his tone.

I was dismayed to find that several of the other soldiers seemed to share in Uthgar's opinion. And I began to realize what Marcus had been saying about Dû Vena Ruösa being a tough crowd.

Luther, however, continued to support me, "He is here because I have asked him to be here Uthgar, and that should be enough." Slowly he turned away from the soldier and addressed my question, "Eighteen years ago the old rebellion was gaining strength again. The Urröbbí was a large part of the new faction and Ronan was there leader. He was a ghost. No one knew who he was or what he looked like. There were just stories. A shadow in the night. A whisper in the dark. From the time between the Great War and then,

Dû Vena Ruösa was the private guard of King Romulás. He had never really recovered from the war, and he had been old and frail for decades. His mind was still sharp, but his body was broken.

Ronan was able to infiltrate our ranks without my father's knowledge. No one knew. No one suspected an elf. When the time to strike came he made his move and assassinated the King. They thought his death would cause the empire to crumble and it almost did. We were banished from the kingdom and the economic system the government had established threatened to collapse. Many refused to stay under the rule of the King's daughter. They call her the Witch Queen and the empire has begun to fester under her rule. No longer having a stake in the empire, we turned all of our efforts toward hunting Ronan.

When the king was killed the elves took it as a personal insult. That one of their own could do something so sinister, it disgusted them. There was an influx of elves to Dû Vena Ruösa's cause. Before then, our ranks were composed mostly of men. Tryson was the first to join and after over three years of hunting Ronan, we cornered him. Tryson was the one who fought and killed him. If the rider truly is Ronan, as I think he is, I believe he wants a chance to exact his revenge."

"Well then we can't just let him go!" I shouted, the pieces of the puzzle starting to fall into place.

Tryson laughed at my exclamation. "Aaron, all will be fine. Even if Luther is right, and this *is* somehow Ronan, I've defeated him before. Besides, whoever the man is, he is still just that, a man. And as such, will have a man's weaknesses." Turning away from me he once again questioned Luther, "What was the deal Luther?"

"He said he wanted 'the elf' in exchange for releasing his captives and leaving the village. You're the only elf here that he knows. Gladía and Lacríel joined our ranks after his death."

"Kind of an odd offer isn't it? He attacked this place without knowing we would come, there had to have been a reason?"

"He seems to think that you have information that he needs."

"No, that cannot be right. Even if I had information, he would know that I would never willingly divulge it."

"You're right, he would know that." Luther's tone was low and steady.

"So what is our move Luther? Do you have an idea what game he is playing?"

"No. But for the moment we play it all the same and see where he leads us. That is, as long as you are willing Tryson?"

"Risking life and limb to play a sinister game with a crazy man who thinks he is an even crazier dead elf? What's not to like?" The elf gave a sparkling smile that spread from the bottom of one pointy ear all the way to the other.

I was nearly speechless at how nonchalantly Tryson was taking all this. But to my surprise it was Uthgar who spoke up. "We can't send him in alone Captain. What is your plan?"

Luther thought for what seemed like an eternity, weighing his words carefully before responding, "He wants Tryson to come to this statue, but it is unrealistic to believe he hasn't chosen that spot for a reason. He will have men ready to prevent us from following him. Because the meeting will be at night, we can expect him to unleash the Mazenkyrie. He knows his foot soldiers alone cannot hold us back. We are at a disadvantage because Ronan knows our strategies, he knows how we operate. He will be expecting us to attack as a unified force and he will expect us to attack from downwind where his beasts cannot smell us coming. What he won't be expecting is for us to attack on two fronts, not with as few men as we have. We will send five men from the north. Their scent should draw the Mazenkyrie together. We will give away our position and then use it to our advantage. It is a risk, but it could allow the rest of us to flank them. And if we are to weaken Ronan's forces we must prevent as many of them as possible from maturing.

"If we are able to flank them we may be able to break an archer around their lines. Tryson, if you can hold him long enough, it could give Gladía enough time to take Ronan down."

"*If* I can hold him long enough?" Tryson retorted. "I'm far more concerned about Gladía missing his shot and striking me instead."

He was immediately smacked in the back of the head by his friend, "Just don't die before I get around their line. All I need is a crow's nest to fire from."

"Waterfalls!" I shouted, my mouth moving before my mind had completely finished formulating the thought.

The whole room went quiet and turned in my direction, like I had just said something that was completely irrelevant… which I suppose I had, but only because they didn't know the forest like I did. This was my chance at redemption. My chance to contribute to a victory.

"Mountain caves." Uthgar snapped back blandly, "See, I can say random words as well. Captain please? This is embarrassing."

Luther turned to me with a look on his face like I had maybe been hit a little harder on the head than originally thought, but I didn't give him time to speak, "No you don't get it, there's a grove not far from that statue, I have been there many times before. There is a pool there that is a miracle of nature. A swim in it heals all wounds."

"La fídal aqúina." Tryson's face lit up like a child's as he said the words. "A pool of life. I did not realize that there was one in Jericho. I must see it."

Ignoring Tryson, Luther finally spoke up again, "That's all good Aaron, but how does this pool's existence help us?"

"Gladía said that he needs a high place to get off a good shot. A place where Ronan's men won't hinder him. The pool is fed by several waterfalls coming down the cliff faces south of the grove. It's the perfect spot. Most villagers don't know how to get to the tops, let alone anyone from the desert. There's only one path and I know it. I can lead him there and he'll have plenty of cover to attack from without being spotted. If Tryson can fight his way to the grove, he'll have two bows covering him instead of one. We can end it from there."

Luther considered what I was saying for a moment, "If we force a distraction north of the statue, how long will it take you to get in position?"

"Not long. I know the route well. Elma and I go to the grove often. We can easily be in position by the time Tryson lures Ronan there."

As Luther took another moment, contemplating the implications of my plan, I allowed my eyes to wander around the room at its occupants. It's strange how many different thoughts and emotions can be transmitted through people's faces, without any words at all. Tryson's face was still lit up like a child's, probably still thinking about the magical 'fetal aqua' or whatever it was he called it. He didn't look like he had a care in the world. Like fighting some evil undead assassin was an everyday occurrence that was simply an amusing part of his morning routine.

Uthgar on the other hand, looked mutinous at the fact that I had come up with a plan that was even being considered. Like if the plan came from my mouth it was doomed to fail, and everyone would die a painful death because of it. Marcus had a thoughtful look on his face that reminded me of Luther and he kept nodding his head like he was impressed that I was stepping up and making myself heard, something he seemed afraid to do. Gladía kept fingering the bow in his hands like he was itching to inflict its deadly force on something, but his face seemed indifferent to what was happening in the room.

On the sill of the window a Peregrine falcon sat scanning the room the same way I was. After a moment, it looked in my direction and tilted its head. Its beady eyes staring me down like I was a worm it wanted to snap up for a late dinner, and as I looked at it, a chill ran down my spine. There was something that Tryson had said to me in passing earlier that was giving me an uneasy feeling, like I was unclean, or being watched by eyes that couldn't be seen. But I couldn't remember for the life of me what it was.

I didn't have long to dwell on it however, because at that moment Luther came to his decision. "Alright Aaron, tomorrow night when the sun sinks beneath the trees we will split. Uthgar, Marcus, Lacríel, Râven and Athéal, you will follow Tryson from the north as he advances to the statue. The rest of us will wait to counter their attack in the trees to the west. As they launch their assault, you must fall back to our location." Turning to me he continued, "As they are advancing Aaron, you must take Gladía to the falls. You must move quickly. Tryson cannot afford for you to be late."

Tryson rolled his eyes, "Why don't I just kill the sand rat and save everyone the trouble."

Luther gave Tryson a scolding look like *now's not the time*, but played it off well, "If you can kill him, kill him. But if not, fall back to the spring as quickly as possible without leaving yourself vulnerable."

"When they see Tryson is only being followed by five men won't they get suspicious?" I could no longer control the uneasy feeling that was growing stronger in the pit of my stomach. "What if they sense a trap?"

Luther looked back at me like questioning the plan was horrible luck. "We must hope that the Mazenkyrie are not smart enough to put that together."

"Do not fear, Aaron." Tryson tried to assure me as he threw a handful of peanuts at the falcon on the sill, "The Mazenkyrie are nothing more than rats with half-formed wings. Their primal instincts force them to act irrationally when a battle is at hand. Until they mature they can be easily manipulated."

The falcon tried to let out a sharp cry but a nut got lodged in its throat and all it could manage was a choking croak. I kept my eyes on it as it spit the nut out on the sill and disappeared into the night. I wished the feeling in my stomach had disappeared with it.

Chapter 21: Another Dumb Idea

The sun was shining, the birds were out, and there was a cool autumn breeze blowing over his stubbly scalp, what was not to like? Other than the multiple bone fractures, the likely internal bleeding and the limp elf draped over his neck like some kind of bizarre scarf that caused pain with every step he took. Although on the bright side Terrick had managed to negotiate a splint for his broken wrist, an extra couple layers of clothing for warmth as well as padding on his ribs, and since he was keeping quiet and leading the Urröbbí to the Blue Rock Mountains like they wanted, they hadn't been hitting him quite as much as usual. All things Terrick considered should fall into the win column. However, as the day wore on the bark splint was starting to chaff, the elf seemed to gain ten pounds with every step and every second brought them closer to marshlands that he was in no way sure he could navigate.

The entire time they had been marching through the forests of Jericho, Terrick had been trying to think of a way he could get himself out of the mess he was in, but nothing useful had made it through his muddled mind. When he had agreed to take the Urröbbí to the mountains it was because he really hadn't had any other options. If he ran out of uses he'd be killed, and faking like he knew where he was going sounded way better than saying *sorry boys you're on your own* and taking a sword in the gut. The problem was as soon as they got to the marshlands and the first warrior dropped out of site through a sink hole they would realize that not only did Terrick not know what he was doing, but he had probably led them all to their death, which Terrick assumed wouldn't make them too happy.

As he walked he found himself almost subconsciously thinking about Aaron. He had been so busy trying to save his own life for the last week he hardly had time to think about anyone else. But now that his only task was placing one foot in front of the other and dragging an elf into the mountains he had time to let his mind wander, and honestly, the mental images of his family were probably the only things keeping him from a screaming insanity. With every painful step he thought of his cousin and wished that he was here with him. Aaron would know what to do. He was always the one with the plans. Plans on how to win at chess. How to talk to girls. How to steal apples without taking a rake to the head. Aaron was the brains while Terrick was the brawn. Jarron always used to joke when they were younger that the two of them together may actually be able to produce the work of one normal human being. Thinking of his family made him smile while taking his mind off the task at hand - the likely final trudge of a dying man.

As he marched he began to wonder if he would have spent his last week at home any differently had he known where he would be now. There were good moments like time he had spent in the fields with his father or sparing with Aaron, but mostly he thought about Sienna. Thought about the way he had made a fool of himself in Dane's tavern, and the way Sienna had gotten embarrassed when he did it. It all seemed rather foolish now, how small of an issue it really was in the grand scheme of things. Here he was marching to his death with his home likely on the brink of destruction and a few weeks earlier he couldn't even build up the courage to talk to a girl. The small kiss he had received before departing the village was nothing more than a tease he didn't deserve. He wasn't worthy of her.

He wondered what it would have been like if he had one last chance. One last moment to talk to her. Would he be able to tell her how he felt? He thought so, after all, at this point what did he have to lose? Maybe Aaron was right and somehow Sienna was able to actually feel something for him other than embarrassment. And if that was the case there was no way he would let another opportunity pass him by. If by some miracle he was able to get himself out of his predicament, he would tell Sienna all the things that he wanted to tell her: that she was beautiful, and funny, and smart, and that he loved her so much it hurt sometimes.

At that moment, while he was lost in blissful thought about the girl of his dreams, he lost track of where he was walking and stepped into a hole, falling to a knee. As he fell he noticed two things simultaneously, one, busting your kneecap on a tree root is not a pleasant way to bring in the afternoon; and two, that the elf noticeably tensed as he fell and almost dropped her. It was one of those reactions that you couldn't control, like gagging when something is caught in your throat, or punching Arctone when he calls you Skipper. As she entered free fall she had sensed it and tensed, grabbing ahold of the one thing she could – him – and that meant that she was awake. You don't notice falling if you're in a week-long coma. At least Terrick assumed that you didn't.

Thinking on his feet he made a split second decision to act like nothing had happened, even though he couldn't help but be a little angered by the elf. Here he was, feeling like he had been trampled by a horse, playing the hero and carrying some stranger league after league while she was only pretending to sleep. Part of him felt like struggling to his feet and dumping the elf right on her butt. Who was she to hitch a ride on him like he was some kind of farm mule? *Terrick's Pony Service! Complete with comfy shoulders for sleeping!*

But the other part of him remembered the bruises on her arms, and the image of her being dragged through Rehorr and took pity on her. She was probably terrified. If the Urröbbí knew she was awake, who knew what they would do her. I mean there had to be a reason the soldiers had brought her with them from the village. The thought sent a shiver down his spine as he continued to trudge along in silence. As the sun began to sink over the distant mountains Terrick began to wonder if this would be the last sunset he'd ever see. A blood stained sky crying out for him as it turned slowly to dark.

…

Night fell quickly in the forest and the temperature dropped with the sun. It was cold enough that you could see the moisture in your breathe. Cold enough that your fingers would turn purple if your hands weren't tucked under your arms. The Urröbbí had made camp for the night and had set up several fires to keep warm, none of which were close enough to Terrick to be anything more than a pleasant tease. Instead, he could be found at the base of a tree close enough to a fire where if a soldier wasn't standing in the way he could at least feel a small amount of the flames warmth radiate in his direction. His arms were wrapped around the elf that, if she was conscious, was doing nothing to protect herself from the bitter cold sting of the night air.

Somewhere through the trees Terrick could hear the sick warrior who he had fought to the brink of death being whipped by his former comrades. They had been dragging him away and beating him on and off for the last two days, feeding him just enough in weeds, mushrooms, and muddy water to keep him alive. The Urröbbí seemed to think that he had deserted the force and apparently the Urröbbían punishment for that was death by slow torture and crappy food. At first Terrick thought it served the guy right. The soldier had attempted to kill him, not to mention the hand he had in braking Lisa's arm. But now, as his cries of pain echoed off the trees like a horn in the night, he found himself almost starting to feel bad for the warrior. After all, he had done nothing but carry out Ronan's orders, and now he was being beating to within an inch of his life more often than old Dane hit on Melinda at the Tavern.

With nearly all of the warriors huddled around fires or interrogating "the deserter", there were multiple times during the early moments of the night where Terrick had contemplated launching some ill-conceived escape attempt. However, he had enough sense to realize intense cold of the night meant that they wouldn't have survived long without a fire. The problem with a fire was that while it was great for warmth, it was also equally useful as a spotlight for anyone searching for you, so he had resigned himself to the idea that he would simply have to figure out some plan for freeing himself in the morning. Everything would be made so much easier if the elf would only wake up and lend a hand or come up with a helpful idea for getting them to safety, heck at this point he would even take her adding some comic relief in his miserable life.

A bone chilling wind blew through the trees and made the fires flicker like distant ghosts. In his arms the elf gave a violent shiver before stiffening up unnaturally, like she was worried she had given herself away, but it was too late. As numb as he was, with his arms draped around her it would have been nearly impossible for Terrick not to notice the elf shaking like a leaf.

"Ugh," Terrick grunted, pushing the elf away from him "Yer just using me you are. You've been awake this whole time haven't you?"

The elf said nothing, but simply rolled to a stop a foot away from him, staying limp as a dead fish the entire time. Her hair spilled over her face in leaf riddled streams.

He stared at her for a moment before realizing that she wasn't about to give in that easily, like *oops, yup, you caught me, sorry for making you carry me for three days through a forest while you walked until your feet bled. You wanna be best friends?*

"And don't think I haven't been on to you for a while now. I felt you tense up when I almost fell earlier." When she again didn't respond he continued, "Fine, lay there and act like you can't hear me, but I'm done doing you favors. You can lay there and freeze for all I care. And it'll probably happen quickly on a night like tonight, especially with them silk clothes on."

Terrick kept waiting for her to say something, but she was either stubbornly choosing to freeze to death, or he had made a horrible judgment call by getting mad and yelling at an unconscious woman. Neither option made Terrick feel good about himself, but he was sore and tired and cold and at the moment, all he wanted was to be in control of an action again, even if it wasn't a good one.

"Ugh!" he grunted again as he rolled closer to the fire and shut his eyes trying to get some sleep. His conscious didn't let him rest for very long however, and his anger with the elf cooled a bit every time the wind blew. If the night was cold for him, it had to be near unbearable for her, and if nothing else, her silence meant that she was one tough woman, and he had to respect that.

He was just about to roll over and gather the elf back into his arms when a voice behind him spoke in a hiss.

"Real chivalrous of you to leave me here to freeze, boy."

Terrick flipped over in a second to see the elf, who still lay on the ground, glaring back in his direction.

"*Boy?*" Terrick growled. If there was one thing he hated more than anything it was being treated like a child. For a moment he imagined Arctone's face on the elf's body, which, aside from being really weird, made him want to pull back and punch her in the face. "This *boy* has spent the last three days carrying you over twenty leagues. The least you could do is show a little gratitude."

"I'll be sure to give you a medal for your valor when we escape this mess." She countered sarcastically, "But in the meantime slide over here so we both don't freeze."

His response was incredulous, "What? You want me to keep you warm after what you've put me through the last two days? I could have let them continue to drag you over roots and stumps."

"But you didn't, and I am… grateful for that." She said the words like they were painful for her to speak. "But right now you are being stubborn."

"*I'm* being stubborn." Terrick couldn't believe her audacity. How could she accuse him of being stubborn after she had pretended to be asleep for three days, and then had not even owned up to it after he caught her in the act?

"Yes," she hissed, still at a whisper. "You know as well as I do that we're too far away from those fires for us to not catch hypothermia at this temperature."

"Hippo-therma-what?" Terrick's brain was starting to cramp up. He couldn't believe how wrong he had been in his initial idea of the elf's character.

"My Gods you're dense. Hypothermia, where we both freeze to death." When Terrick was still slow to comprehend she hissed, "We turn blue and start growing icicles. If we want to last the night we'll have to share body heat."

Terrick could hardly find words for how he was feeling. On one hand, deep down, he knew she was right. If they didn't do something to conserve heat they may not make it through the night. On the other hand, this elf had used then insulted him and he wanted nothing more than to let her freeze. It took an intense internal struggle, but reason finally won. As much as he hated it, she was right, it would be stubborn, and stupid of him to refuse.

"Well then roll yourself over here so we can get to sleep." Terrick finally conceded, and after a few seconds he found himself back in his original position, with his arms draped around the elf. She shivered violently again against him, her skin already like ice to the touch. If she was miserable however, she did a good job of hiding it. It was an odd sensation that Terrick was feeling. He had spent the last week working to free and protect this elf who he expected to be kind, peaceful, and loving, only to find out that she was actually a fiery shrew. And yet, it felt good to him to have his arms wrapped around her.

"What's your name, elf?" Terrick finally asked.

She shivered again before responding, "You should get some sleep."

She didn't speak again for the rest of the night.

...

The temperature rose with the sun the following morning and the fresh heat couldn't come soon enough. Terrick had lost feeling in his hands half way through the night and the sharp tingling sensation that announced its return had him wishing he could simply cut them off. The elf was still wrapped in his arms, her soft body pressed tightly to his own. The feeling was almost... normal, and Terrick kept his eyes shut trying to remember the last moment in his life that had felt anything close to that. The moment of solitude did not last long as he was roughly kicked awake by the long-haired warrior with the scar.

"Wake up." He snarled, "We must be moving now."

"What no breakfast?" Terrick responded sarcastically. When all the warrior did was scowl back at him he continued, "Don't worry about it, I'm not hungry anyway. Time to wake up Blondie." He added, turning to the elf.

When the elf didn't stir he gave her a light shake to which she rolled over limp in the grass again, an exact replica of the previous night.

"Really?" Terrick grumbled exasperatedly, "We're doing this again? Wake up!" When she once again remained motionless he turned and shrugged speechlessly up to the warrior. He didn't really know what he was expecting. It wasn't like the warrior would defend him; the man didn't even know the elf was faking. Instead all he received was a confused look and a shake of the head before the man turned and walked away.

When the warrior was out of sight the elf's eyes shot open. "You can't let them know I'm awake!" She hissed.

"Why the heck not?" Terrick snapped back, starting to get really irritated with the entire situation.

"Just… You'll have to carry me for another day."

"Oh, okay. Well I'd love to, but I have this cramp in my leg from carrying you cross country, and it's really pretty nasty, so it's gonna make jumping through hoops for you pretty tough."

"You are impossible!" She growled through clenched teeth, "Just do what I tell you, trust me." After a pained look she sighed and continued, "I need your help."

Immediately she had won. Terrick would have loved nothing more than to tell her that she could walk her fragile looking butt to the mountains on her own. But for that split second she had looked vulnerable; like she really did need his help and he lost the ability to argue with her.

"Well you don't have to look so upset about asking for help." He threw in harshly. He didn't want her to know that she had already won.

"Who are you talking to?" A voice behind him questioned.

Terrick turned to see the black warrior from the clearing eying him suspiciously.

"No one." He responded quickly as the elf's eyes snapped shut again.

"Ve move now. Drag her vith you."

Terrick bent slowly, scooped the elf back over his shoulders and stared intensely at the warrior. "Ready when you are." He put on the most insolent smile he could manage and marched past the man.

The walk through the forest wasn't any better than it had been the day before. If anything it was worse. Terrick's muscles ached with the exertion of walking such a long distance in such bad shape. It had gotten to the point where even the world around him seemed like it was grasping at straws to survive. The forest seemed to grow grayer and more forlorn with every step, like it was decaying as he marched through it, and he couldn't decide whether it was the awful weather or the depressing state of his life that was making it look so. But he wasn't going to complain or show any sign of weakness. Not even if he was carrying an ungrateful elf with two perfectly good legs for the awesome reason of "just because".

As the minutes melted into hours, the trees became thinner and fewer in number and the Blue Rock Mountains loomed overhead like some giant threatening monster waiting to swallow the small troop whole. What was left of the forest was deathly silent. Any sign of forest life had been left behind for some time. Nothing but the plants lived in this small area on the outskirts of the Jericho forests.

They had entered swamp territory and that meant anything that moved had the ability to kill them. There were no more squirrels, or birds, or fluffy bunnies that made you want to throw out a blanket and have a picnic. Any squirrels, birds, or fluffy bunnies that were unlucky enough to wander here most likely ended up in a larger, not so fluffy something's stomach.

During the times Terrick had been to the swamps before, he had been with Aaron, hunting the wild boar that lived in the northern edge of the swamplands. It was dangerous, the boars were close to four hundred pounds, with ten-inch tusks and a nasty temper, but they both had bows and the ability to step quietly. It would have been hard for an obese pig with a brain the size of an acorn to catch them off guard. That was the northern edge of the swamp and Terrick knew enough to realize that the farther south you traveled, the more dangerous the area became. The desert troop was entering far to the south where things that, until now, had only lived in stories, dwelt.

Where they were entering, boar would be the least of their problems. They were headed straight into swampdragon territory, and for those of you who have never seen a swampdragon face to face, count your blessings, because they would make you want to crawl into bed and snuggle with the aforementioned boar. Swampdragons are the world's most refined hunters, the top of the food chain. For those who have not heard the stories, imagine a ten foot long salamander, with an extra fifteen feet of neck and tail, and a mouth filled with a double row of teeth, sharp and strong enough to shatter a man's femur. Now give the thing four feet covered in rip-your-face-off talons, and glands that secrete a neurotoxin cocktail that'll paralyze you in minutes and you have a really large swampy problem.

They were amphibious, so they could survive in or out of water, but spent most of their time slithering around the swamps, out of sight, and their scales secreted oils that allowed them to cut through the water with ghost-like speed. The males were about half the size of the females and had wings that they could unfurl after breeching the swamps surface, launching them into flight in a heartbeat, but the males aren't really the problem. They usually sized their prey up above water level and, as fast and agile as they are, you can fight what you can see. The problem is always the females. They tended to stay below the surface, and they had become experts at finding brakes in the ground to pop their snake-like heads through and snag an unsuspecting boar, only to drag it back under water so it could take its time feeding. Anyway, let's just say that Terrick wasn't exactly looking forward to traveling through their territory.

He found himself being very careful about where he was stepping, trying his hardest not to make any unnecessary noises. He wasn't really sure why he was bothering with the extra care, the warriors had no idea how dangerous the area was and they were doing nothing to try and conceal their footsteps. All of the noise and jumbled conversation was making Terrick nervous and every time a tree cast a shadow over his face he found himself snapping his head to the sky expecting to be attacked.

Slowly the trees grew few and far between and the swamp came into view. The stench of the swamplands began to overwhelm Terrick. To put it mildly, the place reeked of death. Like a combination of rotting flesh, lizard waste, and the fish nuggets from the tavern. Far from the sweet smell of the trees of Northern Jericho that Terrick had already begun to forget. In this place, every step that you took was a risk.

Terrick stopped moving and turned back to the warriors behind him. "Someone needs to find me a stick. About five foot long should do."

"Vut do you need a stick for? Just keep valking." A dumb looking warrior ordered.

Terrick could barely contain his frustration. "Fine, don't get me a stick and follow me blindly hoping that I can find a path through this place without walking over a sink hole. Because as soon as I fall through the ground into the swamp and become lizard chow, you're on your own. Good luck getting through the rest of it."

The warrior blinked dimly back for a moment before turning and shouting, "Ve need a stick. Find a stick!" to the rest of the men.

It took nearly twenty minutes, but a good sized stick was in Terrick's hand soon enough, and adjusting the elf's weight so that he could balance her with only one of his arms, he began his dangerous task. He tested each step by jamming the stick he had been given into the ground in front of him, the way he and Aaron had done when they had gone hunting boar. The swamps were a tricky place, some areas looked totally safe but the stick went right through the ground because it was nothing more than a layer of thick algae and others looked impossible to pass, only to have the stick prove otherwise.

The going was slow as every inch of land needed poked and prodded and the warriors could only walk where Terrick had first stepped. Several times a stray warrior had wandered a few feet off of the trail only to plummet through the ground into the murky swamp below, never to be seen again. Terrick didn't want to think about what happened to them under the brown muck. Before they started their journey over the swamps Terrick had instructed the warriors that silence was essential and other than the few that had fallen, they had done a fairly good job of not attracting attention to themselves as they passed. Terrick had been keeping his eyes peeled but had only twice seen a pair of reptilian eyes sticking up out of the murky waters of the swamp.

The men had been walking for hours and the Blue Rock Mountains now loomed massively overhead, casting them into permanent shadow. Their base was little over a league away, and Terrick was starting to think he may actually be able to survive another obstacle in his long journey when off to his right in the distance there was a terrible screech. The sound was enough to make Terrick lose his balance and step off course, sinking up to his knee in swamp water. He was able to catch himself, but awkwardly, and one of his shoulders drove up into the elf's stomach, causing her to tense again.

"Will you be careful!" she whispered into his ear almost inaudibly. "I would like to live through the day."

"If this arrangement is bothering you so badly you're more than welcome to carry me for a bit." Terrick mumbled back, quickly pulling his foot out of the water before anything could grab it.

"Just be quiet and watch your step." She fired back.

"You know you're awfully bossy for someone who's askin' for help. Don't you go forgetting that I'm doin' you a favor."

"That was back when I thought you were actually capable of helping without getting us both killed you clumsy ox." She hissed again.

Something in Terrick finally gave way with the elf's insult. It wasn't that he had been asked for one-sided favors, only to be bossed around. It wasn't that he was being forced to cater to an ungrateful elf with a superiority complex. It wasn't even the hurt that came from realizing that the person he had gone out of his way to protect thought so little of him. It was that insult that was the final straw, and the one that made him think of home.

Only one person got to call Terrick a farm animal and get away with it, and that was his baby sister… and this elf was not Lisa.

"That's it!" he shouted before dropping the elf a full six feet to the ground behind him and pointing down at her accusingly. "The elf's awake!"

Every head immediately turned at Terrick's outburst and the ugly long-haired warrior with the scar was in his face in an instant.

"What do you me she's awake?" he ordered, his eyes narrowing as he sized up the seemingly unconscious elf. Terrick was tired of being ordered around. He had been marched all the way out of the forest and half way through the swamplands of Jericho, and he was done with it.

"What do you *think* I mean by she's awake?" he mocked the warrior, who proceeded to lift his blade to Terrick's throat. "Get that away from me!" Terrick continued in his rage, knocking the blade away with his stick. "I mean she's been playing all of you. She's been talking to me the entire time we've been walking!"

"She doesn't look avake." Another warrior imputed dumbly, and Terrick had to hand it to the elf, she was good at feigning unconsciousness.

"Well poke her with that sword a couple times. She'll start moving around." He knew his anger was getting the better of him, but still he just couldn't find the energy to care.

Terrick's words must have been enough for the elf to realize that she would be getting no more help from him because she finally gave in and rolled onto her back before sitting up.

"Thanks for the help boy!" She spat again, "You're a dog."

Terrick raised his eyebrows, "Yea well you can only kick a dog so many times before it bites ya' Blondie. You can do your own walking from now on."

When the elf had first sat up, the look of shock plastered all over their faces, which would have at any other been hilarious, illustrated the effectiveness of the elf's deception. Unfortunately, the long haired warrior recovered quickly enough, taking two steps toward the elf and back-handing her across the face.

"Oiy!" Terrick shouted. As much as he disliked the elf he wasn't about to simply stand by if they started abusing her. "She doesn't deserve that."

Once again Terrick found a sword pointed at his throat. "You stay out of this and keep walking as you were told!" the warrior ordered.

"No, you know what? I think I'm just about done leading you anywhere." Terrick snipped back. "Why don't you just kill me and find your own way through the swamps?"

The warrior drew back his sword, a murderous look on his face as if he would have liked nothing more than to run Terrick through at that instant, but instead he hesitated. The vein on his forehead looked like it was about to explode as he finally he dropped the sword to his side and turned back to the elf. Glancing at another warrior he barked a single word "arm" and the second warrior roughly obeyed, pulling the elf to her feet and holding one of her arms outstretched. She looked terrified.

"Whoa, whoa! What are you doin'?" Terrick stammered.

The warrior rounded on Terrick again; the wicked gleam in his eye working its way into a full blown smile. "You will lead us through the mountains as we agreed!" He shouted.

"Or else what? What'll you do to her?" he stalled, but he already thought he knew the answer.

"Take us where we need to go or I'll take her other hand."

"Her other hand?" Terrick questioned, not quite following

"Yes, the other one. The first one isn't negotiable, you have crossed me for the last time."

Terrick's blood ran cold. He couldn't let anything happen to an innocent woman, no matter how big of a pain she was. He kept trying to think of a way to buy them more time, but to what end? It didn't matter, nothing was coming to him. The warrior had turned back to the elf and had placed the tip of his blade to her arm. The look of horror on her face was too much for him to stand and he was forced to look away from the scene that was unfolding before him, not wanting to witness what would happen next. He tried to focus his attention on something else, anything else, when his eyes finally locked on another pair. Stale, yellow, reptilian eyes, half submerged in the dirty swamp water. As he fought to control his initial shock, he realized it was not just one pair, but five, and all were locked on their position. All of the noise the dispute between Terrick and the warrior must have finally drawn attention to their group.

Terrick snapped his head up as the warrior raised his sword to strike. "Okay!" he yelled. "I'll take you wherever you need to go!"

The warrior looked back at Terrick, but didn't lower his weapon. "Of course you will," he sneered, "But there is a price for your insolence. You cannot stop this from happening." He turned back to the elf and lifted his arms again.

"Yes I can!" Terrick shouted.

This time the warrior lowered his weapon as he turned. "And how are you going to do that? Are you going to hit me with your little stick?" He let out an oily chuckle, apparently enjoying the thought.

Terrick raised the stick and the warrior tensed, like he couldn't believe Terrick was actually dumb enough to attack him with a piece of dead wood. The elf looked even more shocked as they locked eyes for a moment before he made his move. But instead of swinging at the warrior, Terrick heaved the weapon clear over his head causing it to splash right where he had seen the sets of eyes.

The confused look on the warrior's face was worth losing his only way of getting back out of the swamps safely. "Why would you do that?" he questioned, but Terrick never had to respond.

A moment after the words had escaped the warrior's mouth, the water exploded. Five, six, seven... Terrick lost count as a group of winged lizards burst through the surface of the water, the sun glinting savagely off the scaly wings dragging them into the sky. Terrick had never seen a live swampdragon before. They had only been painted canvases and skins that traveling hunters kept as prizes. The real thing was even more terrifying than he imagined. Their murky brown scales and yellow eyes matched the hue of the dirty, swamp water and they were fast. Much faster than anything that large had a right to be.

Terrick only had a second to act in the brief moment of hesitation the swampdragon's appearance had caused. He sprinted forward and tackled the elf at full speed knocking both her and the guard holding her to the ground with a thud. They landed beside the chained warrior, who had spent the last few days in a barely conscious state. He now looked both wide awake, and terrified at the scene unfolding before him. Several of the warriors had run screaming at the site of the monsters and, forgetting their surroundings, dropped through sinkholes into the water almost immediately. Those who had kept their wits about them drew their swords and spears in an attempt to keep the flying creatures at bay.

Terrick had knocked the elf to the ground just as a monster swooped directly over where they had been standing. The dragon snapped the long haired warrior's head in its jaws before plunging back into a hole in the swamp, dragging the struggling body down with it. Everywhere through the swamp chaos had broken out, and the warriors were at a clear disadvantage not being able to maneuver or form a defensive front for fear of falling into the brown water. The dragons commanded the field, diving at individual soldiers before retreating just out of sword point or plunging back into the water with a victim. Occasionally one would stick its head out too far trying to strike and lose its neck to a blade. Others picked their spots more carefully and only attacked the unprotected backsides of the warriors.

"We have to move!" Terrick yelled to the elf over the screams of the raging battle.

The elf nodded wide-eyed and for the first time seemed at a loss for words. In a heartbeat, they were on their feet and had started to weave through the battle-field at full speed toward the mountains. In one hand Terrick held onto the long chain that was attached to the elf's wrists, and in the other he clasped the saber of a deceased warrior that he had found close to where they had fallen.

Just as the warriors had begun to fend off the monsters in the sky, the creatures switched tactics and started attacking from below. Throughout the swamp the long heads of the females started shooting through small gaps in the earth and clasping the exposed ankles of warriors. Sometimes they would be pulled entirely under the surface, other times the gap would be too small and only a leg would disappear as the warrior collapsed in a screaming heap only to be finished by an aerial assault.

"What were you thinking?!?" The elf screamed as they ducked under the snapping jaw of a diving beast, "You're going to get us both killed!"

"Well I didn't see you coming up with any ideas!" Terrick screamed back swinging his saber wildly and cutting a lizard out of the sky. "Unless it's easier to escape with only one hand. In which case I'm sorry for ruining your plans!"

"I can't use the hand you've saved me if I'm dead, boy!"

Terrick wanted to defend his decision but the ground in front of him exploded as another beast emerged. A quick, sloppy, slash of his sword saved his life, but didn't prevent him from being slammed into as the headless swampdragon flopped on top of him pinning him to the ground. The thing weighed a ton, reminding him of the time Aaron had figured out how to get Elma to lay on him as he was sleeping, and causing him to scream out in agony as the pressure on his broken ribs increased. To Terrick's surprise, the elf started to make her way back toward him to help, but he wasn't sure if it was because she cared or because he was still holding on to the other end of the chain that was clasped around her wrists. Either way, with her eyes on the chain she lost track of her surroundings and made one wrong step, falling through the surface of the water and out of sight.

"No!!" Terrick shouted as he tightened his grasp on the chain.

With the weight of the dead swampdragon still crushing him, he summoned the last of his strength and started to slowly reel in the elf. If she was still attached to the other end, he could still save her. It took a few tense seconds but slowly the elf's arms and head popped through the surface of the water and she was able to grab a hold of firm ground.

"Pull harder!" she screamed franticly, grabbing at grass and weeds whose roots were too shallow to stay in the moist ground.

Terrick was pulling with all his might, but something was pulling her back away from him. The elf was in tears as she fought to stay above the water. As the struggle continued a second lizard landed nearby and started to make its way to their location. It was only feet away when a spear stuck in its scaled side and it screeched in pain. Forgetting its prey, the swampdragon turned its attention to its wound where it snapped the spear close to the point before unleashing a terrible roar and diving back into the murky water. Terrick looked in the direction of the throw just in time to see one of the handful of remaining warriors pulled below the surface. He focused all of his remaining energy as his vision started to darken and pulled on the chain with all of his might. The elf was finally pulled onto solid ground, but she still had the mouth of a swampdragon clasped firmly around her ankle. She gave out a cry and kicked it with her free leg causing it to release her and slither back below the surface, but the damage was done. Terrick knew those bites were fatal.

"No!" He pleaded, trying to worm his way out from beneath the dead swampdragon, but it was clear the elf was already running out of time. Her crying had stopped and she was looking even paler than normal.

"Hold on!" he cried again before a sound caught his attention. Terrick looked away from the elf as a fresh wave of pain reverberated through his ribs. Standing over the dead lizard was a second swampdragon. It eyed him momentarily, tilting its reptilian head as if it were trying to decide whether it wanted to eat him then or drag him under the swamp for a late night snack. As it glared, it snapped its jaws twice and tasted the air with its tongue, venomous foam frothing from the corners of its mouth. *So this is where it ends.* Terrick thought to himself. *Unable to defend myself against a giant freakin lizard...*

You know how it's said that your life will flash before your eyes as you die? Well that's crap. All Terrick saw was the swampdragon's horrible, toothy mouth open one last time before a white light blinded him. Whatever the light was, it was so bright that Terrick had to squint to see anything as it caused twenty swampdragons to screech simultaneously in irritation. The load on his ribs lessoned and the sight of the swampdragon was replaced with the craziest image he had ever seen. Out of the sky, and through the light, dropped a man, or at least what looked like a man, except for the fact that the guy was only about four feet tall and had wings. Enormous, pure white, feathery wings. The kind that you would want to make the world's most comfortable pillow out of.

From the waist down the man was clothed in tattered brown pants, with nothing on his feet, like some kind of homeless nomad. But from the waist up, he could have been carved out of granite, every muscle was clealy defined. He looked like four feet of solid trapezoids, deltoids and steroids, as well as fifty other kinds of 'oids' that Terrick didn't even know the names to. He had sandy blond hair that was short and neatly cut, and lightning yellow eyes like pools of gold, that seemed to look straight through Terrick's mind and scorch his soul with an electric jolt. As the man moved towards him, he realized that he was no longer afraid. His mission in this life was complete. This council that the Urröbbí was hunting, whoever they were, would remain safe.

An angel. Terrick thought to himself.

In the blinding light he groped around the grass and found one of the dying elf's hands. He squeezed it as tightly as he could. *I'll see you again in eternity,* he thought, before letting the darkness consume him.

Chapter 22: Cat and Mouse

Word travels fast in a small village so it was not long before Jarron knew of the proposal Ronan had made Luther, as well as the fact that Tryson was going to do everything in his power to get the hostages back safely, even if it meant sacrificing his own life. What Jarron didn't know was that I was going to be taking part in the night's attack, and I didn't really feel it was necessary to inform him. With Lisa a captive and Terrick... I couldn't bring myself to think the words, he was barely holding it together as it was, it would kill him if he knew I was planning on risking my neck as well.

I felt like Luther and Tryson had gone over every detail of our plan a hundred times throughout the day. They had planned an schemed, analyzed attack strategies and formations, thought about what counter attacks and traps the enemy might plan for them, and how to adjust to those attacks. They talked with me about the layout of the forest, what areas could be used to set a trap quickly and what areas to avoid for fear that a trap may be set for them. They had covered every possible angle of the night's mission with a fine-tooth comb and had honed their plan. It was like watching a master chess plot so many moves in advance, that the match was over before it had even begun. In all, I should have felt pretty good about our chances of success. I should have been confident in our ability to save the hostages, but in all honesty, I still had a horrible feeling churning in the pit of my stomach. I still felt like we were being watched, it was the same uneasy feeling I had the previous night when the plan had originally been conceived.

Somehow Ronan and his men had been one step ahead of us the entire time. He had been able to set traps for Terrick and I on our way to Alleron and for Dû Vena Ruösa when we had returned to the village. He had anticipated moves that should have been secret to him. The words spoken by the warrior Terrick and I had captured in the woods – *Ronan always knows* – kept ringing in my ears and the more I tried to shake the feelings of unease and convince myself that everything was going to work out, the tighter my fears twisted in my stomach.

I had a conversation earlier with Marcus about the finer points of the plan. We would be setting out in shifts so that we would all arrive where we needed to be at the correct times. Gladía and I were to leave last, so that Luther's ambush had time to be launched, allowing us a clear passage to the spring. In order for the plan to be successful, the enemy couldn't know that we were with the main body of men.

Tryson would leave first, but it would take him some time to fight his way to the spring. I had tried to press upon Luther that I could get Gladía to the falls earlier without anyone seeing us, but he refused to risk us falling into a trap before everyone else was in position. He was confident that the distraction his men would produce could buy us enough time to skirt around their flank unseen, and with minimal risk. Whereas if we left early and were captured or killed, there would be no way for the rest of the men to know of our fate before it was too late. Marcus had been reassuringly confident in the plan, claiming that when Dû Vena Ruösa had time to actually plan an attack, they couldn't lose.

It was nice to have Marcus around. With Terrick gone he had sort of taken on the role of being my unofficial big brother. I wasn't entirely sure if it was of his own accord or if Luther had assigned him to be my babysitter, but I hoped it was the former. At least he seemed to enjoy himself when he was around me, which was more than I could say about the rest of the soldiers, or even the rest of the villagers for that matter. I knew that none of them truly blamed me for what had happened to Dane, but it still seemed as though I had let the whole village down. Without Terrick, Lisa, and Sienna around to pick me up, I was stuck in a dark haze, and it seemed like I was getting a lot of that pitying look that wasn't really intended as an insult, but it still stung like one.

Marcus had helped to make life seem a little more livable again. He knew that my cousin's absence was taking a heavy toll on me even if I wouldn't admit it and he never let me out of his sight for long. He spent his time alternating between keeping me company and going back to his carving, continuing to intricately sculpt the fine details of the bear. However, he was still reluctant to talk about the carving, other than to say that it was an excellent way to occupy your mind before a battle. He even gave me a spare knife and a small chunk of wood to try and whittle for a bit, and he was right, while I worked the hours slipped away like minutes. The sad part was that in the hours that passed, all I had managed to carve was something that eerily resembled a slightly smaller piece of wood and nothing like the horse that I had been attempting to create. Marcus said that if you tilted your head and squinted a bit it kind of looked like a pig. Let's just say that carving couldn't be added to my list of talents.

Slowly the day wound down, the shadows cast by the trees growing longer as the sun sank beneath the horizon. As the life in the village began to head inside for the night, the men of Dû Vena Ruösa ventured into the outstretched arms of the forest. First it was Tryson, followed by Marcus, Uthgar, Râven, Athéal and an elf whose name I couldn't remember. Soon after that the rest of the men moved out and I was left alone with Gladía. We wouldn't have to wait long to make our move, just long enough to created distance between ourselves and the Luther's men.

As we waited, I pulled the small chunk of wood out of my pocket and played with it while Gladía absentmindedly fingered the tip of one of his arrows. Its shaft was long and made of a red wood that I was unfamiliar with, which was fletched with what looked like the feathers of a swan.

"Where did you get your arrows from?" I finally questioned , anxious to break the silence that suddenly felt very confining.

Gladía looked down at the arrow and studied it like he was trying to recall every detail of its existence. "All of the elves of my clan get our arrows from Mother Tree in Aríamoné." At my look of confusion he gave a little laugh and continued, "My my! Tryson said you knew little of elves but I found that hard to believe until now. It's the great Elf city in the forests north of Ardue`an. When we reach adulthood, eighteen by your standards, every elf is given a branch that they may carve their arrows from if they are to be a warrior. It is a great honor, the wood is strong and flexible, and it makes the best arrows. Very low air resistance and they are said to be unbreakable, though Tryson always manages to find a way. He draws his bow too hard. I myself have never broken one."

The amount of pride in his voice as he talked about his weaponry was unmistakable. It seemed like each arrow was a child of his, and I suppose that in a sense they were, if he had indeed carved each one himself. Looking at the arrow from across the room, it appeared to be flawless. I would have been proud of it as well, had I been the one to craft it.

"And the feathers?" I asked, wanting to hear more about the elf's homeland.

"The feathers are from a Capatchie. It is a bird native to home, much like the red tailed hawk that dwells in this area, but with long white tail feathers. They are the favorite pet of the elves, and are very noble and distinguished creatures."

"Do all elves use those feathers?"

"No, not all." He replied, "Tryson, for one, uses eagle tail feathers."

As the words hit me, I immediately dropped the chunk of wood that I was toying with to the floor. My conscious was screaming warnings that my mind couldn't quite make sense of. It was not so much the knowledge of where Tryson was snagging his tail feathers, I had already known that, but something that he had told me during the same conversation. The idea that had been gnawing at the back of my mind since we had formed our plan the previous night seemed to be just out of the reach of comprehension.

"Are you alright Aaron?" The whole time my mind had be pulling a Terrick and battling with a hazy memory, Gladía had been staring at me like he thought I might become violently ill.

"Tryson told me once that his wife was *friends* with eagles. What did he mean by that?"

Gladía stared at me for another second, "He meant literally that, his wife is friends with a nest of eagles."

"But how is that possible? How can someone be friends with an animal?"

"Well she speaks to them and nests with them. For all intensive purposes she could be a member of their flock." He responded like that should have cleared up the question at once.

"She can *talk* to a family of eagles?" I wanted to be absolutely sure that I understood the elf correctly because the implications of what he was saying could have had terrible consequences. The pieces of the puzzle were starting to fall into place for me and I didn't like the image that it was creating.

"Well, she can talk to any bird, but she prefers to spend her time with one particular family of eagles. She has chosen to nest with them."

Immediately my mind started flying at a hundred leagues a second. Images from the past started flooding back to me. Images of falcons. One distinct peregrine falcon in particular. It really wasn't unusual to see falcons in Jericho Province, but this one kept popping into my mind. I had seen it many times before, always at times when I was having a private conversation or when Ronan had been near.

It had been in the air when the riders first arrived and on top of the barn when Jarron had first sent Terrick and me to Alleron. I had heard its screech on the road before we had been ambushed and saw it again when Luther had fought the cloaked elf. And finally, it was sitting on the window sill when we had planned the night's mission. I had seen it the moment I began to get that queasy feeling in the pit of my stomach - that feeling of being watched - and if Ronan could speak to that falcon, if he could get information from it, then he would have already known about our plan. He could have spent the entire day making adjustments and planning attacks the same way that Luther and Tryson had.

"Gladía, the whole eagle talking thing, that wouldn't be like a special, distinct, one of a kind, kinda thing would it? I mean that's not something a lot of people can do right?"

The elf was still looking at me like he thought I was about to spontaneously combust, but he answered me all the same, "No, it is fairly common. Not everyone can do it, but the ability to telepathically communicate with some form of sentient organism is certainly the most common gift amongst elves."

"We need to catch Luther."

I sprang out of my chair and was half way out of the tavern by the time Gladía reacted, and I was happy to see that when I looked back over my shoulder the elf was right there by my side. I spent the next few minutes quickly running through my revelation and all the times that I had seen the falcon over the last few weeks. I knew that what I was saying sounded crazy, but after everything that we had been through I wasn't about to take any chances and overlook something that could mean failure for our mission.

When I was finished recounting the worries that I had, I was distressed to see that Gladía's expression looked more doubtful than supportive.

Finally he stepped in front of me, trying to prevent me from making up any ground. "I do not know, Aaron. It is possible, but it seems unlikely. Gifts like that are given to elves, not men. I have never known a man who could converse with animals and that rider is definitely a man. It is possible that the falcon's presence has been merely a coincidence."

"No, it hasn't."

Gladía gave me the same sad look that the rest of the village had been giving me for the last three days, and I was sick of it. "Listen Aaron, I simply do not feel that this is a concern that is worth giving away our position. Not when our goal requires stealth and not when all we have to go on is a hunch."

I glared at the elf with my emotions starting to spiral out of control again, "This is *not* a hunch. I know I'm right… I can't fail again!" I shouted thinking about the words that I was determined to prove wrong.

The elf's eyebrows arched high on his forehead at my outburst and I desperately hoped that he would let the comments go. I didn't really feel like explaining the crazy message-sending dreams I had been having. Luckily, the elf just shook his head and looked sadly at me again. "Aaron, the old man was not your fault. You must let it go if you are to grow from the lessons his passing has taught you." He tried to put a hand on my shoulder but I brushed it away. It wasn't Dane that was bothering me, but I chose to let him think he had found the problem.

I tried to search my mind for anything that would give my theory a solid leg to stand on. Every second that we waited would make it harder to catch up to Luther. The thing was that I really didn't have anything more than my gut to go on. So I had seen a falcon a couple of times at odd situations. What did that really mean after all? I didn't want to think that I had allowed myself to get all worked up over nothing, but the feeling in my gut twisted every time I thought of the falcon. That led me to believe that I was right, but all I had to go on was a bird on a windowsill being pelted with nuts... nuts... a shock wave of energy surged through my body. The nuts were the key. I remembered the ride home from Alleron, and I remembered the crazy feeling of worrying that I had not stored enough for the winter

"I've talked to a squirrel before!" I blurted out.

"Maybe you should sit this one out Aaron. Find a nice place to lie down for a while... Perhaps with a lot of pillows." The elf added the last part like I may be a danger to myself. He stared at me like he was seriously worried about my health. Once again he tried to put a hand on my shoulder, and again I brushed him away.

"No, I'm fine! It was on the ride home from Alleron. Anyways, I didn't really talk to it so much as I absorbed its thoughts or something." It was hard to explain the experience. "It was like I *was* the squirrel for a moment; like we were sharing the same mind. I was still me and everything, I mean I was aware of still being human, but I had all the animal's fears and instincts for a moment as well."

For a second the elf's expression softened, and I held out hope that it was because he was starting to buy into my story and not that he thought I had completely gone off the deep end.

"Why didn't you tell anyone about this?" He questioned.

"Really? Because I didn't want everyone looking at me like that." I pointed at the elf's face and his eyebrows crawled back up his forehead under his war helm. "I know what I felt, I know how real it was and I'm tired of getting that look like I've gone crazy. I know that this is more than some random hunch and I really don't care if you believe me. Now I'm going to try and catch Luther and you can either help me, or you can get out of my way."

As I finished, a horn blasted through the night air. The battle had already started and once again I was too late.

"There's nothing we can do for Luther now even if we wanted to." Gladía said, stepping in front of me for a second time.

"We have a responsibility to Tryson, you need to focus on the task at hand and take me to the falls."

It was infuriating. If my gut was right and Ronan already knew the details of our plan he would know where we were heading and even if he didn't know how to find the path to the top of the falls, he could have easily planned for traps to be set along the way. It killed me that I couldn't find a way to assist Luther, but I knew that Gladía was right, he was on his own, and so were we.

Running at top speed it still took us far too long to cover the distance between us and the rest of the men. Through the trees we could see the horrifying scene that was unfolding. Marcus, Uthgar, and the others had locked shields and were using the body of an enormous tree to protect their flank. While it protected them well enough, it unfortunately also meant that they would be unable to retreat. There was a wave of about twenty warriors of the Urröbbi that kept crashing against the four shields only to be pushed away again. The elf whose name I couldn't remember knelt in the middle of the four other soldiers and periodically popped up launching arrows, only to duck down again before a volley of spears lodged themselves into the tree at his back. Behind the rows of attacking warriors, two of the Mazenkryie paced back and forth like a pair of hungry dogs. Their glossy scales shimmered in the dim light of the moon and the thin membranes that were their lips were curled back into growls revealing double rows of razor teeth. They weren't yet attacking but it seemed like it was only a matter of time before one of them found an opening and pounced.

While I watched, the elf pooped up again and fired an arrow that lodged in the shoulder of one of the beasts. It let out an earsplitting howl before turning its head and biting the shaft of the arrow to splinters. To the left Uthgar quickly moved his shield and cut down a warrior before falling back in line with his comrades. Marcus made a similar movement on the right of the line and took the arm clean off one of the warriors. Before he could retreat however, the angered beast charged and smashed against his shield sending him tumbling backwards into the tree. The beast pulled back one of its massive arms and punched the shield so hard it crumpled in the middle like it was made out of nothing more than aluminum.

Before it could strike again however, Athéal landed a thrust of his spear right between its ribs. The creature roared in pain again before crumpling to the ground whimpering and retreated.

I looked at Gladía but he looked like he was just as at a loss for what to do as I was. He seemed stuck between wanting to help his fellow soldiers and wanting to get into position to help Tryson and complete the mission. As I looked back at the one remaining healthy Mazenkryie my stomach twisted with apprehension. If there were only two of the beasts here, where were the other four?

As if on cue, the beast turned its black eyeless pits upward and curled its upper lip back again. I followed its gaze just in time to see two more of the scaly monsters crawling stealthily through the branches of the tree that the soldiers were using to protect their backs. They were only seconds away from being within striking distance. I took the bow from my back and threaded it with an arrow.

"They knew the risks of the mission." Gladía whispered while grabbing hold of my wrist. "Besides, their scales are too thick for arrows to do more than annoy them. And if we give away our position their sacrifice will be in vain."

Gladía made sense, but I was tired of people making sense and I was tired of standing by while the people I cared about were put in harm's way. I lifted my arm again and drew back on the string when another horn sounded just to the side of the battle. With a second blast of the horn Luther and the rest of Dû Vena Ruösa came charging into the fray. They looked like they had been through a battle of their own, but as they charged they completely crushed the flank of the Urröbbían force. The one Mazenkryie still on the ground let out another roar before apparently thinking its life wasn't worth the risk and fleeing back into the black depths of the forest. The two in the tree however finally made their move. One leapt in front of the charging soldiers, attempting to slow their advance, while the other pounced down on the unprotected back of the unnamed elf. He disappeared with a cry beneath a heap of black scales.

I pulled back on the string of my bow again, ready to go to their aid when Gladía grabbed me once more, "We have to move, they have this fight under control."

It wasn't easy, but finally the thought of the trouble Tryson might have been in convinced me to turn my back on the battle and lead Gladía deeper into the forest.

I sprinted at full speed along the path that I had traveled many times before on the back of Elma. I wanted to concentrate solely on reaching the falls so we could take Ronan down, but as we ran my mind kept drifting back to the Mazenkryie. There had only been four of the evil scaly monsters that had attacked Marcus and the small troop of soldiers, and that meant that there were still two more in the forest somewhere. I forced myself to broaden my focus, searching for any sign that the enemy was nearby.

As we neared the falls and I allowed my senses to expand in all directions, I was immediately able to tell that something was off. The smell of the forest was different, like the trees had been covered in some foreign substance. I glanced at the elf that ran by my side but if he had noticed anything was wrong he didn't let it affect the look of concentration on his face. We continued our run and, though our pace didn't change, the way I began to perceive my surroundings did. The world seemed to move in slow motion and the information my eyes began to take in intensified. The way the grass was compacted in certain areas, the way small branches from low lying trees and shrubs were bent and snapped haphazardly meant that something large had moved through the area recently. The fact that there was no hint of night life amongst the animals in this part of the forest, an area that normally seemed to buzz with energy, meant that the large animal had been a predator.

I followed the signs of the forest with my eyes as the scent I had picked up on originally began to intensify. The smell of fetid meat started to make my stomach churn. It was a scent that I had been in the presence of before. Ahead of me the sounds of the falls began to roar through the forest, the path that would lead us to the top of the cliffs was within sight, but I could tell we wouldn't make it there. To the left of the path my eyes locked on a tree that had recently had the bark scraped off of it in several locations. I could tell because the wood underneath still had that fresh look to it. It was moist and the bugs that had once lived under the barks protective cover had not yet finished migrating to a new home in the tree. But something was wrong with the picture it was creating and my sword was in my hand before I had even finished putting the pieces together.

The problem was that the bark didn't look scraped off, like something with claws had tried to climb the tree. Instead it looked pulled off, like something had wanted it to catch our attention, had wanted it to distract us. Gladía had noticed the missing bark the same as I had, but he had misinterpreted it. His bow was drawn and he gazed fiercely from branch to branch in an attempt to locate the creature that had caused the marks.

The hair stood up on the back of my neck as a shiver slowly ran down my spine. I tightened the grip on the pommel of my sword as my palms started to perspire and, as I strained my ears, I heard the sound I shouldn't have been able to hear. It was nothing more than a small intake of breath, but it was enough for me to react. I could feel, rather than see, the beast leap from a tree behind us and my body moved before my mind could command it. I twisted to the side and threw the razor edge of my blade through the air. A sharp cry, louder than anything I had ever heard, rent the air as blood and sinew from one of the thick front limbs of the Mazenkryie coated the ground at my feet with the scent of decay. Wherever it splashed, the ground seemed to boil as a yellow acrid smoke perfumed from the dying grass.

The feral scream of the beast was enough to freeze the blood in my veins, as it radiated fear through my body. It was different from the sound it had bellowed during our first encounter. It was more primal and all the more terrifying. The creature was in pain and now it was angry.

Gladía turned to face my assailant when another cry echoed to our left and a second beast crashed into his side like a tidal wave of fury. With the elf's remarkable agility he was only knocked off balance for a moment, but the contact was enough to send his bow skidding across the ground and into the underbrush of the forest. Regaining his footing he drew a pair of daggers, identical to the ones I had seen Tryson use during the first fighting in Bray's scorched fields. With the speed of a jungle cat he had charged the beast and, after dodging a fist that would have dented a tree trunk, cut two deep gashes under the creature's front right arm. The beast howled and lunged forward, but it was clumsy and too slow for the elf, missing him entirely as Gladía slid back to a safe distance, preparing for a second assault.

The Mazenkryie in front of me had seemed to recover from its initial shock at being wounded and was now circling, crouched low to the ground, like a cat ready to pounce on a mouse. It was an odd position for an animal shaped in its abnormal way, but I had no doubt that when it sprang, I would have no more than a heartbeat to react. Watching the animal made me quickly realize that while I had been able to draw blood with my first swing, it was little more than a flesh wound for something so strong.

I held my sword in a ready position, unsure if it was better to go on the offensive or set back and adopt a defensive tactic against such a foe. I knew that I was not nearly fast enough to charge the creature the way that Gladía had, and hope to not sustain some form of gruesome injury. But holding my position and waiting for the storm to crash against me seemed like an equally hopeless endeavor. I moved slowly and deliberately, circling the beast as it circled me, its growl deepening. Keeping my knees bent I waited for the creature to spring. The sounds of a fight blurred in the background, letting me know that Gladía was doing his best to occupy the other Mazenkryie.

The beast's claws dug into the loose dirt of the forest floor and its muscles tensed into several hundred pounds of coiled energy. The dark creature pounced and I tried to roll to the right, but was too slow. I felt a pair of inch long claws rip through the muscle of my shoulder, causing my left arm to burn like it had been set on fire. I hissed as the pain of the wound coursed through my body thankful the momentum of my roll carried me out of range as the beast slid to a stop. Without hesitation, it had turned around and leapt back in my direction before I could stand. Lying on my back, I jabbed my sword forward causing it to sink three inches deep into the animals left shoulder before the force snapped my blade in two, just above the hilt. It howled in pain a second time before reeling back and lifting a huge black fist. I summersaulted backwards just as the fist smashed a hole the size of my head in the soft dirt where I had lain a moment before. As I got to my feet the Mazenkryie stood back on its hind legs and used one of its massive hands to pull the part of my blade that was still embedded in its shoulder, free of its body. More of the yellow blood dripped from the blade causing the ground to smoke and hiss in protest to the foul substance. The Mazenkryie growled at the blade before hurling it in my direction, missing my head by inches as I fell back to the ground to avoid being impaled by my own broken sword. It landed with a dull thud in the trunk of a tree, which immediately began to smoke as well.

Slowly the beast dropped back down onto all fours, testing its wounded arm and tensing again, preparing for another charge. As it eyed me I scramble back to my feet, but there was no way I would be able to defend myself against another attack with nothing more than a broken blade and I knew the beast would be upon me before I could string an arrow. Its eyeless gaze bore into my soul and its lips curled back into what almost looked like a smile. It knew that I was at its mercy. In my periphery I could see that Gladía was still locked in battle with the other Mazenkryie, so no help would be coming from him. Weaponless and with no sign of back up, I did the only thing that made sense: I turned and ran.

Through the trees and up the path to the falls I ran as fast as my legs could carry me. Weaving through the underbrush of the forest trying to take the path that would slow the wounded Mazenkryie down the most, but it didn't seem to be working. I could still hear the beast's heavy footsteps and raged breathes coming from what seemed like right behind me. Just ahead of me I could see the ivy covered wall that concealed the path that I would need to take to the falls. I approached the wall at full speed, with only fractions of a second separating me from a certain death, and slid feet first into the hole in the rock wall that only I knew existed. Just as the last of my head slid underneath the dangling ivy I heard the loud crunch that told me the Mazenkryie had just had an unpleasant meeting with the cliff face. Quickly, I slid my body farther down the tunnel wanting to get as far out of the reach of the beast as I could.

A minute later I sat panting on the other side of the tunnel, so amazed that I was still alive I could barely stop my hands from shaking. I sat for a moment, sweat dripping down the side of my face, trying to get ahold of myself. *You're alright now.* I thought to myself. *It can't get to you now.* But I was paralyzed. Unable to move for fear that any sound I made would draw more monsters to me like moths to a flame.

It was the cry of a falcon that finally snapped me out of it. With Gladía still occupied, I was the only person who could help Tryson now. I needed to pull it together for his sake. Without running into any further delays I was at a good support location in almost no time. In the middle of the grove, was the sight that I was looking for. Tryson had managed to fight his way from the statue to the spring and seemed to be handling himself well against the much larger dark skinned Ronan. Without thinking I dropped to a knee and threaded an arrow. It would be up to me to end this conflict once and for all. Up to me to save the rest of the village and drive off what was left of the Urröbbí. I pulled back on my bow but was unable to release the string. The two men in the grove danced so wildly it was like they were one undulating being rather than two separate men. They were an entwined mass of blades and flesh spinning and striking with such ferocity that I found it impossible to find an open shot. Tryson moved in ways I would have never thought possible and several times he was so fast it was as if he had disappeared entirely from one spot only to reappear in another, but still, no matter how fast he moved, Ronan's ruby studded blade was always right there to shield him from harm.

The battle raged on for what seemed like an eternity. Tryson bent backward to avoid a strike by Ronan, before stepping forward with a flurry of his own blows. He feinted at Ronan's head before driving his dagger down toward his hip. A second later his other dagger shot towards Ronan's throat, but both strikes were deflected as Ronan twirled his sword in a tight circle.

Spinning to his side, Tryson went to a knee and attempted to sneak his dagger under Ronan's defenses and cut at his unprotected shin, but Ronan was able to dance back out of reach. Luther had told me that the daggers Tryson used were able to enhance his speed and they acted as advertised, but it left him with the disadvantage of having to move inside his enemy's guard and fight in very tight quarters. Against a warrior as skilled as Ronan, this task proved to be nearly impossible, and it was clearly aggravating the elf. He was resorting to increasingly dangerous tactics and it seemed to be getting him nowhere.

Without warning Tryson spun on the spot and hurled one of his daggers at his opponent. It was a desperate and ill-conceived move and it was so unlike Tryson that it seemed to catch Ronan off guard. He sliced his blade through the air a millisecond too late and missed the dagger as it sunk hilt deep in his left bicep. Ronan grimaced but otherwise made no indication that he was in any pain. Tryson tried to take advantage of the moment of confusion and sprinted forward to strike at Ronan's right side, but he swiftly sidestepped the blow and kicked the elf under the ribs. Tryson rolled backwards and sprung gracefully back to his feet while Ronan gritted his teeth and slowly pulled the blade out of his arm. He looked at it for a moment in awe, like he had forgotten that he could still bleed. However, the look of humility quickly turned to disgust and he threw the blade into the woods.

"A poor decision old friend." He sneered at Tryson, who had flipped his remaining dagger upside down in his hand, maneuvering it into a position better suited for defensive fighting rather than his offensive slashing and jabbing.

"To the end." Was all Tryson responded.

I tightened the grip on my bow knowing that my opening would be coming soon. Ronan took a step forward and I drew back the full length of my string, the wounds on my shoulder screaming in agony with the strain. I lined up my shot, exhaled my breath trying to minimize any unwanted bodily movement and as Ronan stepped once more toward Tryson I released my grip. The shot was perfect, sailing straight towards Ronan's head, but the instant before impact a beautiful peregrine falcon dropped out of the sky and with a cry caught the arrow in its breast. As the bird fell to the ground a look of pure rage spread across Ronan's face and he locked eyes with me, sending a clear message. He would punish me… slowly.

I scrambled to string a second arrow, but he had already reengaged Tryson, swinging and hacking with his sword like a man possessed. Tryson deflected a blow before using his off hand to deliver a punch to Ronan's jaw, causing him to stumble backwards. I used the separation to loose another arrow, but with my position being compromised Ronan was prepared and cut the arrow out of the sky.

"Enough!" Ronan screamed and thrust his sword into the ground releasing a wave of energy so strong that Tryson was thrown off his feet. Even from where I knelt atop the falls I could feel the shock wave rush over me.

I threaded a third arrow but froze in disbelief as Ronan's form began to shift. Upon rising, it seemed to ripple and grow hazy, as if he were nothing more than an image in a pool of water that someone had thrown a rock at. His skin seemed to melt off his frame and it grew, if possible, even darker than his normal complexion. He began to shrink in height and his back exploded as two forms shot out from his shoulders. His arms and legs shot backward into his body and began to take on the textured look of feathers. His face grew small and angular and his nose stretched forward and began to hook. The transformation took less than five seconds, but it happened in such disturbingly graphic detail that it nearly made me sick.

He leapt from the ground and a pitch black hawk took flight in my direction. My mind screamed at my legs to turn and run but my body was frozen in place, unable to obey. A moment before reaching my position the hawk's dark feathers began to fuse together and grow back out into limbs as Ronan tumbled out of the sky landing gracefully before me, once again back in human form. I willed my body to move once more and raised my bow in a desperate attempt to get off a last shot, but he was too close. He took two steps and swatted the bow out of my hands like it was nothing more than a child's toy.

"I have been waiting for this." He sneered. A glistening trail of frozen water vapor snaked out of his mouth like the temperature had dropped thirty degrees.

For a moment neither of us moved, we simply sized each other up. I was shocked to see that the wound on his left bicep was completely healed by his transformation. We had no weapons between us, but I figured that wouldn't stop the enormous man from crushing me under his boot like an ant. After all, there he was, master of birds, who could turn into a war hawk at will, and there I was, master of squirrels and all things nutty and terrified. Ronan's sneer grew into a greasy, smooth, evil smile. I didn't have a chance and he knew it. He just wanted to give me time to comprehend the fate that awaited me.

"You will be responsible for the resurrection of my master. Without you, none of this would be possible." I could almost feel the suppressed anger he had for me radiating from his every mannerism.

I probably should have said something bold like *'You'll never take me alive!'* and then attempted to wrestle him backwards off the cliff, but I was not my cousin and as strong as I was in certain areas, hand to hand combat and knuckle busting was one hundred percent Terrick's field of expertise. Instead all I managed to mutter was a weak, "Uh, no."

Ronan gave me another twisted smile and reached out a hand for me. As quickly as I could I knocked his hand away and tried to thrust my left fist up under his jaw. In a heartbeat he reacted, trapping my hand by his side with one arm and grasping me by the throat with his other. I choked as my air was cut off and struggled as I was lifted off of the ground, my right hand clawing frantically at his fingers attempting to loosen his grip.

"You're a bit of a fighter... not much of one, but a bit." he mused, "I would expect nothing less."

He tightened his grip and the world around me started to spin and fade to black. The smells and the sounds of the forest started to diminish into nothingness, and just as I began to lose hope a gust of wind rushed past my head and the air exploded with a scream that sounded more bird than human. I was dropped, choking, to the ground and when my eyes refocused I could see a swan feathered arrow protruding from Ronan's muscular shoulder. His eyes had turned beady and glared deep into the forest as a second arrow whizzed by his ear.

"You!" he hissed, unable to mask the hatred he pumped into the word.

He opened his mouth and another terrible bird-like cry rent the air before he once again transformed into the obsidian hawk and flew away, high over the tree tops back in the direction of the desert and away from his camp.

"Gladía?" I choked, still trying to fill my burning lungs with fresh air. Through the trees I was able to make out the shape of a hooded man moving silently through the darkness of the forest underbrush, and then he was no more.

Chapter 23: Reunion

Gladía arrived by my side shortly after the hooded figure had disappeared from view. Apparently he had been able to overwhelm and kill the Mazenkryie he had been battling; a victory that was not to be understated. Having to hunt and kill eight of those beasts was no small task and that fact that one of them was now out of the way made that mission seem like a slightly less daunting endeavor.

Once I had assured him that I was quite alright, we made our way down to the grove and found Tryson seated by the side of the spring, staring into its mysterious depths. In the dim light the stars were able to sneak through the high canopy, it appeared like a midnight blue mirror, completely undisturbed by the activity around it. The falls by where I had been hiding dropped elegantly into the far side of the pool, sending a flurry of ripples half way across the spring's length before melding seamlessly into its present glasslike state.

"It is a magnificent sight, is it not?" He stated as we approached. "Pools such as these are very rare indeed. The only other one I am aware of is located in Aríamoné. It has been long since I have laid eyes on anything that has reminded me of home." The way he said it was not entirely sad, but more in the way that one would state a fact, such as the weather. Still, for what it was worth, it was the most emotion I had seen any of the elves display since I had been in their presence.

"You miss it don't you?" I asked

Tryson turned his head and smiled at me. "Not so much the place as the people." He stated. Noticing Gladía he continued, "Well, some of the people at least. If I were to see any more of my kin like that one, I fear I would go quite insane."

Gladía flashed a brilliant white smile back, "Tis nice to see you alive as well Tryson." He glanced around the grove like he wasn't sure we were alone. "What happened to Ronan?" he questioned.

Tryson looked back at the spring before answering, "He used magic. An amount of which he should not have been capable. It was enough to make the forest pulse with unnatural energy. The effort of it should have consumed him, and it may have. Everything after the impact is a daze for me, but if he was still alive he would have killed me."

"He's still alive." I cut in. "And I was right." I pointed to the ground halfway across the grove where the peregrine falcon that had become such a pain to my existence still lay motionless with my arrow protruding from its breast. "It intercepted my first shot; saved his life."

Gladía gazed at the bird with an expression of confusion. "This is very troubling. It is rare and dangerous for a human to have this kind of connection with the animals, especially when he is one of our enemies."

"It's worse than that though. After he released the wave of energy... or whatever it was... he transformed." Both of the elves looked at me with questioning expressions, but they didn't interrupt. "His whole body seemed to melt and reform." I said with a shiver, the disturbing image coming back to me. "He shrunk and sprouted feathers and when the shift was complete he had changed into a black war hawk. He flew up to where I was hiding and turned back into himself."

This time, the information was too much, even for Gladía. Turning towards Tryson he questioned "How is that possible? No man could sustain magic of that magnitude, and there has never been a human Shifter."

Tryson assumed the look of a man deep in thought, and when he didn't respond to Gladía's question, the elf turned to me. "Why would he leave the fight with Tryson to attend to you when victory was so near at hand? If Tryson was who he was after, why would he not claim his life while he was indisposed?"

"I was not who he wanted." Tryson finally broke his silence, causing us both to look in his direction. "While he was not at all surprised to see me when I arrived at the statue, he did seem disappointed. He muttered something about my being the wrong elf and what an inconvenience it was before he proceeded to move into some exceedingly boring dialog on how pleasant it would be to gut me anyway. It seemed to amuse him on a near incomprehensible level."

"Have you any idea who the 'right' elf would be?" Gladía probed.

"When he flew to me he said I would be responsible for the resurrection of his master. Whatever that means." I spoke up, remembering Ronan's words. They seemed completely absurd. The idea that I could resurrect anything was dumbfounding when I couldn't even resurrect myself from my bed on most mornings.

The two elves gave each other a meaningful look that was lost on me, before Tryson turned back and asked, "Did he say anything else?"

"No, he was struck by an arrow and flew off. He was headed north I think."

"I suppose that was your handy work." Tryson asked Gladía, to which the elf shook his head.

"It was not my arrow that drove him off. We were intercepted by two of the Mazenkryie. Aaron was the only one who made it to the falls."

Tryson looked at me but all I could do was shrug.

"The arrow was fletched with swan feathers. Other than that, I didn't get a good look at who shot."

After another moment of thought Tryson stood up from the bank of the spring and dusted his pants off. "Alaya aqúina pa nafarí encantalis." He muttered in elfish, before adding, "We should find Luther," and setting off towards the northern edge of the grove, back to the village.

...

When we reached the village we moved straight to the town tavern. It had been deserted since Dane's death, but the commotion of fighting and the howls of the Mazenkryie had stirred the village into realizing that something was amiss, and they had begun to gather with weapons by the tavern in case a second assault became inevitable. We arrived to a blur of questions that Tryson and Gladía answered to the best of their abilities. Out of the crowd Arctone approached and grasped me on the shoulder.

"Aaron, what happened? We heard noises in the forest… you look terrible."

"Thanks Arctone. Tryson was trying to get the hostages back. We were backing him up."

"Well what happened? Where are the rest of the men, and what of the women and children? Are they safe?"

"I don't know." I said flatly sidestepping him before he could accost me with any further questioning. Instead I resumed scanning the crowd for Jarron, and as I feared, I found him standing near the rear, a hand and a half sword strapped to his hip that I was sure he had never before used in his life. His face was gaunt and pale, like a thousand years of worry had zipped through his mind in the last two weeks. As he exhaled a sigh of relief, he looked down towards the ground and shook his head.

"Why must you take unnecessary risks by venturing into situations that are beyond our ability to control?"

"Uncle, I…" I started before Jarron raised a hand cutting me short.

"You are mine, Aaron. As much as Lisa or Te…" His voice caught in his throat as he tried to say his son's name. "The actions that you take carry a weight that you cannot begin to comprehend. If anything were to happen to you tonight I…" His voice broke again. "I would be lost."

"I'm sorry uncle." The amount of emotion that he was showing was sobering. I knew that he would not take my going on this mission lightly, but I didn't expect it to affect him quite the way it had. I was so choked up I could barely speak "I had too… for Lisa."

"I am glad you are alright." He said quietly before turning and making his way back to his home without questioning me about the success or failure of the mission.

I turned my back on the crowd and walked into the empty tavern to collect my thoughts. In my haste to help Luther and Tryson I had forgotten that I may have been hurting the people that still cared about me in the village. Even Arctone, for as out of touch as he was with seemingly all human activity, managed genuine concern when I showed up in the village with only the two elves by my side.

Looking around, the bar seemed cold and empty. The fire had been allowed to die and without Sienna's smile shining out from behind the bar, it was like I had walked into the room of a building I had never been in before; it seemed foreign and unfamiliar. Slowly, I made my way to the back of the room and jumped the bar to examine my wounds from the night in the mirror at the back of the tree.

Upon examination, I saw that the damage was worse than I had anticipated. I realized almost immediately that I should have taken a dip in the spring before heading home. Even after the short amount of time that had passed, my neck was mottled a deep, sickish purple. The thick stripe of discolored skin stretched from one side of my neck to the other, growing darker where Ronan's fingers had applied the most pressure.

Turning my back to the mirror I focus on the tattered cloth that covered my shoulder, which was soaked with far more blood than I had expected. Reaching upward I moved to take my shirt off and the action cause my shoulder to erupt with pain. Slowly, and with more deliberate motions, I was able to work my shirt off with my one good hand and examine the damage. Two deep gashes slid parallel across my upper back like they had been split open by a pair of daggers. From the angle I was looking over my shoulder I couldn't tell how deep the wounds were, but they looked pretty nasty. Blood still seeped from both lacerations, and the edges of each wound had turned a nasty shade of yellowish brown, like the skin had died or had been burnt. One of the two gashes moved directly across the birthmark that had annoyed me since childhood, but now that it was mangled I missed it. It was like a small part of my identity had been destroyed with the mark.

Behind me a commotion broke out outside of the tavern, as startled voices and shouts of surprise began to rise from the crowds midst. Worried that more of the Urröbbí may have shown up at the village I tore myself away from the mirror, grabbed my bow and quiver and ran to the door of the tavern. However, just before I had finished crossing the room, the doors to the tavern were thrown open and Luther walked in, closely followed by Tryson, Uthgar, Athéal, and…

"Sienna!" I shouted dropping my bow to the floor.

The girl looked terrified and a bit ill, which was understandable since the last few days had probably been the longest of her life, but when she saw me her eyes lit up and resumed their usual splendor.

"Aaron!" she shouted back, shaking free of Athéal's grasp and embracing me in a warm hug. Standing up on her toes she put her lips to my ear. "Thank you for coming for us." Her voice quivered like she was about to start crying. Then leaning back she examined me for the first time, noticing the fresh blood that now covered her arm from where she had hugged me. "My Gods you look awful." She said with a smile, causing me to laugh. Somehow, Sienna saying it wasn't nearly as offensive as Arctone.

"Really? I hadn't noticed."

While I had been greeting Sienna, more of the villagers who had been taken earlier in the week had filtered into the tavern. All of them but...

"Where's Lisa?" I asked, turning back to Sienna, but she just looked confused.

"We fought our way to the Urröbbían camp," this time it was Luther who spoke, "but the Mazenkryie had beat us there. They had retreated from our skirmish as soon as our victory seemed inevitable. When we made it to their camp, there were more soldiers waiting. They were disposed of quickly enough, but their presence allowed the Mazenkryie enough time to escape. They must have taken her with them. Why they chose to take her rather than another hostage is beyond me."

The words sunk in like a lead weight. My family still was not safe.

"I am sorry, Aaron." He continued, "We would have tracked them, but Lacríel fell."

My mind shot to the elf that one of the Mazenkryie had jumped on during the night's battle. Behind Luther, Tryson dropped his gaze to the floor.

"With only Athéal, we lacked the ability to track them without any additional source of light. We would have been unable catch them tonight."

Sienna looked back to me, "What do they mean Lisa was taken? She wasn't in the village was she?"

I looked down to the floor, trying to hold off the tears I knew were coming. "She got back the same night you were taken." I said flatly.

Sienna just looked more confused as she started to look around the bar, "But then where's Terrick?"

I found myself unable to respond as the tears started to flow. I couldn't hold them off any longer. I had only been able to make it through the night because my mind had been too occupied to think of my cousin. Sienna didn't have to ask to know what my silence meant.

"Oh Aaron!" She shouted pulling me into another hug as she too broke into tears. We would have stayed that way for the rest of the night, simply trying to comfort each other, had the door not burst open a moment later.

"Where is she? Where is my Sienna?" Anglehurst shouted as he flew into the tavern.

"Father!" Sienna exclaimed back, running to embrace him in the same manner she had me. Seeing them together made me slightly resentful. Lisa should have been able to have a reunion like that with Jarron.

I ripped my eyes away from the scene and turned my attention back to Luther, wiping away the last of my tears and trying once again to suppress the crushing wave of emotion that was still threatening to engulf me. "So what are we going to do now? We have to go after her."

Luther looked around the tavern at all the joyous reunions before responding. "Now is not the appropriate time to discuss the matter. We will speak on this tomorrow, but this village will never be safe as long as Ronan is alive."

I thought about Luther's words and looked back in the direction of Sienna and her father. He looked so happy, but deep down I knew the happiness could not last.

"We can't stay here, can we?" I asked in a low voice.

Luther didn't respond to my question, but then again he didn't have to. I already knew what the answer was.

Chapter 24: Why Don't I Ever Have Nice Dreams?

That night I once again dreamt of the fair elf by the spring in the grove. No new details showed themselves, but once again I was accosted by the grievous message of failure. When I attempted to approach the elf, to ask her what I would fail at or how she knew me, the dream dissolved into nothingness, and I awoke with my head pounding and my shoulder throbbing. Tryson had tended to my wounds the previous night, and Athéal had tried to alleviate some of my pain with magic, but the wound still threatened to become infected and it was sore enough that it prevented me from resting comfortably.

When I finally quieted my mind and my aching shoulder enough to fall back to sleep, a different dream invaded my rest. I found myself standing in the doorway of a dark chamber that led to a room I had never seen before. It was circular and the walls were formed out of beautiful, pearly white marble. Intricate designs were carved into the walls and the skill of the crafter gave the scene an appearance of activity and life. The marble was carved in the pattern of a deep forest, with trees and other forms of vegetation seeming to sprout from the base of the walls. The bark and leaves of the trees were sculpted with such detail that it was easy to imagine I had actually been transported into a stone forest. Around the circle, nearly a dozen wolves made of the same marble were staring out into the room's center, challenging anyone to approach. The cold eyes that would follow the movement of any intruder gave them a dangerous and fearsome look. Their lips curled back into ferocious snarls, baring fangs sharp enough to cut through bone. On the back of their necks, their hackles stood up as if they were preparing to do battle with some impending danger.

The ceiling of the room domed upwards with the branches of the trees, where the leaves changed from the polished white marble to a radiant gold color. From the doorway it was hard to determine if the ceiling was actually made of the rare metal or if it was simply painted that way to give off the imitation of extravagant wealth. Diamond shaped windows no larger than a man's fist were strewn across the domed roof allowing for the dim evening light to paint the floor with eerie, wolfish shadows. As I studied the ceiling I realized that there was no pattern to the diamonds, instead they seemed to have been randomly punched in the marble in the oddest of positions. In the very center of the ceiling a gilded chandelier dangled down into the middle of the room, its flowing appearance gave the illusion that its arms were curving and growing of their own accord, giving the room an even more life-like feel. The chandelier was unlit and the cobwebs that stretched from one branch to the next made it look as though the room had not been visited in some time. It seemed like a great shame that something so beautiful would be placed in a room where it could not be appreciated by all.

As magnificent as the room was, it was startlingly empty. In fact the only object that took up any of the room's vast space was a thick marble dais stationed directly below the chandelier. And it was this dais that drew my attention. Sitting daintily on top of the marble pillar was a bell-shaped glass container that seemed to hum with energy. A faint light was pulsing under the vessel that seemed to draw me closer to it with some form of fierce magnetism. There was nothing I wanted to do more than look underneath the glass and reveal the source of the energy. I took a step into the room when a hand grabbed my wrist from behind and forced me to halt my progress towards the dais. Annoyed, I turned and was surprised to see that it was Sienna who had caused my delay.

She looked absolutely stunning, wearing a green dress that seemed to sparkle in the dim lighting of the room. Her skin was a liquid pool of caramel and glowed with the same energy as the container on the dais. A glow that seemed to be diminished only by that of her eyes, which burned with a fierce intensity that I had never seen from her before. Her face was framed perfectly by her shoulder length coffee colored hair, the small bit of her bangs still draped elegantly over the left side of her face. Her beauty far exceeded anything I had ever before seen. I mean Sienna had always been beautiful, but it was like someone had taken the rough tom-boyish girl of my childhood and placed her in the middle of one of Lisa's fairy tales.

"Are you sure you wish to go on, Aaron?" she asked in a sweet voice, her cherry lips moving in a whisper. "The truth can be a terrible thing and if this is the path that you choose events will be put into motion that cannot be undone. Events that will lead to you discovering the truth. Choosing this path will only lead you down a painful road. Many you care about will suffer and you more than any will feel the pain."

I didn't responded to her question, but simply continued to stare into her mesmerizing eyes.

"Would it not be better to retreat from this place? Would it not be better to stay with me?" As she spoke she stepped forward and slipped her arms around me; one around my waist and the other behind my neck; her fingers tangling themselves into the roots of my disheveled hair. She pulled me in tight to her body so that we were close enough to feel each other's hearts beating, and she exhaled a sweet perfume that smelt of strawberries and fresh grass and made my mind fog over with a thousand thoughts of peace and tranquility.

She moved her face dangerously close to my own, so close that our lips were nearly touching as our eyes locked. Moving slowly while tightening her hold around my waist, she slid her face past mine so that our checks brushed and she pursed her lips next to my ear. Ever so lightly she kissed the base of my jaw sending jolts of electricity through my body and causing the hair on my arms to stand on end. It was a rush of energy equivalent to nothing I had ever experienced.

"This fight does not have to be yours." She whispered into my ear. "Your father did not wish this fate for you."

Shocked, I managed to worm my way out of her grasp and back away toward the center of the room. The humming from the dais grew louder as if it was excited to be so near a person.

"How can you speak about my father? What do you know of him?" I questioned.

Sienna's face grew sad, "The only ones who know of your heritage have long since passed into the void, Aaron. The path to the truth lies behind you, but you do not have to choose it as your own."

"How can you say that? How can I not choose a path that will lead me to my father?"

"By asking yourself if the means justify the ends. Is it worth the suffering that will come as a result of this knowledge? For when the truth is known, you will never be safe."

"What do you mean?" I shouted back, getting frustrated. "How will removing this glass veil put me in danger?"

"He will come Aaron. He will come and he will take it. And you will hunt him because of it. The question will drive you and you will commit yourself to the task. And when you finally find your answer, he will hunt you because of it."

All the information that was being thrown at me was making my head hurt. I felt like Terrick during one of those moments he just snapped and walloped someone for using too many big words.

"But what other choice do I have?" I asked.

"You can let others worry about this room, and you can remain ignorant to the truth." She smiled again before continuing, "You can remain with me. That's what you want isn't it?" Her voice was like honey as she started to move slowly towards me again.

"No…" I responded.

"No?" She put on a fake pouting expression as she continued to close the distance between us. "This isn't what you want?"

"Well yes… I mean no… but Terrick?" I was getting confused. The world was beginning to fuzz at the edges.

"Terrick is missing Aaron. It's just us now." She was now close enough to wrap her arms back around me. "Deep inside you know it's true, Terrick was always the only thing preventing us from being together." And at that moment she laced her hand back through my hair for a second time and pulled me so tightly to her body I thought we may become one. "You want this Aaron." She stated right before our lips touched.

I woke up drenched in sweat, the wound on my shoulder burning like hot coals had been shoved under my skin, doomed to lie awake hating myself for the rest of the night.

Chapter 25: Aaron the Swordsman...ish

The next morning I walked up the stairs to the ground level of my Uncle's tree and found him at the table eating his usual breakfast of wheat mush and goat milk. When he saw me he dropped his spoon into his bowl and leaned back in his chair.

"I could never get you to wake this early when there was field work to be done."

"I had a rough night sleeping." Was all I could say. I didn't understand my dream and I did not want to try and explain it to someone else.

"How is your shoulder feeling?"

I gave a one armed shrug and poured myself a glass of milk. "I've seen better mornings."

"You should go have Gable take a look at it sometime today."

"I'm fine, Uncle." I replied. Gable was the village medic. He spent most of his time locked away in his house trying to invent new medical remedies, none of which were overly effective. "Besides, if I really wanted it better I'd just ride Elma to the spring." I wanted to comfort Jarron, but even as I said it I knew I wouldn't go to the spring. I wanted to keep the wounds as a reminder of what a mistake would cost the next time I came across one of the vile creatures that gave me the ragged cuts.

Jarron gave a curt nod and resumed eating his breakfast He ate in silence for a few minutes before attempting to make small-talk between bites. "Your mother, when she was pregnant with you, she used to wake up every morning, stand right there where you are, and lecture me about feeding Terrick this garbage." He sat back in his chair and laughed to himself. "She'd say 'Jarron, yur a farmer ya' are. Why don't you give that poor boy some carrots, or tomatoes? Somethin' with some flavor.' And I'd look back at her and smile, and I'd say how'sa boy s'pose to become a man eatin' like a rabbit? And I'd say, I'll tell you what makes a man, mush makes a man. It puts hair on your chest I always said.

"And you mother would always say back to me, 'Well you may be able to feed Terrick that mess, but my son will have better.' And then your mother died, and I had to raise you on my own. And I always tried to get you to eat the wheat mush like Terrick and you would have nothing to do with it." He laughed a bit again. "It was like she was still influencing you even after she was gone."

I didn't know what to say. Jarron talked so rarely about my mother that I didn't want him to stop, but I didn't understand why he was telling me this.

"Are you alright Uncle?" I asked

He stayed leaned back in his chair and smiled at me again. "Yea Aaron, I'm fine. Anyway, my point is that your mother was right. You didn't need my mush to become a man; you did that just fine on your own."

It was the first time Jarron had ever said something like that to me. I mean I had always known that he was proud of me; he didn't have to tell me that for me to understand it, it was just that he had never voiced it before. It touched me in a surprisingly strong way.

"You remind me a lot of her." He continued, looking at me with his deep set eyes. "You have her strength. And her bullheadedness." He added with another sad laugh.

"Thank you Uncle." Was all I could muster in reply.

"Your mother also said that we would have to leave this place eventually." Jarron sighed, now looking down at what was left of his food. "I never believed her, but she was adamant about it from the moment she arrived here with you. I guess she was right about that as well."

"What do you mean?" I questioned, confusion evident in my voice.

"I know that we have been fighting for this village, but it is no longer safe here. The men may be gone for now, but eventually they will return, and when they do, they will come with more men, and more weapons, and they will not wait for us to leave peacefully. It won't be like this time. There will be no chance to ride for aid. Our way of life as we know it died when those riders entered our fields."

It was the second time that I had heard this in as many days. Jarron had simply come to the same conclusion as Luther. He was stating what should have been obvious to everyone, but was a thought that, with the victory that had just been won, was unlikely to be accepted by the rest of the villagers.

I looked down at my half-finished glass of milk and thought about everything that had come to pass over the past few weeks. "You're right." I acknowledged, causing Jarron to look up from his meal again in surprise. "Deep down I think I've known we would have to leave for a while." Jarron nodded solemnly and went back to chewing his mush. "It'll be hard to convince the rest of the village that it's best to abandon their homes. They will not want to exchange the trees of Jericho for the stone walls of some city."

"I assume you have spoken to Captain VanDrôck about this feeling of yours." He asked with his mouth full of wheat mush.

"He agrees with you." I confirmed. "Should I go seek his opinion on what to do now?"

Jarron simply nodded into his bowl, and when he spoke again his voice wavered as if he were close to tears. "Even if the rest of the village will not leave, I can't stay here any longer. I have to… I can't lose Lisa too."

A tear rolled from Jarron's cheek into his half-finished bowl of mush.

"We'll find a way Uncle." I responded solemnly. "We'll get her back. I swear it."

Turning to leave, I made it as far as the door before he spoke up. "I am proud of the man you've become Aaron, and your mother would be to."

I had to brush a tear from my eye, but I didn't look back before walking out the door.

…

I found Luther sitting with the rest of his men in a small area east of the sparring field that they had turned into a temporary camp since coming into the village. I told him what Jarron had accepted as the eventual fate of the village to which he agreed, restating his reasons from the previous night. After a quick conversation he told me that he would send a few of his men to gather the villagers for a meeting later that night and that we would go to work convincing the rest of the village that leaving was the safest course of action, and not a foolish endeavor that would lead to the loss of nearly everything they had ever owned.

After Luther had dismissed me I worked my way over to where Marcus was sitting, once again at work on his carving. Beside him sat Tryson who had replaced the somber demeanor that had consumed him during the events of the previous night with the persona of the world's most cheerful elf once again.

"Hello there Aaron." The elf flashed me one of his dazzling smiles. "It is a bit brisk out this morning is it not?"

"That it is Tryson." I replied, before changing the subject. "I've been thinking a lot about what happened last night and I was wondering if you had thought any more about why Ronan would have left you to come after me? Or who he actually hoped to meet in the grove other than you?"

Tryson shrugged, "The only other elf in our company now is Gladía, and he shares no connection to Ronan. It is more likely he saw one of our group and for one reason or another was deceived into thinking that that person was an elf. As to why he would leave the fight once he gained an advantage," he shrugged again, "you may have been the more eminent threat at that moment in time."

His answer seemed reasonable enough, but for some reason I felt that he was holding something back. When he refused to put forth anymore information, I chose not to push the issue. Instead I proceeded onto the real reason for my visit.

"I snapped my sword battling one of the Mazenkryie last night. I suppose that the force of its full weight was too much for my old sword to handle. Anyway, if I am to ever do anymore fighting I need a new blade, and the village doesn't exactly have a surplus of weaponry and –"

"- and you were hoping we had a spare blade we could lend you?" Tryson completed my sentence.

"Well, yea…"

Tryson leaned back against the base of a tree and thought for a moment. "Tis customary to bury our fallen comrades with the arms they carried in life. That way, if the need ever arises, they have a weapon to fight with in the afterlife. The men believe that when they die they will be called to serve in Lord Galahad's army. After all, a warrior in life is a warrior in death. Because of this all the men that have fallen with us here are buried with their broad swords as headstones. Since their weapons are buried with them, spares are rare, unless we are in Alleron."

"Lord Galahad?" I questioned.

This time it was Marcus who spoke up. Sitting down his carving for the first time he looked up at me with a surprised face, "You know not of Lord Galahad? What religion are you Aaron?"

My checks flushed a bit as I tried to conceal my embarrassment, "Umm… the religion of we don't really have one." I said trying to make light of the situation. Then becoming more serious I added, "I mean we believe there are high powers in the universe. We just don't really have names for them or anything. When there is a drought people pray to the God of rain. When crops are scarce we pray to the God of harvests. But there is no real religion here. Is that a problem?" I asked quizzically.

Marcus raised his eyebrows and shrugged like Tryson. "No, not really, only surprising. Just don't go about the other men saying things like that though unless you wish to be lectured to for hours on end. Some of the men here are very devout in their faith."

"That's good to know I guess." I responded before turning back to Tryson, "So that's a no on the sword then?"

"On a sword that you would be comfortable fighting with? Probably. Elves abide by different customs then men. Those of us who spend our lives fighting do not wish to do so in the afterlife. We are buried with our bows so we can hunt, but nothing else. Ranier fought with a Firewind, but it is not a sword many mortals would choose."

"It doesn't have to be a perfect fit; anything I can swing will do for the moment. I just want to be able to defend myself should the need arise."

Tryson stood and walked away into camp and less than five minutes later he returned with a sword sheathed in a lightweight leather scabbard with elven words scrolled down the side. When he handed the blade to me it was lighter than any sword I had ever held. From what I had been told about the weapons most elves use, it made sense that Ranier had used a blade that would not wear on him quickly. Removing the blade from the sheath I was amazed by the dangerous beauty of the weapon. The blade was short, just over two feet in length, and was little more than an inch thick, easily thin enough to slip through joints in an enemy's armor. It stayed that width until an inch from its end, where it slanted backwards to a sleek point. Along the back edge, the blade was partially serrated, I assumed so that it would cause more damage when pulled from a victim and the same elven words that were scrolled on the sheath were mimicked down the length of the blade. The downfall to the blade was that it had no exaggerated pommel to keep an enemy blade from deflecting into your hand, and the hilt was only long enough for a single-handed grip. I had never fought with a sword like it before in my life.

I gripped the Firewind with my right hand and it felt odd. I had always controlled my old sword with two hands. I felt like it gave me more precision in my form, as well as allowing me to strike blows quickly with additional accuracy.

Looking up from his carving again Marcus gestured to the sparring field, "You want to see how it feels?"

"What against you?" I couldn't possibly envision a scenario where that would end well for me, and I really didn't like the prospect of dueling a trained soldier with actual blades.

"Sure." He replied, "You can't very well spar by yourself can you?"

"With actual swords?"

Marcus looked confused and glanced at Tryson who shrugged back, "How else would you spar?"

"Well we have wooden swords stored in the tree at the far end of the field."

Marcus cracked a smile, "And how do you find out if your weapon is suited for you?"

Tryson looked up and laughed his musical laugh, "I suppose they just go into a battle without ever having tested their weapon."

Marcus laughed with him until he looked forward and saw my embarrassed expression. "Oh really? That's what you do then?"

"Kinda." I replied, "We're not exactly like you guys here. In my entire life I've only used my sword four times. Three times in the last three weeks and once to chase a raccoon away from Elma's trough… and I didn't even have to swing it that time." Marcus' shocked look was a bit comical. "Listen, I don't know what it's like in Alleron, but this is the first time anything like this has ever happened in Jericho. Here a sword was always just another tool, like a rake or a hoe. We spar with the wooden swords and that keeps us sharp enough to defend ourselves if bandits were to come riding through. It may not sound like much but its how we get by."

Marcus smiled and shrugged again, "Whatever. Do you want to test that blade or not."

It was odd. Every time I saw the young soldier I could swear that he reminded me of someone, but I could never place it. There was something about the way he smiled, but I pushed the thought from my mind as I accepted his offer. We moved out to the center of the field and I held my new sword at the ready in front of me. Marcus stood across from me but did not draw either of his own weapons that were splayed in an X across his back.

"Are you planning on getting a sword out?" I asked, confused.

"Nah," he responded, "not yet. I want to see how you use the Firewind as an extension of your arm. It's harder to do that when handling a weapon of my own."

"So what, you just want me to attack you?"

"Well I'm assuming you'll use some sort of strategy." He laughed. "But first, we really have to fix your stance. I take it you've never fought one-handed before?"

"No."

"I didn't think so. With a two handed weapon one stands with their shoulders square to their opponent, like you are now. This is so they can reach their weapon with both hands and strike at their enemy comfortably. With a one handed weapon this is unnecessary. You can turn your right shoulder slightly more. This gives your opponent less to strike at, making it easier to defend yourself, as long as you don't allow yourself to be flanked."

I adjusted my stance accordingly before replying, "Like this?"

He flashed me another smile, "It will do for now. Now do your worst, good sir."

I shrugged and stepped forward preparing for an attack. I thought for a moment about how best to use my new weapon, twirling it in a quick circle to test the weight I could not help but feel was off. The blade seemed almost too light and too short to be effective in battle. Bouncing on the balls off my feet a few times I stepped forward and slashed the Firewind down so that it would have cut Marcus from right shoulder to left hip. He easily twisted his body to the side and avoided the blow before stepping back away from me.

"No, no, that's too slow. You have to be faster. You need speed to carry you through a fight with that kind of weapon. It would get battered in a prolonged fight. It was made for quick kills, not for crossing blades. Try again."

The one handed weapon felt unnatural. It was completely against all of my instincts to only guide the blade with one arm and I found my left hand twitching involuntarily in an attempt to grasp the short handle. Although not having to use my left arm saved my shoulder a lot of unnecessary movement that was sure to set off a wave of pain from my still fresh wounds.

As I stepped forward for a second time I tried to put together a combination of what I thought were quick strikes, but it was like Marcus was in my head predicting my every move for every time he was able to bend just out of harm's way. Trying to strike him was like trying to strike a ghost. Finally, I ended my series of blows by lunging forward, thrusting the blade at his left hip, a move that he sidestepped, grabbing my wrist with his left hand while using his right to back hand me lightly in the jaw. I was thrown so off balance by the speed of his attack that I almost fell over.

"Dead." He said with a smile.

Most of the men outside the clearing were too busy cleaning their weapons or carrying on a conversation to realize what was happening between Marcus and I, but Tryson, who had watched the whole thing, let out another peal of laughter.

I stepped away and rubbed my jaw, trying to hide my embarrassment.

"The Firewind is meant for short, quick strikes. Try not to use such large bowing motions. There is too much arm and shoulder in your strikes, and the more movement there is, the more you telegraph where you're going. It takes time but you must build up strength in your wrists and forearms so that your strikes maintain their effectiveness with a minimal amount of movement. And you need to change the way you grip your weapon. You -"

"You hold your sword like you are trying to choke a snake!" Tryson interjected across the field, causing me to scowl back in his direction while he flashed his annoyingly white smile back.

"Tryson's right," Marcus interjected, "you want your grip to be loose but firm. Holding onto your weapon too tightly causes a litany of problems. Remember, your sword was made for one single purpose, you were made for many. Let the sword do the work for you, you are merely the channel for that work. "

"Is that all?" I questioned sarcastically.

"Oh and don't ever lunge like that when you thrust. If you're going to fleche you better land your strike, otherwise you're dead. Now try it again."

This process went on for nearly two hours. I would swing hopelessly at Marcus, and he would instruct me on ways to improve my technique. He was much easier to work with than Arctone and I found myself learning an incredible amount in the relatively short span of time. Eventually, he drew one of his own swords, an impressive looking falchion, and allowed me to duel him for a bit. However, the process resulted in me being disarmed more times than I could count and being slapped more times than I cared to remember. Even worse was the fact that, while I was learning a lot, the whole exercise proved to be nearly pointless, as it ended with both Marcus and Tryson unanimously claiming that the Firewind was not the right sword for me.

"Come here tomorrow and we will work on defensive techniques. If it's a swordsman you want to become, a swordsman we will make you."

"I'll be here too, Aaron." Tryson chimed in.

"Why do you have to be here?" I asked, not sure what he had done during the sparring session other than laugh.

"Oh I do not *have* to, I *want* to. It's always healthy to have a source of comedy in one's life." And the elf chucked again before walking away.

"Try not to mind Tryson too much." Marcus said once we were alone again. "He heckles everyone when they first start learning. I'm afraid it's turned into a kind of sick sport for him."

With that happy thought in mind, I left Marcus and made the long trek back into the heart of the village. To my dismay I could see Uthgar shaking his head at me as I left the field.

Chapter 26: Fading Memories

The moon had worked its way well above the canopy before Luther was able to corral everyone once more in the barn, which had been slowly transformed into a meetinghouse, to discuss the fate of the village. Luther had his mission cut out for him, convincing the people of the best course of action would be an uphill battle at best. After the victory that had been won the previous night, very few people realized the danger that still lingered, and did not understand the need for a meeting in the dead of night. But, after hours of knocking on doors and pleading with grumpy old men, the village sat grumbling, anxiously waiting to hear what was so important. The scene was eerily familiar to the meeting we had convened before Terrick and I had set out to find aide for our village, and I couldn't help but wonder if anyone else could sense that another journey awaited us.

Realizing that the grumbling was not going to end soon enough, I let my mind wander back over the day. I knew that I would have to leave this place, even if no one else did, and wanting to remember all I could. I had spent most of the day after my sparring session, wandering around the village. I tried now to thrust the sights and sounds of the forest, my forest, back into the forefront of my mind. As much as I loved this place, it had become a dull shadow of the beauty I had once known. The memories of all that I had lost seemed to haunt all the places I had grown up loving, and everywhere I went I saw ghosts from my past forcing me to think about all the things I wanted to forget. Walking past the burnt ashes of my tree and the destroyed remains of Elma's pen was hard enough, but coupled with the burnt out husk of the fields where I had worked and wrestled with Terrick every day of my life, and the streams that Lisa used to stick her feet in while reading one of her books, there was almost nowhere I could go to escape the crushing feeling of loss that threatened to overwhelm me. I had tried to take Elma to the spring for a while, simply to remove myself from the memories of village, but even there all I saw were images of Tryson being overwhelmed and a black war hawk vanishing into the night. There was nowhere that I could hide from the torments of my own mind. So it was with great anticipation that I took my seat beside Jarron in the barn to hear the news that was sure to send the village into an uproar.

Luther stood at the front of the barn, resplendent in the freshly polished armor of Alleron. He was flanked by Tryson, Athéal and several other soldiers, waiting for the crowd to quiet down. Eventually the loud talking gave way to anxious murmurs, which finally petered out into silence before Luther began, "I'm sure you are all wondering why I have called you together tonight." When no one responded with anything more than nods of agreement he continued, "I know that you are all thrilled with what was accomplished last night. Many of you have spent the last day happily reunited with a loved one, and my men and I have been more than happy to help that reunion become a reality."

"Thank you Captain!" Anglehurst shouted from the back of the room, wrapping an arm around Sienna.

Luther gave a small smile back in his direction. "You are very much welcome. But I am afraid that we have been unable to fulfill the promise that we gave Aaron when he came riding into Alleron. We promised Aaron that we would save your village from the Urröbbí —"

"And that you did!" Shouted David; an exclamation that caused the rest of the room to applaud.

Luther waved the crowed down before moving on, not at all deterred by the interruption, but he resumed a serious expression before continuing. "I fear that we have not accomplished all that you would have hoped. As I said, in Alleron we promised that we would cleans Jericho of the Urröbbí. That we have done, but we have failed to remove the threat. You were right to rejoice as you were reunited with your friends and family members, but the time for celebration has ended, and the time for being responsible and logical has come. While we have won a great battle, the war is far from over. Ronan still lives and as long as he breathes this village is not safe. More warriors are on their way and a victory in our past does not ensure a victory in our future. The greatest mistake that one can make is to assume that history will repeat itself. Relying on the past is no way to determine the future. I realize that this will be difficult for some of you to accept, but no longer can Northern Jericho be the place that you call home."

Luther waited a moment for the truth to settle over the crowd, and once it had, allowed the inevitable onslaught of questions and angry comments to crash over him. Everyone started talking at once and the noise in the barn reached so high an intensity that I thought my head would explode. Still this needed to happen. The villagers needed to rage and shout and express themselves so that they could be led to the inevitable truth: that Luther was right and that their village was now doomed.

Once the crowd had shouted itself hoarse and the deafening noise quieted, Luther seised the opportunity to once again speak. "You must realize that while we have held back the Urröbbí thus far, they already had reinforcements on the way, and when the tide returns, the waves will smash against the rocks all the harder. There will be more men, they will come with more weapons, and they will not allow time for you to prepare yourselves. My men and I will aide you in whatever way we can, but there are too few of us left to defend against an army. Even if we were to fight them off once more, how many would remain to protect you from a third assault?" The captain paused for an instant, allowing the implications to take root, "Do not fool yourselves into thinking they would stop after two attempts, for there would be a third assault. Ronan will not halt simply because this village has shown resistance. He will attack until he has burnt this forest to ash. His anger and his pride are too great for him to go whimpering back into the desert from whence he came. No, he will not stop, and as such, we must act accordingly.

"There is no way of knowing how far out this new impending danger may be. The second wave of the Urröbbían force may be days, weeks, or even a month out, but we must use what little time we have to gather ourselves and move into a more defendable position."

"We can defend ourselves here!" Chisel objected, "These trees may not seem like much to you, coming from a great city like Alleron, but they are our homes. We can use the time we have to continue fortifying the village. We can cut down more trees, continue building the wall. Make stations for archers. Leaving can't really be an option."

Luther gave the man a sad frown. He understood how difficult it would be for the villagers to accept leaving their homes. "Not only is it an option, but after examining our situation from every possible angle, as an unbiased party, I have deemed it to be the only prudent course of action that we could successfully undertake.

"Yes, we could spend what little time we may have to fortify our surrounding area, but to what end? Ronan has shown us that he is a more than capable magician. I doubt that a wall constructed solely of trees, no matter their size, would remain much of an obstacle for long, and even if it did, the village, while a magnificent spectacle, was not built with thoughts to a defensible perimeter. The village is large and sprawls out over nearly a league. A tree wall was a good idea at the time, but in order to station an archer or lookout in locations surrounding the entire border, it would spread our men far too thin. No, if we were to stay, we would do so knowing that the decision was likely to end in our destruction."

"What would you have us do?" It was Anglehurst who spoke this time. His arm still protectively wrapped around his daughter, like he thought she may be snatched up again at any moment. "Wherever you go, I will leave with you. I will not risk the safety of my daughter again."

Some of the men looked astonished that Anglehurst was giving in to the idea so easily, but Luther simply smiled, "You should gather your belongings. Nothing too strenuous, just what you need so that you can make a living: the items necessary for your survival, or for you to continue your craft in a new location. I suggest that we fall back to the safety of the walls of Alleron."

As the crowd in the barn started shouting in protest, Luther continued, "They have the means and the resources to lend you food and lodging for the time being, and if it becomes a more permanent situation, they have the ability to take you in. Using the defenses of Alleron is the best conclusion I have been able to arrive at. Hopefully, by leaving the village the Urröbbí will deem destroying it unnecessary, thus saving your homes for the future. Once the threat of Ronan has permanently been suppressed, then you would be able to return safely to pick up the pieces. I will not force anyone to leave, but if you choose to stay, you will stay knowing that my men will no longer be here to protect you. As their Captain, I must think for their well being as well as yours."

With that, Luther turned his back on the villagers and walked out into the night, with the rest of his men quickly following suit.

"Can ya' believe that guy?" Johan spoke up sarcastically, "Wantin' us ta leave. Musta lost his mind."

I found it funny that he hadn't had the nerve to speak while Luther was in the room, but acted like a brave man now.

At first no one responded to him, they all seemed to be lost in thought. But after a few minutes Jarron finally stood, "You all can do what you like, the only reasons for me to stay are either buried in the ground or lost in the wilderness. Come the end of this week I'll no longer be here."

He started to walk out of the barn like Luther had, when Bray called him back, "Now wait a minute here Jarron. We should have to discuss this a little. I just got my wife back and now you expect me to go wandering off to Alleron and leave our lives behind?"

"I don't expect you to do anything, Bray." He said sadly, "I'm just voicing what it is I plan to do."

"Well if Luther's men go, and you go draggin' half the others behind you to follow them, how are the rest of us supposed to defend this place!" He started to yell. It surprised me, because Bray was the last guy I expected to put up resistance. "You and them soldiers aren't exactly giving the rest of us much of a choice now are ya'?"

Jarron looked flatly back at Bray, clearly upset that he was being accosted, "Well no I guess we aren't. How's about that?"

Jarron's cavalier tone didn't seem to set well with the rest of the village as the overwhelming uproar over the merits of either staying or going started anew.

As the conversation began to spiral out of control I snuck out the side door and made my way back into the village. The argument was no place for me. The adults would be fighting for hours, and if the matter wasn't about finding herbs or tracking a deer, no one would take my opinion into consideration anyway. Besides, it didn't matter what the rest of the village did, I, like Jarron, already knew what I was going to do. I was going to find Lisa if it took me to my last breath, and I didn't so much care who else came with me. It would be hard to leave some of my friends, but the pain would be dulled knowing what I was leaving to do.

I wandered through the village until I made it back to Jarron's tree. Elma was tethered to one of the strong lower branches and to my surprise Arctone and Erik were sitting next to her, feeding her some sugar cubes which she seemed to be thoroughly enjoying. When they saw me trudge through the trees, Arctone gave me a friendly nod.

"Didn't much feel like sitting through the meeting?" He asked as I approached.

I shook my head and sat down in the moist grass at his side, scooping a sugar cube off the ground and holding it up to Elma, whose pupils were dilated like she was on a drug. She whinnied happily and accepted my offering.

"Why weren't you guys there?" I asked inquisitively.

Erik shrugged, "Dad'll tell me what I need to know later. Toney just didn't care to hear it."

"Toney?" I asked, suppressing a laugh.

Arctone fed Elma another cube, "Decided to try it out for a while." He shrugged, "sounds more adult." We sat in silence for a while before he spoke up again. "You're goin' after her, aren't ya'?" It was phrased as a question but the finality in his voice made me realize he knew the answer.

"Yea." I responded with a tone of determination.

"I figured as much. You know you won't be able to go right away, right?" When I looked confused he continued, "I expect Luther'll tell ya' the same thing."

"What are you talking about?" I questioned, trying to suppress the edge that crept into my voice. There was no way someone like Arctone was going to convince me not to go after Lisa.

Arctone looked at Erik, who just shook his head like *I told you he wouldn't get it.* "Listen Aaron, there's no way you're getting

Lisa back going at 'em head on. There's too many of them and she's the only leverage they've got now. You won't see her again til they dangle her as bait."

Deep down I knew the truth to his statement, but his words just made me more upset, "There's no way I'm going to let them use my cousin as bait!" I shouted.

"Aaron just use your head," this time it was Erik who chimed in. "Sienna didn't even know they had Lisa. They were both gone for three days and she didn't even know Lisa was there."

"They were keeping her separate?" I asked, my mind trying to put together what they were saying.

"See that's exactly what Toney was thinking." He continued. "They must think that can get something through Lisa that they couldn't get through any of their other hostages."

"And if that's the case you think that they'll keep her better protected than the others? You think she'll be harder to get to?"

"Well… yea."

"It doesn't matter." I said stubbornly. "I can't let Jarron lose Terrick and her." At the mention of my cousin's name my eyes started to water.

"Aaron, we know." Arctone started back up, "But just cause the situation looks dim doesn't mean you should throw your life away too. Losing you won't be any easier on the old man than losing Terrick. You have to be smart, kid."

"Oh will you cut it with the kid crap!" I shouted at him, "I'm not much younger than you. You ever wonder why Terrick hit you so much?"

Arctone looked a bit shocked, like he was just realizing how big of a tool he really was, but Erik cut back in before he could say anything, "Aaron, if they need Lisa for something then they aren't likely to hurt her are they?"

I thought for a minute, wanting to argue that what he said was wrong but it made sense. "I guess." I muttered.

"Then all we have to do is wait for them to ask for it again right? We'd never get anywhere near her while they have her… wherever it is they have her. We need to wait for them to bring her back out into the open." When I opened my mouth to argue he continued, "Besides, at least then you might have a place to track her from. Where would you even begin right now? The things that took her could have gone anywhere. They could be back with reinforcements by now."

I hated both of them for being right, but I couldn't find a good leg to stand on for an argument so I just leaned back angrily against the tree and fed Elma another cube.

Finally, after the silence stretched into minutes, Arctone spoke again. "You stay with the soldiers for now, and when the time comes, we'll hunt for her with you."

It took me a minute to realize what he was offering, and when I looked away from Elma I saw the sincerity in his eyes. "Why would you want to come with me?"

Arctone looked back down at the ground like he was embarrassed, "I'm not sure why Erik wants to come, probably because he's an idiot," – Erik shoved him with a slight smile – "but me, well I figure the two of us... all we really have left is each other."

It surprised me to find out that Arctone cared so much. I mean I knew that he had always liked me, but with this, he was treating me like I was family. Suddenly I felt horrible for having yelled at him. He had only been looking out for me in the same way that I was trying to look out for Lisa. Choked up, a small "Thanks," was all I could get out.

He stood up and patted Elma on the back once more. "S'no problem." He said quietly, and then disappeared back into the depths of the forest.

Erik stayed with Elma and me until Jarron finally returned from the meeting. He claimed that all the fighting had accomplish practically nothing, which was as much as I had expected, and that the village was still split down the middle. In Jarron's mind it didn't matter, he was sure that when the time came, angry or not, no one would stay behind by themselves.

The next few days passed by in a haze. People moved hurriedly throughout the village, like it was the bedroom of a dying man. No one wanted to linger for long. Some could be seen making preparations to leave; others simply lock themselves indoors as if they wished to be absorbed by the trees. The jubilation of the victory at the grove had been lost, and in its place was the depressing fog of a village that had just had the life beaten out of it.

Most of my free time was spent with Marcus, learning how to make use of the infuriating windfire that Tryson had given me, while the aforementioned elf stood to the side and heckled. Sometimes Uthgar joined him, but it seemed he enjoyed it for entirely different reasons. Since the first day Marcus had started instructing me, I seemed to improve, and by that I mean I had at least made it to the point where he needed to keep his shield up to prevent any dents in his armor. Still, I was nowhere near good enough to make him break a sweat. Mostly, by the end of each day, I was forced to leave the sparring field bruised, sore, and furious with the increasingly creative jeers that had been thrown my way throughout the session.

It was after one of these particularly painful lessons, where I had completely lost the handle of my sword after overexerting the gashes on my back, that I was surprised to find Sienna waiting for me under the outstretched canopy of my uncle's tree.

"Hey Shorty." I put on a brave smile, trying to mask the discomfort that I was feeling.

Sienna threw on one of her patented smiles, but I could tell it was forced. "Father wants to know if Elma can help carry some of our extra belongings if there's room. It's not anything that we *have* to take, just stuff we'd be sad to leave behind."

I gave a sardonic laugh, "Extra space? You can have all the space. All of my things were lost in the fire and Jarron packs light. I'm not sure how much of Lisa's things he's bringing. Mostly just her clothes and a few books I think."

Sienna bit here bottom lip, "I'm sorry Aaron, I forgot…"

"Forgot what? That my family is all but gone?" The retort slide out before I had a chance to temper it. In my bad mood and my jealousy at the reunion she and Anglehurst had, I managed to completely forget that the last few weeks hadn't exactly been easy on her either. As soon as the words left my mouth I wished I could take them back, but it was too late, Sienna's eyes were already shining with unshed tears.

"Sienna…" I moved forward, embracing her in a hug, and she broke down sobbing on my shoulder, her chest heaving as she inhaled ragged breaths.

"I'm s-sorry Aaron. I m-m-miss T-Terrick too."

I knew she did, it wasn't something that she needed to tell me. After years of flirting with him, and him being to incomprehensibly thick-minded to notice, she had finally given him that kiss. I hadn't forgotten that she was every bit as worried for Terrick and Lisa's safety as I was, and I felt like the world's biggest ass for making her cry.

"S'okay." I mumbled into her thick, dark hair, "I know you do."

For a while we just held each other like that, comforting each other, and I was surprised to find that it was exactly what I needed. Until that point I had been completely avoiding the fact that I had lost my best friend and cousin. I had been trying to put on a bold front and pretend that I was invulnerable to the pain. When I finally accepted the whole situation there in front of my Uncle's withered old tree, all of the stress, soreness, and worry that had been thrumming in the background crashed into me. It hurt at first, but as we sat down in the shade and talked, the pain began to dull into something that was a little more livable. We sat under the tree and talked for hours, and by the time she left, leading Elma through the trees to her home, I felt better than I had in days, and for the first night in as long as I can remember, I slept without a single dream.

…

The next morning saw Jarron and I at the southern edge of the village, standing in the middle of Dû Vena Ruösa's camp, waiting to see whom, if anyone, would show up to make the journey with us to Alleron. The camp was already bustling with activity, and I was happy to see that a majority of the soldiers' horses were nowhere to be seen. Because so many of the villagers had no horse of their own, and the few who did were using them to carry their belongings, the men knew that we would be making the long journey south on foot. They had been kind enough then to offer their own steeds to the villagers who needed extra pack space, or had family members who were either too old, or too young to make the journey without a ride. The fact that so many of the horses were gone had to mean that a majority of the villagers would be joining us.

As we walked into the camp we were met by Tryson and Luther, "I'm glad that you have decided to accompany us back to Alleron," Luther said, "I was worried when we were unable to track your cousin that you may try to take matters into your own hands."

I didn't really feel like going into detail on how close he was to actually being right, so I simply responded with a shrug, "I had some sense talked into me."

"So it seems." He gave me a small smile like he knew more than he was letting on, but didn't elaborate as he turned to discuss something with Marcus.

As the sun began to creep above the canopy, more of the villagers began to arrive at the camp. Some looked upbeat and ready for the journey ahead while others were disgruntled and downtrodden, as if they had been forced to come against their will, which, with the departure of Dû Vena Ruösa, may have actually been the case. Arctone was the first to show up, wearing several of his favorite swords at his hips, and sporting a set of pretty armor that I didn't even know he owned. The few belongings that he brought were strewn in bags over the back of one of Urbank's mares. He greeted me with a nod before seating himself on the grass to wait for whoever else was coming.

To my surprise, the blacksmith, Johan, was the next to arrive with his wife, Selene. One of Dû Vena Ruösa's steeds was trailing behind them loaded with the heavy tools and smaller anvils he would need to continue his craft in Alleron. As he entered the camp, he strolled past Jarron without ever acknowledging him, and followed Arctone's lead by plopping himself on the moist earth beside a tree to wait. Johan was quickly followed by Chisel and his wife, Meg; the older Melinda; Erik, Ebar, and their father Elam; Bray and Illiana (though they looked furious); Urbank and his young daughter Nina; a couple named Argo and Dez, with their daughter Trish, and then finally Anglehurst and Sienna, who greeted me with a smile that finally reminded me of her old confident self. It seemed as though the previous night had helped her get some closure as well.

I was happy to see that a majority of the village had already gathered, and as the families continued to stream into the camp I began to hope that no one would stay behind, but I knew it couldn't last. Eventually, old man Parsons came to the edge of the camp and started saying goodbye to the people who were leaving.

When he reached Jarron and I, he tossed me an apple and smiled, "One for the road." I started to say thanks but he waved me off, "I figured you'd just steal it if I didn't give it to you."

It made me laugh, but it was a hollow feeling. When I asked him why he wasn't coming with us he simply shrugged, claiming that he was too old to want to start over somewhere else, and that a big city like Alleron was likely to swallow him whole. He then said a quick goodbye to Jarron and disappeared back into the village.

Parsons wasn't the only one who refused to leave. Abok was the next to come say goodbye, followed by the village millers, Thom and Lara, with their daughter, Abitha, who had recovered somewhat from her initial attack. In all nearly twenty people had decided to stay, and it was hard thinking that these were faces that I had grown up with that I was likely to never see again. With several tearful goodbyes being said, and stories from the past being relived, it would have been possible for us to stay in the small camp for days, but Luther made a point of announcing that we needed to leave before the hour drew too late. One by one the villagers who were staying behind faded back into the trees, already feeling like nothing more than distant memories of a happier time.

As the last of Abitha's red pigtails disappeared back into the village, a soldier named Borin blew the horn of Alleron and we found ourselves on our way. Slowly marching away from the only place we had even known.

Chapter 27: The Avard Catches the Hawk

The process of leaving the village was painfully slow. With over a hundred refugees in our party it was hard for even Luther to organize our movements. When to eat, when to rest, when to move. It was all difficult. The young and the old needed more rest than the others. Even though they spent most of their time riding a horse, there were muscle aches and saddle sores that needed tending. None but me had ever been in a company of moving soldiers before, and many of them acted as undisciplined as they were; begging for more rest, or more water, or more food, and the required rationing of our supplies made sense to few. By the end of the first day it was easy to see that at our pitiful pace, we would not reach Alleron for well over a week, and that was a problem for the people who insisted on staying well fed.

Slowly, a daily pattern grew for me; in the morning, while most of the villagers were still catching up on their sleep I would practice the sword with Marcus, and in the evenings while most of the village was lagging behind, I would walk ahead on the trail and hunt. Sometimes Erik or a member of Dû Vena Ruösa would come with me. Bagging a deer or a few rabbits each day went a long way to helping us stay provisioned. In the afternoons, I found that I spent most of my time with Sienna. It helped to remind me that not all parts of my past had been lost, and that's where I could be found one afternoon a few days into our journey.

"What's Alleron like?" She asked as we loitered near the back of the pack.

"It's big." I responded, knowing that Sienna had never once been outside the boarders of our small forest, "Much bigger than anything you've seen. It's down in a valley by the sea, so when you get out of the forest you can see the entire city. It's kind of breathtaking the first time you see it. I never imagined anything that large actually existed until I saw it. It makes me wonder what the cities in Ardue`an are like. They must be spectacular."

"Are there no trees inside the city at all?" She questioned, and I could tell the idea of moving out of the normal greenery of our lives was not something that she was looking forward too.

"I'm not sure." I responded honestly, "I didn't have a chance to see the entire city on my last trip. I'm sure there are some trees somewhere. But most of the buildings are built too close together for anything to grow." When her face turned downcast at my words I continued with a smile, "If we can't find any we'll just have to plant some of our own."

That thought brought the beautiful smile back to her face as her imagination ran away with her, "The city will be furious. Trees will be growing up the sides of walls and the roofs of buildings."

I laughed and continued with the idea. "And there will be flowers lining the streets and growing out of people's doorframes; all of the most inconvenient places. People won't know what to do with all the color."

Sienna wrinkled her nose in a cute way, "I'm not ready for all the gray."

"It's not as bad as you think it'll be." I countered, although I knew what she meant. I could still remember the suffocating feeling I had when I first entered the city. "They've found creative ways to brighten their lives. The use flags and drapes and other bright fabrics. It's a poor replacement for the living, breathing plants of the forests, but if you keep an open mind you'll adjust."

"Did you?" she asked.

"No." I stated bluntly with a laugh, "But it's tolerable. The hard part is getting use to the smell of fish. The whole city reeks of it being close to the sea."

Sienna wrinkled her nose again like she could already smell it. "Wonderful." She stated sarcastically. "It'll be like cooking for Dane again."

I gave her a sly smile, "Yea but I don't think they're quite as lenient with their alcohol rules, Miss Fire Whisky."

Sienna opened her mouth in a look of mock affront, "Don't be jealous just because you don't know how to hold your liquor, Aaron. All I did was keep Dane's supply fresh by finishing off the old stock." She said with a shrug. "Nothing wrong with that."

I had to smile at her logic, "Yea okay, whatever helps you feel better about yourself."

She smiled at me again and we walked together for a while longer before Anglehurst called to her and she moved forward to speak with him. A moment later her place beside me was filled by Tryson.

"Pretty young girl you have there." He said with an elfish grin.

"S'nothin." I muttered back. I was still sore about him calling me an 'Avard' during my sparring session earlier that morning, which, from what I could gather, was nothing more than a less coordinated version of a chicken, that the elves raised in Aríamoné.

They cannot fly! He yelled at me. *So they are easy to catch and kill, just like you would be in a battle, Avard!* His comments were immediately followed by me getting slapped in the jaw again by a smiling Marcus, who, for as much as he claimed to like me, really enjoyed hitting me.

"Oh come now, Aaron." He interjected again. "The two of you are quite pleasing together. Like a pair of Capatchies."

"Will you cut it out with the weird elf-bird references?" I pleaded hopelessly, knowing that the chances of him stopping were about as high as my chance of disarming Marcus.

"Alright, Aaron. But all I am saying is that if I was a young unfettered lad and a fair elf wished to be in my company, I would be hard pressed to deny granting her that wish."

"She's off limits Tryson." I muttered, the elf's comments once again bringing the memory of my dead cousin to the forefront of my mind.

"Ah," he sighed, "A life lived with limits yields a limited life. You should do what makes you happy Aaron."

I gave a bitter laugh, "What would make me happy is you not showing up to my sparring sessions anymore."

Tryson waived me off, "Nonsense, you love having me there. And if you spent a little more time hitting Marcus instead of vice versa, I would not have to yell at you so much."

"I'll make a mental note of that." I muttered before changing the subject, "Do you think the Urröbbí will pursue us to Alleron?"

Tryson shrugged, "It does not matter what I believe, Luther believes it, and he is usually right."

"Then won't our presence there put more people in danger?" I suddenly felt sick thinking about all the innocent people we could be dragging into our fight.

Tryson thought for a moment, "There is always danger in every action Aaron. Whether the Urröbbí show up at our doorstep in a week with you amongst us or in a year with you not, I believe that their visit will inevitably come to pass with any course of action. There is no point in delaying the inevitable. But fear not for the safety of Alleron. It has many defenses and has withstood many a battle."

I nodded but didn't add anything more to the conversation, so after a moment the subject was changed again, this time by Tryson, "Gladía gave me an interesting bit of news after our skirmish with Ronan. He says you claim to have spoken to an animal." When I didn't respond immediately he pressed on, "He chalked it up to the concussion you sustained at the hands of the Mazenkryie, and I have to admit, that makes more since than the alternative."

"I know what happened Tryson; I'm not making it up."

The elf nodded, "It is an odd gift for a human to have. I've never heard of it happening before. If it happens again, be sure to tell me about it."

I was glad to see that, unlike Gladía, Tryson was accepting of what I told him. It made me forgive him some for giving me a hard time with my swordplay.

"I will." I responded.

"Good." He said with a smile as he lengthened his stride to catch up with the main body of soldiers. "Oh and Aaron," he said turning around, "limits are what we make them. They can be reshaped at any time."

And with that he disappeared into the crowd of armor-clad men.

...

That night it snowed for the first time of the season. Freezing cold crystals of moisture fell to the ground, which had been chilled hard as a rock. Fires were kept burning all night, and blankets covered shivering villagers who huddled together to make use of one another's body heat. Secretly Erik, Sienna and I had snuck off before going to bed and shared a small bottle of fire whisky that Erik had brought with him from his grandfather's tavern. "For morale." He said as he took a sip of the luminescent amber liquid and passed it to Sienna who accepted it with a smile. I still wasn't fond of drinking, especially after the disaster that was my last encounter with alcohol but I couldn't help but think that a few sips would allow me to make it through the night without freezing to the dirt.

The next morning started with the same routine. I woke early with the moisture of my breath still freezing in the air, and made my way to where Marcus sat, already awake and back to work on his carving. Over the course of the last week he had gotten very near completing it, as the bear had now been completely whittled out of the wood, and he was solely focusing on the kinds of intricate details that only he would be able to notice. In my mind I couldn't have imagined him being able to improve on it any further, but still, every time I saw him he was hard at work on it.

As he saw me approach he carefully wrapped the carving in a cloth and placed it in a small sack by his helm. Standing with a smile he nodded to me, "Do you remember our lesson from yesterday?" he questioned.

"When an enemy thrusts, I should use the momentum of my parry to flow into my next strike." I recited back to him.

"And?" He questioned more.

"And when I block an overhand strike I need to support my blade with my off hand to help keep my wrist more stable."

Marcus looked at me for a moment and then replied, "Good. Remember, you should have a counterstrike prepared for every possible situation."

We talked more about defensive strategies as we walked away from the rest of the camp. We had taken to moving as far as we could into the forest every morning so that the clashing of our swords didn't disturb or startle the rest of the villagers. As we made it through a thicket of trees, I was surprised to see that Tryson wasn't alone as was customary for my training sessions. Instead, Erik stood by his side with a sheepish look on his face. His tired eyes made it clear to me that he was still feeling the aftereffects of the previous night's whiskey indulgence.

"What are you doing here?" I asked in a casual tone as we approached.

"I wanna get better with a sword. The noise you guys have been making has been waking me up the last couple mornings, and I figured if I'm gonna get woken up anyways, I could use the help." He responded before adding, "S'not you guys's fault. I've been a light sleeper since we were attacked. Guess that's to be expected though, right?"

When Erik finished, Marcus added, "He came to me last night. I told him I would be willing to work with both of you."

I nodded to Erik, happy to have a companion to train with. It would nice to work with somebody who couldn't disarm me without even using a weapon.

"Today I told him that he should simply watch us. Try to absorb as much of the information as he can. I'll allow him to use a blade tomorrow." Then turning to me he added, "Are you ready Aaron?"

Nodding to him, I drew the firewind sheathed at my hip. I turned my shoulders as Marcus had taught me and took up a defensive position a few yards from my opponent. Over the last few days I had gotten used to dueling Marcus and I knew that he would stand in front of me all day if I didn't make the first move. Marcus still refused to draw a sword most of the time, but over the last few sessions he had decided to hold a shield, making me feel as though I had to be improving on some small level.

I took a half step forward and prepared to thrust at his unprotected left hip but before I moved more than an inch into my attack he had stepped forward, knocked my sword to the side with his shield and slapped me lightly with his left hand under my jaw.

"Hahaha Avard!" Tryson shouted out with a peal of his musical laughter.

I stepped back from Marcus, put off. "You never attack first." I accused

"What's an Avard?" Erik asked.

Marcus smiled at me, "Don't think for a second you understand my fighting style, Aaron. The key to winning a fight is variation. Do not allow yourself to assume a pattern will hold just because it has been repeated several times. When I strike is up to me, and not anyone else. Besides, your attack was obvious."

"What are you talking about?" I questioned, thoroughly offended. "I hadn't even moved yet!"

"You were about to thrust," he shot back with a sigh, "I presume at my left hip. It would be the most obvious choice."

"Um, no." I responded just to be difficult, but Marcus simply smiled.

"I can't help you if you don't want to help yourself Aaron."

I thought for a moment, the desire to continue my lie flashing across my mind for a second before I realized Marcus would see through it. Slumping my shoulders in acceptance I asked, "How did you know?"

"The way you step forward when you thrust is very different than when you attack in other ways. Your weight noticeably shifts forward and you tilt your wrist toward your target. The latter is almost unperceivable, but I have been trained to pick up on these things. You must try to learn the tells of your enemy as well as your own. There is always something to be caught. No one fights flawlessly."

Nodding solemnly I readied myself a second time. In the background I could hear Tryson explaining several of my less flattering bird-like qualities to Erik… it pissed me off. Taking a deep breath to calm myself I once again stepped towards Marcus; this time making a conscious effort to focus on the way I was moving instead of just what Marcus was doing across from me. This time I moved quicker and kept my weight centered until what I thought was the last possible second. Once again I thrust at Marcus' hip, but he was easily able to deflect the blow with his shield. With my first attack thwarted I moved into a smooth series of strikes. With each blow, I mentally made a note to rid my body of any excess movements using less of my arm and more of my wrist in my attacks.

Each time Marcus was still able to get his shield in front of the blow, but several times, only barely. For the first time I was starting to think that I may actually be able to strike the soldier. Slowly, I began to feel as though I were simply dueling Terrick once more at the sparring field back home and I seized the opportunity to go for the kill. Feigning at Marcus' hip, I chopped upwards at the left side of his head forcing him to come across his body with the shield, spinning as fast as I could I sent a second chop at the right side of his head only to spin back around the right direction, falling to a knee to deliver the third strike in the series at his unprotected shin. Having just blocked by his head, there was no way for him to get his shield out of his line of sight and down across his body to defend against the blow in time. Sure that I had finally won, I put everything I had into the blow… and struck air. At the last moment, Marcus had realized what I was doing and leapt backwards, landing on his back and shoulders. Using his hands, he pushed off the ground, springing back to a standing position, and landing in the spot where my blade had just passed. Out of position and on a knee, Marcus easily kicked the blade out of my grasp and slapped me for a second time under the jaw.

"Damn!" I cursed, outraged that I had been beaten again.

"For all his spins and all his grace, Aaron gets hit in the face!" Tryson sang merrily from the side of the clearing. I picked up a small rock by my feet and threw it at him, which he dodged easily. "With sword or bow or mace or rock, the Avard loses to the hawk!" he sang again in retaliation, grinning from ear to ear.

"Don't pay attention to Tryson. That was actually quite good." Marcus stated in support.

"Not good enough." I mumbled back, disappointed by my loss.

"Only because I am who I am, Aaron. It was a very good move. With a sword of my own it would have been easier to defend against, but I have no doubt that it would have been an effective maneuver against a lesser opponent."

It didn't make me feel a lot better, but the compliment was reassuring nonetheless.

"Remember Aaron," Tryson chimed in from the side, "you must broaden your view. See everything and nothing, and then you will be victorious."

I was caught a little off guard by the elf's comments. It was the first time he had contributed anything other than an annoying attempt at humor to a lesson, and it made me wonder if he had been able to see something that I couldn't, or at least hadn't to this point.

As I readied myself for a third try, I closed my eyes and inhaled deeply, trying to calm my mind. As I slowly exhaled, I opened my eyes and the world seemed to slow, just as it had before the Mazenkryie had attacked the night Gladía and I had attempted to ambush Ronan. I could hear the wind rustling through the trees at the edge of the clearing, and the tactics that Tryson had begun discussing with Erik a few yards from me. I saw the bead of sweat that had slowly rolled from Marcus' brow, and how his grip on his shield shifted as I eyed him. I stepped forward, making sure not to give away my move, and as I did I noticed a slight shift in Marcus' weight. He was leaning forward ever so slightly, which made me almost certain he would once again attempt to strike first. As he thrust his shield in my direction it seemed to come slower than the last time while I continued to move at my normal pace. I easily sidestepped the shield and made a quick cut at his open left hip, which he was able to out maneuver.

Pressing forward I sent a quick strike at his left knee before thrusting once at his heart. As he deflected my thrust I saw his weight shift again as his left hand moved to catch me under the jaw. The almost unperceivable shift in weight gave me just enough time to bend backwards and let the hand miss my face. As I straightened back into a normal stance I stepped away to assess what I had learned. Not having a sword in his hand meant that I had a longer reach then Marcus. This meant that every time he tried to hit me, he needed to advance inside my guard, and every time he did this there was a shift in weight, followed by the slight opening of his hand. All at once I understood what Tryson was telling me. Instead of focusing on my tells I should have been focusing on Marcus'.

Knowing that Marcus could anticipate my moves, I tilted my wrist forward ever so slightly so that he knew I was about to thrust, and as I did I saw it – the shift in his weight. He easily knocked my transparent attack to the side and once again moved to slap me, but this time I was ready. As his hand moved through the air I allowed the momentum of his shield thrust to spin me out away from the blow. Upon completing the turn, I trapped his left arm under my own and pressed the tip of my blade to the back of his exposed neck.

"Dead." I gasped, out of breath from the exhilaration of finally emerging victorious.

Marcus looked shocked at first, like he couldn't believe what had just occurred, and then a broad smile spread across his face. He looked over to Tryson who had started to applaud in approval.

"We may have another hawk on our hands after all." Tryson said with a smile as I released Marcus from my hold.

Looking back to me Marcus asked, "How did you do that?"

"Well I noticed that every time you hit me you had to shift your –" I started, but he cut me off.

"No, not that." He mused, "I've been trying to get you to notice my movements for days. I'm glad to see you finally have, but how did you move like that?"

"What are you talking about?" I asked, bewildered.

"Aaron," Erik spoke up for the first time, "you were like a blur when you spun. I've never seen anyone move that fast."

"What?" I asked again, looking to Tryson for help, but he just smiled and nodded unhelpfully at me like something had just been confirmed.

Finally, looking back to Marcus I just shrugged, "I didn't realize I was doing anything differently other than watching your movements."

"Well however you did it you need to learn to do it more often. You moved like an elf; it was impressive."

"Thanks." I muttered, still unsure what I had done.

"You're welcome." Marcus said while drawing one of the long sabers splayed across his back. Then he smiled, "Now, it looks like I'm done taking it easy on you."

Marcus stepped forward.

I groaned.
Tryson squawked like an Avard.

Chapter 28: A Storyteller Drinks my Soul

It had been four days since I bested Marcus in the clearing, and I hadn't touched him since. Over that time I had tried to channel whatever mysterious power had propelled me to my first victory, but it seemed to have completely deserted me. I was still fast, but just regular Aaron fast, nothing abnormal like before. Fighting Marcus was like trying to fight a monster from your worst nightmare. It was as if he had eight arms and it was impossible for my blade to find its way past any of them. He had allowed me to fight Erik once, but the fight was over quick as I was far his superior, and both Marcus and Tryson deemed it wasn't helping anyone to let me bash him in. Personally, I thought it helped *my* moral quite a lot. But despite my protests, we didn't get a second opportunity to fight. Instead, Marcus had begun training me for only half the time before putting his sword away and walking Erik through the same embarrassing paces that I had gone through.

While Erik worked with Marcus, I was taken to the side to work with Tryson, who was teaching me how to defend myself against knife attacks. I'd love to say that I held my own against the shorter weapons, but our matches were about as evenly matched as me attempting to swordfight Lisa. The elf was so fast and so unpredictable that I rarely managed to see his blade move before it was pressed against my throat. There was no half speed with Tryson; it was just kill-mode all the time, and I had the privilege of being the cutting board.

The days wore on with increasing monotony as the snow started to fall with increasing regularity. The fat flakes were mesmerizing but the cold temperature began to take its toll on our group. The reserve supplies were shrinking quickly and the tempers of villagers and soldiers alike seemed to be dissipating with the food. Nearing the end of our journey, it became increasingly difficult to hunt as a majority of the animals had tucked themselves away in hibernation for the short winter season and with the source of our fresh meat drying up, moral dropped to an all time low. It was with great relief that on the thirteenth day of our journey we emerged from the trees to behold the city of Alleron sprawling across the valley at our feet; its east end opening up to the delta where the Aríalas River merged with the endless sea.

Seeing the city for the first time, Sienna's expression of shock was nothing short of priceless. "It's enormous." She exclaimed breathlessly. Without taking her eyes from the city she grasped my hand as if to make sure that I was still there. Her hand was warm to the touch in the cold winter air.

By the time night began to fall over the city, we found ourselves finally in front of the main gates. Many of the villagers were stared up at Alleron's towering, stale gray walls with amazement and fear as the harsh scents of salted fish and rotting wood assaulting our senses. To my dismay, the gate had already been shut, and the same set of dimwitted guards stood at their front with spears crossed and sabers at their hips. Concern at the incredible number of late arrivals creased the faces of the guards as the remnants of the village advanced, looking weary and travel worn.

As the crowd approached, the short fat guard addressed Luther and stuttered, "Uhh, w-what be yer purpose here s-s-sir?"

Luther gave the guard a reassuring smile but before he could speak Uthgar sneered, "What is his purpose? Do you feign to not recognize a true soldier of Alleron?"

"Uh, baa, umm…" the guard stammered with the color draining from his plump cheeks.

Luther closed his eyes for a moment is if praying for patience, and then explained his presence with much more tact, "We are the troop that was sent to Jericho o're a month ago, we have returned now with what villagers we could convince to follow. We must enter the city. They will need food and shelter for the night."

The guard still looked terrified, but had seemed to regain his ability to speak, "B-but s-sir, we's not suppose ter let no one through after hours s-sir. The gates c-can't open."

"They will open for us." Luther replied, still calm, but assertive with his tone.

"Uhh wait here a moment s-sir." The thin guard stammered when it looked as though his chubby partner may pass out.

"Certainly." Luther replied.

Nodding his thanks, the guard moved to a small, steel door in the side of the wall. He fumbled with his keys for a moment, dropping them once, before unlocking the door and disappearing inside.

Uthgar began to whisper something roughly to Luther, who pursed his lips and held up one of his hands to cut Uthgar off. We waited for nearly twenty minutes before a loud groan, from somewhere behind the walls, cut through the night. The sounds startled several of the villagers, but their fright turned to cheers as the gate slowly began to creep upwards.

As the gates moved, the remaining guard gave an audible sigh of relief, "I guess yers can go through after all." He breathed, quickly moving out of the way in order to allow the villagers to pass.

Once in the city, we walked the same main road I had ridden before, past the gray buildings with their flags and paint. The potted plants had long since died off as the nights had started to frost over with the cold. In their place only bare blankets of frozen soil could be seen. We walked along the avenue for what seemed like hours until we finally arrived at the Lord's Manor. The four members of Dû Vena Ruösa who flanked the entrance and the upper tier of the building stood vigilant as ever, only greeting their Captain with a slight nod before allowing the group of us past them and into the great obsidian building.

We were escorted into a great hall that looked as though it was constructed to support some massive parties, where we waited, examining more of the bizarre artwork that I had seen on my previous visit. We stayed in the solitude of the hall for the remainder of the night. Everyone tried to get what sleep they could but it was difficult lying on the cold, hard, oak floor; our heads resting on the piles of blankets we had used for warmth out in the snow.

By the next morning a man with long dark hair and a familiar smile woke us, and when he introduced himself as Darius I knew immediately who it was. He stood in the entrance to the hall shouting directions that echoed chaotically through the room. Lord Detrick had decreed that the villagers would be given shelter in an area in the far southeastern corner of the city. It was a small area that had been closed down due to its present state of decay and was scheduled to be either renovated or demolished, but our arrival had brought what seemed to be a more beneficial arrangement. The villagers would be allowed to live in the area free of charge, as long as they were willing to work off the fee by making the area "less of a public eye sore". Any further business endeavors the villagers wished to seek, could be run either out of their new homes, or they could purchase business lodgings elsewhere in the city with whatever money they happened to have.

Most of the villagers accepted the arrangement happily, or at least not as begrudgingly as I had expected and after all the echoing shouts and instructions died down, Darius smiled once more and led us out of the Manor and toward our new homes. We marched down the street in a gaggle of people, no one really sure where we were going, but packed as tightly as we were, it took some time for me to work my way to the front of the group where I could finally get close to Darius.

"You're Marcus' brother, aren't you?" I asked.

Darius looked in my direction and smiled once more. He was slightly taller than me with dark eyes and a strong jaw. His build was muscular, like most members of Dû Vena Ruösa, with a large chest and arms that bulged from under his tight-fitting, long sleeved shirt. Even though it was nearly cold enough to snow, he didn't wear a cloak or fur.

Looking at me he responded, "Leave it to my brother to make friends during a battle. I suppose most of the rest of them kept to their own, right?"

"For the most part." I responded, realizing that he was speaking of the other soldiers. "He and Tryson have been helping me with my swordsmanship."

"Oh really? Has it been helping?" he asked.

"I'm honestly not sure." I laughed. "I think I've only hit him once."

Darius gave a shrug, "If you've been able to hit him at all it means you're improving. My brother doesn't get hit." And then he added with a smirk, "Unless it's by me."

We entered the southeastern edge of the city and dreary shacks of building crawled into view. Some had roofs that had partially caved in, while others had walls that had started to buckle under stress that they were clearly not made to withstand. Weaving sluggishly through some of the buildings was a small, dirty branch of the Aríalas River, flowing from somewhere outside of the city, and all I could think was 'How dirty does a place have to be to produce water that shade of brown?'

Unlike the rest of the city, these buildings were constructed with space between them, rather than pressed right up against one another. Dirt passageways could be seen slithering between each decrepit home, adding to their already grimy appearance. It was a far cry from the comfortable trees of Northern Jericho, and the sight of the shambles we were being introduced to was nearly as depressing as leaving the magnificent homes behind.

Darius and I looked back to see the dismal affect the buildings were having on the rest of the village, and he frowned, not knowing what to say, "It's not a lot, I know. But a roof is important this time of year. I'm sure you'll find them manageable."

His words did little to brighten the overcast mood, and one of the older villagers actually started to weep, seeming to leave Darius at a complete loss for words.

Trying to salvage the situation I turned to him, "It's not a lot? It's terrific. I'm gonna go find me one with a skylight!" I chimed with just the right touch of sarcasm. Turning back to the village I continued, "You better hurry or all the riverfront properties'll be gone."

With my words, the mood seemed to lift slightly for several of the villagers, and I could see my uncle shaking his head in the back of the group with a small smile on his face.

I turned and looked back at Darius who gave me a relieved nod of thanks, like if another old guy would have started crying he might have lost it. He shook my hand firmly before trudging back toward the center of the city. With nothing left to do, I wandered into the wreckage that was expected to replace my former life and several of the other villagers slowly followed me. I crossed the dirty river over a bridge that was in surprisingly good shape, considering the disaster of a village that surrounded it, and continued to walk until I found a small building that had at one time been painted green. I stared at it for a long time; the peeling shade of color reminded me ever so briefly of grass. I clenched and unclenched my jaw, hating the loss of my forest, but decided that I would have to make this work for the time being.

Tethering Elma to the corner of an adjacent home that had completely collapsed, I walked into the building through a hole in one of the walls, bypassing the door entirely, and was immediately met by the depressing interior. The walls were cracked and flakes of shale and plaster covered the floor. Cockroaches scattered as I moved throughout the room and a spider that looked large enough to kill and eat a small child lounged lazily over a web that stretched from ceiling to floor. Looking up, I noticed a hole in the ceiling large enough for Elma to fit through, and I thought sadly to myself *well there's your skylight*. The pile of rubble that lay in the corner of the room under the hole was high enough that a tall person like Terrick or Arctone would have been able to stick their head up through it and look outside.

Sighing, I dropped the saddlebags that contained the blankets and other few possessions that had either survived the fire, or had been given to me by other villagers. When I made the noise, the spider scuttled to the upper corner of its web, and I lifted the bow from my shoulder, drew an arrow, and pinned the enormous creature to the wall, where it gave a screeching cry and shuttered, before going still.

The day wore on with villagers moving from shelter to shelter trying to find one that they could make livable and as night fell small improvements could be seen in some of the buildings. Holes in walls and ceilings were covered with unused blankets for temporary solutions and fires were lit inside the bare shale houses for heat, causing smoke to billow from gaps in their respective ceilings. After I had constructed a makeshift bed off the ground and away from the roaches, I climbed up the pile of rubble in the corner of my new home and hoisted myself onto the unstable roof. It was a clear night, and with the sky no longer concealed by a high canopy of trees, I realized for the first time just how many stars surrounded my world. The bright pinpricks of light twinkling in the dark beyond and suddenly a sense of hope filled me. The glimmering lights reminded me that no matter how far away I got from home there would always be something I could take with me. The stars would always remain, firm and unchanging, from their far off homes.

I was drawn from my train of thought by a voice calling out to me from the street below. "Beautiful, isn't it?" the voice asked rhetorically, wonder contained in the tone.

I looked down to see Sienna staring up at me. I smiled back at her, thinking silently that the stars weren't the only beautiful thing out that night, and wondering what she was doing wandering around by herself.

"Couldn't sleep?" I asked.

She nodded before responding, "I haven't slept very well since... well, you know. I was thinking of doing a little exploring. I want to try to find something green other than the shack you're sitting on. Interested?"

"Of course." I replied, jumping straight down from my roof. Why bother going back through the busted interior right?

Together, the two of us crossed back over the muddy river and out of our decrepit corner of the city. Our feet took us wandering slowly through all the places I knew we probably shouldn't, but I couldn't bring myself to care. In the back of my mind I kept trying to stumble upon the poor man's tavern that I had visited the last time I was in the city, right before Uthgar assaulted me, but no matter what path I took I couldn't find it. We looked for hours, searching for anything to remind us that we were still outdoors, but it was like we were trapped in a giant gray mausoleum, and there wasn't a single tree, weed, or blade of grass to be found growing up between the buildings.

We were about to give up hope and head back to the southeast, when we rounded a corner and found ourselves staring at a low-lying building covered from ground to roof in plush green ivy. The vines weaved themselves across the home making it look like the entire building had been ensnared in a giant, green hunter's net. Dark flowers spotted the net here and there, emitting a scent that entranced us and drew us unconsciously closer to the home. A light could be seen flickering through the cracks of the closed shutters and smoke was rising from the chimney in the building's roof, telling us that someone was most certainly home.

"What kind of plant is that?" Sienna asked me, taking in a huge breath of the intoxicating smell.

"No idea." I responded, not exactly getting the most warm and fuzzy vibe from the place.

"We should ask whoever lives here," she continued, taking a few more steps forward, "they're obviously home."

"I don't know Sienna, this place gives me the creeps."

"Nonsense." She said, looking back over her shoulder with a smile, "Really Aaron, shouldn't you be braver?"

She raised her hand to knock on the door, but before she could, it swung open. I wasn't sure if it was the door moving that caused Sienna to scream, or the person standing in the entrance. Cloaked once more in hooded black, the eyeless singer from the tavern stared back at us with gaping dead sockets of vast emptiness. His cracked lips spread into a wide smile as Sienna backed up into me so fast she nearly knocked me over.

"Hello there." The skeletal man chimed, "What is it that you seek? I do not normally receive visitors, especially at night."

"Nothing sir, we were just leaving." I responded quickly as Sienna grabbed my wrist and started attempting to pull me backward, away from the house.

The old man smiled again, "Now, now, the young lady here was just about to knock. Was she not?"

"How did you know I was about to knock?" Sienna questioned.

The man cocked his head slightly, "Ah my dear, I am blind, not deaf. Come in, and we will discuss whatever it is you wished to ask me."

I should have conceded to Sienna and started the journey back home with her, but something about the old man kept me in place.

"What are you doing?" Sienna hissed in my ear, "Let's get out of here."

And this time it was my chance to give her a sarcastic smile, "Come on Sienna," I whispered back, "the guy looks like he's made out of dust and lumpy potatoes. What's he going to do to us?"

"I don't know." She hissed again, "Kill us and suck the marrow from our bones?"

The old man just stood in his doorway smiling, like he knew exactly what we were discussing.

"Really Sienna, shouldn't you be braver?" I asked her mockingly, which caused her to give me an affronted look before finally managing a small smile. "Besides, I'm curious." I confessed.

"Oh now look who's tough all the sudden." She scoffed, but gave in, "Fine, but if you get me killed Aaron so help me I will haunt you forever."

I laughed at her before turning back to the blind man and answering, "We can stay for a bit," before following him into his mysterious home.

The interior of the room was musty and cluttered with junk. Piles of nameless things lay everywhere around the room, and only a narrow path led from the door to a small table at the far end of the room. As we moved through the maze of objects my foot struck something and Sienna gave a small whimper. Looking down I saw an oddly shaped skull, bleached white, morbidly rolling away from where I had accidentally dislodged it.

"What the heck is that?" I asked, starting to believe that Sienna's fear of being eaten might not be far from the truth

Without turning, the man replied, "It is the skull of a tree goblin. You can tell from its small size and the bone calluses on the top that make up the base of the horns."

"Oh Gods, he has goblin skulls." Sienna moaned silently behind me.

"And why do you have it?" I questioned.

"Oh it has its uses." The man brushed off my question before waving us to sit at a table that he promptly rounded, seating himself. "It has been a very long time since an elfling has visited me." He chimed gleefully causing me to start.

"An elfling?" I questioned, glancing at Sienna, "Uhh, we're both humans sir."

"Ahh, well then pardon me, I must be mistaken. After all, you would know better than I." He gave us another creepy smile before once again pointing to the seats in front of him.

Slowly I moved forward, dragging Sienna along, and took a cushioned seat at the small, circular table.

Without turning his head towards Sienna, the old man questioned her, "Now what was it you wanted to ask me, sweetheart?"

It took her a moment to gather her courage, but eventually she responded, "I was curious about the flowers on your house."

"Oh, they're called Aríamums, my dear. Lovely smelling things are they not? Just as long as you don't try to eat one." He gave us another eyeless smile as he dragged his thumb across his throat and cackled, causing Sienna to grimace.

"Why do you grow them on your house if they're dangerous?" I asked.

"Because they make a terrific stew." He responded casually as if that cleared things up, but it only confused me more.

"Well this was… enlightening." I mused, "But I think we're going to be leaving now." And I stood up with Sienna in order to start making my way back through the maze of garbage to the door.

No sooner had we turned to leave did the skeletal man stopped me in my tracks, "I had assumed that you had come seeking answers. I thought the question had driven you here."

I turned, curious as to what the man meant. His empty eyes stared back up at me expectantly, waiting for me to put the pieces together. "What question?"

"You know what question. All you need to do is ask."

I chewed on my tongue for a moment before finally answering, "What will I fail to keep safe?" I thought about the weird dreams that I had been having, the warnings from the elf by the spring.

The skin where the old man should have had eyebrows rose up his forehead slightly, "Interesting, that was not quite the question I expected to hear. Perhaps it is for the best that you will not keep it safe. Have you thought of that? No? Nonetheless, it is good to know where your priorities lie. I was worried you may already be consumed by it."

"Consumed by what?"

"The question." He responded simply, "But it matters not right now. Sit once more and I will examine the query that you have brought before me."

The old man's words had me hooked, and much to Sienna's dismay, forced me to sit back down at the table. As I sat, the man stood and circled the table before moving off into the clutter. For the life of me, I have no idea how he was able to locate it, but from the corner of the room he returned with a plain silver box. As he sat once more I noticed a pair of ornate angel wings that had been engraved on the lid of the case, which was secured with a small lock. The blind bard fiddled with the lock for a moment before lifting the lid to reveal a chalice that was made of a material I had never encountered. The cup seemed to flicker in and out of existence, like it was trying to decide if it was actually real. One second it was clearly visible, with a surface that reflected light like a polished mirror, and then the next, it would catch the light the right way and disappear entirely.

As interesting as the chalice was, it was hard to pay attention to it once I saw what else was lying in the case. An intricately carved, ornate, silver dagger lay beside the cup, its blade shaped to a perfectly razor point. The old man placed his hand over the container and whispered "Comás." And the dagger flipped out of the container and flew into the bard's hand as if it were attracted by a magnet. Sienna jumped at the sight and her grasp on my hand strengthened, but the old man seemed not to notice. Instead he was preoccupied, gently lifting the mirror-like chalice from its case.

"This is called the La Copa Denostrea." The old man intoned, "It is the Cup of Enlightenment. With it, I can see the path that you will travel. See how the God's have chosen to use you."

"This isn't going to be pleasant is it?" Sienna whispered to me, but I couldn't help but ignore her, the cup and dagger had my undivided attention

"I'm going to go ahead and assume that it's not just going to start talking to you." I mused, feeling the tension growing in my chest. When the old man's only response was another creepy, eyeless smile, I continued cautiously, "What's that knife for, buddy?"

"Ingredients must be found." He stated.

"And this is going to be the unpleasant part." Sienna whispered again.

"Umm, what kind of ingredients do you need a knife to get?" I asked cautiously, again ignoring her quip.

"Why, I need the soul of the Seeker." The bard stated, in lieu of an actual answer.

"And there it is." Sienna squeaked for a third time, eyes wide as the full moon.

The old man flashed the knife through the air so fast that I barely noticed it. Desperately, I jumped, attempting to get out of the way and sending my chair tumbling over backwards in the process. "What the heck do you think you're doing?" I shouted at the man, but all he did was slide the chalice across the table in my direction.

I looked down and noticed the knife had left a thin cut down the back of my hand. It was small, no wider than the width of my pinky, and so shallow that I hadn't even noticed he had cut me, but it bled profusely and the crimson liquid drained down my fingers and dripped carelessly on the dusty floor. I looked up at the blade once more, astonished to see that it was as pristine as ever, as if it had never been used.

"Five drops should do." The old man whispered sweetly, "Waste not."

I held my hand out gently over the chalice, watching as my blood dripped in and tarnished its mirror like interior. As the fifth drop fell from my extended fingers, the blood flow staunched itself immediately.

I looked up questioningly and the old man said, "La Copa Denostrea only takes what is required."

Pulling a glass vile from somewhere within his hooded robe, he unscrewed the lid and emptied its bronze contents into the chalice. As the liquid hit the blood it hissed and steamed like it was boiling, before leaving behind a transparent gold liquid in its place. The smell of pine and grass wafted from the chalice, making me suddenly homesick.

"Your soul smells better than most." The man said before grasping the cup and draining its contents in a single gulp, causing Sienna to cringe.

The man sat for a while licking his chapped lips before he shuddered and laid the chalice back down on the table.

As the silence dragged on, my impatience got the better of me, "Well?"

The old man smiled, "You have a long journey ahead of you, restoring the throne to the heir of Romulas. Your failure will be both your beginning and your end, and it will only lead to more questions. These questions, they will be answered over time, but will you like the answers that you receive for them?"

"What you just said, that doesn't make any sense to me." I stated harshly, quickly becoming frustrated, "I thought you said you could answer my question. That's why you drank out of your little glass of destiny wasn't it?"

The man just smiled.

"What will I fail at?"

"You will lead him there, and because of your actions, you will have sealed the fate of the one who returns. Only you can walk this path."

"I'll lead who where?"

"You will lead him into the cold forest; the forest where beasts lie in wait. And in doing so, you will have given your enemy exactly what he wants, and even as he flees from the hounds the resurrection will have started, and none of it would be possible without you."

"My enemy? I'm not going to lead Ronan anywhere."

The man smiled again, "You don't have to. He will get what he wants, and your journey will begin."

"My journey to what? You aren't making any sense."

"Your journey to the truth!" The old man shouted, pushing himself up from the table. "Your journey through rock and sand and woods, to the corners of our world. You will be the centerpiece that others will cling to as the darkness begins to spread. You will seek out that which was lost and claim it as your own. You will find the light and see it restored, and in the end, it will be you who gives him back the power that he seeks. That will be your failure, and you will accept it willingly."

"I'll never give Ronan anything he wants. He's taken everything from me."

The man laughed, "You fear the knight when it is the Prince who should chill your heart."

"The Prince? What Prince?"

"There is no time, you must listen. When you reach the door that cannot be opened, the key will lie in silence. In order to find what was lost, you must lose what was found. Where the sun sets in the east, a secret can be found under rock and root. And in the end, when all hope seems lost, and the connection must be severed, a sacrifice you will give."

"You're mad!" I finally gave in, shaking my head in frustration. Standing, I turned to Sienna, "We're going."

As we made our way through the piles of junk to the door, the man's laughing could still be heard behind us. "A fortnight from now the scales will be unbalanced, and the worlds will embrace. From shadow, the ashes of the past will rise and move to reclaim this world. You must sever his connection to the sha-!" and the door slammed shut behind us.

Chapter 29: The Wolf Room

Returning to my new home that night, I tried to forget everything that had happened at the eyeless man's home. Nothing that had been said made any sense in my mind, and thinking about all the unanswered questions that had been raised only made my brain hurt. I figured the sooner I could put the experience behind me, the better off I would be. Instead of focusing on the bard's pointless riddles, I chose to fully immerse myself in my lessons with Marcus, which had continued even though we were back in Alleron. I had been worried that when we returned to the city he would cease to tutor me, but that proved to be an irrational fear. While I didn't see nearly as much of him, due to his obligations to Dû Vena Ruösa, he still made time every morning to help both myself and Erik with our swordplay, and as the days slipped by I found myself thinking less about my mysterious visit that first night back in the city, and more about familiarizing myself with another new fighting style.

When we had arrived in Alleron, Marcus saw to it that I received a sword that better suited the way I fought. The new weapon was a hand and a half sword, similar to what I had been accustomed to with my old blade. This allowed me to fight with both hands on my weapon if the need arose, a luxury that I had missed dearly whilst wielding the firewind. Marcus still had me train with only one hand on my weapon, but I liked that I now had options.

As time passed, I improved dramatically, even to the point where I had been able to hit Marcus again. It was only a glancing blow, nothing that would have done any real damage in an actual battle, but as Darius had said, any hit landed on Marcus meant that I was improving. It was a beautiful thing, and the clang of my sword against his armor was music to my ears. Right up until the moment he hit me with the hilt of his sword and knocked me unconscious.

I awoke a half an hour later to Tryson's brilliantly white smile leaning over top of me, "It is difficult to slay your opponent whilst you sleep like a babe."

I rubbed my head with a gloved hand and mumbled, "Sleep? Is that what I was doing?" Looking around I found Marcus sitting to my left. "You didn't have to bash my skull in just because I finally hit you."

Marcus looked sheepish, "Sorry about that. I thought you would react in time. You did it again; moved like Tryson does. That's how you snuck past my guard. I'm not sure why you can't sustain it."

I looked hopelessly, at Tryson, still not feeling as though I had done anything out of the ordinary, but he just smiled back at me like the answer should have been obvious to both of us and we were simply being thick headed.

Marcus grabbed my arm and helped to hoist me to my feet, but I wobbled precariously when he let go as spots flashed in front of my eyes. He grabbed my shoulder once more and grimaced, "You need water, and you need to lie down."

With the help of Tryson, Marcus guided me away from the sparring arena and down one of the side streets of Alleron. After a short walk, he shouldered open a door and crossed its threshold, beckoning for me to follow. The room we entered had a warm, homey glow about it and from an adjacent room the smell of freshly baking fish nearly overwhelmed my senses, causing me to salivate, and realize just how hungry I was. Tryson guided me to a well-cushioned armchair and forced me to sit, despite my assertions that I was beginning to feel better.

A moment later, a young woman joined us from the adjacent room and pushed a cold glass of what looked to be carbonated water into my hand. I immediately pressed the glass against my throbbing temple, allowing the perspiration to soak my hair and relief to flow through my body.

"That's for you to drink mister." The woman chided. She was of medium height, with long auburn hair that reached all the way to her waist. She had a cute round face with green eyes and thin lips that were pursed together like a mother watching her child misbehave. The thing that surprised me most about the woman however was that, while she could not have been much older than myself, she was clearly several months pregnant, which seemed wrong to me. It was like trying to picture Sienna with a child. Her age didn't seem to fit with her motherly persona.

"Drink, drink, drink." She scolded again when I didn't move the glass from my temple. "It's medicated, and it should stop most of the symptoms if you only have a mild concussion."

I glanced at Marcus who laughed at my stubbornness, "I'd listen to her if I were you, she knows what she's doing. She's mended my fair share of injuries as well."

The woman turned, "Which happens far too often for my liking." She reproached, slapping the soldier in the chest, which caused him to laugh even harder.

I downed the fizzing liquid, which tasted something like buttered pine needles, while Marcus did his best to sound sincere with an apology. "I'm sorry sweetheart, but you know it comes with the job."

Marcus bent lower and kissed the woman on the cheek, causing her expression to soften instantly. She smiled for a moment before disappearing once more into the room from which she came.

When Marcus noticed my confused expression, he explained, "Pardon my rudeness, that was Angelica, she is my wife."

At my dumbfounded expression Tryson joked, "Perhaps you struck the boy harder than we thought."

I couldn't believe that Marcus had a wife. No one got married young in Jericho, and the idea that it could have almost been Terrick or myself standing there with a wife shocked me. I couldn't imagine being responsible for another human, not with the horrendous job I had done at protecting the people I loved thus far.

Suddenly, I remembered the conversation I had had with Marcus the very first time I had met the young soldier. As he sat under a tree carving a bear from a block of wood, saying that 'it would be ready by the time he arrived', and suddenly everything made sense.

"So wait a minute," I said, trying to get my mind wrapped around the situation, "You're pregnant?" I asked, still in disbelief.

Marcus laughed again, "Well no, *I* am not pregnant, but my wife is. We are to have a son sometime in the next few weeks. He will be our first."

"Congratulations." I sputtered, at a loss for words.

"We were planning on celebrating tonight. You are more than welcome to feast with us while you recover."

I happily accepted Marcus' invitation and spent the next few hours in a constant blur of good conversation, fizzing piney drinks, and Tryson amusing us with several Elven songs that were so beautiful they made your heart stop beating so that it could listen as well. As time passed more people arrived, leaving me with a haze of names I tried desperately to remember – like a tall blond woman named Arnist, who ran an apothecary, a cute older couple that happened to be Angelica's parents, and a fat balding man named Carm, who from what I could garner, spent most of his time simply getting fatter and balder – but then there were others I already knew, like Gladía and Darius, who showed up with a rattle shaped like a mace, which seemed entirely too dangerous for an infant.

"I just knew it would piss off Angie." He whispered to me slyly as Marcus' wife shot daggers at him from across the room.

Soon all the guests had arrived and food appeared from the adjacent room on silver platters, piled high and thick with scrumptious looking food. There were trays with diced potatoes, sprinkled with oils and parsley, platters full of steamed greens that had been buttered and salted, and a plate with three whole salmon still steaming and covered in a glaze that smelt of honey, sugar, and sweet fruit. The fish stared out at the party guests with eyes that had glazed over and scales that were still moist and shimmering. It was far and away the most delicious looking meal I had ever laid eyes on.

As we gathered around the table Darius asked for everyone's attention. "A toast!" He shouted, "Little more than a year ago I thought that my young brother was little more than a hopeless romantic, chasing after a harbor girl that was clearly out of his league. Angelica, it is tragic how far you have lowered your standards."

Angelica gave him a sarcastic smile and wrapped her arm around her husband, "If I wanted to lower my standards I'd be with you, Darius." She said sweetly, causing the rest of the table to laugh.

Darius grinned widely, "But all joking aside, I never would have guessed that Marcus would have not only brainwashed this woman into marrying him, but that I would also now have a nephew on the way. And so I say, may the world welcome young Créos with a warm smile and arms open wide with possibilities. I'm sure that he will live up to the honor and prestige that you yourself are bound to acquire my brother."

"Thank you, Darius." Marcus responded, seemingly glowing.

"No, thank you Marcus. Uncle Darius just has a wonderful ring to it." Darius looked almost as happy as his brother, "How I wish that things could stay this way forever."

"Ah, and here is to hoping they do!" Marcus shouted, "And we grow old together teaching my young one how to vanquish evil like his fearsome uncle and father."

Darius smiled again, "Things always change baby brother, we should enjoy the present while it lasts."

"Ugh," Tryson groaned from the side of the table. "I grow weary of this toast. Babies poop and babies eat, but now I'm hungry so pass the damn meat." He chimed.

"Huzzah!" Darius shouted.

"That was beautiful Tryson." Marcus mused shaking his head derisively.

And so we ate, filling our gullets full of the succulent food before washing it down with small gulps of cider wine. After our trip to Alleron where I had spent my meals chewing on cold pieces of jerky, and the last few days where the villagers had to bargain and trade for nearly every morsel they could gather, my stomach almost couldn't handle all the delicious food, but I forced down as much of it as I could handle anyway, eating until my sides hurt from the exertion of compressing my expanded stomach. The time passed quickly as the food continued to disappear, and the guests started to trickle out into the approaching dark until I found myself sitting with only Marcus, Angelica, and Darius.

"So how did the two of you meet?" I asked curiously.

Angelica smiled and recounted, "Well, I used to spend a lot of my time in the garden. The flowers just made me feel alive."

"Alleron has a garden?" I interrupted.

"Yes, a beautiful one. A long time ago, a sorcerer put a spell on it so that it is always in bloom, no matter the season." She answered dreamily, clearly picturing the garden in her mind, "It's between here and the sparring arena, and that's how we met. Marcus would walk through the garden every day on his way to spar."

"It didn't take her long to find out that my home was on the other side of the city though," Marcus chimed in, "and that I was walking through every day just to see her. Father thought I was out of my mind."

Angelica leaned her head on Marcus' shoulder and sighed, "It is a shame that your father couldn't make it tonight."

Marcus looked solemnly at the table, "He's busy, you know that. He has a lot of responsibilities."

Darius snorted sardonically, "When has he ever made time for any of us?" He asked. Marcus shot him a scolding look in response, but not vocally defend his father. "All I know is you better be there for Créos far more often than he has been for us. A father shouldn't be so absent from his children's lives."

"You're too hard on him Darius, you'll miss him when he's gone." Angelica admonished.

"When he's gone?" Darius scoffed, taking another large quaff of his cider wine, an empty bottle already lying on the table by his side. "He already *is* gone. All that will change when he is dead is that his absences will be less disappointing."

"All right Darius," Marcus sighed standing from the table. Gently, he leaned down to his wife's stomach and spoke to his son, "It looks like it's time for daddy to get your drunk Uncle Darius home."

Darius just shook his head, like his brother was being naive, and drained the rest of his goblet. "I can make it home just fine." He said standing from his chair and roughly kicking it back under the table.

A moment later Darius stormed out the door, with Marcus right on his heels. With only Angelica and I left around the table I promptly said my goodbye and wished both her and the baby well before I too hurried out into the night air, anxious to find Sienna. Within minutes I had arrived at my destination, and after sneaking through a back opening so as to not wake Anglehurst, I found the girl I was looking for, sitting at a table knitting something from a ball of yarn in her lap.

"I found it!" I spoke gleefully once Sienna noticed my presence.

"Found what?"

"That bit of green we've been looking for. And it's not attached to any creepy guy's home." I added as a plus.

Sienna smiled wide and in an instant, had thrown on the extra clothes needed to go out into the cold, early winter air. With it being nighttime and with me only knowing the general location of the garden it took some time, as well as several wrong turns, but eventually we found ourselves standing at the gated entrance to the garden that Angelica had described. The gate was made of wrought iron, sculpted to make it look like ivy, with small leaves and thorns protruding from multiple locations on the bars. Through the gate I could see the beds of flowers, still in full bloom, as though they were trapped in an eternal spring, even as flakes of snow landed on their extended petals.

Standing beside me, Sienna seemed to be in a trance. Slowly, she pushed the gate open and stepped through, leaving me to quietly follow in her wake. The garden truly was beautiful; the circular plot of land was divided evenly between twelve different beds of flowers and shrubs. The flowers ranged from the familiar - carnations, roses, lilies, lilacs, and bright blue flowers called crasanisses that were native to Jericho, to exotic varieties that I had never seen before. The barrage of color rivaled the leaves of Jericho in the fall, and was arranged so that they complimented one another to perfection instead of drowning each other out. In the center of each segment of flowers a short peach tree grew, branching out to shade and protect the flowers beneath it. Vines grew up around the trunk of each tree, clusters of grapes or strawberries protruding from under patches of oval leaves.

Each segment was separated by thin marble walkways, all of which converged on a single point; an odd, white, marble dome, that protruded from the middle of the garden like the head of some giant baby trying to rise from the earth. Small holes dotted the dome with no discernable pattern. Some were grouped together while others were separated by much greater distances.

I turned to see Sienna smiling at me. "Peaches, Aaron... can you believe it? I never thought I'd see one."

I was thrilled that Sienna was so happy. "Pssh, see one? How would you like to taste one?"

Sienna's eyes grew wide and her smile stretched from ear to ear. "Aaron, you little thief!" she accused in mock disapproval.

I glanced around the garden to make sure that we weren't being watched, before carefully maneuvering my way through the flowers to the base of a tree. Plucking two of the ripest peaches I could find, I made my way back to her.

She took one and felt the fuzz like it was the most precious substance in the world before grinning at me, "Shall we take a seat?"

We wandered down the rows of flowers before climbing onto the dome, careful not to step in any of its holes, and once we were at the top, seated ourselves to enjoy our snack. The peach was like nothing I had ever tasted, so sweet and juicy, I wanted each bite to last for an eternity. Sienna kept sighing after every bite like she might faint from overexposure to pure deliciousness. It seemed like a near tragedy when several drops of juice ran down my hand and fell against the white marble.

I finished my peach and looked up at the stars for a minute at total peace, before having to laugh at Sienna, "I know it's good Shorty, but you don't have to hum."

Sienna looked questioningly at me, "I'm not humming."

I looked around, realizing that unless Sienna had a second mouth hidden somewhere it would be impossible to talk and hum at the same time. "Then where is that sound coming from?"

"Peaches aren't hallucinogenic are they?" she asked while looking at the pit as if she longed to devour it as well.

"No. Seriously, you can't hear that?" I asked again, to which she just shrugged and shook her head.

It took me another few minutes of straining my ears to realize that the humming was coming from the beneath me; from somewhere down inside the giant marble dome that we had been sitting on. I bent low and placed an ear against the marble, causing the sound to intensify before I slowly made my way to one of the holes that spotted the dome. Reaching the first one I came to, I peered over the edge and squinted into the darkness. It only took a moment for my eyes to adjust and for me to recoil from what I saw. In the center of the room, almost directly under where I was looking, stood a dais that was glowing with a faint amount of light; light which came from beneath a bell-shaped glass container. I knew at once that I was staring into the room from my dream, and that supposedly, the answer to who my father was could be found under that glass vessel.

"I have to get in that room." I said, more to myself than to Sienna.

"Are you sure there isn't something wrong with these peaches?" Sienna asked again, looking at me with a worried expression before finally throwing her pit back into the garden.

"The peaches are fine Sienna."

"I'm not worried about the peaches."

"*I'm* fine. Don't worry about me either. Just… follow me."

I glanced quickly around the garden and found an old stone building that looked as though it extended underground. Making a snap decision, I started towards it with the hope that it would somehow lead to the room. Rounding a corner, I found the building's door but after leaning a shoulder into it, quickly realized that it was locked. A pair of deep foot prints in front of the door told me that someone was, for whatever reason, standing in this one place for an extended period of time; likely a sentinel, like the members of Dû Vena Ruösa who stood watch in front of the Lord's Manor. Looking around to make sure there was no one in sight, I took a step forward and kicked the door by the handle with all the force I could muster. The wood frame splintered and the heavy door swung open.

Sienna's face was in shock, "Okay, stealing the peaches was one thing, but I think we're officially doing something we're not supposed to."

The worry was thick in her voice, but I was too curious about the room to pay much heed to her concerns. "We're always doing something we're not supposed to. It'll be alright." I said, walking cautiously through the door.

Sienna followed reluctantly, but didn't give up that easily. "Aaron, what's gotten into you?"

I turned a corner and found a set of shale stairs that led underground and started my descent. "There's something I'm supposed to find in that room. I just have to get into it."

"Oh thanks, that clears everything up. Let's just continue kicking in doors then." Sienna retorted, still obviously worried.

A second later I reached the bottom of the stairs and upon finding the door locked, immediately took her sarcastic advice, splintering it by the doorknob.

"I wasn't being serious!" She shouted, hitting me in the back. I knew how worried she was, but my curiosity caused me to ignore her and continued on.

Even though the basement was dark, my eyesight was good enough to make out the cold stone hallway I was traveling through. Running my hand against the wall, I realized the stones were damp, like water was seeping through the rocks, and I could hear dripping from up ahead. I took a second to get my bearings and figure out which direction I was facing, and upon realizing that I would need to make a right, found the first door that allowed it and forced it open, surprised that is wasn't locked.

The door swung back to reveal a dark chamber around the size of the foyer in the Lord's Manor. Along one wall was a small table that was bare but had two empty chairs pushed neatly underneath. At the far end of the room was another door, but it was slightly ajar, with a faint trace of light leaking through the open crack. Once again the indistinct humming reached my ears.

I walked to the far end of the room with Sienna clinging to the back of my winter cloak. As we moved closer I noticed a dark liquid pooling beneath the door. Sienna had to have noticed it as well because her vice-like grip tightened before asking. "Aaron, what's that under the door?"

"I don't know. It could be water." In the dark it was impossible to visually determine what the pool was made of.

"Water isn't that dark, Aaron." Sienna responded, officially sounding scared.

I bent down and stuck two fingers in the liquid, which was sticky to the touch. Placing my fingers close to my nose told me all I needed to know. The churning of my stomach told me exactly what the liquid was, so I wasn't surprised when I pushed the door the rest of the way open to reveal a heavily armed member of Dû Vena Ruösa slumped against the wall of the next corridor. Sienna gave a small whimper of fright, but held it together reasonably well for the circumstances. In the dark, I couldn't tell where the soldier was bleeding from, but it didn't much matter. I put my fingers to the man's cold neck, feeling for the pulse I knew I'd never find.

"He's dead." I stated coldly.

It was then that I looked up and saw it; the dais with the bell-shaped container, still glowing and humming with energy, just as it had in my dream. I stepped over the soldier's body and walked forward into the circular room. From every open area in the room, the cold eyes of the marble pack of wolves glared back at me, challenging me to move closer to the dais. Looking around I counted ten of them, scattered between marble trees and thickets of delicately carved grass. In each of the cardinal directions another passageway branched from the room, leading away from the dais. Looking up at the domed ceiling, I was finally able to understand the reason for the holes. Each one lined up with a group of stars, letting just enough light into the room to allow for a ghostly appearance.

"Aaron, stay with me." Sienna spoke up from the door behind me. When she spoke a chill went up my spine, reminding me of the words she whispered to me in my dream. As I turned to look back at her I was relieved to see that she was still wearing her traveling cloak and terrified expression, rather than the stunning green dress and look of seduction of my nightmare.

"We shouldn't be here." She continued, but I had already made up my mind.

"It'll be alright Sienna. I promise." I assured her before resuming my slow march forward.

With every step, the humming seemed to intensify, begging me to unveil what lay hidden beneath. It grew louder until a step away from the dais and I could no longer tell if it was humming or growling. I glanced around the room once more to make sure that my stone companions remained as they were, before lifting a gloved hand to remove the small container and hopefully make sense of the dream, when Sienna's words came back to me:

The truth can be a terrible thing, and if this is the path that you choose events will be put into motion that cannot be undone. Events that will lead to you discovering the truth. Choosing this path will only lead you down a painful road. Many you care about will suffer, and you more than any will feel the pain.

It wasn't until that moment that I realized I had been holding my breath. My chest started to tighten, and suddenly I didn't feel much like knowing 'the truth', whatever that was. Slowly, I pulled my hand away from the glass vale, which hummed with disappointment. I sighed, relieved that I had come to my decision, but as soon as I took a step away from the dais, the container exploded, sending shards of glass in every direction. I jumped in shock and covered my ears as an alarm sounded. I turned back to Sienna in time to see steel bars closing off every path out of the room.

"Get out of here!" I shouted to her, and she gave me a wide-eyed nod before disappearing into the darkness of the last room.

From the passageway at the opposite end of the chamber I could hear voices approaching and I knew that I was running out of time. Stepping forward once more I looked down at the dais and was surprised. I'm not sure what I was expecting, a picture with a caption saying *Hi son, I'm your daddy!* But I at least expected the hidden object to make since to me. This was supposed to be the big hint, the thing that finally gave me an answer, and instead, all I had was more questions. Resting on the dais was nothing more than a completely unspectacular fragment of metal. It looked like a quarter of a larger circle that had been roughly broken away from the rest. There were small engravings in the fragment, but without light, or the rest of the object, they were impossible to decipher. I was forced to believe that there had to be something incredibly magical about it for it to be so protected because it looked like little more than garbage to me.

Part of me wanted to pick the relic up and examine it further, or throw it against a wall in frustration, but as the voices continued to draw nearer I decided that it would be a bad idea to be caught in a sealed room, holding whatever it was that was being so heavily guarded. Instead, I took a step back from the dais and waited. Waited as the voices drew closer. Waited as the first of the soldiers burst through a door at the far end of the room. Waited as Uthgar pressed his smiling face against the bars that kept me imprisoned.

"Well, well, look what we have here." He sneered, as the chandelier in the center of the room burst into light.

I shielded my eyes while they adjusted, but I didn't need them to hear the laughing coming from the soldiers behind him.

"Will you shut up and let me out of here?" I said with all the vehemence I could muster. "One of your men, the guard to the room, he's dead." I added. Instantly the laughing stopped and metal scratched metal as the key holder fumbled. In the light from the amazing chandelier, the room looked less intimidating and more magnificent, like it should have been the chambers for a noble king rather than the tiny dais. My time to examine the room was cut short though as the bars retracted back into the ceiling and Uthgar roughly dragged me from the building while his companions went to find the dead guard.

"What were you doing in the Wolf Room?" He questioned coarsely as we exited back into the night air.

"I was in the garden and I heard humming coming from inside the dome." I answered honestly, "I was curious so I checked it out."

"How did you get in?"

"The door was kicked in. I thought someone might be in trouble." I lied.

"Like the guard you slew." He hissed, squeezing my arm until it started to go numb.

"Are you kidding me? I don't even have a sword with me."

"No matter, Lord Detrick will know what to do with you."

Great I thought to myself. With the way Uthgar was likely to tell the story I would be lucky to escape this incident with a best-case-scenario whipping, or a worst-case-scenario hanging. Within what seemed like no time, we passed the guards at the front of the Manor and entered its magnificent halls. Through the building we marched, up the stairs, and past the bizarre collection of artwork, until at last Uthgar threw open the door to the Lord's chamber.

"Lord Detrick I found –" he started, but snapped his mouth shut when he realized Lord Detrick was in the midst of a meeting with Luther. I was thrilled to see that the Captain was there. I knew as long as Luther remained in the room, I would receive a fair chance to tell my side of the story.

"Well?" Bo huffed, clearly irritated by our intrusion.

"I found the boy in the Wolf Room. He had broken in and slain a guard." Uthgar stated, clearly enjoying the reaction that he received, with Bo's look of outrage and Luther's look of shock.

"I didn't kill anyone." I argued back, "I didn't even have my sword on me."

"He could have discarded it somewhere my lord." Uthgar rebutted.

"Discarded it where?" I was irate, "Down the throat of a stone wolf?"

"I know not the tricks your mind can conjure." Uthgar hissed back again.

"Silence!" Lord Detrick ordered harshly. "The matter can be sorted out later. We have more pressing issues at the moment."

"More pressing issues?" Uthgar questioned, "Need I remind you what has been placed in our charge?"

"Oh come off it!" I shouted, "I didn't even try to take the metal, it looks like a piece of junk anyway."

At my words the room fell silent, and I became distinctly aware that everyone had their eyes locked on me.

"What?" I asked when the silence became palpable.

I looked at Luther, and noticed that even his stone face betrayed a look of surprise, "You saw the fragment?" He asked.

"Yea, why? What's so special about it?"

"Nothing." Lord Detrick interjected a little too quickly before turning back to Uthgar, "See Uthgar, the boy did not take anything. No harm, no foul. You are dismissed."

"No foul!" Uthgar shouted, clearly outraged that I was getting away with nothing more than a slap on the wrist, and I had to admit, I was a little surprised as well. It made me curious as to why I was being let off so easily. "Sir, I beg you to reconsider. This child must be reprimanded. What could be more important at the moment?"

"Uthgar, stand down!" Luther ordered.

"It's quite fine Luther." Lord Detrick spoke up again. "*This* is what happens to be more pressing." He said, holding up a black arrow fletched with the feathers of a raven. "We pulled this from the hip of one of our scouts this morning. He rode like that for two days."

"What is that?" I asked, trying desperately to keep the fear out of my voice.

Luther looked back at me, "It's a Urröbbían arrow."

"And that means what?"

Luther looked older than I ever remembered him looking, "It means their force will be here within the week."

Chapter 30: The Angel of Annoying Vagueness

The first thing Terrick noticed was how uncomfortable he was. Not uncomfortable because of his injuries. In fact, he wasn't experiencing any discomfort from his injuries whatsoever. Terrick assumed that this was a convenient side effect of being dead – no more pain. What he didn't understand was why, if he was dead, he could not find a more comfortable place to lie down and enjoy his eternal slumber. He had always figured that the afterlife would be a place of relaxation, like sleeping on a cloud. Instead, his back ached as though he had been lying on a bed of rock for two weeks.

He opened his eyes slowly and was shocked to find that he couldn't see anything. Everything around him was the same blanket of white. Terrick had to fight off the tightening in his chest as he began to panic. *This is great, not only am I dead, I'm blind!* He thought to himself.

His anxiety intensified until his eyes adjusted and he realized the whiteness was not quite so enveloping. It seemed to fluctuate and drift both through and around itself. Slowly he raised his hand and moved it in front of his face, relieved to find that he could still make out the familiar shape. As he moved his arm through the white, small droplets of moisture collected on his hand, and he realized that what he had been seeing was nothing more than a fine mist.

I really am in a cloud! He thought to himself, followed closely by, *Wow, clouds are way less comfortable than I thought they'd be.*

Terrick sat in silence for a while, reflecting on his life, but he quickly became bored dwelling on the past, and the monotony of his misty white surroundings started to annoy him. He spent several minutes trying to examine his new world but gave up the endeavor as futile since the thick mist prevented him from seeing anything more than a foot in front of his face. To the touch his bed felt exactly how he thought it felt, like a rock, and he had to fight the urge to stand several times for fear that, if he managed to get his feet under him, he would take a wrong step and plummet back down to the earth below. He wasn't sure if the dead could die – weird thought right? – but he wasn't exactly ready to find out.

Just when he was starting to think that the afterlife was by far the most boring experience he had ever had, the mist began to clear. The small particles of moisture began to drift away from him as if they were being carried away by a strong breeze that Terrick couldn't feel. As the droplets vanished from sight, a golden glow slowly replaced it. The glow seemed to come from everywhere and nowhere at the same time. It completely surrounded him, but he was unable to pinpoint its origin. As the mist cleared and the glow continued to deepen, the structure that he was seated upon also began to change. It grew softer and more comfortable, and once his vision improved he was able to make out a plush mattress and the outline of a gilded bedframe.

This is more like it. He thought to himself again.

He was about to lie back down on the bed for a short relaxing nap when a small flicker of movement in the far corner of his field of vision caught his attention. Not moving from his bed, he waited tensely for the mist to finish clearing. As it thinned a shape began to come into view, slowly growing with the light. It started as two short legs attached to a more massive, shapeless upper body and ending with a small head, but as the last bit of white mist crept out of view, the undefined mass developed into a beautiful set of snow white wings. He had been unable to make out what they were originally because they were furled against the back of the bizarre man. The same man he had seen during his last few seconds in the marshes.

The man cocked his head to the side and stared at Terrick with his smooth golden eyes, eyes like circlets of frozen lightning in a bleached white sky, matching the golden glow of the background, which Terrick was now able to see was a gloriously ornate chamber. The golden walls extended upwards for fifty feet before slanting into a sharp baroque ceiling. Golden chandeliers hung down from the ceiling in several locations like the hands of some metal giant reaching down to grab him. The large, square room was wide enough to encompass a dozen of the trees from Jericho, canopy and all.

Stained glass windows dotted the walls of the chamber, refracting the bright outside light and separating it into an array of color. Between the windows along the base of the room several alcoves led into areas that Terrick could not see. A pair of circular columns flanked the entrance to each, adding to the ornate interior. The sight of the room was amazing, but even the beautifully carved columns were nothing compared to the detail of the walls.

The gold walls were patterned with designs and glyphs the likes of which Terrick had never seen. He supposed that the stream of writing was important for one reason or another, but the meaning of it escaped him. Each line of glyphs was punctuated with a golden candleholder that branched out from the wall like the stems of some precious flower. They grew out at different angles throughout the room, each one ending with a different variety of petals. Some took the form of orchids, others chrysanthemums, lilies or roses. Some of them had thorns, while others were smooth and unblemished. In the center of each of the hundreds of golden flowers, where the pistil should be, a candle sprouted upwards. None were lit in the bright daylight, but Terrick could begin to imagine how breathtaking they would appear cutting through the inky blackness of night.

Taking in all the information he could from the room, Terrick turned his attention back to the short man who leaned against the side of a pillar and stared back in his direction. He was exactly the same as Terrick remembered him, with the same tattered brown pants and bulging muscles that seemed to ripple annoyingly from places Terrick didn't even know muscles existed. However, now that Terrick was closer to the man he could see that there was something odd about his skin. It was like the man had permanent goose bumps, which gave his flesh textured look, not unlike the scales of a reptile. The bumps added to the man's already bizarre appearance. Terrick really wasn't sure how much time had elapsed but it had to have been enough for the strange man to find a shirt, and the fact that he hadn't seemed a little self-absorbed to Terrick, like he was trying to show off. The man looked like the world's most buff vagabond, and the appearance did not match the lodging.

Maybe it's against angel code to wear a shirt. Terrick thought to himself. *Or maybe it's just hard to find clothing that's wing accessible.*

Almost as if he knew what Terrick was thinking, the man pushed himself away from the pillar and straightened. After taking a step forward he stopped and cracked his neck, unfurling his wings in the process like he was stretching before returning them to their original position and squatting down like a bird of prey on a perch. The man never spoke, but simply continued to stare intensely in Terrick's direction like Terrick was a field mouse he hadn't quite worked up the energy to move in and snack on yet.

Finally Terrick worked up the nerve to ask. "Who are you?"

The man cocked his head again and clicked his tongue twice but did not immediately respond. It wasn't until the silence had dragged on long enough for Terrick to begin wondering if the man was even capable of speech, that he spoke up.

"Who am I?" he responded whimsically in a voice as smooth as melted butter.

"Yea, you know... your name?" Terrick repeated.

"My name?" The man seemed to ponder the question for a moment before responding. "I am the All Seer, the Falcon, the Wind, but you may call me The Gray, for I am what exists between the lightness and the darkness. I am the side that cannot be chosen; the war that cannot be won."

Terrick waited a moment for the man to elaborate and when he didn't, responded derisively, "Oh... Well that's nice. Thank you for the clarity. So you're like an angel or something, right?"

If the man thought the question was odd, he didn't show it. "Possibly." Was all he said, never shifting his expression or taking his eyes off Terrick.

"Possibly? What does that mean?"

"It means that depending on the definition you wish to apply to the term 'angel', I could possibly be one."

"I mean, you know, you're like a guardian of the afterlife; a soldier of the Gods from the olden stories."

"Then no. By your narrow delineation I am not."

"Well then what are you?"

"I am the All Seer, the Falcon, the –"

"Yea, yea I got all that." Terrick interrupted. "I mean you're not like a living being are you?"

"I am neither living nor dead. I am what I am because I have to be. I am the side that cannot be chosen."

"So what, are you in between then?" Terrick asked with a laugh.

"Yes." Was the man's only response, quickly putting a stop to Terrick's small bout of laughter.

"What do you mean yes?" Terrick asked bluntly.

"I mean yes. Is that not the term used for the positive affirmation of a statement in your patois?"

Terrick shut his eyes and took a deep, calming breath, trying to keep the confusing words from swimming in his brain. "Never mind." He finally replied, before deciding to at least figure out where he was and changed the topic, "Where am I?"

"There are many answers to the question that you ask. Which would you like?"

"How 'bout the simplest?" Terrick responded sardonically.

"You are in the present." The man said flatly, once again causing Terrick to shut his eyes in frustration.

"Maybe a little less simple."

The angel man paused for a moment before answering, "Through my presence you have entered the convergence, and as such, your physical being has been permitted to exist in multiple dimensions simultaneously. To be brief, in this world you are in my home, La'Anthril. In your world you are in the range of massifs north of the Allerian Sea. I believe your appellation for them is Blue Rock."

"We're in the Blue Rock Mountains? How can a structure like this exist in the mountains without people knowing of it? This is huge, it would reflect the light well enough to be seen for leagues."

"It does not exist in the Mountains as you know them."

"But you just said – "

"That in *your* world we are at that location. This structure is not of your world."

"What do you mean it's not of my world? Am I dead?"

"No"

"I'm not?" A wave of shock and relief flowed through his body before his mind clouded over once more in confusion.

"You are not. I could feel the disturbance your struggle with the Lycazul caused. Its energy rippled through this realm unsettling the tranquility of my home."

"Lycazul?" Terrick asked growing weary of the way the angel-man talked.

The man cocked his head again, his twitchy movements reminding Terrick even more of a bird. "The water-breeders, winged scales, long-necks."

"The swampdragons?"

For the first time the man blinked and when he did Terrick was glad he didn't make a habit of it. When he blinked, he actually seemed to blink twice; the first time, in a way that any normal human would blink, but the second was with a pair of glossy-looking, transparent inner eyelids which added to the man's reptilian appearance. The blink took only a split second, but it was more than long enough to make Terrick's stomach do a flip, and for him to grow uneasy in the man's presence. Everything in Terrick's experience told him that things of a reptilian nature were bad. They were venomous and sneaky creatures whose thirst for blood led them to be cannibalistic in nature. They damaged healthy crops and killed livestock. Liars and thieves were referred to as snakes and they were never to be trusted. Not to mention he had almost been killed by the Lyca…whatever they were called.

"The Lycazul share a relatively minute quantity of resemblances with dragons. They have completely nonrelated sets of cardiovascular systems and their skeletal structures differ in nearly every single significant detail most notably in relation to their cranial maxilla and squamosal where the bone fans out far less in the Lycazul." The man didn't sound offended; he simply stated the facts like he was trying to educate a child.

"Hey guy, they're both flying lizards, alright." Terrick defended himself to which the man simply snapped his jaws shut twice in quick succession and turned his gaze away from Terrick. Without the glare of the angel-man on him, Terrick's thoughts began to wander back to the fight he had just apparently survived and for the first time the image of the dying elf came back to him. "I wasn't alone on the swamp. There was an elf with me."

"She will live. I have done what I can to heal both of you of your ailments. I believe that shall suffice." The man nodded, looking back in Terrick's direction and sending a second satisfying wave of relief through his body. "When the disturbance reached me here I became aware that there was an elf in mortal danger and I – "

"How could you tell we were in danger?"

The man stared back at Terrick for some time gas if deciding whether to acknowledge the interruption, but his facial features remained in the same expressionless mask they always were. "Not you, her. I could tell that *she* was in danger. Every action in your world has and equal and opposite reaction here, in this world. The movements you make send energy rushing backwards through space and that energy can be collected and interpreted whenever I deem it a worthy endeavor. If I wished, I could observe every wing beat of a butterfly on the far corner of your land. However, this would be a tragic misappropriation of my time, so I am often disinclined to engage in the practice. The meaningless happenings of your world do not interest me in the slightest. There is enough conflict and tension for me to deal with here. However, I sense that our worlds are on the verge of a cataclysmic embrace, and as such I have allotted a small portion of my consciousness the task of filtering this energy for occurrences of significance. The dying struggle of this elf would most certainly alert me, and as such, I came."

"You keep saying *my* world like there's more than one of them. What are you talking about?"

"There are." The angel-man stated, "There are three worlds that overlap and envelope the energy of this celestial orb."

"You're crazy." Terrick blurted out, making to stand for the first time. "Thanks for fixin' me up and everything, but I'm outta here." And with that he strode to the far side of the room and pressed himself against a door of shining, jewel-studded gold, but as hard as he pushed, the door would not budge. Sighing he took a step back and once again faced the angel-man. "Why won't this door open?"

"Because right now you are pressing yourself against a solid rock face." The man said back. "That door is of my realm, and only I can open it."

Terrick clinched his fists contemplating charging the man and beating a straight answer out of him. "What are you talking about *your* world? There is only one – "

Terrick cut himself off as the scene around him began to shift. The golden glow of the walls began to fade and the color of the ceiling began to clear away like paint being drawn off a canvas. Where there was once a magnificent stained glass window there was now an enormous, snow-covered rock spire pointing up to a misty morning sky. Terrick took a step back toward the door and his hand brushed against cold rock. Turning, he saw that the angel-man hadn't been lying. Where the door once stood there was now a sheer cliff face extending a hundred meters upward to some unknown location. Turning back to the man, Terrick saw that he actually was perched on a thick horizontal tree branch that jutted out oddly from the solid rock face. Terrick clinched his fists and took a step toward him only to cry out in shock as the marble floor that he had just traversed opened up into an endless, black crevasse, leaving him standing precariously on a ledge with only a few inches between him and a sheer drop.

Looking back to where he had been lying just moments before, the bed had been replaced by a boulder the size of Aaron's bedroom, and beyond that the mist had cleared up enough that he could start to make out the tops of a vast, rolling forest spread out before him as far as the eye could see. The forest was a sea of green leading to the base of the mountain where a few miles of bare, dying land could be seen. Terrick immediately knew that he was looking down at the sprawling forests of Jericho and the cursed swamps that he had just attempted to cross. He had not been able to come to that realization earlier because the morning fog was too thick for him to see anything. A stunning bout of vertigo launched an assault on Terrick's stomach as he saw how high he was, miles above the sea of trees, with air so thin the act of getting sick was starting to tire him.

I must be higher up in the Blue Rock's than any other man in history. Terrick thought to himself, and he scanned the horizon one last time before the golden room once again materialized around him.

"How?" He questioned, still trying to catch his breath.

"As I stated earlier, my presence has allowed you to enter the convergence."

"And that means what exactly?"

"You are in the world between worlds, the land that stretches from that of the living to that of the dead, the side that cannot be chosen."

"You keep saying that, 'the side that can't be chosen', what does that mean?"

"The living dwell with the living and the dead sleep with the dead. This is the side that cannot be chosen. No one may come here voluntarily. They must be brought here, as I brought you."

"So what, this is like purgatory?"

"That is not the appellation I would apply to it, but as far as your reasoning is capable, yes. We call this world Du Fidal Antaro, The Life Shadow."

"So what does that make you?"

"It is the charge of those of my heritage to govern and bring harmony to this land. We are here to prevent its occupants from disturbing the other worlds."

"And why did you bring us here?"

"I needed time to heal the elf of her infirmities, and the laws that govern my kind prevent me from lingering in the mortal world. We can interfere in the affairs of mortals but once every millennia."

"And you used it to save us?" Terrick wondered out loud. He had no idea how long a millennia was, but it sounded like a long time. He couldn't help but wonder what was so special about him and the elf that would cause some otherworldly angel-guy to waste his one chance at altering human affairs.

"Not to save you," the man corrected, his eyes seeming to grow a colder shade of gold, "to save her. I have decided to spare your life, and yet I question whether it was the right decision. I sense a great darkness inside you, and I fear that your jaded heart may lead to you being easily corrupted."

"Hey there!" Terrick shouted starting to walk towards the man, his fists clenched again. "You have no idea who I – "

The angel-man held up one of his hands and Terrick froze in place, unable to move, or continue speaking. The veins that bulged out of the man's arms and chest seemed to pulse with intensity from the effort of whatever it was he was doing, and his face contorted to express a mixture of annoyance and sadness.

"You may not be an angry person, but anger resides in the depths of your heart all the same. That anger will be what fuels you to fight when all hope seems to be lost, but it is a weaknesses greater than any can overcome. Time heals many things, but not the wounds that you will hold on to so desperately in your heart. I fear that by allowing you to live I am undoing the good I have accomplished with my act." He lowered his arm and Terrick was freed from the crushing power that had grasped him.

"Well then why not just kill me!" Terrick shouted, letting the frustration flow from him. "Why allow me to live?"

"Because," he replied, his face resuming its masklike quality, "I have only the power to preserve life, not destroy it, and I cannot violate the laws of my race any easier than you could grow wings and fly from this place. You will leave here, but you can never return to the west, for if you return, all that was achieved today may be lost, and the darkness that you hold inside will be unleashed on your land."

"You have no right to tell me not to return to my home." Terrick spoke in a harsh whisper. "I will return."

"For the sake of all our worlds, I hope not. Now sleep." The angel-man waved his hand and Terrick dropped to the floor, darkness overtaking him.

Chapter 31: Songs Sung and a War Begun

Knowing that our new sanctuary was about to be invaded caused all the anxiety and fear I had buried after the attack on Jericho bubbled back up to the surface. The apprehension that came with the fear sent my brain reeling and only various points of the rest of the conversation between Luther and Lord Detrick made it through the fog in my head. Apparently, a scout had been patrolling the wilderness in Northern Jericho only to find the village in ruins. Leaving immediately to relay the news, he found a path from the village where the vegetation had been trampled by what could only have been an enormous force. However, he misjudged the distance they had covered after destroying the village and stumbled upon their rear guard less than a day's march out. From his vantage point, he couldn't see the entire force, but estimated their numbers to be in the thousands. In desperation, several of their archers let fly, and one managed to get lucky, catching the scout in the hip as he fled back into the trees. It was a clean hit that didn't strike any bone, so the scout would recover in time, but he had been lucky to escape with his life and was presently sleeping off his ordeal in the infirmary. What seemed to worry Luther more than anything, even more than the size of the impending force, was the report that as the scout fled, he was followed for several leagues by a beast in the sky; a shadow that blotted out the sun. Luther knew as well as I did what that meant; at least one of the Mazenkryie had reached maturity.

Much to Uthgar's chagrin, Luther escorted me from the meeting, essentially unpunished for my transgressions, with the exception that I was to never again set foot in the Wolf Room. An investigation was ordered in an attempt to determine who had killed the guard from Dû Vena Ruösa, but Luther did not seem optimistic that its conclusion would yield anything more than a dead end.

"Anyone good enough to fight their way into the Wolf Room and survive is smart enough not to leave any evidence behind." He stated before quickly changing the subject back to my transgressions. "Tell me about the medallion you saw."

I could tell Luther was attempting to be nonchalant about his question, but my mind jumped to the way everyone had grown quiet for a moment when I first mentioned the medallion. That reaction, coupled with his question, made me wonder why he was so curious about a dull metal shard he had likely seen hundreds of times.

Deciding it would be wisest to hide my suspicions, I matched his pretense and replied, "It didn't look like much; just an old broken fragment of metal. There was some kind of writing on it, Elfish maybe, but nothing else. Why?"

Luther shrugged, "I've never seen it before. I was simply curious."

"You've never seen it before?" I was surprised. If the metal was important enough to be protected, I would have thought the Captain of the Guard would at least know what it was he was protecting.

"No one is permitted in the Wolf Room other than Lord Detrick and whomever he assigns to guard it."

"Not even you?"

Luther smiled down at me. "No Aaron, there are some places even I am not permitted to enter. Typically, to enter the room outside of an official capacity carries the penalty of death."

"Wait, death? I could have been killed for going in there?" I asked, astonished at his answer and finally realizing why Uthgar had been so disappointed by the mere slap on the wrist I received.

"Yes. I suppose Lord Detrick pardoned you because you are new to Alleron and our laws were never fully explained to you. His friendship with your uncle likely played a role as well."

"What's so important about that medal that people are executed for going into the room where it is held?" I asked.

Luther stared at me pensively for a moment before answering, "It is better if you do not know. But the fragment is highly magical, and dangerous. Just understand that there is a very good reason for the law to be structured the way it is."

Luther didn't elaborate as he continued to lead me in the direction of our new village, so I decided it would probably be best to change the subject.

"What will we do about the Urröbbí?" I questioned.

"We will fortify the city the same way we always do during dark times. Preparations are already underway. Lord Detrick has sensed that battle would come to our doorstep ever since we departed for your village. They have had time to import both supplies and men from Arebock and Westphall. The armory is fully stocked and the barracks are cramped. When the Urröbbí arrive we will be well rested and ready for battle."

"How will the people of Jericho be expected to assist?" I asked, curious as to the role I would play in the upcoming battle.

"I have not had a chance to speak with my generals yet, but you will be utilized in whatever manner we deem gives us the best strategic advantage. There are several members of your village who are respectable with the bow. The most advantageous plan will probably see you placed on the rooftops near the city walls."

A mixture of relief and disappointment shot through me as I realized I was happy to be stationed outside the primary range of fighting, but saddened by the fact that I would not be able to use my new found skills with a blade.

Luther saw my face and gave a small laugh, "Fear not Aaron, there will be plenty of victims for you to exact your revenge no matter where I position you." And with that he led me back across the small muddy river and into the desolate village that was my new home.

…

The next morning, after seeking out and calming Sienna who had been a nervous wreck since my capture, I strapped my sword to my hip and threw my bow over my shoulder before setting out to rouse Erik. We made our way to the practice field in silence, surprised when we arrived and found Marcus nowhere in sight. Not sure what else to do, I put Erik through the paces that Marcus normally started him with, trying to remember the specifics of how he had instructed me. It was odd; I hadn't realized how much I had learned until I was forced to teach someone else. Surprisingly, I found myself making miniscule adjustments to Erik's stance, the way he held his weapon, and even the way he followed through with a particular strike. It gave me a sense of pride seeing that I was able to help Erik without being annoyingly belittling like Arctone.

We practiced this way for a while, working together and sometimes dueling until finally, when we were about to leave, Tryson appeared before us.

"And so the Avard thinks he can finally fly." He mused at my teaching.

"I think I did alright." I replied, defending myself before changing my tone to ask, "Where's Marcus?"

"He is busy making preparations and will not be able to attend the next few days. He sends his apologies. In the meantime, I am here to tend to something entirely different. I am aware that you possess some skill with that bow of yours. I need to determine exactly how much."

"I can hit a boar at over fifty yards." I claimed with pride.

"Terrific," Tryson chimed, "I'll be sure to instruct all of your foes to stay at least that far from you at all times." When I seemed put off, he continued, "In a siege setting, anyone can loose an arrow into a crowd of soldiers and hit something, but few can stick an arrow between the chinks in a man's armor whilst that man is running, or climbing a siege ladder."

"I can hit the boar in the eye." I continued, annoyance coloring my tone. "Every time."

Tryson looked from me to Erik who responded shyly, "I can hit a target if that's what you're askin'." Then he turned to me, "Why did he just say the word siege?"

"The Urröbbí are on their way here." I stated flatly, causing him to turn a shade of pale green.

"Oh… Well that's good." He responded quietly.

Tryson gave us both one quick look to make sure we were finished before he pulled the magnificent bow from his back, strung an arrow, and let it fly. The arrow traveled the length of the arena, before lodging itself into a wooden pole with a thud.

"Hit the arrow." He said.

Erik laughed for a moment but stopped abruptly when he saw the confused look on Tryson's face. "So he isn't joking then, huh?" He questioned rhetorically.

In response, a second arrow was released from somewhere behind us, and upon reaching the pole, cleanly split Tryson's first arrow in two, causing Erik's jaw to drop in amazement. Looking behind us I saw a short hooded figure approaching with an oddly compacted bow in hand.

"This is Ambria." Tryson introduced, "She is the best archer in Alleron, and she will see to it that your fellow villagers are properly trained."

She? Erik mouthed to me.

Slowly the hood was pulled back to reveal long, fiery red hair that fell in curls down the sides of a pale face, like rivers of fire on a snowy plain. Ambria had a small rounded face with a pointed chin, and intense green, slanted eyes that seemed to hold you in place. She was petite, so it amazed me that she had been able to launch her arrow with such force.

"Most people call me Bria." She introduced herself, curling her cherry lips into a smile, and holding out a hand that Erik seemed too mesmerized to shake. I could hardly blame him, the woman was absolutely stunning.

"I'm Aaron," I responded, taking her hand, "He's Erik."

She gave me another quick smile before walking past us.

"I think I'm in love." Erik whispered to me, but I didn't respond. Instead, I was busy focusing on the arrow that was maybe forty yards away. I took the bow from my shoulder and threaded an arrow. I had never tried to skewer an arrow before, but archery was something I had always excelled at, and this was a moment to show my worth, and to finally become more than just a boy playing soldier to Tryson. I pulled back on the bowstring, keeping my elbow high and drawing the feathers back past my chin. I inhaled slowly and blew the air back out, calming myself for the shot, envisioning the path that I wished for my arrow to take. Making a minor adjustment, I removed my forefinger from the shaft and Bria screamed. I jerked at the last moment and my arrow lodged itself in the wood beam two feet above the other arrows.

"What was that for?" I asked roughly, perturbed by the distraction.

"War is not calm." She said with another smile, "The archer next to you was just hit with a dart and he cried out in agony. Now you have just wasted an arrow. Every shot counts, there can be no mistakes, and there *will* be distractions. Many more than you can imagine."

"Yea, but I'll be prepared for them then." I shot back.

"Will you?" Bria shrugged, brushing her hair back behind a pointed ear. For some reason I wasn't at all surprised that she was an elf. With her high cheekbones and the slight slant to her eyes, she had the same exotic beauty that Tryson and Gladía exhibited.

I took another deep breath and pulled back on a second arrow, at the last minute she screamed again, but it didn't matter. The arrow flew true, and thudded in the wood, skimming off one of the Capatchie feathers that fletched Bria's arrow. It wasn't a perfect shot, but it was the best I could have hoped for.

Bria gave me a shrewd look before flashing me another stunning smile and giving me a little giggle, "Oh this one will do just fine." She mused, before turning to Erik, "And what can you do?"

Erik still seemed to be in a trance, staring at Bria like Terrick always looked at Sienna, and causing Tryson to slap him in the back of the head. "Pick up your jaw and look respectable." He ordered, but I could tell he was amused. He had probably seen Bria have this effect on people before.

Slowly, Erik lifted his bow, readied, and released. It wasn't a pretty shot, sticking into the pole several inches inside my first shot, but it was better than I thought he would perform under the female elf's gaze.

"That was a good shot right?" Erik asked hopefully.

"Oh it was just fine sweetie." Bria announced in a fawning voice, like a parent pandering to a child, before glancing back at me, "How are the rest of the people from your village?"

"Erik is about the standard." I stated, "But we have far more capable archers than swordsmen."

"Any more like you?" she questioned.

"Not as good as me." I answered honestly.

"What a pity." She frowned, giving a pouty expression that caused my face to flush. Turning to Erik she continued, putting on another transparently sweet face, "You would just be a *darling* if you let the rest of your villagers know that they would do well to report here for training in an hour. Can you do that for me?"

"Of course!" Erik responded eagerly, like obeying her wishes would simply be the greatest honor in the world.

"Aww, so sweet!" Bria said back in a voice as sweet as honey, "Run along now darling."

Erik stumbled over himself leaving the arena to do her bidding.

Now with only me in the arena, she stared at me for several uncomfortable minutes, like she was trying to observe every inch of my body, and to my chagrin it caused my face to flush an even brighter shade of red.

"Pull another arrow please." She said, and I followed her order, not quite as enthusiastically as Erik, but still quickly enough that I fumbled with my arrow for a moment before stringing it.

Pulling the arrow back to my jaw I held my form and waited for her to say something. She slowly walked around me, making casual adjustments to how I stood or held my weapon, and I was distinctly aware of every time she touched me. Moving my hand a fraction of a centimeter. Gently pushing my hips slightly forward. She touched my neck and I accidentally released the arrow. It flew through the air and split my first arrow in two, once again barely missing Bria's.

"Aww, you fired early." She said gently from behind me, allowing one thin finger to trace its way slowly down my shoulder, "I wasn't finished adjusting you yet." And then she whispered into my ear, "Don't worry darling, it happens to most men."

At her words I could feel the blood rushing to my face, but I was saved by a voice behind me, "I thought you were here to teach him, not flirt with him Ambria."

Bria turned and scowled, but it was quickly replaced by her sweet expression, "How lovely to see you this evening Marcus."

Looking at Tryson, Marcus continued, "You were just going to let her keep toying with him weren't you?"

"Oh come now Marcus, I was only doing as instructed." Bria stated innocently.

Tryson simply shrugged, "I wanted to see if she could break his focus. And it *is* always entertaining to watch."

"And it clearly didn't work." Marcus continued, "His shot was still true. I don't think you will be able to improve much on what he is already capable of doing."

Tryson smiled, "I feel you are correct. Aaron is quite the archer."

"Well in that case you wouldn't mind me stealing him from you?" Marcus questioned.

Bria put on her fake pouting expression again, once more brushing a lock of her crimson hair behind a pointed ear, "Oh but Marcus, we were just starting to have fun."

"That would be fine." Tryson concluded with a nod, ignoring Bria's comment.

A feeling of relief passed through my mind as I left the arena with Marcus, and it wasn't long before he turned to me. "Ambria is a good instructor, but don't let her play games with you."

"Thanks for the warning." I replied back, "The two of you don't get along, do you?"

Marcus gave an abrasive laugh, "Is it that obvious? I don't like the way she can manipulate people. Darius courted her nearly a year ago. My father and I both vocalized our displeasure with his choice. Ambria doesn't talk to you unless she wants something, and she's notoriously good at getting what she wants. We assumed she was merely using him, and I must admit I still haven't quite forgiven her for the way she toyed with my brother."

I listened remembering how Erik had acted around Bria, and wondering if it had been a similar situation with Darius. I wouldn't have liked for Terrick to be seen running around like a puppy dog all day for the affection of an elf, and I could understand why Marcus disproved.

As we walked on we continued to make small talk, while I noticed the subtle differences in the city. On the roofs of the buildings near the center of the city, people could be seen scurrying around, carrying heavy beams. Marcus informed me that runners had been sent out this morning to inform the cities inhabitants of the impending war. Now that everyone knew what was coming, people had been set to work on defenses for the city. The beams that I was seeing were to be used for building catapults that could be fired well over the outer walls. Several dozen of the war machines were being constructed at the moment at different locations throughout the city, and it made me feel safer knowing that the weapons would be ready when our enemy arrived.

As we walked we moved by the old tavern that I had seen on my first trip into the city. With the time of day and the necessity of the defense projects, it was nearly deserted, but I made a mental note to remember its location for the future. When the tavern first came into view, I caught a glimpse of a man cloaked in green, but as we marched closer he was nowhere to be seen and I was forced to assume that my mind was simply playing tricks on me. I put the moment behind me and continued to follow Marcus. Finally, after walking for over an hour, we made it close enough to the northern wall of the city that I could see the stone fortification through the last few remaining buildings. That was when Marcus stopped moving.

"I have talked to the Captain, and he has decided that this is where we are likely to place you and the rest of the villagers that Bria deems skilled enough with a bow to not waste arrows. From these roof tops you should be close enough to the enemy to inflict damage, but far enough back that if the outer walls are breeched, you can still be out of direct hand to hand combat, behind the second gate."

"I've improved with the blade." I added hopefully.

Marcus smiled, "That wasn't meant as a slight Aaron. You should not wish to rush into battle, you're more skilled with the bow, and if you embrace that proficiency it will serve you well."

I lowered my head, knowing that he was right. "You sound just like Luther." I said, causing Marcus to laugh.

"Perhaps he is starting to rub off on me. Try as I might to resist."

"Certainly that's not a bad thing." I responded, but Marcus simply shrugged, so I continued, "Where will you be stationed?"

"I will be with the rest of Dû Vena Ruösa protecting the wall. The wall will be lined with sword and spearmen. We will make the outsides of our resistance and try to prevent them from flanking us. If the Urröbbí were to breech the walls we want the leak to be in the center, where there will be a surplus of men and arrows to help stem the tide. We will cover this wall the heaviest because we expect the Urröbbí to attack from the north. That would make the most strategic sense because, if needed, they could then make a quick retreat back into the forest. We've reinforced the gate with Elvin steal, so it should withstand nearly anything they can throw at it."

"What if they attack from the river?" I asked knowing that the docks were almost completely exposed.

"They won't." Marcus responded confidently, "We will bring several of our war vessels up stream as far as we can. They wouldn't want to come within firing range of their scorpions. It would leave them too vulnerable. No, their attack will be from the north. They could circle to the east, but there is not an eastern gate, so any attack would have to be centered entirely around siege ladders and in only a small area, unless they were able to cross to the south shore. Plus in the north they can use the wind to give their arrows extra distance while hampering how far we can fire our own."

As Marcus explained the battle strategies of Alleron, a young girl ran by us, clearly distressed. Marcus ignored her crying, but I followed the girl with my eyes. As she approached a door close behind us, a woman who could have only been the girl's mother came out. The woman fell to her knees and wiped away one of the child's tears.

"What's wrong, my dear?" She asked, trying to console the girl.

"Benjamin told me forest people were coming to get us!" The girl cried.

Her mother smiled kindly, "There is nothing to be afraid of. We are protected by good people here, and good people always win."

"But what if the good people lose?" The girl asked again, still not comforted.

"The good people can't lose, for it is their nature to succeed. Just like the sun. Did you know that every day the sun has to fight its way back up to the sky?"

"No." The girl responded in awe.

"It's true." The mother said. "Every night when the sun goes to sleep the moon comes out and tries to keep him away with his army of stars."

The girl gasped, "What does the sun do mommy?"

"Well the sun is a fierce warrior sweetheart, and he's not about to let a few stars keep him hidden away." And then the mother began to sing;

Rise, rise, rising sun, cooks the morning dew.
It rises high with the songs of birds, and lights the sky so blue.
Waking up the animals so they can come and play.
The rise, rise, rising sun, greets them with his day.

Rise, rise, rising sun, keeps us safe and warm.
Protects us from the sneaky moon who tries to steal the morn'.
But every night the sun must sleep, promising to return,
As the rise, rise, rising sun, a page of life to turn.

Sleep, sleep, sleepy sun, resting in his bed.
The stars come out and run about and try to keep him hid.
You see the moon and stars like it dark so they can shine the brighter.
But the rise, rise, rising sun, knows we need it lighter.

Fight, fight, fighting sun, surrounded by the stars.
They close in and try to win the sky that should be ours.
They fight for hours upon hour, but you know what happens then?

The child's mother stopped singing for a moment to let the little girl guess, "No mommy, what happens?"

The mother smiled widely and finished her song in a whisper;

The rise, rise, rising sun, rises once again.

"And every morning the sun rises and it never lets us down. So you see my child, good always wins. And if the sun can win every single night against all those stars and the big bad moon, we here can keep the bad people away as well." The child smiled widely for the first time as her mother wrapped her in a hug, "Now go inside and get cleaned up for dinner." The mother ordered before they both disappeared through the door. By the time I realized I had missed the last of Marcus' descriptions and refocused my attention, he was dismissing me. I felt badly for allowing my mind to wander, but still, I couldn't help the feeling of peace that swept through me with that mother's song. For some reason, it made the entire situation seem less bleak.

I thought about the crying girl and her soothing mother the rest of the way back to the arena. The woman's strength and confidence was able to even still a few of my own fears and I realized that if everyone's will was as strong as that woman's then the city walls were in no danger of being breeched.

As I walked into the sparring arena I was greeted by the sight of nearly forty of the villagers loosing arrows at targets that Tryson and Bria had set up. The two of them sat in between several of the targets throwing small rocks at the villagers so that they were forced to move from side to side whenever they weren't firing. Behind them, a third man whom I didn't know, walked with a pair of swords, clanging them together or screaming at inopportune moments, trying to scare or alarm people who were attempting to concentrate on their targets.

Near the end of the line of villagers, I saw Jarron pelted with a rock.

"You have to keep your eyes focused on the sky while you're reloading!" Tryson shouted over the noise, "If that were an arrow you'd be dead."

Jarron grimaced and rubbed his brow before he continued practicing. Further down the line I was surprised to see Sienna standing next to her father with a bow that I didn't even know she owned. Nimbly, she sidestepped a rock and fired an arrow. It was a weak shot, but it stuck in the outside of one of the targets all the same. Next to her, Erik kept getting hit by rocks from Tryson as he kept starring at Bria in between shots like he was hoping she would notice him, or smile, or hit him with a stone. Arctone was nowhere to be seen, but that was to be expected. Being one of the few villagers who were far better with a sword, I assumed Luther would have other plans for him.

I continued watching the spectacle for a while before a bit of movement caught my attention. In the upper corner of the arena, a red tailed hawk had landed to observe the commotion. I watched it for a moment as it scanned the field, before it turned and locked eyes with me. In a moment I was lost. I felt myself change, becoming wilder, more primitive. My nest was too close to this place. It had been a long time since the two legs had gathered here in more than a small number, but there were too many threats here now. Too many to ward off if they attacked the nest. I needed to fly back and move the younglings. I needed to fly!

I leapt from the rafter and spread my wings, but then I realized, I didn't have wings at all. I came back to myself a moment before I hit the rough, frozen, dirt, scraping the side of my face. I must have jumped from where I was standing on the steps a moment before. I looked up from the ground preparing for the worst, but was relieved to see that with all the noise, no one had noticed my swan dive from the steps. No one except Tryson, who had momentarily stopped throwing stones, to keep his eyes locked on me. As the hawk gave a cry he shifted his eyes to the sky and watched it fly out of sight before returning the gaze to me.

Quickly, I stood and left the arena, not even worrying to brush myself off, or stop the slow trickle of blood that hard started to slide down my raw cheek. I made it back to my makeshift home and laid in bed for the rest of the day, trying to understand what was happening to me, but never coming up with an answer.

...

The rest of the week passed quickly, and the snow started falling heavily, blanketing the ground in a layer of fresh white powder. Most of the villagers were spending their days in the arena, practicing with Tryson, and as I was actively trying to avoid the elf, I wound up spending a majority of my time either by myself, or in the always pleasant company of 'Toney'. Close to the end of the week, Darius stopped by to give me a beaten looking shirt of mail, a small whetstone for sharpening my blade and an extra ream of twenty arrows to add to my quiver.

When I asked him about the mail, he responded, "It won't stop a broadsword, but if an arrow sticks you, you'll be happy you're wearing it."

He said that everyone in the village would be receiving one for their help defending the city, and that I was in charge of making sure that all the stubborn old men decided to actually wear them, a task that I grudgingly accepted simply because I liked Darius, and he didn't seem too thrilled with his role as delivery boy.

It wasn't until late one night that Sienna finally found me sheltered in the corner of my home, honing my sword with the whetstone.

"Hey Shorty." I said out of habit as she entered through the hole in my wall that I still had not fixed.

"Hey. Haven't seen much of you lately." She said casually, "I don't like it when you get depressed and hide away."

"I'm not depressed." I rebutted, to which she simply gave me a disapproving frown. "And I'm not hiding."

"Then what are you doing?" She asked.

"Sharpening a sword."

"You know what I mean." She urged on, not accepting my sarcastic answer.

I thought for a moment, before setting down my whetstone, "You're not gonna let this be, are you?"

"Nope." Was all she said as she smiled and sat down next to me.

I sighed and waited several long minutes to respond, "It's just, I think about home, and all the people that I lost the last time we were attacked." I swallowed hard, "I don't want to lose anyone else."

It was an honest admission. Sienna grabbed my hand and laced her fingers through my own, "What makes you think you will?"

"Its war Sienna, there's always losses." When Sienna didn't respond I continued, "And what the hell are you doing with a bow?"

It was her turn to avoid a real answer, "Well you know, I wanted to be prepared for the next time you decide to drag me along as you break into a creepy dungeon where someone's been recently killed."

I gave her a stare that told her how worried I really was and she finally admitted. "I want to be able to defend myself, Aaron. People without weapons can be hurt just as easily as people with them. I don't necessarily want to fight, but I don't want to be anyone's prisoner ever again."

It took me a while, but I finally decided that it was a fair answer. I kept forgetting that Sienna had spent the longest week of her life in the clutches of the Urröbbí. She squeezed my hand and I locked eyes with her for a moment that was long enough to cause my stomach to flutter. I hated myself for it.

Looking away I said with a whisper, "I don't want to lose you."

She smiled at me again, "You won't."

A moment after she spoke, the night was rent by a piercing screech. A sound cold enough to chill the marrow of your bones. It was immediately followed by a second screech, and then a third. I sprung to my feet as the ring of the Manor bell began to echo through the city in alarm. The time had finally come. They were here.

"Go to the center of the city." I ordered Sienna, "If you can fight your way onto a boat, do it."

To my relief Sienna didn't argue, but simply nodded and embraced me in a firm hug. "Be smart," she said, "and keep yourself safe." And then she was gone out the hole in my wall.

In a moment, I was garbed in my mail outfit with my sword at my hip and my bow and quiver over my shoulder. I ran out of my home and began my sprint to the northern edge of the city. Weaving my way past several other villagers, I managed to run into Arctone, who was once again dressed in the fine armor he had taken from Jericho. He nodded to me before branching off down a different side street to some unknown destination on the wall. It took an inordinate amount of time in the darkness, but eventually I did find my way to the building that would lead me to the rooftops, which would finally give me a view of my enemy. As I emerged out onto the roof of the building, large snowflakes began to fall, graying the darkness and giving an eerie, otherworldly look to the forest at the edge of the valley.

For the longest time there was nothing to see. Men kept appearing on the rooftops beside me, or on the outer wall that was only three rooftops away. A majority of the men had on rough looking mail armor like the ones that had been given to my fellow refugees from Jericho, but dispersed throughout these men were units of other soldiers. I knew that most of Dû Vena Ruösa's men were stationed at the northeast and northwest corners of the city, but I could see several of their finely armored figures patrolling the center of the wall as well, helping to give structure and order to the cities defenses. Elsewhere on the wall, I saw a unit of soldiers garbed in cold looking, gold colored armor, and on a rooftop to my left, there was a unit suited similarly, but in black, with red bracers. I assumed that these were some of the soldiers that had traveled from Arebock and Westphall.

Together all of the soldiers formed a formidable looking force standing watch over the valley, four or five men deep in some places. On several of the outer towers, I could see men hurrying to load the enormous scorpions that I had noticed on my first trip into the city, and I couldn't help but wonder what the purpose of the giant steel arrows was. Behind me, in the distance I could hear the creaks and groans that let me know the giant war machines were being armed and readied. To my left, I noticed that Erik had finally arrived by my side. He gave me a curt nod before turning his gaze to the forest in an attempt to see what dangers approached. It was odd to see my friend dressed in mail and a helm when I had never seen him in anything other than his thick leather hunting tunic, and it made me regret that he had to be standing next to me in battle. On my right, I saw Jarron, dressed similarly, and breathing heavily in the cold night air. Separating us stood an old man from the city that I had never seen before, his gnarled beard, the same gray as the night sky, poked out from under his helm at odd angles.

When the Urröbbí attacked in Jericho, I had thought that it was the worst moment of my life; watching that battle had been terrifying. But now, standing on the edge of a war I could do nothing to prevent was far worse. The anxiety, and anticipation, of what would come next nearly suffocated me; blanketing me even more completely than the cold that caused my muscles to ache and my joints to stiffen. Together we stared out over the forest as another fierce cry echoed over the treetops. It was closer this time, much closer, and I could sense Erik tensing beside me.

On my right, the old man whom I did not know began to sing:

O're hills and glades the fog has settled, wishing me to feel its presence.
Darkness comes to shroud my home and press its weight upon me.
And in this time I pray for peace and wait for judgment's call.
The man who once was just a boy has lived to see the ending fall.

Out of the trees the first row of Urröbbían soldiers marched, their footsteps echoing off of the frozen ground. Their bodies seemed to be nothing more than an undefined mass, shifting fluidly in the shadowy distance. As more men bled out of the forest, larger shapes could be seen marching with them as well, and still, the man continued to sing:

On angels wings the sky seems smaller, oh world of green and blue.
To fly so high and burn so bright, to live life free of all its troubles.
Never once had reason to prepare for Galihad's white hall.
The man who once was just a boy has lived to see the ending fall.

By the hundreds the soldiers marched through the darkness, until there were too many rows of them to count. But unlike in Jericho, these men had come prepared for the elements, as well as for all-out war. No longer were they wearing light cloaks with no means of protection. Instead, they were covered from head to foot in rough black armor that stood out in stark contrasted to the snow covered valley they now traversed. Every man carried a thin shield that covered him from neck to knee, and would make good bow shots difficult at best. Behind them some of the larger shapes materialized into war machines; catapults that would be capable of returning fire on the city once in position. Other figures formed large undefined armored shapes that walked hunched over on two legs.

    Mountain trolls. I thought to myself, it was the only thing they could be. Larger than ten men and as thick around as a tree. I glanced up at one of the towers and saw men pointing and redirecting one of the enormous crossbows. I now knew what the weapons were for. It was about the only hope we had of bringing down one of the massive creatures, each of which carried a large club with its end covered in spikes as long as a short sword.

In time all things shall wane and fade. Indeed they'll fade away.
Whether earth or plant or flesh of bone, the fog will come to claim.
In glory sweet the blade is swung to bring truth to us all.
The man who once was just a boy has lived to see the ending fall.

    Little more than a long bowshot away from the outer wall the first row of soldiers halted. Some thousands of men stretched across the length of the valley, and I wondered if any of the faces shielded by black helms betrayed the fear that I held inside. With all the men stretched out in front of my eyes, I found it hard to comprehend how the desert could have housed and hidden so many of them. Behind the last line of men I was able to make out five men on horseback. Five men I knew to be Ronan and four of his dreaded Mazenkryie.

O're hills and glades the fog has settled, calling me to join my fathers.
I brace myself to heed its call and ponder whether it's too late to fight.
And in this time I pray for peace and wait for judgment's call.
The man who once was just a boy has lived to see the ending fall.

    For the fourth time a cry rent the night air, and out of the forest a mass lifted itself, on wings large enough to encompass one of the war machines. It soared over the tree tops and made a pass high above the walls of the city. Its body was the same as always; its canine head was attached by a short neck, its long muscular front limbs and shorter, thicker, hind legs flexed behind it as it flew, scanning the city. From its elevation I couldn't see them, but I knew from talking to Luther that each hand would now contain fresh talons that would be used to cut its prey to ribbons. It made two circles over the city before returning to land beside the five other horsemen.

A moment later eight fires were simultaneously light, one behind each of the distant war machines, and I knew the beginning was near. Beside me the man finished his haunting song:

And in this time I pray for peace and wait for judgment's call.
The man who once was just a boy has lived to see the ending fall.

Chapter 32: Judgment's Call

BOOM!

The ground shook as the building behind me exploded. A fiery missile had collided violently with its roof, immediately crumbling two thirds of its structure and causing me to hope that its inhabitants had made it to the interior of the city. As the Urröbbí's first volley fell upon us, Alleron's catapults began to return fire. The dark boulders that they flung were impossible to see as they glided through the air, but the thuds they made as they crushed frozen earth and armored bodies beneath them told us when they landed. I threaded my first arrow and watched the scene unfold before me, knowing that I was powerless to act until the soldiers moved within my range.

It was clear that the Urröbbían force had underestimated the range of the cities weapons, for their front few rows of soldiers were battered by the falling missiles, most of which landed hard, sticking in the cold earth and only killing a handful of soldiers, but others managed to roll after striking the ground, inflicting far more damage. One such boulder rolled to the feet of a mountain troll who angrily picked the stone up with both hands and heaved it half the distance back to the city, before bellowing into the night.

"Archers! On my signal!" Boomed the voice of Tryson. It resonated throughout the city, almost as if it had been intensified by magic. On the front wall, I saw a single member of Dû Vena Ruösa with a bow raised, and arrow drawn. I decided that this had to be the elf, even though I was unable to make out the details of his weapon from my distance.

To my left, another building burst apart when a flaming mass, the size of a small boat, smashed violently into its side. Several of the sharp-eyed archers stationed on its roof managed to jump to an adjacent building before the impact, but most of them were not so lucky. My mind raced as I wondered if there was anyone I knew in the burning wreckage of the destroyed building, and with a pang in my heart, I force myself to focus once more on the battle in front of me.

As a forth cry from the Mazenkryie rang out, the force began to march forward in a slowly undulating mass. As they marched their shields were held high in an effort to deflect the storm of arrows our archers would release. The far less disciplined trolls bellowed and moved about, occasionally knocking their fellow soldiers out of formation and even crushing unfortunate men under their giant feet.

"Hold your fire!" Tryson yelled out for a second time, "Let them come!"

A fireball flew over my head and crashed somewhere in the center of the city. In the valley below, one of the city's catapults had a lucky shot as the large form of a troll crumpled under a massive boulder. I raised my bow high a little high, trying to calculate the trajectory I would have to release my arrow in order to effectively strike my target. In a moment of good fortune, the wind had fallen deathly silent, choosing not to hinder my efforts, and as the soldiers continued to march closer, we continued to wait. We waited until the first soldiers had nearly disappeared below the wall that stretched in front of us, and then...

"Loose!" Tryson's magically enhanced voice cracked through the night, and at once hundreds of arrows launched themselves into the sky, black against the falling snow.

In the inky blackness it was impossible to follow my arrow, so I was unsure whether it was by my hand or another's, but the soldier I targeted fell to the ground, along with dozens of others. The clang of arrowhead on shield echoed over the valley and the Urröbbí broke into a run.

"Loose!" Tryson yelled again, and I released another arrow.

Dozens more of the soldiers fell, unprotected by the body length shields that had become useful only for gathering momentum for in their run. Several of the trolls bellowed as arrows stuck in their chest and legs, but they would be nothing more than pinpricks to the beast's thick skin, unlikely even to draw blood. In one of the towers, a giant scorpion fired with a lightning-like crack, sending its missile into the night and impaling a troll, who stumbled for a moment before falling to the frozen ground. Farther off a second ballista missed its target but still managed to skewer half a dozen soldiers.

"Fire at will!" Tryson's voice could be heard again, "Aim for the soldiers, not the trolls!"

I released a third arrow, and then a forth, and then a fifth, each time allowing myself to find a target that would be an easy kill, and every time I loosed an arrow my vision seemed to get better. I could see the small gaps in the soldier's armor; could count the snowflakes that fell on my arrow point as I tensed and prepared the fire. The soldiers continued to run, but it seemed as if their feet were sticking to the icy ground, keeping them in place for longer periods of time.

"Arrows!" I heard my uncle yell, and looked up from my sixth target just in time to see a blanket of black arrows cross the snow covered trees in the distance. Without hesitation I dropped to a knee and lifted the small shield that I had placed at my feet. One second, then another, I waited with bated breath before the harsh clangs of enemy arrows could be heard falling on shields throughout the city. Two arrows thudded against my shield, the sudden impact stinging my arm in the cold. A third black arrow scraped a layer of leather off the thick sole of my shoe. To my right I heard a scream, and I looked over in time to see the old man, who had started the battle with a song, crumple to the ground in pain, an arrow imbedded in his thigh. A moment later a second arrow caught him in the neck and he fell silent. As the thudding of arrows quieted, I lowered my shield and resumed my attack, barely chancing a glance to either side in order to assure myself that Erik and Jarron were still standing.

The scene was chaos. Deep within the city I heard a crash that signaled the death of another building. A fire had broken out somewhere in the east, but I assume it would eventually put itself out, unable to spread around its shale barriers. I loosed ten more arrows, periodically covering myself from volleys lofted at us from the enemy's archers. All around me cries of agony could be heard, issued forth from the lips of the wounded, ghosts of voices that belonged to bodies that were hidden beneath the sea of men who still stood. Once more, the towers fired their giant steel arrows, and several of the trolls were killed or wounded. One of the larger trolls managed to pick an arrow right out of the sky however, and flipping it around threw it right back at the tower it came from. The heavy, steel arrow destroying the roof and the war machine, causing the building to cave in on those inside.

The clanks of siege ladders locking into place on the forward wall resounded louder than Tryson's voice, making the fight even more real if that was possible. It had been one thing firing arrows at the faceless masses outside of the walls, but now that those masses were attempting to infest the great city a feeling close to panic tightened in my throat, making it hard to swallow. In front of me, the elf I assumed to be Tryson threaded three arrows at once in a desperate attempt to clear the ladders; quickly reloading two more times before dropping his bow and drawing the double daggers sheathed at his shoulders. In front of the elf, I saw the first head pop over the city wall despite Tryson's attempts. Knowing I had to help, I loosed an arrow, lodging it deep in one of the eyehole of the unfortunate soldier's helm. My shot missed the elf by less than a foot and caused the body to go limp as it tumbled backward out of sight.

The elf turned to me and Tryson's magically enhanced voice boomed out, "That one was mine Aaron!"

How he knew it was my shot was beyond me, and despite the rebuke in his voice, I could faintly make out the trace of the approving smile that stretched beneath his helm before he turned back and finished off the next warrior whose head appeared.

Off to the right, a troll had finally reached the base of the wall and its giant spiked club came crashing down on the battlements. The top two feet of the club extended over the wall and killed a soldier who was unable to get out of the way. As the troll continued to batter the wall, chunks of stone crumbled off the fortification's face, weakening the walkway behind it. Frustration welled inside of me, for as much as I wanted to help, I realized there was nothing I could do while the troll's head was still covered by the top of the wall. Instead, I turned my attention back to the unrelenting stream of men that poured toward the wall, and continued loosing my arrows.

While I was doing what I could to hold back the horde, I started to study the rest of the battle. Amongst the hordes of soldiers in black who attacked the walls, something was missing. A thought was tingling at the back of my mind but it took me longer than it should to acknowledge the reason for the feeling. As I loosed an arrow that dropped another crazed warrior off the top of the wall, I realized that the horsemen at the rear of the Urröbbían line were no longer anywhere in sight, and neither was the winged beast. A fear I had never felt began to blossom in my chest. The one mature Mazenkryie was a dangerous factor to lose track of. I threaded another arrow and scanned the sky, hoping to find a trace of the beast in the darkness, but was unable to locate it anywhere. Relaxing, I prepared to resume my attack, when over the din of clashing blades I heard the soft thud of wings pounding the air. I turned to the side just in time to see the beast crash into a group of soldiers who had been defending against several siege ladders. The collision sent several of the soldiers tumbling over the edges of the wall, while two others were lifted effortlessly off the ground. The Mazenkryie's thick hind legs hit the ground for only a moment before it pushed off and launched itself back into the sky, carrying the two helpless solders with it.

I fired as soon as I saw it, but the beast was too fast, dodging the arrow before dropping the two soldiers fifty feet back down to the wall where they crushed several other men. The beast cried and the will of several of the soldiers broke. Some of the men tried to break rank and scatter farther down the line, allowing enemy soldiers to start flooding onto the wall for the first time. Several of the braver men tried to retake the section, but a second pass of the Mazenkryie pushed those who didn't tumble over the wall back from where they came.

Tryson's voice boomed out once more, "Close that hole in the line!"

I'm not sure why, but for some reason I felt he was talking to me. I drew an arrow and fired it through the neck plate of one soldier. Immediately, I laced a second and sent it through the eye of another. I ran forward and leapt the short distance to the house in front of me before releasing a third arrow and taking down another victim. Continuing to move forward I jumped to the last roof separating me from the outer wall and at the last minute had to slide to avoid a third pass of the Mazenkryie. Still on my back, two of the Urröbbí jumped the gap to my roof and closed in on me. Knowing I couldn't get my bow strung and up fast enough, I reached for my sword, only to find it stuck fast in its sheath, the cold and the frost working against me. I tried to scramble backward but it was unnecessary as the two warriors were littered with arrows from the villagers behind me. I glance back and saw several of them including Erik leaping forward to follow me. My uncle stood back, his bow at the ready, letting me know he had released one of the arrows that saved my life.

Getting to my feet I was finally able to draw the sword at my hip. Two members of Dû Vena Ruösa and several other soldiers approached from the western flank to staunch the flood of the Urröbbí onto the wall. They collided with the men at the same time I finally made the leap to the outer wall. A black sword cut through the air to meet me as I landed, but I parried the blow easily and countered with a strike that brought the soldier crumpling to the ground. As another faceless enemy replaced him, I quickly glanced to the side and noticed Uthgar and Râven fighting their way through soldiers as if they were nothing more than sparring dummies, bodies littered the wall at their feet. The soldier in front of me jabbed at my hip and landed a glancing blow that cut through a layer of my chain mail and left it hanging from my side like a flap of skin, but still protecting me from the strike. Quickly, I knocked the soldier's next strike to the side and used my momentum to spin, bringing my sword down in an arch and cutting the soldier from neck to nipple, dropping him on the spot.

At my side, Erik had finally arrived with me at the outer wall, and I greet him with a nod, taking my eyes off the battle just long enough to be struck hard with an arrow in the sternum. The mail I was wearing kept the arrow from killing me but it was enough to take me to the ground and knock the wind from my lungs. I gasped desperately for air as another solder stepped over me, bringing his blade down in an arch at my head. A moment before contact I raise my arm to absorb the blow with the steel bracer on my wrist. Before he could swing a second time I thrust the point of my blade into his exposed shin where it stopped abruptly after contacting the bone.

The man howled in pain and drop to the ground where Uthgar subsequently finished him off.

"Get your archers back to the building!" He yelled at me as I struggled to my feet. "You're in the way here."

I wanted to fight Uthgar, but he had already turned away from me to engage the next wave of soldiers fighting their way to the top of the wall. Another cry of the Mazenkryie blended with the sounds of the battle as the creature prepared to make another pass at the soldiers on the wall. I scanned the sky, but was unable to find the monster against the dark, cloudy night sky, fragmented by flakes of snow. Frustrated by the elusiveness of the beast, I looked down and spotted Tryson, his eyes locked on something that I couldn't see. The elf sprinted forward to the nearest watchtower and ran three steps up its side before leaping into the air. In the blink of an eye he was gone, as well as two of the soldiers that were close to where he had been standing on the wall. The Mazenkryie cried out in anger at the unwelcome elf that was hitching a ride and flew high out over the city, dropping the other two soldiers as it gained altitude.

With Uthgar and Râven closing the gap in the wall I grabbed Erik and started to pull him back to where we came from when a sudden light behind me lit up the wall like the noonday sun. I turned in time to see Uthgar scramble to the side as fiery missile crashed into the front of the wall, destroying a siege tower in the process, and causing the wall to disintegrate below my feet. In an instant, I was falling. One, two, three times I collided with different pieces of the crumbling wall before landing hard on the frozen ground inside the city. The sounds of the war meant nothing as the world spun in front of me. Snow blended with armor, and smoke swirled into night, as my head throbbed with a furious pounding. In the distance I could hear the clash of sword on shield, mixed with the wails of the dying and wounded. Someone was calling my name. My eyes finally found Erik, and I forced them to focus. He was lying motionless on the ground by a building. To his immediate right, Râven lay moaning, his leg sticking out from under him at an extreme angle, the bone protruding out the back of his calve as blood pooled on the ground in stark contrast to the dazzling white snow. The heat from it sent small wisps of steam rising from the ground as it caused the snow to melt.

I turned back to what was left of the wall in time to see the Urröbbí scrambling over the rubble in droves, an enormous mountain troll in their midst. With its strides the troll was over the threshold in seconds and standing over Râven. In a rush I got to my feet pulling the bow from my shoulder and loosing an arrow at the giant that lodged in his chest, but I could have been throwing snowballs at it for all the good it did me. The troll took another step like it didn't even notice the shaft sticking out of its rough, gray flesh, and impaled Râven with an enormous spear. The strike was so hard it moved straight through the soldier, burying its point deep in the ground.

Furious, I stepped forward and released a second arrow, hitting the monster between the eyes and finally getting its attention. It howled and scratched clumsily at its face before turning away from Râven to glare at me. Taking another step I fired a third arrow, hitting it in almost the exact same place. The troll screamed in rage and stumbled toward me, until it was close enough to attack. I reached back for another arrow, hoping to send my forth shot through its eye when I realized my quiver was empty.

"Shit." I muttered to myself, as a giant hand swatted me like a gnat and sent me flying through though the wooden door of a nearby building, where I crashed through a table and rolled to the back wall, struggling to remain conscious. Outside the building I heard the troll roar again, and felt the ground shake as I saw the monster fall to the ground outside the window, the form of a man in green tumbling off its back. A second later I was dragged to my feet.

Someone was saying something to me, but it sounded like "Aar ookay eed otta ere." So I just smiled and fell over again.

"Damn." I heard the person curse before I was hoisted over a shoulder and carried out the back of the building.

After a few minutes I found myself propped up against a wall in the streets of the city, where I was finally able to clear my head. Slowly Darius' face finally came into focus in front of me.

"Are you still out of it?" He asked seriously, "Because I'm getting tired of carrying your ass."

"I'm… where are we?" I slurred. The sounds of the battle seemed far off in the distance, but that could have just been the ringing in my ears.

"Deeper in the city, I had to get you away from the hole in the wall."

"Erik?" I asked, trying to think, "Where's Erik?"

"Who?" Darius asked confused.

"By the wall. I need to get back to the wall." I tried to stand up but Darius' hand forced me back down.

"Listen, forget the wall, everyone by that hole is dead! They've closed the second level gates anyway; you couldn't get back to there even if you wanted to."

"Well then what do we do now?" I asked, trying to absorb the fact that my friend was now trapped outside, vulnerable to the enemy.

"The Captain called the banners back to the second set of rooftops to set up a new defensive line. They gave the order to collapse the first row. We need to work our way back upstairs to them. Are you okay to move?"

"I'll survive." I muttered, the fog finally starting to lift from my mind.

As I started to get my feet under me, I heard several loud collisions far off in the west. Darius looked in the direction of the sounds, an expression on his face, like he was fighting some intense internal struggle.

"What was that?" I questioned.

"One of the war ships was firing. It doesn't matter." He responded.

"Why would they be firing, all the Urröbbí are attacking in the north?"

Darius shook his head, "It's probably nothing. I mean it was only three shots. Someone probably fired them on accident. All sailors are idiots."

He hoisted me the rest of the way to my feet but his assurances did little to allay the feeling in my stomach that told me something was wrong. I thought back to the battle in Jericho, how

Ronan had sacrificed his men in order to make it inside the village so he could take hostages.

"Shadow games." I whispered, almost to myself. "It's all a farce."

"What is?" Darius questioned, looking at me like I had lost my mind.

"The battle." I said, realization and confidence fixed in my tone, "The whole thing. All the soldiers, the war machines, everything. It's just a show. It's just to take our eyes off of the real threat."

Darius looked angry, "This *farce* you speak of is taking men's lives, and threatening to overrun the city. We're needed in battle."

"Forget the battle!" I shouted. "It's just a diversion. Sacrifice the pawns so a small force goes unnoticed."

"What are you talking about?"

My mind was racing, the answer just on the tip of my tongue. If the battle didn't matter, what did? What was in the city that would better be acquired through diversion and stealth? My mind flashed to a marble room. A room with stone wolves standing guard.

"I know what they're after."

Chapter 33: Happy Endings

I raced through the streets, my fear kicking my brain into overdrive and laying the path I needed to take out like a map in my mind. Knowing I would never make it in time, I whistled for Elma, clear and sharp over the sounds of the distant battle. Darius was close on my heels, but he didn't seem too happy about it.

"You know about the medallion?" He asked, surprised.

I slowed down my pace enough for Darius to catch me and quickly explained to him about that night; about Sienna, the peach in the garden, the humming I had heard from atop the dome, and finally, about finding my way into the Wolf Room. When I told him he looked perturbed for a moment like he couldn't believe he was following me on my ridiculous hunch, and I was thankful when he didn't put his argument into words. Instead we continued to sprint.

When we were a third of the way into the city, Elma came bolting out through an alley where she came to a stop and whinnied, her beautiful mane flowing in the wind… Have I mentioned how much I love my horse? Even with Elma's sudden appearance, we didn't stop. Vaulting onto her back, I pulled Darius up with me, and pointed Elma in the direction we needed to take. Without any prodding, she understood and broke into a gallop. Even with two riders, Elma made short work of the remaining distance and in no time I found myself standing in front of the door I had kicked in only a week earlier.

"Why isn't there a guard here?" I asked, not believing that they would leave the fragment unprotected.

"I told you, they have every available body in the north fighting, and we're standing in the center of the city like a couple of cravens. We should head back toward the second gate."

"Go if you want to." I told him, "But I'm getting down into that room, this is the thing they want."

"There isn't anyone here." Darius rebutted, throwing up his hands in an incredulous gesture.

"They don't have to be here. There are four entrances. If they know a different one they could already be inside." I took a step forward and kicked the newly refurbished door in for a second time before starting down the dark hallway.

"Why are you so stubborn?" He shouted. "Lord Detrick will have your head for breaking in here again."

"I said you don't have to come with me." I called back over my shoulder.

Darius huffed, begrudgingly following my lead, "If you're going in there so will I. If I can't change your mind maybe I can at least keep you from getting killed."

Slowly, we crept our way through the underground tunnels, retracing the steps that had lead me to my destination before, and soon enough, we found ourselves standing at the entrance to the Wolf Room. With the holes in the ceiling it was as cold in the room as it was outside. A new glass cover stood on the dais in the middle of the room, its contents still humming with the same energy as before. Only the light dusting of snow that had blown in through the holes in the ceiling and frosted over the dais made the scene any different from my previous visit. Around the room the wolves continued to stare out into space, the coating of snow having no dampening effect on their ominous and threatening appearance. Instead, the glittering snow reflected the light of the half lit chandelier, casting unsettling shadows into every corner of the room. As I approached the center of the room, my breath misting in front of me, they seemed to come alive, hackles raised, the hint of a growl emanating from their maws. The only change to the room was a small log that was propped up against the wall of an alcove leading to a door on the opposite end of the chamber. Nothing seemed amiss at all until…

BOOM!

The door Darius and I had passed through only moments ago burst open. In an instant my sword was in my hand, and I was prepared to race into battle when I forced myself to stop.

"Marcus?" I asked, not being able to help the confusion that was clearly written across my face. A moment later, Luther followed in his steps.

"Father." Darius said in a flat voice.

"Father?" I questioned back, more confused than ever. And then it finally hit me; every time I had seen Marcus or Darius and their eyes or their smile reminded me of someone. It had been Luther. Their long hair had disguised their similarities enough that I had never been able to put it together before, but now, with them all in the same room, it seemed blatantly obvious.

"Yea Aaron." Darius muttered back, "The father who's never around." Then directing his attention to his father, he spat, "What are you doing here?"

"We heard the ships firing." Luther spoke, brushing off his son's abrasive comment. "I figured this was what Ronan would be after. There have been far too many coincidences as of late."

"I was thinking the same thing," I spoke up, "That's what brought Darius and me here."

"That's very astute of you Aaron; you're learning to think like a soldier." Luther's compliment made me face flush. "Marcus, Darius, Aaron, make sure the other three doors are secured. I'll take care of this one."

Turning, I made my way to one of the doors and checked to see if it was locked. I rattled the handle and gave the door a tug when the crash of shattering glass caused me to snap around. For the second time in a week an alarm began to blare into the night, like a war horn being blown from the center of the room. I turned in time to see the steel bars close in front of me, trapping me between the steel and the locked door. To my right Marcus was caged the same way I was, but in the center of the room Darius stood over the shattered vessel with sword in hand, the metal fragment glowing golden on the dais in front of him. Luther stood inside the bars to his own alcove, having just made it back into the room. To my left I finally realized what the log was for. It had stopped the bars half way down from the ceiling, leaving one route free to escape the room.

"What are you doing, Darius?" Marcus questioned from behind his cell, a look of shock on his face.

"You weren't supposed to be here." Darius deadpanned, "None of us were. This room was supposed to be empty."

"What are you doing, Darius?" Marcus repeated, more slowly this time.

"I have to protect you Marcus. You weren't supposed to be here."

You will lead him into the cold forest. The forest where beasts lay in wait. And he will take it. The words from the eyeless man rang in my head as I looked around the room at the marble trees, frost sticking to every inch of the room. The eyes of the wolves seemed to bore into my soul.

"Why is your blade drawn son?" Luther asked quietly. He had the look of a defeated man. A look that said his heart had been crushed.

"We don't have much time father. I'm taking the fragment with me for my master. He was planning on doing it himself, but Aaron was too bull-headed to go back to the real fighting. If you stand in my way, I will kill you." There wasn't a hint of jest in Darius' voice.

"Why?" was all Luther could ask, followed closely by, "how could you?"

"*How could I?*" Darius repeated in disgust. "How could I what? Betray you? You are nothing to me!" He shouted.

"I love you." Luther's voice was little more than a whisper.

"You love is held solely for your station, nothing more. Certainly, it was never held for me and never for Marcus! You could have been with us whenever you wanted, but your precious *Bear Pack* was always first. Everywhere I go, I hear stories of how great and noble my father is, and I don't even know him! I have no father! And when I finally earn my right to stand by your side, you turned me away."

Darius' words sounded eerily familiar to the first time I had questioned Marcus about his father. It was sad to see Luther reduced to this. In my time around him he had always treated me well. I couldn't believe his own child felt this way.

"Everything I've ever done, I've done to keep you and your brother safe." Luther tried to defend his actions, but while his soft voice held the same conviction, it couldn't match the angry power of his son's.

"Oh spare me your noble words and protective instincts." Darius spat. In his rage he kicked the dais and it tumbled to the ground, sending the fragment skidding across the floor, a mere foot from my reach. "You sound like a quivering mother. We did not need your protection, we needed your acknowledgement! I will be made a general for this. I will command armies! And when the sun finally sets on this land, I will be made a Lord, and then I will be able to make sure that no child is left alone to fend for his brothers. Negligence should be punished, father, and I plan to do just that. Draw your sword."

"Darius, please don't do this." Marcus pleaded from his cage, but his brother simply ignored him.

"Son, I will not draw swords against you. I know that there have been times after your mother died, where I could not always be there for you and Marcus. But just because one leaves, does not mean they won't return, or that their absence is any easier to suffer through. It pained me terribly to be parted from you and Marcus. Every moment that I was away was spent thinking of your faces. I love you both too dearly to place into words. Whatever it is you want Darius, my resignation from the pack, a place at my side in battle, titles, I will see that you receive it. Please," Luther was pleading, his normally cool face corrupt with emotion, "please, just put down the sword. There are other ways to solve our problems."

Darius' expression changed, "You will give it up for me?" he asked.

"In an instant." Luther responded.

Darius' sword dropped an inch, "And we can be the family we were meant to be?"

"I swear. Just drop the sword."

Darius' arm slowly went limp, and a moment later the sword left his fingers and clattered harmlessly to the floor. Luther strode forward and embraced his son like he was finally seeing him for the first time, but Darius only put one arm around his father in return in response. The other slowly reached for something at his hip.

"Darius, no!" Marcus shouted, but it was too late. The knife was already planted firmly through the gap in the back of Luther's armor, causing him to gasp in pain.

"The hour is late for halfhearted promises. Nothing can change the past that I have lost." Darius hissed in Luther's ear, and then he added, "Epsus de undíum father."

From the next cage over I heard Marcus howl, his rage echoing off every inch of the carved marble walls. Even though I couldn't see him, I could tell from the pounding that he was trying to kick in the door to the back of his cell, but the doors down here weren't like the ones on the outside of the building, the wood of these doors was plated with metal, it would not break.

As Darius removed his arms from around his father, Luther crumbled to the floor. Turning back to the wreckage of the dais he cursed, and began feeling around in the broken glass like a blind man, as his brother's rage finally began to subside into broken defeat.

"Why?" Marcus mumbled from his prison.

Darius didn't even look up, "Don't even pretend that you had any love lost for our father Marcus."

"It didn't have to end this way." There was a pleading in Marcus' tone that I couldn't ignore.

"End?" Darius questioned, "Who said anything about it ending here brother? This is merely the beginning."

Looking at Luther, his blood dying the floor a sickening color as it pooled on the icy, white floor like a crimson mirror, was heartbreaking. I realized then that he had been like a second father to me through everything that had happened since I first rode to Alleron. Seeing his lifeless body on the cold stone floor was no easier than if it would have been Jarron in his place, and yet, I couldn't feel anything akin to sadness. Instead, I felt like an intruder. A fly on the wall of someone else's worst nightmare. Somehow, the expression on Marcus' face was even more difficult to look at than the broken body of his father.

"How I wish things could stay like this forever." Marcus whispered, remembering the words that Darius had said during his toast. "You knew this was going to happen didn't you?"

"It wasn't supposed to be this way Marcus. You have to believe me. I was just told to scout the building and place the log below the gate." For the first time, Darius was the one to plead for understanding. "None of you were supposed to be here. I would never do anything to harm you brother."

"You were to be Créos' Godfather. I always thought the two of us would have a happier ending than this."

Darius' face lost some of its color at the mention of his unborn nephew, but he kept his composure, "If a happy ending is what you seek, Marcus, do not let the story end here."

Behind Darius a door creaked open, and slowly, the large dark form of Ronan bent beneath the wedged gate and entered the room, followed closely by two surly looking soldiers carrying longbows.

"You." I hissed.

"Me." He agreed with a wicked smile, his unnaturally deep voice echoing off the hard stone walls. Upon seeing Luther's body he turned to Darius, "I see you've ridden me one of my most formidable opponents. I suppose thanks are in order, although I had quite hoped to accomplish that pleasant task on my own. You've done well Darius, but we must be quick. The spell caster approaches."

Darius was still haplessly groping around on the ground, but he paused to look back at Ronan, "Foramére? He is nothing compared to you."

Ronan sighed like he had grown weary of educating children, "Yes, but if he were to bring the building down on our heads it would make things exceedingly more difficult, not to mention inconvenient. Doubtless, he has already sensed my presence. It would be most prudent if we were no longer here when he arrives. Aroughha," he spoke to one of the bowmen, "kill the soldier."

Darius was on his feet in an instant, rage lining his face, sword back in his hand, its tip pointed at Ronan's throat. "My brother is not to be touched."

"My my," Ronan tisked, "For a young man who clearly has no issue severing family ties," he glanced once more at Luther, "you certainly are stubborn on this point. Surely you realize that attacking me would accomplish little more than sealing your own demise."

"He is no family of mine." Marcus spat, contesting Darius' worry.

"You see?" Ronan continued with a sly sneer, "The young war monger will not even claim you."

"He isn't to be touched." Darius repeated simply, ignoring his brother's slight, while not releasing any of the tension in his arm.

"What of the other?" The bowman questioned.

"No Aroughha, I would prefer to take that one alive. He could be of good use to my master later. Tragically, it seems there will be no killing for you this evening; I know how very much you were looking forward to it."

The bowman slumped his shoulders and whined stupidly, "I never get to kill anyone."

"I want you to know I'm going to find my cousin, and I'm going to kill you." I growled at Ronan, my words portraying bravery that I in no way felt.

"Oh I plan for you to find her. I must admit that capturing the young girl was a stroke of dumb luck, I had no idea she was your relation until I rode with her into the field. I could almost feel the heat of your anger rising from your body as you saw me with her." Ronan replied with an evil smile. "But not to worry, I'll even tell you where to look. She's right where you left her, the forests of Northern Jericho. Do be a good boy and try to rescue her; I've grown weary of her mouth." Turning to Darius he continued, "Grab the fragment and let us be on our way."

"I can't seem to find it master." Darius grimaced, which shocked me because he was kneeling no more than two strides from it as it shown bright gold from the floor, amidst the shards of broken glass.

"Ah yes, how simple of me." Ronan replied as though Darius' inability to locate an object mere feet from him made perfect sense.

He strode forward and reached to pick up the fragment, but as his large, ebony hand contacted the metal, the humming in the room began to intensify. Or at least what I thought was humming, that is until the first one moved. The humming became a growl as first one, and then another wolf broke free from the outer marble wall and shook the loose snow from their backs.

Ronan's eyes grew wide as he backed toward the half open gate, "Well isn't that unexpected." He quipped. The stone wolves locked eyes with the four men in the center of the room as their growls thundered off of the domed marble ceiling loud enough to drown out the alarm that still rang out through the city.

A terrified Darius sidestepped behind the bowman named Aroughha, "We should be leaving now." He hissed as he turned and sprinted from the room, closely followed by Ronan.

The two archers weren't quite as lucky. As their companions ran from the room the wolves pounced. Aroughha launched an arrow that bounced harmlessly off the head of one wolf before he was quickly overwhelmed by two others. The second archer fell screaming before he could even get a shot off. Their terrified shrieks were quickly silenced as the stone beasts ripped at their throats, leaving fine sprays of blood to further taint the room, before they joined the rest of their stone pack in pursuit of Darius and Ronan.

He will take the piece and even as he flees from the hounds, the resurrection will have started, and none of it would be possible without you. Those words and Marcus' silent sobs rang through my head for the rest of the night, haunting me, and forcing me to ponder, what had I just helped to resurrect?

Chapter 34: The Amazing Alliance of People who Hate Each Other

It was dark when Terrick woke, a suppressed groan escaping his lips as his back throbbed. *Birdman needs to work a little bit on his hospitality,* he thought harshly, as he sat up gingerly from the stone floor where he had slept. Groping around in the dark, his hand chanced upon a soft, furry object and he froze, fear momentarily getting the best of him. *If Birdman stuck me in the same cave as a bear, I'm going to rip his wings off and feed them to him.* Slowly, he gave the fur a tug and realized that it was only loosely draped over a rock. As he pulled the pelt from its resting place, something clattered to the ground beside him. Reaching toward the sound, his hand found the cold steel of a blade, and relief flooded through him. At least the Birdman hadn't decided to abandon him completely defenseless.

Cautiously, he glanced around in an attempt to get his bearings. It was pitch black where he lay, but to his left, there was a circle of white light in the distance. Curious, and anxious to be out of the cave, he hulled himself up from the cold ground, grabbing the fur and blade in the process, and walked toward the light. As Terrick approached, the light began to grow and the temperature started to fall. It dropped so much that it forced him to stop and wrap the surprisingly warm fur around his shivering shoulders. The light on the other side was so bright it blinded Terrick. Groping forward, eyes squinted against the glare, he was surprised when one hand plunged through the semi-solid snow built up around the entrance to the cave.

Pushing forward again, Terrick made it through the entrance before straightening up and brushing his wet hands of on his trousers before using them in an attempt to shield his eyes from some of the glare reflecting off the brilliant, sparkling snow. It took nearly five minutes, with the wind biting at him violently, for his eyes to adjust to the light, and when they finally did, he was able to take in the scene in front of him. The first thing he noticed was the mountains; they seemed to be all around him, everywhere he looked, like he was standing inside the mouth of some enormous beast who was preparing to swallow him. He also noticed that he was above the tree line. In front of him, the snow-covered ground sloped steeply downward for thirty or forty meters before a forest of evergreens and aspen erupted from the mountainside. He wasn't high enough on the mountain to see what lay down in the valley below the treetops, so he had no way to be sure where exactly he was in reference to the view Birdman had shown him the last time he was conscious. He knew the land west of the Blue Rock Mountains well enough that he could find his way home if he got a good view of the valley floor, but the way the mountain rose up around him led him to believe that he was no longer on the western side of the mountains.

Looking behind him up the steep slope of the mountain, he started to think that it might be a good idea to climb higher in an attempt to get a better view of his surroundings. After all, it wouldn't do him much good to go wandering through the forest without any real sense of direction. Examining the fur and the blade that he had found in his cave, he saw that the sword was nothing more than a common saber, similar to the one he had taken during his failed escape from the swamplands. The fur was a traveling cloak, thick, black and soft. It was a tough hide and reminded him of a shaggy bear, or even a great Blackwolf. He had no idea how he had received it, but wrapping it around his shoulders cause the wind to lose its sting, and for that he was thoroughly grateful.

Tucking the thin saber through his belt to keep it out of his way, he prepared to climb the cold face of the mountain when a heavy crunch behind him caught his attention. He turned at the last minute, only to see a blur of black, and feel the heavy weight crash against his chest. Down the slope both he and the black object tumbled, trying desperately to regain a solid hold on the ground and halt their fall, but it wasn't until he crashed backwards into a tree that he finally came to a stop. Pain coursed up his spine and he writhed on the ground for a moment, biting his lip to keep from howling. A moment later the weight was on him again. He rolled to the left trying to free himself as he felt something grasping at the sword at his hip. Forgetting his pain, he threw his elbow backward, connecting three times before the object was forced to release him. Rolling away he managed to struggle to his feet, causing another wave of pain to pulse up his back. To his left, the black bundle also made its way to its feet.

"You!" Terrick shouted, "What are you doing here?"

Standing several feet from him, and wearing an identical fur cloak, was the warrior who had been accused of desertion and beaten by his fellow desert soldiers. He didn't look nearly as bruised as he had the last time they had fought. *And Birdman had the nerve to question healing me!* Terrick thought angrily.

"I could ask you ze same question?" He returned.

"I don't have any idea where we are. I was gonna try to figure it out before you decided to attack me, for the third time." Terrick thought for a moment before adding, "You really aren't very good at your job, are you?"

The warrior whose name Terrick had forgotten sneered, "Alvays vith funny comments. You vill cease comments ven you cease to move. This vill be very soon."

"Really?" Terrick waved his saber to make sure the warrior wasn't being completely oblivious to the fact that he was armed, "and how do you figure to accomplish that task?"

The warrior said nothing, but simply flexed his fingers, opening and closing them into fists.

"I assure you, that's very menacing and all, but I have a blade, and you have naught but bone and flesh. I'll cut you to ribbons."

"I seem to recall you saying that the last time ve fought as vell. Yet, here I still stand."

The warrior took a hesitant step forward, and Terrick had to admit, if the man was nothing else he was brave. *Foolishly brave, until it takes him to his grave.* Terrick thought, raising his saber and moving to meet his enemy. *This time I won't show him Aaron's mercy.* A step away, Terrick sent a downward slice toward the warrior's right shoulder. The man stepped left before moving under the blow to the right and driving a fist into Terrick's kidney, dropping him to a knee. Terrick growled in frustration, surprised by the agility that the warrior exhibited for such a large man. Still, he recovered quickly enough, getting back to his feet and swiping wildly with the saber, as the warrior danced back out of reach.

"Hold still so I can kill you." Terrick grumbled, causing the warrior to merely smile cunningly.

As he started to move forward a second time, the warrior's smile was replaced by something that resembled fear. The reaction caused Terrick's confidence to grow, until he heard the growling.

Terrick stopped mere feet from the warrior and glanced behind him, back toward the forest. At first he saw nothing in its vast green depths, but the low growling had given way to the rolling rumble of something large and dangerous. A minute passed by as the two stood side by side, forgetting the fight that had consumed their minds only moments ago, as the growling seemed to surround them.

Taking another step away from the forest, Terrick broke the silence, "Something tells me we're not gonna like what comes out of there." The warrior beside him merely grunted in agreement while slowly beginning to edge his way behind Terrick.

To his right, there was a glimpse of white before the trees once again obscured it. Another glimpse was seen to his left, then a third close to the second, causing Terrick to take another step in retreat. In front of him the snarling grew louder, until a great Whitewolf emerged from the forest. The wolf was the size of a small horse, and white as the purest snow making its blood red eyes stand out in stark contrast. As it slowly stalked forward, it raised its hackles, and bared its fangs. Great drops of saliva fell from its open maw. The Whitewolf was joined by a second, and then a third, and before Terrick knew it, there were six of the beasts moving to encircle him and the warrior. The first wolf snapped its jaws twice and Terrick lashed out with his saber, but he failed to connect as the wolf fell back beyond his reach and resumed its growl.

"Don't hurt them!" A familiar voice yelled from behind them.

Terrick stole a quick peek over his shoulder in the direction of the voice and saw the elf. For the first time since Terrick had met her she wasn't covered in bruises, with dead leaves and mud caked in her hair. Instead, she radiated power and beauty. She was garbed in a white fur, similar to the ones he and the warrior were wearing, with the exception that hers had a hood that was pulled to cover the top of her head. The hood of her cloak was made out of the head of a

Whitewolf, and gave her the appearance that she was speaking to them from the inside of one of the beast's mouths. Her golden-blond hair streamed down past her shoulders and over the front of the fur, mimicking the slaver of the wolves threatening to devour them.

"Yea, sorry Blondie, I'm a little more worried about *them* hurting *me*." Terrick replied, swiping his blade through the air once more as a second wolf snapped at him.

"You cannot hurt them, they are sacred." She fought on.

Terrick glanced back at her angrily, "Then why are you wearing one as a coat?"

"The Whitewolves are protectors." She explained calmly, as if nothing was amiss. "They protect the forests in their lives. This one chooses to protect me in its death."

"Yea, I'm sure it chose that." Terrick scoffed, "Why do the sacred, all-protecting wolves look like they want to eat us?"

"Look at the two of you," She chided, "you look like the enemy. Take off your cloaks."

Terrick glanced down at himself. He had forgotten that he was wearing the fur of a Blackwolf.

"Ze she-elf lies. She vould have us both killed." The warrior hissed into his ear, never taking his eyes from the wolves that circled them.

Terrick thought the warrior might not be far from the truth, but his mind flashed back to the moment in the swamps; the moment when he had been pinned by a swampdragon and she had started to make her way back to him. If only he knew if she was coming back to help, or to yank her chain from his grasp. He paused for a moment longer before slowly setting down his saber and removing his cloak, tossing it to the ground a foot in front of the lead wolf. For a moment, the growling stopped while the Whitewolf inspected the cloak, making sure the pile of furs was really dead, but a moment later the wolf straightened up and continued baring its fangs.

Terrick took another step back and whispered to the warrior through clenched teeth, "Take off your cloak before you get us both killed."

Slowly, the warrior repeated Terrick's actions. When the wolves were finished sniffing the second cloak, they eyed the two men once more before turning and disappearing back into the forest.

Terrick finally exhaled, only now realizing that he was holding his breath. "Thank you," he muttered to the warrior.

The man grunted once more before replying, "If ve both die now, I cannot kill you later."

Terrick ignored the comment while reclaiming his saber and walking up the slope to the elf. "You have any idea where we are?" He snapped, the question coming out a bit harsher than he intended.

The elf gave him a cool stare before responding, "We are on the eastern peaks of the mountains. I believe the Farion Woods lie beyond the next ridge of mountain tops."

"How do you know we're on the east?"

She gave an exasperated sigh, pointed to her right and simply stated, "The sun moves up, not down."

It was something Terrick hadn't even noticed, but still he took a moment to squint stupidly at the sun as if he would be able to confirm its movements in the few seconds it took him to go practically blind. "Awesome," he said, "so how do you propose we get out of here?"

"We?" The elf shot back, a faux confusion and sweetness blended with the sarcasm lacing her tone. "I assumed since I was ever such a burden to you on the journey here you would be happy to leave me behind."

She said it genuinely enough, but Terrick knew that she was trying to goad him, "Let's see, I don't know the area, but you seem to know it just fine. And I know how you'd just love to watch me wonder off into the forest alone so I could be eaten by your pack of mountain protectors, but I think I'm gonna stick with you Blondie."

The elf's eyes flashed dangerously, "Do not call me that."

"Well, then what should I call you? What's your name?" Terrick said exasperatedly.

The elf took a long time to look Terrick over before finally responding, "You may call me Lily."

I may call you that, but that's not your real name. Terrick thought to himself before responding sarcastically, "Aww, like the flower? That's cute." He reached out to give her a condescending pat on the shoulder, but before he knew it, she had grabbed his wrist and twisted him so violently he thought for sure his arm would be yanked from its socket. She moved faster than he thought was possible and in a flash, a short inch and a half blade was pressed against his throat.

"Like a flower that could kill you." She whispered into his ear before pushing him away from her.

Terrick rubbed his shoulder, still slightly in shock of what had just transpired. "Well that wasn't very flower-like." He mumbled under his breath.

"I'm sorry, what was that?" she asked coyly.

"I said these mountains'll be quite a hike. We should get going."

"I thought so." She said with a smug smile.

"Where'd you get the skinner?" Terrick asked, glancing at the knife that had just been pressed to his throat.

The elf glanced at it as well. It was a thin blade, likely meant for nothing more than peeling potatoes or skinning vegetables. "It was with my cloak when I awoke here." She finally answered.

"Vhy didn't I get a blade?" The sullen warrior, who had finally decided to join them on the slope,   mumbled.

Terrick had completely forgotten that the man was even there. "What are you still doing here? You can go. I don't feel much like killing anyone right now."

The warrior had fastened his cloak back around his shoulders and he glanced nervously back at the forest. "I haf no veapon. I vill die in ze forest." He admitted.

"Well if you linger around me any longer you'll die just the same, so you best be on your way."

The warrior looked from Terrick to the elf, but didn't say another word.

"It will be easier to survive together than apart." The elf stated, causing Terrick to turn, mouth gaping like a fish out of water.

"You want him to come with us? He's tried to kill me, *three times*." Terrick hissed so only she could her.

Lily merely scowled back before finally claiming, "I think I like him already. Unfortunately, he is unarmed, so it is unlikely he will be trying to kill you for a fourth time."

With that, she spun on her heel and walked down the slope, passed a stunned Terrick. After a few steps she turned back and added sarcastically, "Besides, a big strong man like you should be able to take care of himself."

Terrific. Terrick thought to himself as he trudged after the two into the depths of the forest, refastening his fur as he walked. *I liked her better when she was pretending to sleep.*

Chapter 35: The Changing of the Guard

I woke up under the scratchy wool blanket that covered the makeshift bed in my crumbling home. It had been over a week since the battle had ended. Others had told me that it had been a massacre at the wall. Thousands of the Urröbbí had died in the fighting, compared to a fourth as many members of the city guard. But that did not make any of the losses easier to comprehend. All of it had been a ruse. All those men had died defending against an enemy that had been designed for the slaughter. The only good that seemed to come from the battle came at the hand of Tryson. The elf had been found walking the walls of the city after the battle, wearing one of the thick black wings of the Mazenkryie he had slew like some morbid black cape. If nothing else, at least there was one less of those monsters to worry over. Thankfully, Erik had also been found. Somehow he had managed to work his way into a ground level home and hide under an overturned wooden countertop while the enemy flooded in around him. My uncle had told me the Urröbbí announced the retreat shortly after the city's alarm sounded. He didn't know about the fragment that had been stolen, so he didn't realize the real reason for the retreat. Once Ronan had what he wanted, there was no need to continue the carnage.

The next few days were spent collecting the bodies of the dead and tending to the wounded. Men from Alleron were given individual funeral pyres south of the city's outer walls, while members of the Urröbbían army were piled in the north and set to flame. The bones of soldiers, who had come from Westphall and Arebock, were to be returned to their homes with an honor guard. Finally, Luther had his own pyre in the center of the city days after the battle had ended. Râven and six other members of Dû Vena Ruösa had smaller pyres lit around their leader's. Their ashes were to be set in shallow graves in the western end of the city, their broadswords set to mark their final resting places.

I hadn't attended the ceremony. It had all been too much for me. Instead, I willed away the day with Sienna, sitting atop the domed roof to the Wolf Room, in the middle of the garden. It was the only time I had managed to see Sienna, she had seemed to spend every hour of every day since the battle, honing her skill with a bow in the practice range. The stone wolves had given chase throughout the city, one had even ripped a chunk out of Darius' calf, but eventually they returned with nothing but snarls. It had surprised me that they didn't go back to their resting place in the cold marble room. Instead the seven who hadn't been shattered roamed the city streets in a constantly agitated stone pack. Tryson had told me that they would never rest until they claimed the thief who had escaped them. "Whitewolves are protectors." was all he offered as an explanation.

The King of Alleron, some fat oaf from Westphall, had decreed that, as the city remained safe, no retaliatory strike was to be issued. "There was to be no more bloodshed on his watch," his raven-sent note had read. He apparently regarded the battle as a crushing victory that would send a message to Alleron's enemies. He was unable to grasp the idea that they had stolen something that may have been worth going after.

In my humble opinion, thought him a right ass. Retaliation or no, I would return to Jericho and rescue my cousin. Whether I acted alone or with help was of no concern, there were just several stops I had to make first, and I had needed to wait until tonight to make them. Tonight was the night when the members of Dû Vena Ruösa would formally anoint their new Captain. It was a forgone conclusion in most people's minds that the honor would pass to Tryson, and I didn't much care, but I found I needed to talk to the elf one more time before I departed, and he had been locked in a room with his brothers in arms for the last four nights. His would have to be the last visit I paid before I left the city.

Deciding against facing everything just yet, I pulled the wool blanket over my head and shut my eyes again. I had spent a lot of my time since the battle acting sullen and keeping to my room and I wasn't quite ready to change that yet. It wasn't until the sun had crept up high enough to shine brightly through the hole in my ceiling that I had never repaired, that I finally threw off the cover and forced myself out of bed. Fastening a long brown traveling cloak about my shoulders and pulling the hood tightly over my head I walked through the hole in my wall and whistled for Elma. She came trotting to my side and whinnied restlessly as I fixed the old saddle on her back. She was intelligent enough to know that I was ready to leave the city, even if no one else had figured out my decision. I ate a few pieces of dry bread while I fed her a pair of sugar cubes.

"Just one more day girl." I whispered, running my fingers through her mane. "One more day and we'll put this place to our backs. Just you and me girl. How does that sound?"

Elma snorted and shook her head in response as if to say I'd be going alone if we were headed somewhere that didn't have sugar cubes.

Putting on a weary smile, I reassured her, "It won't be that bad, I promise."

I patted her one more time and hopped into my place on her back, nudging her with my heels to urge her forward. Together we wound our way through the crumbling buildings in the southeastern corner of the city. My first stop was only a short distance away, and Elma made it there in a matter of minutes. I dismounted and knocked on a recently replaced wooden door. A moment later, it opened to reveal Jarron, and he ushered me in with a sad smile, almost as though he had been dreading this visit.

"I thought you were going to come two days past." He started, taking up a seat in a hansom oak chair that was uniquely fashioned in such a way that it could only have been made by Chisel. Looking up at me, he continued, "When the week passed I had begun to hope you may stay."

"You know I can't," was all I replied as Jarron once again stood. He was nearly as restless as Elma. I had told him earlier in the week about what Ronan had said about Lisa, and how I was planning to return to Jericho to free her. At the time he had taken what I said with a solemn expression, but I knew that eventually he would try to dissuade me.

"Wine?" He asked me, grabbing a skin from a nearby counter.

His offer nearly caused me to laugh. He had never offered me a drink before. "You know I'm not of age Uncle."

Jarron shrugged, "You've fought in a war. You're man enough to have a drink. Besides, at present we aren't in Jericho. Its laws don't apply here."

Gently, I took the skin from him and took a long sip of the fine red liquid. It was dry, with a taste of blackberries, sage, and oak, and it made my mouth feel as though it were full of cotton, but it was still surprisingly refreshing, nothing like the fire whiskey I had before.

"Did I ever tell you that I grew up here in this city?" Jarron asked, the unexpected information nearly causing me to spit up my second sip of wine. He had never mentioned anything like that before that I could recall. When I shook my head he continued, his eyes glossed over and distant as he recalled events that had long ago passed. "I thought not. I grew up just north of the Lord's Manor. My father was a squire to Lord Barian Detrick. I grew up playing Knights and Thieves with Bo, and stealing peaches from the gardens. It was a good childhood."

I was confused; Jarron had never talked about his childhood before. "What made you leave?"

Jarron sat back down with a heavy sigh as he answered, "Lord Barian was a noble man. Not the best of men, but noble, and he put his honor before anything else. He held my father in high esteem, and taught him about honor and duty. He taught him that the Gods come first in a man's life, duty came second, and family came third." He leaned back in his chair, and took a sip of wine from the skin, "My aunt also worked in the Lord's Manor. She was a maid. Menial work; cleaning rooms, skinning vegetables, maintaining the artwork. She loved the art more than anything.

"One night, her son crept into the Manor and attempted to steal one of the paintings. He was caught and taken to Lord Barian while others woke his mother. In Alleron, the penalty for thievery was always the loss of a hand. My aunt was obviously distraught, and when she asked her boy why he did it, he said it was to be her birthday present. Lord Barian felt for my aunt, but the law was the law. Duty came before friends and family, and the boy was to lose the hand. My aunt disagreed with his order of things. She talked my father into trying to help her flee the city with her son. In the escape, my aunt killed another squire who was in the wrong place at the wrong time.

"When they were caught, Lord Barian was irate. All those years, duty second, family third, and somehow my father mixed up the order. He should have never conceded to go along with her mad plan. The law was the law, and the penalty for murder was death. My cousin lost his hand, my aunt was to be beheaded, and my father was to watch. The night before the execution my father took your mother and I from the city and told us to wait for him in the northern woods. He was going to get my aunt and we were going to leave for Jericho where we would be safe. I was fifteen at the time, your mother was eleven. We waited for hours. The sun sunk in the sky and rose again before anyone left the northern gates, and when someone finally did, it was my friend Bo who came, riding out on his stallion. He told us that our father had been caught, and our aunt killed. He told me that our father was to be put to the block next. Duty second, family third. I tried to get back to the city to rescue my father, but Bo kept me from the gate, told me I needed to stay with Brianna. He knew if I went back, I would get the block same as my father."

Finally I knew where Jarron was going with his story and I couldn't believe his implication. "You think if I go riding off to save Lisa I'm going to be killed." It wasn't a question. "You think I should leave her. Your own daughter."

Jarron took another draw from the skin and looked down at the table, "It is true that Bo likely saved my life that day. Lord Barian was a strict man, and he never bent the rules. If I would have gone after my father, I would have been caught, and he would have had me executed." I gazed at him in shock, not believing that he would have me abandon Lisa, but he continued talking before I could interrupt him. "Bo saved my life that day, but there isn't a day that goes by when I don't regret not trying to save my father. I've had to live with that regret my whole life. Terrick is gone from me, and I never had a chance to save him. Lisa is gone from me now as well, and it is likely that anyone who goes after her will meet the same fate as Terrick, but I can't ask you to live with the same ache that I have held in my heart for the last thirty eight years."

I looked at my uncle tentatively, "You're gonna let me go?" I asked surprised, "You're not trying to stop me?"

Jarron shook his head, suddenly looking older than I had ever seen him, "More than that. Aaron, you're all I have left right now. I can't ask you to do this for me with a clear heart. Lord Barian always said duty second, family third, but he didn't understand that it *is* a man's duty to take care of his family. He didn't understand that sometimes, those two things are one in the same. It's *my* duty to care for Lisa. I'm going with you."

I looked at Jarron in disbelief. My uncle was near worthless with a sword, and his bow work was modest at best, but I couldn't take this from him. Not after what he had just told me. I couldn't ask him to stay behind while I risked my own life. Instead I just nodded and took another draw from the wineskin.

Standing from the table, I made my way to the door before turning back to my uncle, "I plan on leaving before first light tomorrow. I'll meet you at the north gate."

Without looking back, I climbed on Elma's back and without any prompting she started to walk. As I relaxed into the steady sway of my horse, I processed what Jarron had told me. *Does he really believe it is better to die than live with regret?* I wondered as I made my way to the sparring arena for my next stop. Dismounting from Elma once more I walked onto the open pitch. It was nearly empty. Two men worked on swordplay in the far corner of the area while Sienna stood with her bow, loosing arrow after arrow at a battered old target while Bria looked on, eating an apple and making it look like an art form. The arrows were scattered all over the target, but it looked as though she had far more hits than misses. When she saw me approaching she smiled and lay down her bow.

"Hey Shorty."

I gave my customary greeting, but it must not have been as enthusiastic as usual, because her smile faded, "What's wrong?"

I glanced at Bria who returned my look with a seductive smile and wave before I turned back to Sienna and asked if we could talk in private. Once we were finally out of earshot, I turned to her and blurted out, "I'm leaving for Jericho tomorrow."

She gave me a confused look before responding in a hopeful voice, "Why, are people heading back?"

Grudgingly, I explained what had happened the night of the battle, about how Darius betrayed the city and how Ronan had taunted me by saying Lisa was still alive and in Jericho. I had been planning on telling her earlier, but she was so happy to see me alive after the battle that I hadn't been able to bring up the horrible way the fight had ended for me.

By the time a finished telling her about Lisa the look on her face was one of pure outrage. "You *can't* do this." She said sternly, her voice barely lower than a yell.

"I have to try Sienna. I can't just let them have my cousin."

"Oh don't be so thick headed Aaron, you're smarter than that!" Now she was yelling. "You know exactly why he told you that! He knows you'll just go running off to play the hero, when really you'll just get yourself killed!"

Her yelling made my own anger bubble up to the surface and at that point I couldn't take the extra stress, "Well what would you have me do?" I shouted back.

"Nothing." Her response was flat, but she was deadly serious.

"How can that be an option?"

"How can it not be an option?" She rebutted, "I know that Lisa being gone is horrible, but I'm not going to let you go kill yourself so you can feel all noble!"

"I'm not really asking your permission Sienna. I'm leaving tomorrow whether you're okay with it or not. I just didn't want to leave without saying goodbye."

"*Saying goodbye?*" She spit the words back at me like they were poison. "You're an idiot if you think you're going to save anyone Aaron. Can't you see he's trying to trap you?"

"It doesn't matter if it's a trap!" I shouted back, "Can you even imagine what this has been like for her! And maybe you could live with yourself if she was to die with us doing nothing, but I can't!"

Sienna looked as though I had slapped her, tears welling up in her eyes. "You think I don't worry about Lisa? Unlike you, I can imagine *exactly* what it's been like for her. It's terrifying, and horrible, and you worry every day that you may not be around the next, and you pray that someone, somewhere, is coming for you, but that only matters if that someone is still around after the saving is done, and if you die you haven't done Lisa any good. If you want to walk right into a trap that's your own choice Aaron, but don't you dare come to me and ask me to say goodbye to you when you know damn well you're never coming back to say hello again!"

She started to storm away from me when I yelled after her, "You said goodbye to Terrick!"

Sienna stopped in her tracks, turning slowly with disbelief covering her face. Her disbelief turned to anger as she stalked toward me with all the malice of the stone wolf pack. I assumed she was going to start yelling again but instead her hand pulled back and smacked me hard enough across the face to cause me to stagger.

"Don't you dare talk to me about Terrick!" She hissed, tears streaming from her red eyes, "Terrick didn't have a choice, you do." Turning on her heel again she grabbed her bow and stormed away once more, leaving me to cup my reddening cheek in the palm of my hand.

Finding nothing else to say, I simply walked away, unable to decide what stung more, my cheek or my pride. The last thing I wanted to do was hurt Sienna, but it was frustrating that she didn't understand my need to find Lisa. Rounding a corner to the arena I saw Elma but when I approached she snorted at me and stepped away.

"Aw listen, I already feel like a right ass, I don't need to hear it from you too."

Reluctantly she allowed me to remount, and we made our way deeper into the city. The whole area had taken on a look of post-war celebration. The snow-covered streets were littered with people chatting with neighbors or drinking from wineskins. It was amazing how palpable the change in the environment was from just a week and a half earlier, and I tried to allow the infectious atmosphere to lift my spirits. I wondered around the town for hours, as the sun past quickly overhead, enjoying the colorful banners of the city one last time. It was a pleasant scene, but I would be happy to make my way back into the dense forest greenery on the morrow.

I stopped by the tavern as the evening sun began to make its way back down to the horizon and listened to a few tattered musicians play an assortment of odd flutes. I sat by the bar and watched the different acts as increasingly filthy men and women took to the stage to try and earn a few extra coppers. Wanting to get one last warm meal in me before beginning my journey back home, I rode to the Setting Sun and feasted on a honeyed goose leg with cranberry sauce and a piping hot vegetable pie with creamed chicken. I paid Barrman twice what I owed him and he gave me a sweet smelling cinnamon apple tart that I was too full to eat, but he refused to take back. Pocketing the tart, I rode to my third stop and dismounted in front of a rickety building covered in flowering vines.

A rush of anxiety hit me as soon as I crept close enough to knock and as I raised my hand I found myself hesitating, still not entirely sure I wanted to make this visit. The hard oak door didn't seem to share in my trepidation however, as it swung open of its own accord, ushering me into the dimly lit entrance. Carefully measuring every step and quieting the voice in my mind that was screaming at me to just go back to Elma, I crossed the threshold of the building and began to weave my way through the piles of rubbish. Cautiously I followed the same path Sienna and I had traveled on our previous visit and upon entering the small room with the decrepit table, I laid eyes upon the dark hooded figure I was searching for. As before, he was seated at the table's head and part of me wondered if he had ever managed to move since my last visit. The same stench of decay filled my nose as I drew closer, and upon my approach, the hooded man tilted his deep, eyeless face in my direction to give me a disconcerting half-smile.

"You were right about everything." I said, trying not to let memories from the night he 'drank my soul' sap my courage.

"Was I now?" He rasped; the black pits of his face seeming to bore into my soul, "About everything? I guess I was."

"How did you know?"

"Hmmm." Was all the man said back.

"Why didn't you tell me Darius would betray me? Why didn't you tell me it was him I'd lead to the medallion?" I tried to keep my calm, but anger crept into my tone. I couldn't help but think that the bard's vagueness had cost Luther his life.

"Hmmm, medallion... Yes, that seems so very familiar. But I am sorry boy, I see only shadows and circumstances, never names... never names. I see only what the fates wish for me to see, the action is yours."

"What do you mean the action is mine?"

The old man in the cloak sat unmoving for a long time before answering, "In times past, men of action would ask if their fates are already chosen, and that answer is no. But at the same time their fates can be gleaned, solely because they are men of action."

"What does that mean? How does it apply to me?" Curiosity blended with my growing frustration at the bard's half-answers.

"You claim I was right about everything yet things that I have said have not come to pass. If you wished, you could bar yourself in a chamber and never return to the light of the world, or you could take blade to throat and avoid the truths that lie ahead of you. If you were to do this, nothing I have said would come to pass. But you will not imprison yourself, nor shall you take your own life."

"How do you know I won't?" I argued for the sake of being difficult.

The old man gave another wrinkly smile, recognized my question for what it was. "For you are a being of action, and a being of great destiny. Already you are planning to act on the impulses of your heart. You find that you can no longer stay here while your questions go unanswered. It is why you have come here to me tonight, is it not?"

As much as I hated to admit it, the man was right. "You listed several things for me to watch for, that means I will return from Jericho safely right? If I'm dead, then your predictions and warnings can't come true."

"How do you know your path will lead to Jericho?"

"I have to go." I stated with finality, my opinion on the subject inflexible.

"*Have* to go and *will* go are two different things indeed."

"But when I go, no harm will befall me?" I pressed on, choosing to ignore the blind man's semantic argument.

This caused the bard to frown, giving him an even more skeletal appearance, "A false sense of security will lead you not where you wish to go. A careless man leads a short life. I have mentioned things to guide you, but only if you make intelligent choices."

I took a deep breath realizing that I wouldn't get a straight answer and decided to move on to my next question, "Who is my father?"

"Ahh, and so we come to the question at last." The man sighed.

"You won't tell me, will you?" I asked, but it wasn't really a question.

"Perchance I do not know." He responded. "Perchance no one does."

Well then how is the medallion connected to him?" I had been thinking of my weird dream, down in the depths of the Wolf Room for some time now. Thinking of the message that the 'dream Sienna' had sent me; about how uncovering the veil would lead me down a road to my father, but I had yet to understand anything special about the medallion that would tell me anything worthwhile.

"I never mentioned the medallion, or your father."

"But you know how they are connected." It was a statement, not a question.

"Ahh," he sighed again with a slight disappointment in his voice, "have you not guessed already?" He looked at me with his vacant eye sockets for a moment before he added, "No, perhaps not."

"Guessed what? What's so special about it?"

"The Medallion of Light holds many powers. A gift from the Gods, to the redeemed of faith. Yet evil has corrupted its virtue. It has been guarded dearly by the Bears for many a year, and still it sees fit to return to its master."

Guarded by Bears. I thought to myself before finally making the connection. "Captain VanDrôck said he had never seen the medallion."

"Perhaps it was beyond his ability to see." The old man riddled for a reply.

"What does that mean?" I snapped back. I wasn't sure how much trouble I could get into for assaulting a skeleton, but I found myself dangerously close to taking the risk.

"Think child, you know what I say."

I took a moment to compose myself before thinking about how Luther had spoken of the medallion, and then of how Darius had searched the floor of the Wolf Room, unable to locate the prize that was only feet from his face. "Why can't anyone see the medallion but me?"

"There are many who can lay eyes on the medallion, but you have found the vein of truth that lies near the heart of your question."

I thought a moment longer before I realized that Ronan had located the medallion just fine. "Why could Ronan see it but not the VanDrôcks?"

The old man was silent again for a long time before replying, "Perhaps you share more in common with this Ronan than you do with the Bears."

His words touched a nerve, "I have nothing in common with Ronan," I spat at the blind man, causing him to tilt his head to the side and clap his jaws shut twice in quick succession. The twitchy movement looked odd and nonhuman, and it caused my stomach to creep into my throat. I changed the subject quickly to avoid his eyeless glare, "You called the fragment 'The Medallion of Light'. I heard you sing of it once. Who was it made for?"

The old man hissed before responding, "The Dark One."

"And this 'Dark One' is dead, right?" I continued.

"He was vanquished." The old man's agitation with the subject was clear in his response.

"What would be the point of stealing the piece that was here in Alleron?"

"The shadow looms large over life. The kiss of worlds will lead to war. The connection to the shadow must be severed." The skeletal man seemed to be growing angry, and it was making me increasingly nervous.

Standing from the table I started to back out of the room. When I reached the edge of the junk piles I asked my final question, "How does someone like Ronan come back from the dead?"

The man's face was twisted with rage, "The dead must sleep with the dead!" He shouted, "You must sever his connection to the shadow!"

The man stood from his seat and flipped the rickety table with a strength I would have never thought possible. The strange odds and ends on the table flew across the room and the decrepit wood hit the ground so hard it shattered to splinters. Taking that as my cue to leave, I ran the last few feet through the encumbering mess and out the door, jumping into Elma's saddle without missing a beat. She took off down the snow-covered street at a gallop, but all I could think about were the questions I hadn't managed to find any answers for.

While I was with the blind seer the sun had dropped below the outer buildings of the city, and the dark red and purple hues of the setting sun had begun to creep into the sky. Moving as fast as Elma could carry me without slipping on the icy streets, I made my way to the Lord's Manor to meet Tryson once his conclave with the other senior members of Dû Vena Ruösa had ended.

When I reached the Manor, four soldiers in the gleaming armor of Dû Vena Ruösa stood guard in their usual places at the front of the building. A man named Aermon admitted me only to have me wait for the end of the meeting in the Manor's enormous atrium. Even at the late hour, it took longer than expected for the gathering to come to a conclusion, and when Tryson finally emerged from a side chamber with the likes of Athéal, Gladía, Host, and several others, he had a look of weariness shrouding him that I had never before seen the elf wear. When he spotted me seated on a hard oaken bench on the opposite side of the atrium he gave a solemn nod and waved for me to follow him.

The elf led me through a side hallway that was covered in more of the same bizarre artwork as the rest of the building; pictures of great feasts and greater fields of battle, of lightning filled skies and stormy kraken filled seas, and of beasts and animals whose shapes I could have never imagined.. Eventually, Tryson opened a door to a small room with a single mahogany table in its center. The room was plainly furnished; the table and its six matching chairs were the only objects within. The chairs were exquisite, each had clawed bear paws carved into the armrests and a great bear's head carved into the head of the backing. Tryson offered me a seat before rounding the table and taking up one opposite me. After seating himself, he flashed me one of his familiar smiles, but it was clear to see that the act was forced.

"Been a long couple days has it?" I observed causing him to scoff.

"Glad to see there is still nothing that slips by your keen intellect. It has indeed Aaron, but duty must come before my own comforts." Tryson admitted before cutting to the point, "What is it you wish to ask?"

I opened my mouth to speak but closed it again hurriedly, remaining silent for a long time, weighing my words. I had known what question I was going to ask for a while, but now that the time had come, I didn't know how best to approach the subject. Tryson waited patiently for me to speak, but when I didn't he prodded, "Whatever you have to say Aaron is alright. Just ask it."

Chewing my tongue for a moment more I finally gave in, "You and Luther have been keeping things from me haven't you?"

"Yes." The elf said plainly, surprising me with his honesty.

"Yes," I repeated to myself, the word tasted bitterer than I expected, "Why?"

"For our protection." Tryson responded, now surprising me in a different way.

"What do you mean? Protection from whom? Ronan? How would not telling me things protect us from him?"

Tryson shook his head, the silver blond hair shimmering as it moved through the flickering candle light of the room, "Protection from you, Aaron. We did not know if we could trust you, and you could potentially be a very dangerous enemy."

Tryson's words stunned me, "*Me? Dangerous?* How am I a danger to anyone but myself?"

The elf leaned back into his seat, "You will be more powerful that you can understand. The last of your kind brought

Ardue`an crumbling to its knees. We needed to make sure you would not be prone to the same lust for power."

"What do you mean the last of my kind? I'm a farmer from Jericho, there's nothing special about me."

Tryson smiled at me like I was amusing him, "Surely you do not believe that Aaron. You are different from other men. You know this to be true."

I thought back to the squirrel on the ride home from Alleron, and the hawk in the training arena, "Different and special are just nicer words for the same thing; crazy."

This time the elf actually let out a pearl of his musical laughter, "You are most certainly not going crazy Aaron, but you *are* different. The way you sometimes move when you fight with Marcus, or the way you ran when your village was burning. The fact that you could see the fragmented medallion in the Wolf Room. And for how long have you been communicating with animals?" He stated all these differences like they were definitive proof of what he was saying.

"Alright, fine, so I'm different, I still don't know how that makes me any more threatening than anyone else."

"You are a half-breed." Tryson said bluntly, "and that makes you infinitely more dangerous than others."

"A half-breed? What does that even mean? I'm no different than anyone else from Jericho. No different than Erik, or Arctone, or Terrick." I didn't understand what Tryson was trying to tell me. I had lived my whole life with the other villagers from Jericho, and while I was more skilled in certain areas than others, there was nothing that dramatically separated me from anyone else.

"Erik and Arctone and Terrick could not do any of the things I have just mentioned." After a short pause he continued, "but I can, and so can Gladía."

"So what, are you trying to tell me I've been an elf my whole life and just haven't been smart enough to realize it?" I laughed at the thought. "That I've grown my hair long to hide my pointed ears?"

"No, you are undoubtedly human, but there is also no denying that you have elf blood. That is what makes you different, and that is what made you a potential threat."

I sat dumbfounded by Tryson's accusations, trying desperately to keep myself in a state of calm while absorbing everything he was telling me. "My uncle is a human, as was my mother. I'm human." I continued stubbornly.

"Yes, but elven blood runs through your veins nonetheless. This means your father must have been an elf."

"My father…" I said aloud to myself, thinking of what my dream in the Wolf Room had told me. "My being able to see the medallion…"

"- is exclusively an elven trait, Aaron. Mortals cannot see that which is gifted by the Gods."

I thought about how Darius scrambled through the broken glass for the medallion that was just beyond his reach, never being able to find it. "Why could Ronan see it then?"

"If Luther was right about this truly being *the* Ronan Hazarra, which I now believe is acurate, than his ability to see the fragment would make since. Ronan was an elf in his previous life. If somehow he was able to find a way back to this world, it would make sense for him to carry his elven traits with him into his new mortal body."

"So you really think I'm part elf?" I was still having trouble wrapping my brain around the idea.

"I am certain of it. These differences that you are experiencing, I assume that they have only just begun to express themselves, likely in the last few months. Am I correct in that assessment?"

I thought back over the past few months before answering, "It started around the time the riders came to Jericho."

"After your seventeenth name-day?" He paused while I nodded in agreement, before continuing, "As a human you are considered a man by the age of seventeen, you can still develop further, but this is around the time you reach physical maturity. An elf reaches physical maturity around their eighteenth name-day. You didn't start developing your elven traits until you were finished with your human ones. These elven traits, as well as others, will continue to be honed and developed until you turn eighteen. At that time I assume your development will switch back over to the human variety."

"Are the dreams an elven trait as well?" I asked, curious as to their origin.

"What dreams?" It was the first time Tryson looked confused.

"Never mind." I said quickly, deciding to chance the subject desperate to keep something private. "I still don't see how this makes me a threat to anyone."

"You don't?" Tryson asked with sincerity. When I didn't alter my question, he sighed heavily and begin with an explanation, "Being a half-breed allows you to utilize the best traits of both races. You will grow to be far faster than any human, and you will be able to use the animals to benefit you in your tasks. Yet you will have the strength of a man, which mean you will not wear down under attacks, while you may simply be able to overpower other opponents. You may be able to wield a sword with an elves speed and grace, while we can use not but knives. You could develop all the strengths of an elf with none of the weaknesses, which means that if you are trained correctly, you will be better adapted to defeat either man or elf in battle. This is what will make you either an important ally or an imposing foe."

I thought about what he was telling me before I responded, "And you wanted to know which I was. You wanted to make sure you were training a friend and not an enemy."

"Yes, but there is no way for us to know with any certainty."

"What do you mean? Of course I'm not your enemy. Ronan has taken everything from me."

"That only makes you a friend as long as we share a common enemy." When his comment visibly stung me he continued, softening his words, "I know you have a good heart Aaron, and that is why Dû Vena Ruösa is prepared to take the risk with you. But you must understand King Romulas' son, the only other half-breed of record, was reportedly a carefree youth for the first hundred years of his life. He was liked and respected, and gave good and honest counsel, but the longer he sat in his father's shadow the more bitter he became. You have elven blood Aaron, that makes you immortal, and there is no guarantee that you will not eventually become dissatisfied with your station. Having the best traits of both races will make you well suited for a crown, and the weak masses that search desperately for a leader will look to you for guidance. When the time comes, will you be able to turn them away and resist the allure of power?"

I'm immortal? The thought had never crossed my mind. It was a strange thing to have your life redefined so drastically by another. "I have no desire to rule over anyone." I claimed, defending myself.

"Yet." Was Tryson's only response.

After taking a moment to think on everything he had told me I confessed, "It won't matter much what Dû Vena Ruösa thinks of me, I'm not planning on staying around Alleron long enough for you to give me any more training."

Tryson seemed unsurprised, letting me know I wasn't quite as unpredictable as I had thought. Voicing his knowledge with a knowing smile he asked, "Planning on returning to Jericho so soon?"

I nodded in response, "I have to. For Lisa."

"And you assume Dû Vena Ruösa plans to allow it's potentially most important asset to wander alone into enemy hands?" His smile widened, allowing his white teeth to sparkle in the dim light like he thought the idea was amusing.

"Well, I'll have Jarron with me." I said stubbornly, not sure what he was trying to say.

"Oh, well I am glad to see you will be well protected. What does he plan on defending you with, a pitchfork and a garden hoe? No, that will not do."

"Well I'm going whether you wish it or not." I said defensively.

Tryson laughed, "I will not stand in your way. In fact, I think I will ride by your side."

I opened my mouth to argue again, but shut it just as fast as Tryson's words sank in. "You... you're gonna come with me? But your King, he said there would be no retaliatory measures taken."

"Well then it is a good thing Dû Vena Ruösa is an entity separate from the rule of Alleron."

"But as Captain of the Guard, don't you have to stay with the rest of your men?"

"I am not the new Captain of Dû Vena Ruösa Aaron." Tryson confessed with another smile, "I have declined the offer. The title will pass to Gladía."

"What? Why?" I stammered.

Tryson sighed, "You are right; our Captain must stay with the men here in the city. I joined Dû Vena Ruösa to avenge the death of King Romulas. Now I feel my new task will be to avenge Luther's death, and that I cannot do standing guard at Lord Detrick's Manor. I will ride with you to Jericho Aaron, as will Marcus, and several others, but your former home in Northern Jericho will not be our only stop."

"What do you mean?"

Tryson smiled but did not expand on what he had said. "You should go home and rest Aaron, tomorrow will be a long day of riding." I knew I would not get anything more from the elf so I bowed my head in a silent thank you before leaving the Manor in a slight daze, my head swimming with everything I had learned.

As I turned Elma in the direction of our village I reveled in the cool night air, air that felt much less oppressive and suffocating than it had the night of the battle. For the first time in over a week I smiled, allowing myself to enjoy the cold, biting wind that tossed my hair wildly behind me. I was excited to know that my task would not be undertaken alone. It would be nice to have familiar faces, as well as good fighters with me for what lie ahead. Even Elma seemed to understand the change in my mood, holding her head higher as she trotted through the empty streets. My mind was so preoccupied by my conversation with Tryson that I nearly didn't notice the two men who stood just outside the entrance to my home.

"You fixin' on leavin' without us there, kid?" Arctone asked pointedly. Erik stood to his left, his arms crossed against his chest, his short sword strapped to his hip.

"Shut up, Arctone." I ordered, trying to force my way past him to no avail. When he made it clear I wasn't getting by him without an explanation I stepped back and admitted, "I don't want you and Erik getting yourselves in trouble just to try and help me. If either of you were killed, it would be on me. I don't think I could live with that."

"Well then it's a good thing you don't have much of a choice in the matter." Arctone rebutted, "We said we would help you when you went after Lisa, and we meant it. You're gonna need help."

"I'll have help." I said obstinately, "Tryson and some of Dû Vena Ruösa are coming with me."

Erik stepped forward, clearly upset, "Oh, so these strangers are good enough to help you but your friends aren't? We fought in that battle too you know, and we survived it just as well as you."

"That's not what I meant, Erik. You know that. How did you even find out I was leaving?"

"Sienna told us." Arctone confessed, "You have her a right mess, you do. How could you get her all stirred up like that?"

At the mention of Sienna all the fight went out of me, "I know. I just wanted to say goodbye."

"Well that was a stupid idea." Arctone snapped, "She always throws on a smile when you're around, but Erik's seen her. She cries all the time. She's been a wreck since Terrick left and didn't come back, and now it seems to her you're plannin' on goin' off and doin' the same thing. She came to us to try and change your mind. It didn't help her at all when she found out we're planning to go with you."

"What do you want from me? I couldn't just leave her."

"Well it would have made things easier." Erik added his two cents.

"What do we want from you?" Arctone repeated the question, "We want you to accept the fact that you're not getting rid of us that easily."

I looked at them both for a long time, trying to think of a way to convince them to stay behind, but when no good argument came to me, I was forced to give in, "If you're not at the north gate before first light we'll leave without you."

Erik smiled for the first time, "We'll be the first two there," he promised, before patting me on the shoulder and walking past me in the direction of his home. Arctone gave me a good long look before he was finally convinced that I had accepted their company, and gave a stiff nod before following in Erik's wake.

A long while later I lay in bed, unable to sleep. The wool blanket seemed to chaff against my bare chest. Somewhere in the distance a raven cried out. The sound rippled through the night air and caused me to shiver. Realizing that sleep was not coming to me I kicked off the blanket and walked from my home into the bitter cold night. The full moon shone overhead, bright enough with the thousands of stars to cast a light glow across the land. I walked to the edge of the muddy river and looked down into its murky depths, like I expected the dark water to present the answers to my wandering mind. In the moonlight the river didn't look muddy, it shown like liquid glass, a mirror that rippled as it flowed slowly to the east in order to meet up with the main branch of the Aríalas River.

I stood on the snowy bank and looked down at my reflection in the black pool. Slowly I traced my fingers over the muscles in my chest and arms, before pushing the hair behind one of my ears to feel that it was still rounded. Its weird having you're whole identity changed for you over the course of a single conversation, like I was suddenly going to be a different person. I didn't feel any different. Looking at the reflection, I was still the same man I was in Jericho, same hair, same eyes. Nothing had changed, yet now I was supposed to believe that deep down there was something in me to be feared; something even Luther had feared. The idea didn't sit right.

If only Ronan shared that fear, I thought to myself, wishing that I could control whatever new gifts I was likely to have by being a half-breed… *Half-breed,* I rolled the thought around in my head a few more times like it would suddenly fit, suddenly make sense, instead the concept still seemed alien to me, making me feel like I was something unnatural. But then a new thought worked its way into my mind. *If unnatural is what I am, than unnatural is what I will become.* This joined the blurring ideas and suddenly became the only one that really made sense. I would embrace the life that had been thrust upon me, embrace the destiny that was mine to have. If I was to be feared, than I would have my enemies fear me. No longer would I be still, waiting for Ronan, or the Urröbbí to bring the fight to me. No longer would I feel like a pawn in a chess match, being moved at others commands. I would take control of my own actions, and follow my own orders, and bring the fight to their lands. All those who had torn my life apart would rue the day they set foot in Jericho, and in the end, it would be me they looked up at while their lives ended. My hand that sent them forward into eternity.

"You have a long journey ahead of you, restoring the throne to the heir of Romulas." The eyeless man had told me. I did not know where my journey would lead me, or if it would actually end with a throne being restored, but I knew where it would begin. *It will begin with me finding Lisa.* I thought to myself, looking down at my undulating reflection. *It will begin with Ronan learning to fear me.*

Chapter 36: Darkness Falls

He landed in the sand at the base of the cliff, his knees flexing just enough to absorb the impact of the fall. The fortress in the distance looked larger than it had at the top of the cliff. It was closer than he remembered. He inhaled deeply as his body pulsed with energy. They had captured a second piece, he could feel it; feel the strength that flowed back into his limbs, feel his mind grow sharper. He took another breath as he allowed the sensation to wash over him. It wouldn't be long now. Not when compared to the decades through which he slept; fighting to return. Soon the world would be within his grasp once more. All would bow to the true king.

Slowly, he reached into a hidden pocket in his cloak, extracting a small wooden creature and examining it in his hand. It was a scorpion, no larger than a silver coin, but carved so intricately that it almost seemed to be alive. Its eight legs were flexed and its pedipalps were stretched out in front of it, like it was preparing to attack some invisible foe. Quickly, he inverted his hand and dropped the carving onto the sandy desert floor, where it lay motionless. Minutes blurred into hours as he waited patiently. If there was one thing he had learned during his imprisonment, it was patience.

He heard it from a distance, and closed his eyes. The periodic clicks grew louder and more frequent as he waited, sounding almost irritated, like a beast waiting to escape is cage. The carving at his feet responded to the sounds with agitation. The pinchers clicked open and shut, testing its newfound motion, then the legs and metasoma followed suit. Its stinger curled and arched over its body, needing something to strike at, to poison. He lifted his right hand for a second time and closed it into a fist. In reaction to the movement, the wooden scorpion burrowed its way into the sand.

Taking another deep breath he whispered into the perpetual darkness "Rise my friends," and the sand began to boil at his feet.

Waves of energy rippled across its vast surface like rain falling on an ocean, and the tremors excited him. He opened his fist, lifting his hand into the air in the same motion, and as he did so, the sand erupted like a thousand explosions erupting simultaneously. Soon the distance between him and the fortress was alive with beasts emerging from the pot marked sand. Pinchers large enough to cut a man in half fought their way out into the air. Hard, jet-black exoskeletons appeared in all directions and it caused the wild gleam in his eyes to grow brighter. Beside him the sand trembled again, and out of it emerged what he had been waiting for. This scorpion was larger than the others. Each pincher the size of a horse, with violent, serrated edges. Its exoskeleton was enormous, and built up in the back like a hardened throne. From its backside its metasoma extended, poison red streaks stretching up to a stinger long enough to impale a wild boar. As it extracted itself from the sand it opened and closed its pinchers in agitation.

He stepped towards the beast and patted it gently, as if it were a beloved pet. "Orotheous," he smiled, "king of the Arachnida. I have missed you my old friend."

The beast clicked its pinchers twice more in response, pleased to be back with its master. It lowered one if its massive claws to the desert floor and waited for his master to climb on. The scorpion slowly lifted him onto its back, placing him directly in front of the creature's throne-like exoskeleton. After he had settled into his seat, the scorpion began to crawl forward, and as it did so, the sea of arachnids parted in front of them, lowering the front of their hardened bodies into an awful bow of respect, and he was pleased to see that they still remembered the order of things after all these years.

As he rode to the fortress he thought about what still needed to be accomplished. With two pieces now in his possession, there were only five left to acquire. The dwarves would be easy. Those inbred miners care for no one but themselves. They would be simple enough to manipulate. For enough jewels and riches they may even become his allies. He needn't worry about acquiring their assets. His thoughts turned to the elves. Creatures who, for all their subtleties and supposed wisdom, were ready to crumble. They live their lives oblivious to the knifepoint on which they balance. With the right push those *noble elves* would be sent spiraling into a war solely to protect their false sense of righteousness. They too were nothing more than pebble in the path of a tidal wave. The Red Forest would be a different matter, not even he knew what lay in its untamed depths, in the land of no return. His last, and most enjoyable task, would be his brother... Very few knew of the old King's second son, but it could not be hidden from him. Even now, he could feel his presence, could feel every move he made as an act of defiance. The Elfling would bow to him in the end. He would not be an issue. No, the only thing that stood between him and his goal was time, and time was something he had an abundance of.

The war, *his* war, was only just beginning.

25590635R00239

Made in the USA
Charleston, SC
09 January 2014